Classic Novels

THE ADVENTURES OF .
SIR LAUNCELOT GREAVES
AND
THE ADVENTURES OF .
AN ATOM . . .

Dawdle's Victory over Captain Crowe.
(See p. 187.)

The Adventures of
Sir Launcelot Greaves

AND THE

Adventures of an Atom

BY

TOBIAS SMOLLETT

WITH ILLUSTRATIONS BY
GEORGE CRUIKSHANK, ETC.

Philadelphia { GEORGE W. JACOBS & CO. ~ Publishers

PRINTED IN GREAT BRITAIN

ILLUSTRATIONS

THE ADVENTURES

OF

SIR LAUNCELOT GREAVES

CHAPTER I

In which certain Personages of this delightful History are
introduced to the Reader's Acquaintance.

IT was on the great northern road from York to London,
about the beginning of the month of October, and the hour
of eight in the evening, that four travellers were, by a violent
shower of rain, driven for shelter into a little public-house
on the side of the highway, distinguished by a sign which
was said to exhibit the figure of a black lion. The kitchen,
in which they assembled, was the only room for entertainment
in the house, paved with red bricks, remarkably clean,
furnished with three or four Windsor chairs, adorned with
shining plates of pewter, and copper saucepans, nicely
scoured, that even dazzled the eyes of the beholder; while
a cheerful fire of sea-coal blazed in the chimney Three
of the travellers, who arrived on horseback, having seen their
cattle properly accommodated in the stable, agreed to pass
the time, until the weather should clear up, over a bowl of
rumbo, which was accordingly prepared. But the fourth,
refusing to join their company, took his station at the opposite

side of the chimney, and called for a pint of twopenny, with which he indulged himself apart. At a little distance, on his left hand, there was another group, consisting of the landlady, a decent widow, her two daughters, the older of whom seemed to be about the age of fifteen, and a country lad, who served both as waiter and ostler.

The social triumvirate was composed of Mr. Fillet, a country practitioner in surgery and midwifery, Captain Crowe, and his nephew Mr. Thomas Clarke, an attorney. Fillet was a man of some education, and a great deal of experience, shrewd, sly, and sensible. Captain Crowe had commanded a merchant ship in the Mediterranean trade for many years, and saved some money by dint of frugality and traffic. He was an excellent seaman, brave, active, friendly in his way, and scrupulously honest; but as little acquainted with the world as a sucking child; whimsical, impatient, and so impetuous, that he could not help breaking in upon the conversation, whatever it might be, with repeated interruptions, that seemed to burst from him by involuntary impulse. When he himself attempted to speak he never finished his period; but made such a number of abrupt transitions, that his discourse seemed to be an unconnected series of unfinished sentences, the meaning of which it was not easy to decipher.

His nephew, Tom Clarke, was a young fellow, whose goodness of heart even the exercise of his profession had not been able to corrupt. Before strangers he never owned himself an attorney without blushing, though he had no reason to blush for his own practice, for he constantly refused to engage in the cause of any client whose character was equivocal, and was never known to act with such industry as when concerned for the widow and orphan, or any other object that sued *in forma pauperis*. Indeed, he was so replete with human kindness, that as often as an affecting story or circumstance was told in his hearing, it overflowed at his eyes. Being of a warm complexion, he was very susceptible of passion, and somewhat libertine in his amours. In other respects, he piqued himself on understanding the practice of the courts, and in private company he took pleasure in laying down the law; but he was an indifferent orator, and tediously circumstantial in his explanations. His stature was rather diminutive; but, upon the whole, he had some title to the character of a pretty, dapper, little fellow.

The solitary guest had something very forbidding in his aspect, which was contracted by an habitual frown. His eyes were small and red, and so deep set in the sockets, that each appeared like the unextinguished snuff of a farthing candle, gleaming through the horn of a dark lanthorn. His nostrils were elevated in scorn, as if his sense of smelling had been perpetually offended by some unsavoury odour; and he looked as if he wanted to shrink within himself from the impertinence of society. He wore a black periwig as straight as the pinions of a raven, and this was covered with a hat flapped, and fastened to his head by a speckled handkerchief tied under his chin. He was wrapped in a great coat of brown frieze, under which he seemed to conceal a small bundle. His name was Ferret, and his character distinguished by three peculiarities. He was never seen to smile; he was never heard to speak in praise of any person whatsoever; and he was never known to give a direct answer to any question that was asked; but seemed, on all occasions, to be actuated by the most perverse spirit of contradiction.

Captain Crowe, having remarked that it was squally weather, asked how far it was to the next market town, and understanding that the distance was not less than six miles, said he had a good mind to come to an anchor for the night, if so be as he could have a tolerable *berth* in this here harbour. Mr. Fillet, perceiving by his style that he was a seafaring gentleman, observed that their landlady was not used to lodge such company, and expressed some surprise that he, who had no doubt endured so many storms and hardships at sea, should think much of travelling five or six miles a-horseback by moonlight. "For my part," said he, "I ride in all weathers, and at all hours without minding cold, wet, wind, or darkness. My constitution is so case-hardened that I believe I could live all the year at Spitzbergen. With respect to this road, I know every foot of it so exactly that I'll engage to travel forty miles upon it blindfold, without making one false step; and if you have faith enough to put yourselves under my auspices, I will conduct you safe to an elegant inn, where you will meet with the best accommodation." "Thank you, brother," replied the captain, "we are much beholden to you for your courteous offer; but, howsomever, you must not think I mind foul weather more than my neighbours. I have worked hard aloft and alow in many a taut gale; but this here is the case, d'ye see, we have run down a long day's reckoning; our beasts have had a hard spell, and as for my own hap, brother, I doubt my bottom-planks have lost some of their sheathing, being as how I a'n't used to that kind of scrubbing."

The doctor, who had practised aboard a man-of-war in his youth, and was perfectly well acquainted with the captain's dialect, assured him that if his bottom was damaged he would *new pay* it with an excellent salve, which he always carried about him to guard against such accidents on the road. But Tom Clarke, who seemed to have cast the eyes of affection upon the landlady's eldest daughter, Dolly, objected to their proceeding farther without rest and refreshment, as they had already travelled fifty miles since morning; and he was sure his uncle must be fatigued both in mind and body, from vexation, as well as from hard exercise, to which he had not been accustomed. Fillet then desisted, saying, he was sorry to find the captain had any cause of vexation; but he hoped it was not an incurable evil. This expression was accompanied with a look of curiosity, which Mr. Clarke was glad of an occasion to gratify; for, as we have hinted above, he was a very communicative gentleman, and the affair which now lay upon his stomach interested him nearly.

"I'll assure you, sir," said he, "this here gentleman, Captain Crowe, who is my mother's own brother, has been cruelly used by some of his relations. He bears as good a character as any captain of a ship on the Royal Exchange, and has undergone a variety of hardships at sea. What d'ye think, now, of his bursting all his sinews, and making his eyes start out of his head, in pulling his ship off a rock, whereby he saved to his owners——" Here he was interrupted by the captain, who exclaimed, " Belay, Tom, belay ; pr'ythee, don't veer out such a deal of jaw. Clap a stopper on thy cable and bring thyself up, my lad—what a deal of stuff thou hast pumped up concerning bursting and starting, and pulling ships. Laud have mercy upon us !—look ye here, brother—look ye here—mind these poor crippled joints ; two fingers on the starboard, and three on the larboard hand ; crooked, d'ye see, like the knees of a bilander. I'll tell you what, brother, you seem to be a— ship deep laden—rich cargo—current setting into the bay—hard gale—lee shore—all hands in the boat—tow round the headland—self pulling for dear blood against the whole crew—snap go the finger-braces—crack went the eye-blocks. Bounce daylight—flash starlight—down I foundered, dark as hell—whiz went my ears, and my head spun like a whirligig. That don't signify—I'm a Yorkshire boy, as the saying is—all my life at sea, brother, by reason of an old grandmother and maiden aunt, a couple of old stinking—kept me these forty years out of my grandfather's estate. Hearing as how they had taken their departure, came ashore, hired horses, and clapped on all my canvas, steering to the northward, to take possession of my—— But it don't signify talking—these two old piratical—had held a palaver with a lawyer—an attorney, Tom, d'ye mind me, an attorney—and by his assistance hove me out of my inheritance. That is all, brother—hove me out of five hundred pounds a year—that's all—what signifies—but such windfalls we don't every day pick up along shore. Fill about, brother—yes, by the L—d ! those two smuggling harridans, with the assistance of an attorney—an attorney, Tom—hove me out of five hundred a year." " Yes, indeed, sir," added Mr. Clarke, " those two malicious old women docked the intail, and left the estate to an alien."

Here Mr. Ferret thought proper to intermingle in the conversation with a " *Pish*, what dost talk of docking the intail ? Dost not know that by the statute Westm. 2. 13 Ed. the will and intention of the donor must be fulfilled, and the tenant in *tail* shall not alien after issue had, or before." " Give me leave, sir," replied Tom, " I presume you are a practitioner in the law. Now, you know, that in the case of a contingent *remainder*, the intail may be destroyed by levying a fine, and suffering a recovery, or otherwise destroying the particular estate, before the contingency happens. If *feoffees*, who possess an estate only during the life of a son, where divers *remainders* are limited over, make a *feoffment* in fee to him, by the *feoffment*, all the future *remainders* are destroyed. Indeed, a person in *remainder* may have a writ of intrusion, if any do intrude after the death of a tenant for life, and the writ *ex gravi querela* lies to execute a device in *remainder* after the death of a tenant in tail without issue." " Spoke like a true disciple of Geber," cries Ferret. " No, sir," replied Mr. Clarke, " Counsellor Caper is in the conveyancing way—I was clerk to Serjeant Croker." " Ay, now you may set up for yourself," resumed the other ; " for you can prate as unintelligibly as the best of them."

" Perhaps," said Tom, " I do not make myself understood ; if so be as how that is the case, let us change the position, and suppose that this here case is a *tail after a possibility of issue extinct*. If a tenant in *tail* after a possibility make a *feoffment* of his land, he in reversion may enter for the forfeiture. Then we must make a distinction between *general tail* and *special tail*. It is the word *body* that makes the *intail :* there must be a *body* in the *tail*, devised to heirs male or female, otherwise it is a fee-simple, because it is not limited of what *body*. Thus a corporation cannot be seized in *tail*. For example, here is a young woman— what is your name, my dear ? " " Dolly," answered the daughter, with a curtsey. " Here's Dolly—I seize Dolly in *tail*—Dolly, I seize you in *tail* "—" Sha't then," cried Dolly, pouting. " I am seized of land in fee—I settle on Dolly in *tail*."

Dolly, who did not comprehend the nature of the illustration, understood him in a literal sense, and, in a whimpering tone, exclaimed, " Sha't then, I tell thee, cursed tuoad ! " Tom, however, was so transported with his subject, that he took no notice of poor Dolly's mistake, but proceeded in his harangue upon the different kinds of *tails, remainders,* and *seisins,* when he was interrupted by a noise that alarmed the whole company. The rain had been succeeded by a storm of wind that howled around the house with the most savage impetuosity, and the heavens were overcast in such a manner that not one star appeared, so that all without was darkness and uproar. This aggravated the horror of divers loud screams, which even the noise of the blast could not exclude from the ears of our astonished travellers. Captain Crowe called out, " Avast, avast ! " Tom Clarke sat silent, staring wildly, with his mouth still open ; the surgeon himself seemed startled, and Ferret's countenance betrayed evident marks of confusion. The ostler moved nearer the chimney, and the good woman of the house, with her two daughters, crept closer to the company.

After some pause, the captain starting up, " These," said he, " be signals of distress. Some poor souls in danger of foundering—let us bear up a-head, and see if we can give them any assistance." The landlady begged him, for Christ's sake, not to think of going out, for it was a spirit that would lead him astray into fens and rivers, and certainly do him a mischief. Crowe seemed to be staggered by this remonstrance, which his nephew reinforced, observing, that it might be a stratagem of rogues to decoy them into the fields, that they might rob them under the cloud of night. Thus exhorted, he resumed his seat, and Mr. Ferret began to make very severe strictures upon the folly and fear of those who believed and trembled at the visitation of spirits, ghosts, and goblins. He said he would engage with twelve pennyworth of phosphorus to frighten a whole parish out of their senses; then he expatiated on the pusillanimity of the nation in general, ridiculed the militia, censured the Government, and dropped some hints about a change of hands, which the captain could not, and the doctor would not, comprehend.

Tom Clarke, from the freedom of his discourse, concluded he was a ministerial spy, and communicated his opinion to his uncle in a whisper, while this misanthrope continued to pour forth his invectives with a fluency peculiar to himself. The truth is, Mr. Ferret had been a party writer, not from principle, but employment, and had felt the rod of power, in order to avoid a second exertion of which he now found it convenient to skulk about in the country, for he had received intimation of a warrant from the Secretary of State, who wanted to be better acquainted with his person. Notwithstanding the ticklish nature of his situation, it was become so habitual to him to think and speak in a certain manner, that even before strangers whose principles and connections he could not possibly know he hardly ever opened his mouth without uttering some direct or implied sarcasm against the Government.

He had already proceeded a considerable way in demonstrating that the nation was bankrupt and beggared, and that those who stood at the helm were steering full into the gulf of inevitable destruction, when his lecture was suddenly suspended by a violent knocking at the door, which threatened the whole house with inevitable demolition. Captain Crowe, believing they should be instantly boarded, unsheathed his hanger, and stood in a posture of defence. Mr. Fillet armed himself with the poker, which happened to be red hot, the ostler pulled down a rusty firelock, that hung by the roof over a flitch of bacon. Tom Clarke perceiving the landlady and her children distracted with terror, conducted them, out of mere compassion, below stairs into the cellar; and as for Mr. Ferret, he prudently withdrew into an adjoining pantry.

But as a personage of great importance in this entertaining history was forced to remain some time at the door before he could gain admittance, so must the reader wait with patience for the next chapter, in which he will see the cause of this disturbance explained much to his comfort and edification.

CHAPTER II

In which the Hero of these Adventures makes his First Appearance on the Stage of Action.

THE outward door of the Black Lion had already sustained two dreadful shocks, but at the third it flew open, and in stalked an apparition that smote the hearts of our travellers with fear and trepidation. It was the figure of a man armed cap-à-pie, bearing on his shoulders a bundle dropping with water, which afterwards appeared to be the body of a man that seemed to have been drowned, and fished up from the bottom of the neighbouring river.

Having deposited his burden carefully on the floor, he addressed himself to the company in these words : " Be not surprised, good people, at this unusual appearance, which I shall take an opportunity to explain, and forgive the rude and boisterous manner in which I have demand d, and indeed forced admittance ; the violence of my intrusion was the effect of necessity. In crossing the river, my squire and his horse were swept away by the stream, and, with some difficulty, I have been able to drag him ashore, though I am afraid my assistance reached him too late, for since I brought him to land he has given no signs of life."

Here he was interrupted by a groan, which issued from the chest of the squire, and terrified the spectators as much as it comforted the master. After some recollection, Mr. Fillet began to undress the body, which was laid in a blanket on the floor, and rolled from side to side by his direction. A considerable quantity of water being discharged from the mouth of this unfortunate squire, he uttered a hideous roar, and, opening his eyes, stared wildly around. Then the surgeon undertook for his recovery; and his master went forth with the ostler in quest of the horses, which he had left by the side of the river. His back was no sooner turned than Ferret, who had been peeping from behind the pantry-door, ventured to rejoin the company; pronouncing with a smile, or rather grin, of contempt, "Hey-day! what precious mummery is this? What, are we to have the farce of Hamlet's ghost?" "Adzooks," cried the captain, "my kinsman Tom has dropped astern—hope in God a-has not bulged to, and gone to bottom." "Pish," exclaimed the misanthrope, "there's no danger; the young lawyer is only seizing Dolly in tail."

Certain it is, Dolly squeaked at that instant in the cellar; and Clarke, appearing soon after in some confusion, declared she had been frightened by a flash of lightning. But this assertion was not confirmed by the young lady herself, who eyed him with a sullen regard, indicating displeasure, though not indifference; and when questioned by her mother, replied, "A doan't maind what a-says, so a doan't, vor all his goalden jacket, then."

In the meantime the surgeon had performed the operation of phlebotomy on the squire, who was lifted into a chair, and supported by the landlady for that purpose; but he had not as yet given any sign of having retrieved the use of his senses. And here Mr. Fillet could not help contemplating, with surprise, the strange figure and accoutrements of his patient, who seemed in age to be turned of fifty. His stature was below the middle size; he was thick, squat, and brawny, with a small protuberance on one shoulder, and a prominent belly, which, in consequence of the water he had swallowed, now strutted beyond its usual dimensions. His forehead was remarkably convex, and so very low that his black bushy hair descended within an inch of his nose; but this did not conceal the wrinkles of his front, which were manifold. His small glimmering eyes resembled those of the Hampshire porker, that turns up the soil with his projecting snout. His cheeks were shrivelled and puckered at the corners, like the seams of a regimental

coat as it comes from the hands of the contractor. His nose
bore a strong analogy in shape to a tennis-ball, and in colour
to a mulberry ; for all the water of the river had not been
able to quench the natural fire of that feature. His upper
jaw was furnished with two long white sharp-pointed teeth
or fangs, such as the reader may have observed in the chaps
of a wolf, or full-grown mastiff, and an anatomist would
describe as a preternatural elongation of the *dentes canini.*
His chin was so long, so peaked, and incurvated, as to form
in profile, with his impending forehead, the exact resemblance
of a moon in the first quarter. With respect to his equipage,
he had a leathern cap upon his head, faced like those worn
by marines, and exhibiting in embroidery the figure of a
crescent. His coat was of white cloth, faced with black,
and cut in a very antique fashion ; and, in lieu of a waistcoat,
he wore a buff jerkin. His feet were cased with loose
buskins, which,though they rose almost to his knee, could not
hide that curvature, known by the appellation of bandy
legs. A large string of bandaliers garnished a broad belt
that graced his shoulders, from whence depended an instrument of war, which was something between a back-sword
and a cutlass ; and a case of pistols was stuck in his girdle.
   Such was the figure which the whole company now
surveyed with admiration. After some pause, he seemed to
recover his recollection. He rolled about his eyes around,
and, attentively surveying every individual, exclaimed, in a
strange tone, " Bodikins ! where's Gilbert ? " This interrogation did not savour much of sanity, especially when
accompanied with a wild stare, which is generally interpreted
as a sure sign of a disturbed understanding. Nevertheless,
the surgeon endeavoured to assist his recollection. " Come,"
said he, " have a good heart. How dost do, friend ? "
" Do ! " replied the squire, " do as well as I can.—That's
a lie too ; I might have done better. I had no business
to be here." " You ought to thank God and your master,"
resumed the surgeon, " for the providential escape you have
had." " Thank my master ! " cried the squire, " thank
the devil ! Go and teach your grannum to crack filberds. I

know who I'm bound to pray for, and who I ought to curse the longest day I have to live."

Here the captain interposing, " Nay, brother," said he, " you are bound to pray for this here gentleman as your sheet-anchor ; for, if so be as he had not cleared your stowage of the water you had taken in at your upper works, and lightened your veins, d'ye see, by taking away some of your blood, adad ! you had driven before the gale, and never been brought up in this world again, d'ye see." " What, then you would persuade me," replied the patient, " that the only way to save my life was to shed my precious blood ? Look ye, friend, it shall not be lost blood to me.—I take you all to witness, that there surgeon, or apothecary, or farrier, or dog-doctor, or whatsoever he may be, has robbed me of the balsam of life.—He has not left so much blood in my body as would fatten a starved flea.—Oh that there was a lawyer here to serve him with a *siserari* ! "

Then, fixing his eyes upon Ferret, he proceeded : "An't you a limb of the law, friend ?—No, I cry you mercy, you look more like a showman or a conjurer." Ferret, nettled at this address, answered, " It would be well for you, that I could conjure a little common sense into that numskull of yours." " If I want that commodity," rejoined the squire, " I must go to another market, I trow.—You legerdemain men be more like to conjure the money from our pockets than sense into our skulls. Vor my own part, I was once cheated of vorty good shillings by one of your broother cups and balls." In all probability he would have descended to particulars had he not been seized with a return of his nausea, which obliged him to call for a bumper of brandy. This remedy being swallowed, the tumult in his stomach subsided. He desired he might be put to bed without delay, and that half a dozen eggs and a pound of bacon might, in a couple of hours, be dressed for his supper.

He was accordingly led off the scene by the landlady and her daughter ; and Mr. Ferret had just time to observe the fellow was a composition, in which he did not know whether knave or fool most predominated, when the master returned from the stable. He had taken off his helmet, and now displayed a very engaging countenance. His age did not seem to exceed thirty. He was tall, and seemingly robust; his face long and oval, his nose aquiline, his mouth furnished with a set of elegant teeth, white as the drifted snow, his complexion clear, and his aspect noble. His chestnut hair loosely flowed in short natural curls, and his grey eyes shone with such vivacity as plainly showed that his reason was a little discomposed. Such an appearance prepossessed the greater part of the company in his favour. He bowed round with the most polite and affable address; inquired about his squire, and, being informed of the pains Mr. Fillet had taken for his recovery, insisted upon that gentleman's accepting a handsome gratuity. Then, in consideration of the cold bath he had undergone, he was prevailed upon to take the post of honour; namely, the great chair fronting the fire, which was reinforced with a billet of wood for his comfort and convenience.

Perceiving his fellow-travellers, either overawed into silence by his presence, or struck dumb with admiration at his equipage, he accosted them in these words, while an agreeable smile dimpled on his cheek:

"The good company wonders, no doubt, to see a man cased in armour, such as hath been for above a whole century disused in this and every other country of Europe; and perhaps they will be still more surprised when they hear that man profess himself a novitiate of that military order, which hath of old been distinguished in Great Britain, as well as through all Christendom, by the name of knights-errant. Yes, gentleman, in that painful and thorny path of toil and danger I have begun my career, a candidate for honest fame; determined, as far as in me lies, to honour and assert the efforts of virtue; to combat vice in all her forms, redress injuries, chastise oppression, protect the helpless and forlorn, relieve the indigent, exert my best endeavours in the cause of innocence and beauty, and dedicate my talents, such as they are, to the service of my country."

"What!" said Ferret, "you set up for a modern Don

Quixote ? The scheme is rather too stale and extravagant. What was a humorous romance and well-timed satire in Spain near two hundred years ago will make but a sorry jest, and appear equally insipid and absurd when really acted from affectation, at this time of day, in a country like England."

The knight, eyeing this censor with a look of disdain, replied, in a solemn, lofty tone : " He that from affectation imitates the extravagancies recorded of Don Quixote is an impostor equally wicked and contemptible. He that counterfeits madness, unless he dissembles, like the elder Brutus, for some virtuous purpose, not only debases his own soul, but acts as a traitor to Heaven, by denying the divinity that is within him. I am neither an affected imitator of Don Quixote, nor, as I trust in Heaven, visited by that spirit of lunacy so admirably displayed in the fictitious character exhibited by the inimitable Cervantes. I have not yet encountered a windmill for a giant, nor mistaken this public-house for a magnificent castle ; neither do I believe this gentleman to be the constable ; nor that worthy practitioner to be Master Elizabat, the surgeon recorded in Amadis de Gaul ; nor you to be the enchanter Alquife, nor any other sage of history or romance ; I see and distinguish objects as they are discerned and described by other men. I reason without prejudice, can endure contradiction, and, as the company perceives, even bear impertinent censure without passion or resentment. I quarrel with none but the foes of virtue and decorum, against whom I have declared perpetual war, and them I will everywhere attack as the natural enemies of mankind."

" But that war," said the cynic, " may soon be brought to a conclusion, and your adventures close in Bridewell, provided you meet with some determined constable, who will seize your worship as a vagrant, according to the statute."

" Heaven and earth ! " cried the stranger, starting up, and laying his hand on his sword, " do I live to hear myself insulted with such an opprobrious epithet, and refrain from trampling into dust the insolent calumniator ? "

The tone in which these words were pronounced, and the indignation that flashed from the eyes of the speaker, intimidated every individual of the society, and reduced Ferret to a temporary privation of all his faculties. His eyes retired within their sockets; his complexion, which was naturally of a copper hue, now shifted to a leaden colour; his teeth began to chatter; and all his limbs were agitated by a sudden palsy. The knight observed his condition, and resumed his seat, saying, " I was to blame; my vengeance must be reserved for very different objects. Friend, you have nothing to fear—the sudden gust of passion is now blown over. Recollect yourself, and I will reason calmly on the observation you have made."

This was a very seasonable declaration to Mr. Ferret, who opened his eyes, and wiped his forehead, while the other proceeded in these terms: " You say I am in danger of being apprehended as a vagrant. I am not so ignorant of the laws of my country, but that I know the description of those who fall within the legal meaning of this odious term. You must give me leave to inform you, friend, that I am neither bearward, fencer, stroller, gipsy, mountebank, nor mendicant; nor do I practise subtle craft, to deceive and impose upon the king's lieges; nor can I be held as an idle disorderly person, travelling from place to place, collecting monies by virtue of counterfeited passes, briefs, and other false pretences; in what respect, therefore, am I to be deemed a vagrant? Answer boldly without fear or scruple."

To this interrogation the misanthrope replied, with a faltering accent, " If not a vagrant, you incur the penalty for riding armed in affray of the peace."—" But, instead of riding armed in affray of the peace," resumed the other, " I ride in preservation of the peace, and gentlemen are allowed by the law to wear armour for their defence. Some ride with blunderbusses, some with pistols, some with swords, according to their various inclinations. Mine is to wear the armour of my forefathers. Perhaps I use them for exercise, in order to accustom myself to fatigue, and

the emissaries of France, both in word and writing, who exaggerate our necessary burdens, magnify our dangers, extol the power of our enemies, deride our victories, extenuate our conquests, condemn the measures of our government, and scatter the seeds of dissatisfaction through the land. Such domestic traitors are doubly the objects of detestation ;—first, in perverting truth, and, secondly, in propagating falsehood, to the prejudice of that community of which they have professed themselves members. One of these is well known by the name of Ferret, an old, rancorous, incorrigible instrument of sedition. Happy it is for him that he has never fallen in my way ; for, notwithstanding the maxims of forbearance which I have adopted, the indignation which the character of that caitiff inspires, would probably impel me to some act of violence, and I should crush him like an ungrateful viper, that gnawed the bosom which warmed it into life ! "

These last words were pronounced with a wildness of look that even bordered upon frenzy. The misanthrope once more retired to the pantry for shelter, and the rest of the guests were evidently disconcerted.

Mr. Fillet, in order to change the conversation, which was likely to produce serious consequences, expressed uncommon satisfaction at the remarks which the knight had made, signified his approbation of the honourable office he had undertaken, declared himself happy in having seen such an accomplished cavalier, and observed that nothing was wanting to render him a complete knight-errant but some celebrated beauty, the mistress of his heart, whose idea might animate his breast, and strengthen his arm to the utmost exertion of valour. He added, that love was the soul of chivalry.

The stranger started at this discourse. He turned his eyes on the surgeon with a fixed regard, his countenance changed, a torrent of tears gushed down his cheeks, his head sank upon his bosom, he heaved a profound sigh, and remained in silence with all the external marks of unutterable sorrow. The company were, in some measure, infected by his despondence, concerning the cause of which, however, they would not venture to inquire.

By this time the landlady, having disposed of the squire, desired to know, with many curtsies, if his honour would not choose to put off his wet garments, assuring him that she had a very good feather bed at his service, upon which many gentlevolks of the virst quality had lain, that the sheets were well aired, and that Dolly would warm them for his worship with a pan of coals. This hospitable offer being repeated, he seemed to wake from a trance of grief, arose from his seat, and, bowing courteously to the company, withdrew.

Captain Crowe, whose faculty of speech had been all this time absorbed in amazement, now broke into the conversation with a volley of interjections. " Split my snatchblock ! —Odd's firkin !—Splice my old shoes !—I have sailed the salt seas, brother, since I was no higher than the Triton's taffrel—east, west, north, and south, as the saying is—Blacks, Indians, Moors, Morattos, and Sepoys—but, smite my timbers ! such a man of war——"

Here he was interrupted by his nephew, Tom Clarke, who had disappeared at the knight's first entrance, and now produced himself with an eagerness in his look, while the tears started in his eyes. " Lord bless my soul ! " cried he, " I know that gentleman and his servant as well as I know my own father ! I am his own godson, uncle ; he stood for me when he was a boy. Yes, indeed, sir, my father was steward to the estate. I may say I was bred up in the family of Sir Everhard Greaves, who has been dead these two years. This is the only son, Sir Launcelot, the best-natured, worthy, generous gentleman—I care not who knows it. I love him as well as if he was my own flesh and blood——"

At this period Tom, whose heart was of the melting mood, began to sob and weep plenteously, from pure affection. Crowe, who was not very subject to these tendernesses, d—ed him for a chicken-hearted lubber, repeating, with much peevishness, " What dost cry for ? What dost cry for, noddy ? " The surgeon, impatient to know the story of Sir Launcelot, which he had heard imperfectly recounted, begged that Mr. Clarke would compose himself, and relate it as circumstantially as his memory would retain the particulars, and Tom, wiping his eyes, promised to give him that satisfaction, which the reader, if he be so minded, may partake in the next chapter.

CHAPTER III

Which the Reader, on perusal, may wish were *Chapter the last.*

THE doctor prescribed a *repetatur* of the julep, and mixed the ingredients, *secundum artem*; Tom Clarke hemmed thrice to clear his pipes; while the rest of the company, including Dolly and her mother, who had by this time administered to the knight, composed themselves into earnest and hushed attention. Then the young lawyer began his narrative to this effect :

" I tell ye what, gemmen, I don't pretend in this here case to flourish and harangue like a—having never been called to—but what of that, d'ye see ? Perhaps I may know as much as—facts are facts, as the saying is. I shall tell, repeat, and relate a plain story—matters of fact, d'ye see, without rhetoric, oratory, ornament, or embellishment ; without repetition, tautology, circumlocution, or going about the bush ; facts which I shall aver, partly on the testimony of my own knowledge, and partly from the information of responsible evidences of good repute and credit, any circumstance known to the contrary notwithstanding. For as the law saith, if so be as how there is *an exception* to evidence, that *exception* is in its nature but a denial of what is taken to be good by the other party, and *exceptio in non exceptis, firmat regulam*, d'ye see ? But, howsomever, in regard to this here affair, we need not be so scrupulous as if we were pleading before a judge *sedente curia*."

Ferret, whose curiosity was rather more eager than that of any other person in this audience, being provoked by this preamble, dashed the pipe he had just filled in pieces against the grate, and after having pronounced the interjection *pish!* with an acrimony of aspect altogether peculiar to himself, " If," said he, " impertinence and folly were felony by the statute, there would be no want of unexceptionable evidence to hang such an eternal babbler."—" Anan, babbler ! " cried Tom, reddening with passion, and starting up. " I'd have you to know, sir, that I can bite as well as babble, and that, if I am so minded, I can run upon the foot after my game without being in fault, as the saying is, and, which is more, I can shake an old fox by the collar."

How far this young lawyer might have proceeded to prove himself staunch on the person of the misanthrope, if he had not been prevented, we shall not determine ; but the whole company were alarmed at his looks and expressions. Dolly's rosy cheeks assumed an ash colour, while she ran between the disputants, crying, " Naay, naay—vor the love of God doan't then, doan't then ! " But Captain Crowe exerted a parental authority over his nephew, saying, " Avast, Tom, avast ! Snug's the word—we'll have no boarding, d'ye see. Haul forward thy chair again, take thy berth, and proceed with thy story in a direct course, without yawing like a Dutch yanky."

Tom, thus tutored, recollected himself, resumed his seat, and, after some pause, plunged at once into the current of narration. " I told you before, gemmen, that the gentleman in armour was the only son of Sir Everhard Greaves, who possessed a free estate of five thousand a year in our country, and was respected by all his neighbours as much for his personal merit as for his family fortune. With respect to his son Launcelot, whom you have seen, I can remember nothing until he returned from the university, about the age of seventeen, and then I myself was not more than ten years old. The young gemman was at that time in mourning for his mother ; though, God knows, Sir Everhard had more cause to rejoice than to be afflicted at her death :—for, among friends " (here he lowered his voice, and looked round the kitchen), " she was very whimsical, expensive,

ill-tempered, and, I'm afraid, a little—upon the—flighty
order—a little touched or so;—but mum for that—the
lady is now dead; and it is my maxim, *de mortuis nil nisi
bonum.*   The young squire was even then very handsome,
and looked remarkably well in his weepers ; but he had an
awkward air and shambling gait, stooped mortally, and was
so shy and silent that he would not look a stranger in the face,
nor open his mouth before company.   Whenever he spied
a horse or carriage at the gate, he would make his escape
into the garden, and from thence into the park ; where
many is the good time and often he has been found sitting
under a tree, with a book in his hand, reading Greek, Latin,
and other foreign linguas.

"Sir Everhard himself was no great scholar, and my
father had forgotten his classical learning ; and so the rector
of the parish was desired to examine young Launcelot.
It was a long time before he found an opportunity ; the
squire always gave him the slip.   At length the parson
catched him in bed of a morning, and, locking the door,
to it they went tooth and nail.   What passed betwixt
them the Lord in heaven knows ; but when the doctor
came forth, he looked wild and haggard as if he had seen a
ghost, his face as white as paper, and his lips trembling
like an aspen-leaf.   'Parson,' said the knight, 'what is the
matter ?—how dost find my son ?   I hope he won't turn
out a ninny, and disgrace his family ? '   The doctor, wiping
the sweat from his forehead, replied, with some hesitation,
'he could not tell, he hoped the best—the squire was to
be sure a very extraordinary young gentleman.'   But the
father urging him to give an explicit answer, he frankly
declared, that, in his opinion, the son would turn out either
a mirror of wisdom, or a monument of folly ; for his genius
and disposition were altogether preternatural.   The knight
was sorely vexed at this declaration, and signified his displeasure by saying the doctor, like a true priest, dealt in
mysteries and oracles, that would admit of different and
indeed contrary interpretations.   He afterwards consulted
my father, who had served as a steward upon the estate for

bove thirty years, and acquired a considerable share of his avour. 'Will Clarke,' said he, with tears in his eyes, 'what hall I do with this unfortunate lad? I would to God he iad never been born; for I fear he will bring my grey hairs vith sorrow to the grave. When I am gone, he will throw iway the estate, and bring himself to infamy and ruin, by :eeping company with rooks and beggars.—O Will! I could orgive extravagance in a young man; but it breaks my heart :o see my only son give such repeated proofs of a mean spirit ind sordid disposition!'

" Here the old gentleman shed a flood of tears, and not vithout some shadow of reason. By this time Launcelot vas grown so reserved to his father that he seldom saw him)r any of his relations, except when he was in a manner forced :o appear at table, and there his bashfulness seemed every iay to increase. On the other hand, he had formed some 7ery strange connections. Every morning he visited the itable, where he not only conversed with the grooms and helpers, but scraped acquaintance with the horses; he fed his favourites with his own hand, stroked, caressed, and rode them by turns, till at last they grew so familiar, that, even when they were afield at grass, and saw him at a distance, they would toss their manes, whinny like so many colts at sight of the dam, and, galloping up to the place where he stood, smell him all over.

" You must know that I myself, though a child, was his companion in all these excursions. He took a liking to me on account of my being his godson, and gave me more money than I knew what to do with. He had always plenty of cash for the asking, as my father was ordered to supply him liberally, the knight thinking that a command of money might help to raise his thoughts to a proper consideration of his own importance. He never could endure a common beggar that was not either in a state of infancy or of old age; but in other respects he made the guineas fly in such a manner as looked more like madness than generosity. He had no communication with your rich yeomen, but rather treated them and their families with studied contempt, because forsooth they pretended to assume the dress and manners of the gentry.

" They kept their footmen, their saddle horses, and chaises ; their wives and daughters appeared in their jewels, their silks, and their satins, their negligees and trollopees ; their clumsy shanks, like so many shins of beef, were cased in silk hose and embroidered slippers ; their raw red fingers, gross as the pipes of a chamber organ, which had been employed in milking the cows, in twirling the mop or churn-staff, being adorned with diamonds, were taught to thrum the pandola, and even to touch the keys of the harpsichord ! Nay, in every village they kept a rout, and set up an assembly ; and in one place a hog-butcher was master of the ceremonies.

" I have heard Mr. Greaves ridicule them for their vanity and awkward imitation ; and therefore, I believe, he avoided all concerns with them, even when they endeavoured to engage his attention. It was the lower sort of people with whom he chiefly conversed, such as ploughmen, ditchers, and other day-labourers. To every cottager in the parish he was a bounteous benefactor. He was, in the literal sense of the word, a careful overseer of the poor, for he went from house to house, industriously inquiring into the distresses of the people. He repaired their huts, clothed their backs, filled their bellies, and supplied them with necessaries for exercising their industry and different occupations.

" I'll give you one instance now, as a specimen of his character : he and I, strolling one day on the side of a common, saw two boys picking hips and haws from the hedges, one seemed to be about five, and the other a year older ; they were both barefoot and ragged, but at the same time fat, fair, and in good condition. 'Who do you belong to ? ' said Mr. Greaves. ' To Mary Stile,' replied the oldest, ' the widow that rents one of them housen.' ' And how dost live, my boy ? Thou lookest fresh and jolly,' resumed the squire. ' Lived well enough till yester-day,' answered the child. ' And pray what happened yesterday, my boy ? ' continued Mr. Greaves. ' Happened!' said he, 'why, mammy had a coople of little Welsh keawes, that gi'en milk enough to fill all our bellies; mammy's, and mine, and Dick's here, and my two little sisters' at hoam. Yesterday the squire seized the keawes for rent, God rot'un! Mammy's gone to bed sick and sulky, my two sisters be crying at hoam vor vood, and Dick and I be come hither to pick haws and bullies."

" My godfather's face grew red as scarlet; he took one of the children in either hand, and leading them towards the house, found Sir Everhard talking with my father before the gate. Instead of avoiding the old gentleman, as usual, he brushed up to him with a spirit he had never shown before, and presenting the two ragged boys, ' Surely, sir,' said he, ' you will not countenance that there ruffian, your steward, in oppressing the widow and fatherless ? On pretence of distraining for the rent of a cottage, he has robbed the mother of these and other poor infant-orphans of two cows, which afforded them their whole sustenance. Shall you be concerned in tearing the hard-earned morsel from the mouth of indigence ? Shall your name, which has been so long mentioned as a blessing, be now detested as a curse by the poor, the helpless, and forlorn ? The father of these babes was once your gamekeeper, who died of a consumption caught in your service. You see they are almost naked. I found them plucking haws and sloes, in order to appease their hunger. The wretched mother is starving in a cold cottage, distracted with the cries of other two infants, clamorous for food; and while her heart is bursting with anguish and despair, she invokes Heaven to avenge the widow's cause upon the head of her unrelenting landlord ! '

" This unexpected address brought tears into the eyes of the good old gentleman. ' Will Clarke,' said he to my father, ' how durst you abuse my authority at this rate ? You who know I have always been a protector, not an oppressor of the needy and unfortunate. I charge you go immediately and comfort this poor woman with imme-diate relief; instead of her own cows, let her have two of the best milch cows of my dairy; they shall graze in my parks

in summer, and be foddered with my hay in winter.—
She shall sit rent free for life, and I will take care of these her
poor orphans.'

" This was a very affecting scene. Mr. Launcelot took his
father's hand and kissed it, while the tears ran down his
cheeks ; and Sir Everhard embraced his son with great
tenderness, crying, ' My dear boy ! God be praised for having
given you such a feeling heart.' My father himself was
moved, thof a practitioner of the law, and consequently
used to distresses. He declared that he had given no
directions to distrain, and that the bailiff must have done it
by his own authority. ' If that be the case,' said the young
squire, ' let the inhuman rascal be turned out of our service.'

" Well, gemmen, all the children were immediately clothed
and fed, and the poor widow had well-nigh run distracted
with joy. The old knight, being of a humane temper
himself, was pleased to see such proofs of his son's generosity.
He was not angry at his spending his money, but at squan-
dering away his time among the dregs of the people. For
you must know, he not only made matches, portioned poor
maidens, and set up young couples that came together
without money, but he mingled in every rustic diversion,
and bore away the prize in every contest. He excelled
every swain of that district in feats of strength and activity ;
in leaping, running, wrestling, cricket, cudgel-playing, and
pitching the bar ; and was confessed to be, out of sight,
the best dancer at all wakes and holidays. Happy was the
country-girl who could engage the young squire as her
partner ! To be sure, it was a comely sight for to see as
how the buxom country-lasses, fresh and fragrant and
blushing like the rose, in their best apparel dight, their
white hose, and clean short dimity petticoats, their gaudy
gowns of printed cotton, their top-knots and stomachers,
bedizened with bunches of ribbons of various colours, green,
pink, and yellow, to see them crowned with garlands, and
assembled on May-day, to dance before Squire Launcelot, as
he made his morning's progress through the village. Then
all the young peasants made their appearance with cockades,

suited to the fancies of their several sweethearts, and boughs of flowering hawthorn. The children sported about like flocks of frisking lambs, or the young fry swarming under the sunny bank of some meandering river. The old men and women, in their holiday garments, stood at their doors to receive their benefactor, and poured forth blessings on him as he passed. The children welcomed him with their shrill shouts, the damsels with songs of praise, and the young men, with the pipe and tabor, marched before him to the Maypole, which was bedecked with flowers and bloom. There the rural dance began. A plentiful dinner, with oceans of good liquor, was bespoke at the White Hart. The whole village was regaled at the squire's expense ; and both the day and the night was spent in mirth and pleasure.

" Lord help you ! he could not rest if he thought there was an aching heart in the whole parish. Every paltry cottage was in a little time converted into a pretty, snug, comfortable habitation, with a wooden porch at the door, glass casements in the windows, and a little garden behind, well stored with greens, roots, and salads. In a word, the poor's rate was reduced to a mere trifle, and one would have thought the golden age was revived in Yorkshire. But, as I told you before, the old knight could not bear to see his only son so wholly attached to these lowly pleasures, while he industriously shunned all opportunities of appearing in that superior sphere to which he was designed by nature and by fortune. He imputed his conduct to meanness of spirit, and advised with my father touching the properest expedient to wean his affections from such low-born pursuits. My father counselled him to send the young gentleman up to London, to be entered as a student in the Temple, and recommended him to the superintendence of some person who knew the town, and might engage him insensibly in such amusements and connections as would soon lift his ideas above the humble objects on which they had been hitherto employed.

" This advice appeared so salutary that it was followed without the least hesitation. The young squire himself

3

was perfectly well satisfied with the proposal ; and in a few
days he set out for the great city. But there was not a dry
eye in the parish at his departure, although he prevailed
upon his father to pay in his absence all the pensions he had
granted to those who could not live on the fruit of their
own industry. In what manner he spent his time in London
it is none of my business to inquire, thof I know pretty well
what kind of lives are led by gemmen of your Inns of Court.
I myself once belonged to Serjeants' Inn, and was perhaps
as good a wit and a critic as any Templar of them all. Nay,
as for that matter, thof I despise vanity, I can aver with a
safe conscience that I had once the honour to belong to the
society called *the Town*. We were all of us attorney's clerks,
gemmen, and had our meetings at an ale-house in Butcher
Row, where we regulated the diversions of the theatre.

" But to return from this digression : Sir Everhard
Greaves did not seem to be very well pleased with the
conduct of his son at London. He got notice of some
irregularities and scrapes into which he had fallen, and the
squire seldom wrote to his father, except to draw upon him
for money, which he did so fast that in eighteen months the
old gentleman lost all patience.

" At this period Squire Darnel chanced to die, leaving
an only daughter, a minor, heiress of three thousand a year,
under the guardianship of her Uncle Anthony, whose brutal
character all the world knows. The breath was no sooner
out of his brother's body than he resolved, if possible, to
succeed him in Parliament as representative for the borough
of Ashenton. Now you must know that this borough had
been for many years a bone of contention between the
families of Greaves and Darnel, and at length the difference
was compromised by the interposition of friends, on condition
that Sir Everhard and Squire Darnel should alternately
represent the place in Parliament. They agreed to this
compromise for their mutual convenience, but they were
never heartily reconciled. Their political principles did not
tally, and their wives looked upon each other as rivals in
fortune and magnificence. So that there was no intercourse

between them, thof they lived in the same neighbourhood. On the contrary, in all disputes, they constantly headed the opposite parties. Sir Everhard, understanding that Anthony Darnel had begun to canvass, and was putting every iron in the fire, in violation and contempt of the *pactum familiæ* before mentioned, fell into a violent passion, that brought on a severe fit of the gout, by which he was disabled from giving personal attention to his own interest. My father, indeed, employed all his diligence and address, and spared neither money, time, nor constitution, till at length he drank himself into a consumption, which was the death of him. But, after all, there is a great difference between a steward and a principal. Mr. Darnel attended in *propria persona*, flattered and caressed the women, feasted the electors, hired mobs, made processions, and scattered about his money in such a manner that our friends durst hardly show their heads in public.

" At this very crisis our young squire, to whom his father had written an account of the transaction, arrived unexpectedly at Greavesbury Hall, and had a long private conference with Sir Everhard. The news of his return spread like wildfire through all that part of the country. Bonfires were made, and the bells set a-ringing in several towns and steeples, and next morning above seven hundred people were assembled at the gate, with music, flags, and streamers, to welcome their young squire, and accompany him to the borough of Ashenton. He set out on foot with his retinue, and entered one end of the town just as Mr. Darnel's mob had come in at the other. Both arrived about the same time at the market-place ; but Mr. Darnel, mounting first into the balcony of the town-house, made a long speech to the people in favour of his own pretensions, not without some invidious reflections glanced at Sir Everhard, his competitor.

" We did not much mind the acclamations of his party, which we knew had been hired for the purpose, but we were in some pain for Mr. Greaves, who had not been used to speak in public. He took his turn, however, in the balcony,

and, uncovering his head, bowed all round with the most
engaging courtesy. He was dressed in a green frock, trimmed
with gold, and his own dark hair flowed about his ears in
natural curls, while his face was overspread with a blush,
that improved the glow of youth to a deeper crimson, and
I daresay set many a female heart a-palpitating. When he
made his first appearance, there was just such a humming
and clapping of hands as you may have heard when the
celebrated Garrick comes upon the stage in *King Lear*, or
King Richard, or any other top character. But how agreeably
were we disappointed when our young gentleman made such
an oration as would not have disgraced a Pitt, an Egmont,
or a Murray ! While he spoke, all was hushed in admiration
and attention ; you could have almost heard a feather drop
to the ground. It would have charmed you to hear with
what modesty he recounted the services which his father
and grandfather had done to the corporation ; with what
eloquence he expatiated upon the shameful infraction of
the treaty subsisting between the two families, and with
what keen and spirited strokes of satire he retorted the
sarcasms of Darnel.

" He no sooner concluded his harangue than there was
such a burst of applause as seemed to rend the very sky.
Our music immediately struck up, our people advanced with
their ensigns, and, as every man had a good cudgel, broken
heads would have ensued, had not Mr. Darnel and his party
thought proper to retreat with uncommon despatch. He
never offered to make another public entrance, as he saw
the torrent ran so violently against him, but sat down with
his loss, and withdrew his opposition, though at bottom
extremely mortified and incensed. Sir Everhard was unanimously elected, and appeared to be the happiest man upon
earth ; for besides the pleasure arising from his victory
over this competitor, he was now fully satisfied that his son,
instead of disgracing, would do honour to his family. It
would have moved a heart of stone to see with what a tender
transport of paternal joy he received his dear Launcelot,
after having heard of his deportment and success at Ashenton,

where, by the bye, he gave a ball to the ladies, and displayed as much elegance and politeness as if he had been bred at the court of Versailles.

"This joyous season was of short duration. In a little time all the happiness of the family was overcast by a sad incident, which hath left such an unfortunate impression upon the mind of the young gentleman as, I am afraid, will never be effaced. Mr. Darnel's niece and ward, the great heiress, whose name is Aurelia, was the most celebrated beauty of the whole country; if I said the whole kingdom, or indeed all Europe, perhaps I should barely do her justice. I don't pretend to be a limner, gemmen, nor does it become me to delineate such excellence, but surely I may presume to repeat from the play—

> Oh! she is all that painting can express,
> Or youthful poets fancy when they love?

"At that time she might be about seventeen, tall and fair, and so exquisitely shaped. You may talk of your Venus de Medicis, your Dianas, your Nymphs, and Galateas, but if Praxiteles, and Roubilliac, and Wilton were to lay their heads together, in order to make a complete pattern of beauty, they would hardly reach her model of perfection. As for complexion, poets will talk of blending the lily with the rose, and bring in a parcel of similes of cowslips, carnations, pinks, and daisies. There's Dolly, now, has got a very good complexion. Indeed, she's the very picture of health and innocence—you are, indeed, my pretty lass; but *parva componere magnis*. Miss Darnel is all amazing beauty, delicacy, and dignity! Then the softness and expression of her fine blue eyes, her pouting lips of coral hue, her neck, that rises like a tower of polished alabaster between two mounts of snow. I tell you what, gemmen, it don't signify talking; if e'er a one of you was to meet this young lady alone, in the midst of a heath or common, or any unfrequented place, he would down on his knees, and think he kneeled before some supernatural being. I'll tell you more: she not only resembles an angel in beauty, but a saint in

goodness, and a hermit in humility—so void of all pride
and affectation, so soft and sweet, and affable and humane !
Lord ! I could tell such instances of her charity !

" Sure enough, she and Sir Launcelot were formed by
nature for each other. Howsoever, the cruel hand of fortune
hath intervened, and severed them for ever. Every soul
that knew them both said it was a thousand pities but they
should come together, and extinguish, in their happy union,
the mutual animosity of the two families, which had so often
embroiled the whole neighbourhood. Nothing was heard
but the praises of Miss Aurelia Darnel and Mr. Launcelot
Greaves, and no doubt the parties were prepossessed, by
this applause, in favour of each other. At length Mr.
Greaves went one Sunday to her parish church, but though
the greater part of the congregation watched their looks,
they could not perceive that she took the least notice of him,
or that he seemed to be struck with her appearance. He
afterwards had an opportunity of seeing her, more at leisure,
at the York assembly during the races ; but this opportunity
was productive of no good effect, because he had that same
day quarrelled with her uncle on the turf.

" An old grudge, you know, gemmen, is soon inflamed
to a fresh rupture. It was thought Mr. Darnel came on
purpose to show his resentment. They differed about a
bet upon Miss Cleverlegs, and, in the course of the dispute,
Mr. Darnel called him a petulant boy. The young squire,
who was as hasty as gunpowder, told him he was man enough
to chastise him for his insolence, and would do it on the spot
if he thought it would not interrupt the diversion. In all
probability they would have come to points immediately,
had not the gentlemen interposed, so that nothing further
passed, but abundance of foul language on the part of Mr.
Anthony, and a repeated defiance to single combat.

" Mr. Greaves, making a low bow, retired from the field,
and in the evening danced at the assembly with a young
lady from the bishopric, seemingly in good temper and
spirits, without having any words with Mr. Darnel, who
was also present. But in the morning he visited that proud

neighbour betimes; and they had almost reached a grove of trees on the north side of the town, when they were suddenly overtaken by half a dozen gentlemen, who had watched their motions. It was in vain for them to dissemble their design, which could not now take effect. They gave up their pistols, and a reconciliation was patched up by the pressing remonstrances of their common friends; but Mr. Darnel's hatred still rankled at bottom, and soon broke out in the sequel. About three months after this transaction, his niece Aurelia, with her mother, having been to visit a lady in the chariot, the horses being young, and not used to the traces, were startled at the braying of a jackass on the common, and, taking fright, ran away with the carriage like lightning. The coachman was thrown from the box, and the ladies screamed piteously for help. Mr. Greaves chanced to be a-horseback on the other side of an enclosure, when he heard their shrieks, and riding up to the hedge, knew the chariot, and saw their disaster. The horses were then running full speed in such a direction as to drive headlong over a precipice into a stone quarry, where they and the chariot and the ladies must be dashed to pieces.

"You may conceive, gemmen, what his thoughts were when he saw such a fine young lady, in the flower of her age, just plunging into eternity; when he saw the lovely Aurelia on the brink of being precipitated among rocks, where her delicate limbs must be mangled and torn asunder; when he perceived that, before he could ride round by the gate, the tragedy would be finished. The fence was so thick and high, flanked with a broad ditch on the outside, that he could not hope to clear it, although he was mounted on Scipio, bred out of Miss Cowslip, the sire Muley, and his grandsire the famous Arabian Mustapha. Scipio was bred by my father, who would not have taken a hundred guineas for him from any other person but the young squire. Indeed, I have heard my poor father say——"

By this time Ferret's impatience was become so outrageous that he exclaimed in a furious tone, " D—n your father, and his horse, and his colt into the bargain ! "

Tom made no reply, but began to strip with great expedition. Captain Crowe was so choked with passion that he could utter nothing but disjointed sentences. He rose from his seat, brandished his horsewhip, and, seizing his nephew by the collar, cried, " Odd's heartlikins ! sirrah, I have a good mind—— Devil fire your running tackle, you land-lubber ! Can't you steer without all this tacking hither and thither, and the Lord knows whither ? 'Noint my block ! I'd give thee a rope's end for thy supper if it wan't——"

Dolly had conceived a sneaking kindness for the young lawyer, and thinking him in danger of being roughly handled, flew to his relief. She twisted her hand in Crowe's neckcloth without ceremony, crying, " Sha't then, I tell thee, old codger—who kears a vig vor thy voolish tantrums ? "

While Crowe looked black in the face, and ran the risk of strangulation under the grip of this Amazon, Mr. Clarke, having disengaged himself of his hat, wig, coat, and waistcoat, advanced in an elegant attitude of manual offence towards the misanthrope, who snatched up a gridiron from the chimney corner, and Discord seemed to clap her sooty wings in expectation of battle. But as the reader may have more than once already cursed the unconscionable length of this chapter, we must postpone to the next opportunity the incidents that succeeded this denunciation of war.

CHAPTER IV

In which it appears that the Knight, when heartily set in
for sleeping, was not easily disturbed.

In all probability the kitchen of the Black Lion, from a domestic temple of society and good fellowship, would have been converted into a scene or stage of sanguinary dispute, had not Pallas, or Discretion, interposed in the person of Mr. Fillet, and with the assistance of the ostler disarmed the combatants, not only of their arms, but also of their resentment.

The impetuosity of Mr. Clarke was a little checked at
sight of the gridiron, which Ferret brandished with uncommon dexterity; a circumstance from whence the company were, upon reflection, induced to believe that before
he plunged into the sea of politics he had occasionally figured
in the character of that facetious droll, who accompanies
your itinerant physicians, under the familiar appellation of
Merry-Andrew, or Jack-pudding, and on a wooden stage
entertains the populace with a solo on the salt-box, or a
sonata on the tongs and gridiron. Be that as it may, the
young lawyer seemed to be a little discomposed at the
glancing of this extraordinary weapon of offence, which the
fair hands of Dolly had scoured, until it had shone as bright
as the shield of Achilles; or as the emblem of good old
English fare, which hangs by a red ribbon round the neck
of that thrice-honoured sage's head, in velvet bonnet cased,
who presides by rotation at the genial board, distinguished
by the title of the. *Beef-steak   Club*: where the delicate
rumps irresistibly attract the stranger's eye, and, while they
seem to cry, " Come cut me—come cut me," constrain, by
wondrous sympathy, each mouth to overflow. Where the
obliging and humorous Jemmy B——t, the gentle Billy
H——d, replete with human kindness, and the generous
Johnny B——d, respected and beloved by all the world,
attend as the priests and ministers of mirth, good cheer,
and jollity, and assist with culinary art the raw, unpractised,
awkward guest.

·· But to return from this digressive simile. The ostler
no sooner stepped between those menacing antagonists
than Tom Clarke very quietly resumed his clothes, and Mr.
Ferret resigned the gridiron without further question.
The doctor did not find it quite so easy to release the throat
of Captain Crowe from the masculine grasp of the virago
Dolly, whose fingers could not be disengaged until the honest
seaman was almost at the last gasp. After some pause,
during which he panted for breath, and untied his neckcloth, " D—n thee, for a brimstone galley," cried he;
" I was never so grappled withal since I knew a card from

a compass. Adzooks ! the jade has so tautened my rigging, d'ye see, that I—— Snatch my bow-lines, if I come athwart thy hawser, I'll turn thy keel upwards—or mayhap set thee a-driving under thy bare poles—I will—I will, you hell-fire, saucy—I will."

Dolly made no reply, but seeing Mr. Clarke sit down again with great composure, took her station likewise at the opposite side of the apartment. Then Mr. Fillet requested the lawyer to proceed with his story, which, after three hems, he accordingly prosecuted in these words :

"I told you, gemmen, that Mr. Greaves was mounted on Scipio, when he saw Miss Darnel and her mother in danger of being hurried over a precipice. Without reflecting a moment, he gave Scipio the spur, and at one spring he cleared five-and-twenty feet, over hedge and ditch and every obstruction. Then he rode full speed, in order to turn the coach-horses ; and, finding them quite wild and furious, endeavoured to drive against the counter of the hither horse, which he missed, and staked poor Scipio on the pole of the coach. The shock was so great that the coach-horses made a full stop within ten yards of the quarry, and Mr. Greaves was thrown forwards towards the coach-box, which mounting with admirable dexterity he seized the reins before the horses could recover of their fright. At that instant the coachman came running up, and loosed them from the traces with the utmost despatch. Mr. Greaves had now time to give his attention to the ladies, who were well-nigh distracted with fear. He no sooner opened the chariot door than Aurelia, with a wildness of look, sprang into his arms, and, clasping him round the neck, fainted away. I leave you to guess, gemmen, what were his feelings at this instant. The mother was not so discomposed but that she could contribute to the recovery of her daughter, whom the young squire still supported in his embrace. At length she retrieved the use of her senses, and, perceiving the situation in which she was, the blood revisited her face with a redoubled glow, while she desired him to set her down upon the turf.

"Mrs. Darnel, far from being shy or reserved in her compliments of acknowledgments, kissed Mr. Launcelot without ceremony, the tears of gratitude running down her cheeks; she called him her dear son, her generous deliverer, who, at the hazard of his own life, had saved her and her child from the most dismal fate that could be imagined.

"Mr. Greaves was so much transported on this occasion that he could not help disclosing a passion which he had hitherto industriously concealed. 'What I have done,' said he, 'was but a common office of humanity, which I would have performed for any of my fellow-creatures; but for the preservation of Miss Aurelia Darnel, I would at any time sacrifice my life with pleasure.' The young lady did not hear this declaration unmoved. Her face was again flushed, and her eyes sparkled with pleasure. Nor was the youth's confession disagreeable to the good lady, her mother, who, at one glance, perceived all the advantages of such a union between the two families.

"Mr. Greaves proposed to send the coachman to his father's stable for a pair of sober horses, that could be depended upon, to draw the ladies home to their own habitation; but they declined the offer, and chose to walk, as the distance was not great. He then insisted upon his being their conductor, and, each taking him under the arm, supported them to their own gate, where such an apparition filled all the domestics with astonishment. Mrs. Darnel, taking him by the hand, led him into the house, where she welcomed him with another affectionate embrace, and indulged him with an ambrosial kiss of Aurelia, saying, 'But for you we had both been by this time in eternity. Sure it was Heaven that sent you as an angel to our assistance!' She kindly inquired if he had himself sustained any damage in administering that desperate remedy to which they owed their lives. She entertained him with a small collation; and in the course of the conversation lamented the animosity which had so long divided two neighbouring families of such influence and character. He was not slow in signifying his approbation of her remarks, and expressing the most eager desire of seeing all those unhappy differences removed. In a word, they parted with mutual satisfaction.

" Just as he advanced from the outward gate, on his return to Greavesbury Hall, he was met by Anthony Darnel on horseback, who, riding up to him with marks of surprise and resentment, saluted him with, ' Your servant, sir. Have you any commands for me ? ' The other replying with an air of indifference, ' None at all,' Mr. Darnel asked what had procured him the honour of a visit. The young gentleman, perceiving by the manner in which he spoke that the old quarrel was not yet extinguished, answered, with equal disdain, that the visit was not intended for him, and that, if he wanted to know the cause of it, he might inform himself by his own servants.' ' So I shall,' cried the uncle of Aurelia ; ' and perhaps let you know my sentiments of the matter.' ' Hereafter as it may be,' said the youth, who, turning out of the avenue, walked home, and made his father acquainted with the particulars of this adventure.

" The old gentleman chid him for his rashness, but seemed pleased with the success of his attempt ; and still more so when he understood his sentiments of Aurelia and the deportment of the ladies.

" Next day the son sent over a servant with a compliment to inquire about their health, and the messenger, being seen by Mr. Darnel, was told that the ladies were indisposed, and did not choose to be troubled with messages. The mother was really seized with a fever, produced by the agitation of her spirits, which every day became more and more violent, until the physicians despaired of her life. Believing that her end approached, she sent a trusty servant to Mr. Greaves, desiring that she might see him without delay, and he immediately set out with the messenger, who introduced him in the dark.

" He found the old lady in bed almost exhausted, and the fair Aurelia sitting by her overwhelmed with grief, her lovely hair in the utmost disorder, and her charming eyes inflamed with weeping. The good lady beckoning

Mr. Launcelot to approach, and directing all the attendants to quit the room, except a favourite maid, from whom I learned the story, she took him by the hand, and fixing her eyes upon him with all the fondness of a mother, shed some tears in silence, while the same marks of sorrow trickled down his cheeks. After this affecting pause, ' My dear son,' said she, ' oh that I could have lived to see you so indeed ! You find me hastening to the goal of life.' Here the tender-hearted Aurelia, being unable to contain herself longer, broke out into a violent passion of grief, and wept aloud. The mother, waiting patiently till she had thus given vent to her anguish, calmly entreated her to resign herself submissively to the will of Heaven ; then turning to Mr. Launcelot, ' I had indulged,' said she, ' a fond hope of seeing you allied to my family. This is no time for me to insist upon the ceremonies and forms of a vain world. Aurelia looks upon you with the eyes of tender prepossession.' No sooner had she pronounced these words than he threw himself on his knees before the young lady, and pressing her hand to his lips, breathed the softest expressions which the most delicate love could suggest. ' I know,' resumed the mother, ' that your passion is mutually sincere, and I should die satisfied if I thought your union would not be opposed ; but that violent man, my brother-in-law, who is Aurelia's, sole guardian, will thwart her wishes with every obstacle that brutal resentment and implacable malice can contrive. Mr. Greaves, I have long admired your virtues, and am confident that I can depend upon your honour. You shall give me your word, that when I am gone you will take no steps in this affair without the concurrence of your father, and endeavour, by all fair and honourable means, to vanquish the prejudices, and obtain the consent of her uncle ; the rest we must leave to the dispensation of Providence.'

" The squire promised, in the most solemn and fervent manner, to obey all her injunctions, as the last dictates of a parent whom he should never cease to honour. Then she favoured them both with a great deal of salutary advice touching their conduct before and after marriage, and presented him with a ring as a memorial of her affection; at the same time he pulled another off his finger, and made a tender of it as a pledge of his love to Aurelia, whom her mother permitted to receive this token. Finally, he took a last farewell of the good matron, and returned to his father with the particulars of this interview.

" In two days Mrs. Darnel departed this life, and Aurelia was removed to the house of a relation, where her grief had like to have proved fatal to her constitution.

" In the meantime the mother was no sooner committed to the earth, than Mr. Greaves, mindful of her exhortations, began to take measures for a reconciliation with the guardian. He engaged several gentlemen to interpose their good offices, but they always met with the most mortifying repulse, and at last Anthony Darnel declared that his hatred to the house of Greaves was hereditary, habitual, and unconquerable. He swore he would spend his heart's blood to perpetuate the quarrel, and that, sooner than his niece should match with young Launcelot, he would sacrifice her with his own hand.

" The young gentleman, finding his prejudice so rancorous and invincible, left off making any further advances, and, since he found it impossible to obtain his consent, resolved to cultivate the good graces of Aurelia, and wed her in despite of her implacable guardian. He found means to establish a literary correspondence with her as soon as her grief was a little abated, and even to effect an interview, after her return to her own house; but he soon had reason to repent of his indulgence. The uncle entertained spies upon the young lady, who gave him an account of this meeting, in consequence of which she was suddenly hurried to some distant part of the country, which we never could discover.

" It was then we thought Mr. Launcelot a little disordered in his brain, his grief was so wild, and his passion so impetuous. He refused all sustenance, neglected his person, renounced his amusements, rode out in the rain, sometimes bareheaded, strolled about the fields all night, and became

so peevish that none of the domestics durst speak to him
without the hazard of broken bones. Having played these
pranks for about three weeks, to the unspeakable chagrin
of his father, and the astonishment of all that knew him,
he suddenly grew calm, and his good-humour returned.
But this, as your seafaring people say, was a deceitful calm,
that soon ushered in a dreadful storm.

"He had long sought an opportunity to tamper with
some of Mr. Darnel's servants, who could inform him of
the place where Aurelia was confined; but there was not
one about the family who could give him that satisfaction,
for the persons who accompanied her remained as a watch
upon her motions, and none of the other domestics were
privy to the transaction. All attempts proving fruitless,
he could no longer restrain his impatience, but throwing
himself in the way of the uncle, upbraided him in such harsh
terms, that a formal challenge ensued. They agreed to
decide their difference without witnesses, and one morning,
before sunrise, met on that very common where Mr. Greaves
had saved the life of Aurelia. The first pistol was fired
on each side without any effect, but Mr. Darnel's second
wounded the young squire in the flank; nevertheless, having
a pistol in reserve, he desired his antagonist to ask his life.
The other, instead of submitting, drew his sword, and Mr.
Greaves, firing his piece into the air, followed his example.
The contest then became very hot, though of short continuance. Darnel being disarmed at the first onset, our
young squire gave him back the sword, which he was base
enough to use a second time against his conqueror. Such
an instance of repeated ingratitude and brutal ferocity
divested Mr. Greaves of his temper and forbearance. He
attacked Mr. Anthony with great fury, and at the first lunge
ran him up to the hilt, at the same time seized with his left
hand the shell of his enemy's sword, which he broke in
disdain. Mr. Darnel having fallen, the other immediately
mounted his horse, which he had tied to a tree before the
engagement, and, riding full speed to Ashenton, sent a
surgeon to Anthony's assistance. He afterwards ingenuously

had promised the presentation to another clergyman. In the meantime, Sir Launcelot, chancing one Sunday to ride through a lane, perceived a horse saddled and bridled, feeding on the side of a fence, and, casting his eyes around, beheld on the other side of the hedge an object lying extended on the ground, which he took to be the body of a murdered traveller. He forthwith alighted, and, leaping into the field, descried a man at full length, wrapped in a greatcoat and writhing in agony. Approaching nearer, he found it was a clergyman, in his gown and cassock. When he inquired into the case, and offered his assistance, the stranger rose up, thanked him for his courtesy, and declared that he was now very well. The knight, who thought there was something mysterious in this incident, expressed a desire to know the cause of his rolling in the grass in that manner, and the clergyman, who knew his person, made no scruple in gratifying his curiosity. 'You must know, sir,' said he, 'I serve the curacy of your own parish, for which the late incumbent paid me twenty pounds a year ; but this sum being scarce sufficient to maintain my wife and children, who are five in number, I agreed to read prayers in the afternoon at another church, about four miles from hence, and for this additional duty I receive ten pounds more. As I keep a horse, it was formerly an agreeable exercise rather than a toil, but of late years I have been afflicted with a rupture, for which I consulted the most eminent operators in the kingdom ; but I have no cause to rejoice in the effects of their advice, though one of them assured me I was completely cured. The malady is now more troublesome than ever, and often comes upon me so violently while I am on horseback, that I am forced to alight, and lie down upon the ground, until the cause of the disorder can for the time be reduced.'

" Sir Launcelot not only condoled with him upon his misfortune, but desired him to throw up the second cure, and he would pay him ten pounds a year out of his own pocket. 'Your generosity confounds me, good sir,' replied the clerygman, 'and yet I ought not to be surprised at any instance of benevolence in Sir Launcelot Greaves; but I will check the fulness of my heart. I shall only observe that your good intention towards me can hardly take effect. The gentleman, who is to succeed the late incumbent, has given me notice to quit the premises, as he hath provided a friend of his own for the curacy.'—'What!' cried the knight, ' does he mean to take your bread from you without assigning any other reason ? '—'Surely, sir,' replied the ecclesiastic, ' I know of no other reason. I hope my morals are irreproachable, and that I have done my duty with a conscientious regard. I may venture an appeal to the parishioners, among whom I have lived these seventeen years. After all, it is natural for every man to favour his own friends in preference to strangers. As for me, I propose to try my fortune in the great city, and I doubt not but Providence will provide for me and my little ones.'

" To this declaration Sir Launcelot made no reply, but, riding home, set on foot a strict inquiry into the character of this man, whose name was Jenkins. He found that he was a reputed scholar, equally remarkable for his modesty and good life ; that he visited the sick, assisted the needy, compromised disputes among his neighbours, and spent his time in such a manner as would have done honour to any Christian divine. Thus informed, the knight sent for the gentleman to whom the living had been promised, and accosted him to this effect : ' Mr. Tootle, I have a favour to ask of you. The person who serves the cure of this parish is a man of good character, beloved by the people, and has a large family. I shall be obliged to you if you will continue him in the curacy.' The other told him he was sorry he could not comply with his request, being that he had already promised the curacy to a friend of his own. ' No matter,' replied Sir Launcelot, ' since I have not interest with you, I will endeavour to provide for Mr. Jenkins in some other way.'

" That same afternoon he walked over to the curate's house, and told him that he had spoken in his behalf to Dr. Tootle, but the curacy was pre-engaged. The good man having made a thousand acknowledgments for the

trouble his honour had taken, ' I have not interest sufficient
to make you curate,' said the knight, ' but I can give you
the living itself, and that you shall have.' So saying, he
retired, leaving Mr. Jenkins incapable of uttering one
syllable, so powerfully was he struck with this unexpected
turn of good fortune. The presentation was immediately
made out, and in a few days Mr. Jenkins was put in possession
of his benefice, to the inexpressible joy of the congregation.

" Hitherto everything went right, and every unprejudiced
person commended the knight's conduct, but in a little
time his generosity seemed to overleap the bounds of discretion, and even in some cases might be thought tending
to a breach of the king's peace. For example, he compelled,
vi et armis, a rich farmer's son to marry the daughter of a
cottager, whom the young fellow had debauched. Indeed,
it seems there was a promise of marriage in the case, though
it could not be legally ascertained. The wench took on
dismally, and her parents had recourse to Sir Launcelot,
who, sending for the delinquent, expostulated with him
severely on the injury he had done the young woman, and
exhorted him to save her life and reputation by performing
his promise, in which case he, Sir Launcelot, would give her
three hundred pounds to her portion. Whether the farmer
thought there was something interested in this uncommon
offer, or was a little elevated by the consciousness of his
father's wealth, he rejected the proposal with rustic disdain,
and said, if so be as how the wench would swear the child
to him, he would settle it with the parish ; but declared,
that no squire in the land should oblige him to buckle with
such a cracked pitcher. This resolution, however, he could
not maintain ; for in less than two hours the rector of the
parish had direction to publish the banns, and the ceremony
was performed in due course.

" Now, though we know not precisely the nature of the
arguments that were used with the farmer, we may conclude
they were of the minatory species, for the young fellow could
not, for some time, look any person in the face.

" The knight acted as the general redresser of grievances.

If a woman complained to him of being ill-treated by her husband, he first inquired into the foundation of the complaint, and, if he found it just, catechised the defendant. If the warning had no effect, and the man proceeded to fresh acts of violence, then his judge took the execution of the law in his own hand, and horsewhipped the party. Thus he involved himself in several law-suits, that drained him of pretty large sums of money. He seemed particularly incensed at the least appearance of oppression, and supported divers poor tenants against the extortion of their landlords. Nay, he has been known to travel two hundred miles as a volunteer, to offer his assistance in the cause of a person who he heard was by chicanery and oppression wronged of a considerable estate. He accordingly took her under his protection, relieved her distresses, and was at a vast expense in bringing the suit to a determination ; which being unfavourable to his client, he resolved to bring an appeal into the House of Lords, and certainly would have executed his purpose, if the gentlewoman had not died in the interim."

At this period Ferret interrupted the narrator, by observing that the said Greaves was a common nuisance, and ought to be prosecuted on the statute of barratry.

" No, sir," resumed Mr. Clarke, " he cannot be convicted of barratry, unless he is always at variance with some person or other, a mover of suits and quarrels, who disturbs the peace under colour of law. Therefore he is in the indictment styled, *Communis malefactor, calumniator, et seminator litium.*"

" Pr'ythee, truce with thy definitions," cried Ferret, " and make an end to thy long-winded story. Thou hast no title to be so tedious, until thou comest to have a coif in the Court of Common Pleas."

Tom smiled contemptuously, and had just opened his mouth to proceed, when the company were disturbed by a hideous repetition of groans, that seemed to issue from the chamber in which the body of the squire was deposited. The landlady snatched the candle, and ran into the room, followed by the doctor and the rest, and this accident naturally

suspended the narration.   In like manner we shall conclude
the chapter, that the reader may have time to breathe and
digest what he has already heard.

CHAPTER V

In which this Recapitulation draws to a close.

WHEN the landlady entered the room from whence the
groaning proceeded, she found the squire lying on his back,
under the dominion of the nightmare, which rode him so
hard that he not only groaned and snorted, but the sweat
ran down his face in streams.   The perturbation of his
brain, occasioned by this pressure, and the fright he had
lately undergone, gave rise to a very terrible dream, in which
he fancied himself apprehended for a robbery.   The horror
of the gallows was strong upon him, when he was suddenly
awaked by a violent shock from the doctor, and the company
broke in upon his view, still perverted by fear and bedimmed
by slumber.   His dream was now realised by a full persuasion
that he was surrounded by the constable and his gang.   The
first object that presented itself to his disordered view was
the figure of Ferret, who might very well have passed for
the finisher of the law ;   against him, therefore, the first
effort of his despair was directed.   He started upon the
floor, and seizing a certain utensil, that shall be nameless,
launched it at the misanthrope with such violence that had
he not cautiously slipped his head aside, it is supposed that
actual fire would have been produced from the collision of
two such hard and solid substances.   All future mischief
was prevented by the strength and agility of Captain Crowe,
who, springing upon the assailant, pinioned his arms to his
sides, crying, " Oh, d—n ye, if you are for running a-head,
I'll soon bring you to your bearings."

The squire, thus restrained, soon recollected himself, and
gazing upon every individual in the apartment, " Wounds ! "
said he, " I've had an ugly dream.   I thought, for all the

world, they were carrying me to Newgate, and that there was Jack Ketch coom to vetch me before my taim."

Ferret, who was the person he had thus distinguished, eyeing him with a look of the most emphatic malevolence, told him it was very natural for a knave to dream of Newgate, and that he hoped to see the day when his dream would be found a true prophecy, and the commonwealth purged of all such rogues and vagabonds. But it could not be expected that the vulgar would be honest and conscientious, while the great were distinguished by profligacy and corruption. The squire was disposed to make a practical reply to this insinuation, when Mr. Ferret prudently withdrew himself from the scene of altercation. The good woman of the house persuaded his antagonist to take out his nap, assuring him that the eggs and bacon, with a mug of excellent ale, should be forthcoming in due season. The affair being thus fortunately adjusted, the guests returned to the kitchen, and Mr. Clarke resumed his story to this effect:

"You'll please to take notice, gemmen, that, besides the instances I have alleged of Sir Launcelot's extravagant benevolence, I could recount a great many others of the same nature, and particularly the laudable vengeance he took of a country lawyer. I'm sorry that any such miscreant should belong to the profession. He was clerk of the assize, gemmen, in a certain town, not a great way distant; and having a blank pardon left by the judges for some criminals whose cases were attended with favourable circumstances, he would not insert the name of one who could not procure a guinea for the fee; and the poor fellow, who had only stole an hour-glass out of a shoemaker's window, was actually executed, after a long respite, during which he had been permitted to go abroad, and earn his subsistence by his daily labour.

"Sir Launcelot being informed of this barbarous act of avarice, and having some ground that bordered on the lawyer's estate, not only rendered him contemptible and infamous, by exposing him as often as they met on the grand jury, but also, being vested with the property of the

great tithe, proved such a troublesome neighbour, sometimes
by making waste among his hay and corn, sometimes by
instituting suits against him for petty trespasses, that he was
fairly obliged to quit his habitation, and remove into another
part of the kingdom.

"All these avocations could not divert Sir Launcelot
from the execution of a wild scheme, which has carried his
extravagance to such a pitch that I am afraid, if a statute—
you understand me, gemmen—were sued, the jury would—I
don't choose to explain myself further on this circumstance.
Be that as it may, the servants at Greavesbury Hall were
not a little confounded, when their master took down from
the family armoury a complete suit of armour, which
belonged to his great-grandfather, Sir Marmaduke Greaves,
a great warrior who lost his life in the service of his king.
This armour being scoured, repaired, and altered, so as
to fit Sir Launcelot, a certain knight, whom I don't choose
to name, because I believe he cannot be proved *compos mentis*,
came down, seemingly on a visit, with two attendants ; and,
on the evening of the festival of St. George, the armour
being carried into the chapel, Sir Launcelot (Lord have
mercy upon us !) remained all night in that dismal place
alone, and without light, though it was confidently reported
all over the country, that the place was haunted by the
spirit of his great-great-uncle, who, being lunatic, had
cut his throat from ear to ear, and was found dead on the
communion table."

It was observed, that while Mr. Clarke rehearsed this
circumstance, his eyes began to stare and his teeth to chatter ;
while Dolly, whose looks were fixed invariably on this
narrator, growing pale, and hitching her joint-stool nearer
the chimney, exclaimed, in a frightened tone, " Moother,
moother, in the neame of God, look to 'un ! how a quakes !
as I'm a precious saoul, a looks as if a saw something." Tom
forced a smile, and thus proceeded :

"While Sir Launcelot tarried within the chapel, with
the doors all locked, the other knight stalked round and
round it on the outside, with his sword drawn, to the terror

of divers persons who were present at the ceremony. As soon as day broke he opened one of the doors, and going in to Sir Launcelot, read a book for some time, which we did suppose to be the constitutions of knight-errantry. Then we heard a loud slap, which echoed through the whole chapel, and the stranger pronounce, with an audible and solemn voice, 'In the name of God, St. Michael, and St. George, I dub thee knight—be faithful, bold, and fortunate.' You cannot imagine, gemmen, what an effect this strange ceremony had upon the people who were assembled. They gazed at one another in silent horror, and when Sir Launcelot came forth completely armed, took to their heels in a body, and fled with the utmost precipitation. I myself was overturned in the crowd, and this was the case with that very individual person who now serves him as squire. He was so frightened that he could not rise, but lay roaring in such a manner that the knight came up and gave him a thwack with his lance across the shoulders, which roused him with a vengeance. For my own part I freely own I was not unmoved at seeing such a figure come stalking out of a church in the grey of the morning ; for it recalled to my remembrance the idea of the ghost in Hamlet, which I had seen acted in Drury Lane, when I made my first trip to London, and I had not yet got rid of the impression.

"Sir Launcelot, attended by the other knight, proceeded to the stable, from whence, with his own hands, he drew forth one of his best horses, a fine mettlesome sorrel, who had got blood in him, ornamented with rich trappings. In a trice, the two knights, and the other two trangers, who now appeared to be trumpeters, were mounted. Sir Launcelot's armour was lacquered black, and on his shield was represented the moon in her first quarter, with the motto, *Impleat orbem*. The trumpets having sounded a charge, the stranger pronounced with a loud voice, 'God preserve this gallant knight in all his honourable achievements ; and may he long continue to press the sides of his now adopted steed, which I denominate Bronzomarte, hoping that he will rival in swiftness and spirit Bayardo,

Brigliadoro, or any other steed of past or present chivalry!"
After another flourish of the trumpets, all four clapped
spurs to their horses, Sir Launcelot couching his lance,
and galloped to and fro, as if they had been mad, to the terror
and astonishment of all the spectators.

"What should have induced our knight to choose this
here man for his squire is not easy to determine ; for, of all
the servants about the house, he was the least likely either
to please his master, or engage in such an undertaking.
His name is Timothy Crabshaw, and he acted in the capacity
of whipper-in to Sir Everhard. He afterwards married the
daughter of a poor cottager, by whom he has several children,
and was employed about the house as a ploughman and
carter. To be sure, the fellow has a dry sort of humour
about him; but he was universally hated among the servants,
for his abusive tongue and perverse disposition, which often
brought him into trouble ; for, though the fellow is as strong
as an elephant, he has no more courage naturally than a
chicken ; I say naturally, because, since his being a member
of knight-errantry, he has done some things that appear
altogether incredible and preternatural.

"Timothy kept such a bawling, after he had received
the blow from Sir Launcelot, that everybody on the field
thought that some of his bones were broken ; and his
wife, with five bantlings, came snivelling to the knight,
who ordered her to send the husband directly to his house.
Tim accordingly went thither, groaning piteously all the
way, creeping along, with his body bent like a Greenland
canoe. As soon as he entered the court, the outward
door was shut, and Sir Launcelot, coming downstairs with
a horsewhip in his hand, asked what was the matter with
him that he complained so dismally ? To this question
he replied, that it was as common as duck-weed in his
country for a man to complain when his bones were broken.
' What should have broken your bones ? ' said the knight.
' I cannot guess,' answered the other, ' unless it was that
delicate switch that your honour in your mad pranks handled
so dexterously upon my carcass.' Sir Launcelot then told

him there was nothing so good for a bruise as a sweat;
and he had the remedy in his hand. Timothy, eyeing the
horsewhip askance, observed that there was another still
more speedy, to wit, a moderate pill of lead, with a sufficient
dose of gunpowder. ' No, rascal,' cried the knight; ' that
must be reserved for your betters.' So saying, he employed
the instrument so effectually, that Crabshaw soon forgot
his fractured ribs, and capered about with great agility.

" When he had been disciplined in this manner to some
purpose, the knight told him he might retire, but ordered
him to return next morning, when he should have a repetition
of the medicine, provided he did not find himself capable
of walking in an erect posture.

" The gate was no sooner thrown open, than Timothy
ran home with all the speed of a greyhound, and corrected
his wife, by whose advice he had pretended to be so grievously
damaged in his person.

" Nobody dreamed that he would next day present himself
at Greavesbury Hall; nevertheless, he was there very early
in the morning, and even closeted a whole hour altogether
with Sir Launcelot. He came out, making wry faces, and
several times slapped himself on the forehead, crying,
' Bodikins! thof he be crazy, I an't, that I an't ?' When he
was asked what was the matter, he said, he believed the devil
had got in him, and he should never be his own man again.

" That same day the knight carried him to Ashenton,
where he bespoke those acccoutrements which he now
wears; and while these were making, it was thought the
poor fellow would have run distracted. He did nothing but
growl, and curse and swear to himself, run backwards and
forwards between his own hut and Greavesbury Hall, and
quarrel with the horses in the stable. At length, his wife
and family were removed into a snug farmhouse, that happened to be empty, and care taken that they should be
comfortably maintained.

" These precautions being taken, the knight, one morning,
at daybreak, mounted Bronzomarte, and Crabshaw, as his
squire, ascended the back of a clumsy cart-horse, called

this ferocious commander. 'What, d'ye think to frighten
us with your pewter piss-pot on your skull, and your lacquered
pot-lid on your arm ?   Get out of the way, and be d—ned,
or I'll raise with my halbert such a clutter upon your target,
that you'll remember it the longest day you have to live.'
At that instant, Crabshaw arriving upon Gilbert, ' So,
rascal,' said Sir Launcelot, ' you are returned.   Go and beat
in that scoundrel's drum-head.'

" The squire, who saw no weapons of offence about the
drummer but a sword, which he hoped the owner durst not
draw, and being resolved to exert himself in making atonement for his desertion, advanced to execute his master's
orders; but Gilbert, who liked not the noise, refused to
proceed in the ordinary way.   Then the squire, turning
his tail to the drummer, he advanced in a retrograde motion,
and with one kick of his heels not only broke the drum into
a thousand pieces, but laid the drummer in the mire, with
such a blow upon his hip-bone that he halted all the days
of his life.   The recruits, perceiving the discomfiture of
their leader, armed themselves with stones, the sergeant
raised his halbert in a posture of defence, and immediately
a severe action ensued.   By this time Crabshaw had drawn
his sword, and begun to lay about him like a devil incarnate ;
but, in a little time, he was saluted by a volley of stones, one
of which knocked out two of his grinders, and brought him
to the earth, where he had like to have found no quarter,
for the whole company crowded about him, with their
cudgels brandished ;   and perhaps he owed his preservation
to their pressing so hard that they hindered one another
from using their weapons.

" Sir Launcelot, seeing with indignation the unworthy
treatment his squire had received, and scorning to stain his
lance with the blood of plebeians, instead of couching it at
the rest, seized it by the middle, and fetching one blow at
the sergeant, broke in twain the halbert which he had raised
as a quarter-staff for his defence.   The second stroke encountered his pate, which being the hardest part about him,
sustained the shock without damage, but the third, lighting

The Alarm of Crowe and Fillet at the Appearance
of Sir Launcelot.

on his ribs, he honoured the giver with immediate prostra-
tion. The general being thus overthrown, Sir Launcelot
advanced to the relief of Crabshaw, and handled his weapon
so effectually that the whole body of the enemy were disabled
or routed, before one cudgel had touched the carcass of the
fallen squire. As for the corporal, instead of standing by
his commanding officer, he had overleaped the hedge, and
run to the constable of an adjoining village for assistance.
Accordingly, before Crabshaw could be properly remounted,
the peace officer arrived with his posse, and by the corporal
was charged with Sir Launcelot and his squire as two highwaymen. The constable, astonished at the martial figure
of the knight, and intimidated at sight of the havoc he had
made, contented himself with standing at a distance, displaying the badge of his office, and reminding the knight
that he represented His Majesty's person.

"Sir Launcelot, seeing the poor man in great agitation,
assured him that his design was to enforce, not violate, the
laws of his country, and that he and his squire would attend
him to the next justice of peace; but, in the meantime, he,
in his turn, charged the peace officer with the sergeant and
drummer, who had begun the fray.

"The justice had been a pettifogger, and was a sycophant
to a nobleman in the neighbourhood, who had a post at
court. He therefore thought he should oblige his patron
by showing his respect for *the military*; but treated our
knight with the most boorish insolence, and refused to admit
him into his house until he had surrendered all his weapons
of offence to the constable. Sir Launcelot and his squire
being found the aggressors, the justice insisted upon making
out their mittimus if they did not find bail immediately;
and could hardly be prevailed upon to agree that they should
remain at the house of the constable, who, being a publican,
undertook to keep them in safe custody, until the knight
could write to his steward. Meanwhile he was bound over
to the peace, and the sergeant with his drummer were told
they had a good action against him for assault and battery,
either by information or indictment.

" They were not, however, so fond of the law as the justice seemed to be. Their sentiments had taken a turn in favour of Sir Launcelot, during the course of his examination, by which it appeared that he was really a gentleman of fashion and fortune; and they resolved to compromise the affair without the intervention of his worship. Accordingly, the sergeant repaired to the constable's house, where the knight was lodged, and humbled himself before his honour, protesting, with many oaths, that, if he had known his quality, he would have beaten the drummer's brains about his ears for presuming to give his honour or his horse the least disturbance, thof the fellow, he believed, was sufficiently punished in being a cripple for life.

" Sir Launcelot admitted of his apologies, and taking compassion on the fellow who had suffered so severely for his folly, resolved to provide for his maintenance. Upon the representation of the parties to the justice the warrant was next day discharged, and the knight returned to his own house, attended by the sergeant and the drummer mounted on horseback, the recruits being left to the corporal's charge.

" The halberdier found the good effects of Sir Launcelot's liberality, and his companion being rendered unfit for his majesty's service by the heels of Gilbert is now entertained at Greavesbury Hall, where he will probably remain for life.

" As for Crabshaw, his master gave him to understand that if he did not think him pretty well chastised for his presumption and flight, by the discipline he had undergone in the last two adventures, he would turn him out of his service with disgrace. Timothy said he believed it would be the greatest favour he could do him to turn him out of a service in which he knew he should be rib-roasted every day, and murdered at last.

" In this situation were things at Greavesbury Hall about a month ago, when I crossed the country to Ferrybridge, where I met my uncle. Probably this is the first incident of their second excursion, for the distance between this here house and Sir Launcelot's estate does not exceed fourscore or ninety miles."

CHAPTER VI

In which the Reader will perceive that in some Cases Madness is catching.

MR. CLARKE having made an end of his narrative, the surgeon thanked him for the entertainment he had received, and Mr. Ferret shrugged up his shoulders in silent disapprobation. As for Captain Crowe, who used at such pauses to pour in a broadside of dismembered remarks, linked together like chain-shot, he spoke not a syllable for some time, but, lighting a fresh pipe at the candle, began to roll such voluminous clouds of smoke as in an instant filled the whole apartment, and rendered himself invisible to the whole company. Though he thus shrouded himself from their view, he did not long remain concealed from their hearing. They first heard a strange dissonant cackle, which the doctor knew to be a sea-laugh, and this was followed by an eager exclamation of " Rare pastime, strike my yards and topmasts !—I've a good mind—why shouldn't—many a losing voyage I've—smite my taffrel but I wool——"

By this time he had relaxed so much in his fumigation, that the tip of his nose and one eye reappeared ; and as he had drawn his wig forwards, so as to cover his whole forehead, the figure that now saluted their eyes was much more ferocious and terrible than the fire-breathing chimera of the ancients. Notwithstanding this dreadful appearance, there was no indignation in his heart, but, on the contrary, an agreeable curiosity, which he was determined to gratify.

Addressing himself to Mr. Fillot, " Pr'ythee, doctor," said he, " canst tell whether a man, without being rated a lord or a baron, or what d'ye call um, d'ye see, mayn't take to the highway in the way of a frolic, d'ye see ? Adad ! for my own part, brother, I'm resolved as how to cruise a bit in the way of an arrant—if so be as I can't at once be commander, mayhap I may be bore upon the books as a petty officer or the like, d'ye see ? "

" Now, the Lord forbid ! " cried Clarke, with tears in his

5

eyes. " I'd rather see you dead than brought to such a
dilemma." " Mayhap thou wouldst," answered the uncle,
" for then, my lad, there would be some picking—aha ! dost
thou tip me the traveller, my boy ? " Tom assured him
he scorned any such mercenary views. " I am only concerned," said he, " that you should take any step that might
tend to the disgrace of yourself or your family ; and I say
again I had rather die than live to see you reckoned any
otherwise than compos." " Die and be d—ned ! you shambling half-timber'd son of a ——," cried the choleric Crowe.
" Dost talk to me of keeping a reckoning and compass ? I
could keep a reckoning and box my compass long enough
before thy keel-stone was laid. Sam Crowe is not come
here to ask thy counsel how to steer his course." " Lord !
sir," resumed the nephew, " consider what people will say.
All the world will think you mad." " Set thy heart at ease,
Tom," cried the seaman, " I'll have a trip to and again in
this here channel. Mad ! what then ? I think for my part
one half of the nation is mad—and the other not very sound.
I don't see why I han't as good a right to be mad as another
man. But, doctor, as I was saying, I'd be bound to you,
if you would direct me where I can buy that same tackle
that an arrant must wear. As for the matter of the long
pole, headed with iron, I'd never desire better than a good
boat-hook, and could make a special good target of that there
tin sconce that holds the candle. Mayhap any blacksmith
will hammer me a skull-cap, d'ye see, out of an old brass
kettle, and I can call my horse by the name of my ship, which
was *Mufti*."

The surgeon was one of those wags who can laugh inwardly,
without exhibiting the least outward mark of mirth or
satisfaction. He at once perceived the amusement which
might be drawn from this strange disposition of the sailor,
together with the most likely means which could be used
to divert him from such an extravagant pursuit. He therefore tipped Clarke the wink with one side of his face, while
the other was very gravely turned to the captain, whom he
addressed to thsi effect. " It is not far from hence to

Sheffield, where you might be fitted completely in half a day—then you must wake your armour in church or chapel, and be dubbed. As for this last ceremony, it may be performed by any person whatsoever. Don Quixote was dubbed by his landlord, and there are many instances on record of errants obliging and compelling the next person they met to cross their shoulders and dub them knights. I myself would undertake to be your godfather, and I have interest enough to procure the keys of the parish church that stands hard by ; besides, this is the eve of St. Martin, who was himself a knight errant, and therefore a proper patron to a novitiate. I wish we could borrow Sir Launcelot's armour for the occasion."

Crowe, being struck with this hint, started up, and laying his fingers on his lips to enjoin silence, walked off softly on his tiptoes to listen at the door of our knight's apartment and judge whether or not he was asleep. Mr. Fillet took this opportunity to tell his nephew that it would be in vain for him to combat this humour with reason and argument, but the most effectual way of diverting him from the plan of knight-errantry would be to frighten him heartily while he should keep his vigil in the church, towards the accomplishment of which purpose he craved the assistance of the misanthrope as well as the nephew. Clarke seemed to relish the scheme, and observed that his uncle, though endued with courage enough to face any human danger, had at bottom a strong fund of superstition, which he had acquired, or at least improved, in the course of a sea-life. Ferret, who perhaps would not have gone ten paces out of his road to save Crowe from the gallows, nevertheless engaged as an auxiliary, merely in hope of seeing a fellow-creature miserable, and even undertook to be the principal agent in this adventure. For this office indeed he was better qualified than they could have imagined. In the bundle which he kept under his greatcoat, there was, together with divers nostrums, a small vial of liquid phosphorus, sufficient, as he had already observed, to frighten a whole neighbourhood out of their senses.

In order to concert the previous measures without being overheard, these confederates retired with a candle and lantern into the stable ; and their backs were scarce turned when Captain Crowe came in loaded with pieces of the knight's armour, which he had conveyed from the apartment of Sir Launcelot, whom he had left fast asleep.

Understanding that the rest of the company were gone out for a moment, he could not resist the inclination he felt of communicating his intention to the landlady, who, with her daughter, had been too much engaged in preparing Crabshaw's supper to know the purport of their conversation. The good woman, being informed of the captain's design to remain alone all night in the church, began to oppose it with all her rhetoric. She said it was setting his Maker at defiance, and a wilful running into temptation. She assured him that all the country knew that the church was haunted by spirits and hobgoblins ; that lights had been seen in every corner of it, and a tall woman in white had one night appeared upon the top of the tower ; that dreadful shrieks were often heard to come from the south aisle, where a murdered man had been buried ; that she herself had seen the cross on the steeple all a-fire, and one evening as she passed a-horseback close by the stile at the entrance into the churchyard, the horse stood still, sweating and trembling, and had no power to proceed, until she had repeated the Lord's Prayer.

These remarks made a strong impression on the imagination of Crowe, who asked in some confusion if she had got that same prayer in print ? She made no answer, but reaching the Prayer-Book from a shelf, and turning up the leaf, put it into his hand ; then the captain, having adjusted his spectacles, began to read, or rather spell aloud, with equal eagerness and solemnity. He had refreshed his memory so well as to remember the whole, when the doctor, returning with his companions, gave him to understand that he had procured the key of the chancel, where he might watch his armour as well as in the body of the church, and that he was ready to conduct him to the spot. Crowe was not now quite so forward as he had appeared before to achieve this adventure. He began to start objections with respect to the borrowed armour, he wanted to stipulate the comforts of a can of flip and a candle's end during his vigil, and hinted something of the damage he might sustain from your malicious imps of darkness.

The doctor told him the constitutions of chivalry absolutely required that he should be left in the dark alone, and fasting, to spend the night in pious meditations; but if he had any fears which disturbed his conscience, he had much better desist, and give up all thoughts of knight-errantry, which could not consist with the least shadow of apprehension. The captain, stung by this remark, replied not a word, but gathering up the armour into a bundle, threw it on his back, and set out for the place of probation, preceded by Clarke with the lantern. When they arrived at the church, Fillet, who had procured the key from the sexton, who was his patient, opened the door, and conducted our novice into the middle of the chancel, where the armour was deposited. Then bidding Crowe draw his hanger, committed him to the protection of Heaven, assuring him he would come back, and find him either dead or alive by daybreak, and perform the remaining part of the ceremony. So saying, he and the other associates shook him by the hand and took their leave, after the surgeon had tilted up the lantern to take a view of his visage, which was pale and haggard.

Before the door was locked upon him, he called aloud, "Hilloa! doctor, hip—another word, d'ye see." They forthwith returned to know what he wanted, and found him already in a sweat. "Hark ye, brother," said he, wiping his face, "I do suppose as how one may pass away the time in whistling the Black Joke, or singing Black-eyed Susan, or some such sorrowful ditty." "By no means," cried the doctor; "such pastimes are neither suitable to the place, nor the occasion, which is altogether a religious exercise. If you have got any psalms by heart, you may sing a stave or two, or repeat the Doxology."—"Would I had Tom Laverick here," replied our novitiate; "he would sing your anthems like a seamew—a had been a clerk a-shore—many's the time and often I've given him a rope's end for singing psalms in the larboard watch. Would I had hired the son of a b—h to have taught me a cast of his office—but it cannot be holp, brother—if we can't go large, we must haul up a wind, as the saying is ; if we can't sing, we must pray." The company again left him to his devotion, and returned to the public-house, in order to execute the essential part of their project.

CHAPTER VII.

In which the Knight resumes his Importance.

Doctor Fillet having borrowed a couple of sheets from the landlady, dressed the misanthrope and Tom Clarke in ghostly apparel, which was reinforced by a few drops of liquid phosphorus, from Ferret's vial, rubbed on the foreheads of the two adventurers. Thus equipped, they returned to the church with their conductor, who entered with them softly at an aisle which was opposite to a place where the novice kept watch. They stole unperceived through the body of the church ; and though it was so dark that they could not distinguish the captain with the eye, they heard the sound of his steps, as he walked backwards and forwards on the pavement with uncommon expedition, and an ejaculation now and then escaped in a murmur from his lips.

The triumvirate having taken their station with a large pew in their front, the two ghosts uncovered their heads, which by the help of the phosphorus exhibited a pale and lambent flame, extremely dismal and ghastly to the view; then Ferret in a squeaking tone, exclaimed, " Samuel Crowe ! Samuel Crowe ! " The captain hearing himself accosted in this manner, at such a time, and in such a place, replied, " Hilloah " ; and turning his eyes towards the quarter whence the voice seemed to proceed, beheld the terrible apparition. This no sooner saluted his view than his hair bristled up, his knees began to knock, and his teeth to chatter, while he cried aloud, " In the name of God, where are you bound, ho ? " To this hail the misanthrope answered, " We are the spirits of thy grandmother Jane and thy aunt Bridget."

At mention of these names, Crowe's terrors began to give way to his resentment, and he pronounced in a quick tone of surprise, mixed with indignation, " What d'ye want ? what d'ye want ? what d'ye want, ho ? " The spirit replied, " We are sent to warn thee of thy fate." " From whence, ho ? " cried the captain, whose choler had by this time well-nigh triumphed over his fear. " From heaven," said the voice. " Ye lie, ye b—s of hell ! " did our novice exclaim ; " ye are d—ned for heaving me out of my right, five fathom and a half by the lead, in burning brimstone. Don't I see the blue flames come out of your hawse holes ?— mayhap you may be the devil himself, for aught I know— but I trust in the Lord, d'ye see—I never disrated a kinsman, d'ye see, so don't come alongside of me—put about on th'other tack, d'ye see—you need not clap hard a-weather, for you'll soon get to hell again with a flowing sail."

So saying, he had recourse to his Paternoster ; but per- ceiving the apparitions approach, he thundered out, " Avast —avast—sheer off, ye babes of hell, or I'll be foul of your forelights." He accordingly sprang forwards with his hanger, and very probably would have set the spirits on their way to the other world, had he not fallen over a pew in the dark, and entangled himself so much among the benches, that he could not immediately recover his footing. The triumvirate took this opportunity to retire ; and such was the precipitation of Ferret in his retreat, that he en- countered a post by which his right eye sustained considerable damage ; a circumstance which induced him to inveigh bitterly against his own folly, as well as the impertinence of his companions, who had inveigled him into such a troublesome adventure. Neither he nor Clarke could be prevailed upon to revisit the novice. The doctor himself thought his disease was desperate; and, mounting his horse, returned to his own habitation.

Ferret, finding all the beds in the public-house were occupied, composed himself to sleep in a Windsor chair at the chimney corner; and Mr. Clarke, whose disposition was extremely amorous, resolved to renew his practices on the heart of Dolly. He had reconnoitred the apartments in which the bodies of the knight and his squire were deposited, and discovered close by the top of the staircase a sort of a closet or hovel, just large enough to contain a truckle bed, which, from some other particulars, he supposed to be the bedchamber of his beloved Dolly, who had by this time retired to her repose. Full of this idea, and instigated by the demon of desire, Mr. Thomas crept softly upstairs, and lifting the latch of the closet door, his heart began to palpitate with joyous expectation; but before he could breathe the gentle effusions of his love, the supposed damsel started up and seizing him by the collar with a Herculean grip, uttered, in the voice of Crabshaw, "It wan't for nothing that I dreamed of Newgate, sirrah; but I'd have thee to know, an arrant squire is not to be robbed by such a peddling thief as thee—here I'll howld thee vast, an the devil were in thy doublet—help! murder! vire! help!"

It was impossible for Mr. Clarke to disengage himself, and equally impracticable to speak in his own vindication; so that here he stood trembling and half throttled, until the whole house being alarmed, the landlady and her ostler ran upstairs with a candle. When the light rendered objects visible, an equal astonishment prevailed on all sides; Crabshaw was confounded at sight of Mr. Clarke, whose person he well knew; and releasing him instantly from his grasp, "Bodikins!" cried he, "I believe as how this hause is haunted—who thought to meet with Measter Laawyer Clarke at midnight, and so far from hoam?" The landlady could not comprehend the meaning of this encounter; nor could Tom conceive how Crabshaw had transported himself thither from the room below, in which he saw him quietly reposed. Yet nothing was more easy than to explain this mystery: the apartment below was the chamber which the hostess and her daughter reserved for their own convenience; and this particular having been intimated to the squire while he was at supper, he had resigned his bed quietly, and been conducted hither in the absence of the company. Tom, recollecting himself as well as he could, professed himself of Crabshaw's opinion, that the house was haunted, declaring that he could not well account for his being there in the dark; and leaving those that were assembled to discuss this knotty point, retired downstairs in hope of meeting with his charmer, whom accordingly he found in the kitchen just risen, and wrapped in a loose dishabille.

The noise of Crabshaw's cries had awakened and aroused his master, who, rising suddenly in the dark, snatched up his sword that lay by his bedside, and hastened to the scene of tumult, where all their mouths were opened at once, to explain the cause of the disturbance, and make an apology for breaking his honour's rest. He said nothing, but taking the candle in his hand, beckoned his squire to follow him into his apartment, resolving to arm and take horse immediately. Crabshaw understood his meaning; and while he shuffled on his clothes, yawning hideously all the while, wished the lawyer at the devil for having visited him so unseasonably, and even cursed himself for the noise he had made, in consequence of which he foresaw he should now be obliged to forfeit his night's rest, and travel in the dark, exposed to the inclemencies of the weather. " Pox rot thee, Tom Clarke, for a wicked lawyer ! " said he to himself ; " hadst thou been hanged at Bartlemy-tide, I should this night have slept in peace, that I should—an I would there was a blister on this plaguy tongue of mine for making such a hollo-ballo, that I do—five gallons of cold water has my poor belly been drenched with since night fell, so as my reins and my liver are all one as if they were turned into ice, and my whole harslet shakes and shivers like a vial of quicksilver. I have been dragged, half-drowned like a rotten ewe, from the bottom of a river ; and who knows but I may be next dragged quite dead from the bottom of a coal-pit—if so be as I am, I shall go to hell to be sure, for being consarned like in my own moorder, that I will, so I will ; for, a plague on it ! I had no business with the vagaries of this crazy-peated measter of mine, a pox on him, say I."

He had just finished this soliloquy as he entered the apartment of his master, who desired to know what was become of his armour. Timothy, understanding that it had been left in the room when the knight undressed, began to scratch his head in great perplexity, and at last declared it as his opinion that it must have been carried off by witchcraft. Then he related his adventure with Tom Clarke, who he said was conveyed to his bedside he knew not how ; and concluded with affirming they were no better than Papishes who did not believe in witchcraft. Sir Launcelot could not help smiling at his simplicity ; but assuming a peremptory air, he commanded him to fetch the armour without delay, that he might afterwards saddle the horses, in order to prosecute their journey.

Timothy retired in great tribulation to the kitchen, where, finding the misanthrope, whom the noise had also disturbed, and, still impressed with the notion of his being a conjurer, he offered him a shilling if he would cast a figure, and let him know what was become of his master's armour.

Ferret, in hope of producing more mischief, informed him without hesitation, that one of the company had conveyed it into the chancel of the church, where he would now find it deposited ; at the same time presenting him with the key, which Mr. Fillet had left in his custody.

The squire, who was none of those who set hobgoblins at defiance, being afraid to enter the church alone at these hours, bargained with the ostler to accompany and light him with a lantern. Thus attended, he advanced to the place where the armour lay in a heap, and loaded it upon the back of his attendant without molestation, the lance being shouldered over the whole. In this equipage they were just going to retire, when the ostler, hearing a noise

at some distance, wheeled about with such velocity, that
one end of the spear saluting Crabshaw's pate, the poor
squire measured his length on the ground; and, crushing
the lantern in his fall, the light was extinguished. The
other, terrified at these effects of his own sudden motion,
threw down his burden, and would have betaken himself
to flight, had not Crabshaw laid fast hold on his leg, that
he himself might not be deserted. The sound of the pieces
clattering on the pavement roused Captain Crowe from a
trance or slumber, in which he had lain since the apparition
vanished; and he hallooed, or rather bellowed, with vast
vociferation. Timothy and his friend were so intimidated
by this terrific strain, that they thought no more of the
armour, but ran home arm in arm, and appeared in the
kitchen with all the marks of horror and consternation.

When Sir Launcelot came forth wrapped in his cloak,
and demanded his arms, Crabshaw declared that the devil
had them in possession; and this assertion was confirmed
by the ostler, who pretended to know the devil by his roar.
Ferret sat in his corner, maintaining the most mortifying
silence, and enjoying the impatience of the knight, who
in vain requested an explanation of this mystery. At length
his eyes began to lighten, when, seizing Crabshaw in one
hand, and the ostler in the other, he swore by Heaven
he would dash their souls out, and raze the house to the
foundation, if they did not instantly disclose the particulars
of this transaction. The good woman fell on her knees,
protesting, in the name of the Lord, that she was innocent
as the child unborn, thof she had lent the captain a Prayer-
Book to learn the Lord's prayer, a candle and lantern to
light him to the church, and a couple of clean sheets, for
the use of the other gentlemen. The knight was more and
more puzzled by this declaration; when Mr. Clarke, coming
into the kitchen, presented himself with a low obeisance to
his old patron.

Sir Launcelot's anger was immediately converted into
surprise. He set at liberty the squire and the ostler, and
stretching out his hand to the lawyer, " My good friend

Clarke," said he, " how came you hither ? Can you solve
this knotty point which has involved us all in such confusion ? "

Tom forthwith began a very circumstantial recapitulation
of what had happened to his uncle ; in what manner he had
been disappointed of the estate, how he had accidentally seen
his honour, been enamoured of his character, and become
ambitious of following his example. Then he related the
particulars of the plan which had been laid down to divert
him from his design, and concluded with assuring the knight
that the captain was a very honest man, though he seemed
to be a little disordered in his intellects. " I believe it,"
replied Sir Launcelot ; " madness and honesty are not
incompatible—indeed, I feel it by experience."

Tom proceeded to ask pardon, in his uncle's name, for
having made so free with the knight's armour, and begged
his honour, for the love of God, would use his authority
with Crowe, that he might quit all thoughts of knight-
errantry, for which he was by no means qualified ; for,
being totally ignorant of the laws of the land, he would be
continually committing trespasses, and bring himself into
trouble. He said, in case he should prove refractory, he
might be apprehended by virtue of a friendly warrant, for
having feloniously carried off the knight's accoutrements.
" Taking away another man's movables," said he, " and
personal goods against the will of the owner, is *furtum* and
felony according to the statute. Different indeed from
robbery, which implies putting in fear in the king's highway,
*in alta via regia violenter et felonice captum et asportatum,
in magnum terrorem*, etc., for if the robbery be laid in the
indictment, as done *in quadam via pedestri*, in a footpath,
the offender will not be ousted of his clergy. It must be
in alta via regia, and your honour will please to take notice,
that robberies committed on the river Thames are adjudged
as done in *alta via regia*, for the king's highstream is all
the same as the king's highway."

Sir Launcelot could not help smiling at Tom's learned
investigation. He congratulated him on the progress he

ıad made in the study of the law. He expressed his concern ıt the strange turn the captain had taken, and promised to ıse his influence in persuading him to desist from the pre-ɔosterous design he had formed.

The lawyer, thus assured, repaired immediately to the ҫhurch, accompanied by the squire, and held a parley with ıis uncle, who, when he understood that the knight in person lesired a conference, surrendered up the arms quietly, and ːeturned to the public-house.

Sir Launcelot received the honest seaman with his usual ҫomplacency, and perceiving great discomposure in his ⅼooks, said he was sorry to hear he had passed such a dis-ıgreeable night to so little purpose. Crowe, having recruited his spirits with a bumper of brandy, thanked him for his ҫoncern, and observed, that he had passed many a hard night in his time, but such another as this he would not be bound to weather for the command of the whole British navy. " I have seen Davy Jones in the shape of a blue flame, d'ye see, hopping to and fro on the sprit-sail yardarm ; and I've seen your Jacks-o'-the-Lanthorn and Wills-o'-the-Wisp, ɑnd many such spirits, both by sea and land. But to-night I've been boarded by all the devils and d—ned souls in hell, squeaking and squalling, and glimmering and glaring. Bounce went the door—crack went the pew—crash came the tackle—white-sheeted ghosts dancing in one corner by the glow-worm's light—black devils hobbling in another—Lord have mercy upon us ! and I was hailed, Tom, I was, by my grandmother Jane, and my Aunt Bridget, d'ye see—a couple of d—n'd—but they're roasting ; that's one comfort, my lad."

When he had thus disburdened his conscience, Sir Launcelot introduced the subject of the new occupation at which he aspired. " I understand," said he, " that you are desirous of treading the paths of errantry, which, I assure you, are thorny and troublesome. Nevertheless, as your purpose is to exercise your humanity and benevolence, so your ambition is commendable. But towards the practice of chivalry, there is something more required than the

virtues of courage and generosity. A knight-errant ought
to understand the sciences, to be master of ethics or morality,
to be well versed in theology, a complete casuist, and minutely
acquainted with the laws of his country. He should not
only be patient of cold, hunger, and fatigue, righteous, just,
and valiant, but also chaste, religious, temperate, polite, and
conversable, and have all his passions under the rein, except
love, whose empire he should submissively acknowledge."
He said this was the very essence of chivalry, and no man
had ever made such a profession of arms, without first having
placed his affection upon some beauteous object, for whose
honour, and at whose command, he would cheerfully encounter the most dreadful perils.

He took notice, that nothing could be more irregular than
the manner in which Crowe had attempted to keep his vigil.
For he had never served his novitiate—he had not prepared
himself with abstinence and prayer—he had not provided
a qualified godfather for the ceremony of dubbing—he had
no armour of his own to wake ; but, on the very threshold of
chivalry, which is the perfection of justice, had unjustly
purloined the arms of another knight.   That this was a mere
mockery of a religious institution, and therefore unpleasing
in the sight of Heaven—witness the demons and hobgoblins
that were permitted to disturb and torment him in his trial.

Crowe, having listened to these remarks with earnest
attention, replied after some hesitation, "I am bound to
you, brother, for your kind and Christian counsel. I doubt
as how I've steered by a wrong chart, d'ye see. As for the
matter of the sciences, to be sure I know Plain Sailing and
Mercator, and am an indifferent good seaman, thof I say it
that should not say it.   But as to all the rest, no better than
the viol-block or the geer-capstan. Religion I han't much
overhauled, and we tars laugh at your polite conversation,
thof, mayhap, we can chaunt a few ballads to keep the hands
awake in the night watch ; then for chastity, brother, I
doubt that's not expected in a sailor just come ashore after
a long voyage—sure all those poor hearts won't be d—ned
for steering in the wake of nature. As for a sweetheart, Bet

Mizen of St. Catherine's would fit me to a hair. She and I are old messmates, and what signifies talking, brother, she knows already the trim of my vessel, d'ye see." He concluded with saying he thought he wa'n't too old to learn, and if Sir Launcelot would take him in tow as his tender, he would stand by him all weathers, and it should not cost his consort a farthing's expense.

The knight said he did not think himself of consequence enough to have such a pupil, but should always be ready to give him his best advice ; as a specimen of which, he exhorted him to weigh all the circumstances, and deliberate calmly and leisurely, before he actually engaged in such a boisterous profession, assuring him that if, at the end of three months, his resolution should continue, he would take upon himself the office of his instructor. In the meantime he gratified the hostess for his lodging, put on his armour, took leave of the company, and, mounting Bronzomarte, proceeded southerly, being attended by his squire Crabshaw, grumbling, on the back of Gilbert.

CHAPTER VIII

Which is within a hair's-breadth of proving highly interesting.

LEAVING Captain Crowe and his nephew for the present, though they, and even the misanthrope, will reappear in due season, we are now obliged to attend the progress of the knight, who proceeded in a southerly direction, insensible of the storm that blew, as well as of the darkness, which was horrible. For some time Crabshaw ejaculated curses in silence, till at length his anger gave way to his fear, which waxed so strong upon him that he could no longer resist the desire of alleviating it, by entering into a conversation with his master. By way of introduction he gave Gilbert the spur, directing him towards the flank of Bronzomarte, which he encountered with such a shock that the knight was almost dismounted.

When Sir Launcelot, with some warmth, asked the reason
of this attack, the squire replied in these words : " The
devil, God bless us ! mun be playing his pranks with Gilbert
too, as sure as I'm a living soul.   I'se wager a teaster, the
foul fiend has left the seaman, and got into Gilbert, that he
has.   When a has passed through an ass and a horse, I'se
marvel what beast a will get into next."—" Probably into
a mule," said the knight ; " in that case, you will be in some
danger, but I can at any time dispossess you with a horsewhip."—" Ay, ay," answered Timothy, " your honour has
a mortal good hand at giving a flap with a fox's tail, as the
saying is.   'Tis a wonderment you did not try your hand on
that there wiseacre that stole your honour's harness, and
wants to be an arrant with a murrain to 'un.   Lord help his
fool's head ! it becomes him as a sow doth a cart saddle."—
" There is no guilt in infirmity," said the knight ; " I punish
the vicious only."—" I would your honour would punish
Gilbert then," cried the squire, " for 'tis the most vicious
tuoad that ever I laid a leg over   But as to that same seafaring man, what may his distemper be ? "

" Madness," answered Sir Launcelot.—" Bodikins," exclaimed the squire, " I doubt as how other volks are leame
of the same leg.   But it an't vor such small gentry as he to
be mad ; they mun leave that to their betters."—" You
seem to hint at me, Crabshaw.   Do you really think I am
mad ? "—" I may say as how I have looked your honour in
the mouth, and a sorry dog should I be if I did not know
your humours as well as I know e'er a beast in the steable
at Greavesbury Hall."—" Since you are so well acquainted
with my madness," said the knight, " what opinion have
you of yourself, who serve and follow a lunatic ? "—" I hope
I han't served your honour for nothing, but I shall inherit
some of your cast vagaries—when your honour is pleased to
be mad, I should be very sorry to be found right in my
senses.   Timothy Crabshaw will never eat the bread of
unthankfulness.   It shall never be said of him that he was
wiser than his measter.   As for the matter of following a
madman, we may see your honour's face is made of a fiddle ;

every one that looks on you loves you." This compliment
the knight returned by saying, "If my face is a fiddle,
Crabshaw, your tongue is a fiddlestick that plays upon it—
yet your music is very disagreeable—you don't keep time."
—"Nor you neither, measter," cried Timothy, "or we
shouldn't be here wandering about under a cloud of night,
like sheep-stealers or evil spirits with troubled consciences."

Here the discourse was interrupted by a sudden disaster,
in consequence of which the squire uttered an inarticulate
roar, that startled the knight himself, who was very little
subject to the sensation of fear.   But his surprise was changed
into vexation when he perceived Gilbert without a rider
passing by, and kicking his heels with great agility.   He
forthwith turned his steed, and riding back a few paces,
found Crabshaw rising from the ground.   When he asked
what was become of his horse, he answered in a whimpering
tone, "Horse! would I could once see him fairly carrion
for the hounds!   For my part I believe as how 'tis no horse,
but a devil incarnate, and yet I've been worse mounted, that
I have—I'd like to have rid a horse that was foaled of an
acorn."

This accident happened in a hollow way, overshadowed
with trees, one of which the storm had blown down, so that
it lay over the road, and one of its boughs projecting hori-
zontally encountered the squire as he trotted along in the
dark.   Chancing to hitch under his long chin, he could not
disengage himself, but hung suspended like a flitch of bacon;
while Gilbert, pushing forward, left him dangling, and, by
his awkward gambols, seemed to be pleased with the joke.
This capricious animal was not retaken without the personal
endeavours of the knight; for Crabshaw absolutely refusing
to budge a foot from his honour's side, he was obliged to
alight and fasten Bronzomarte to a tree.   Then they set out
together, and, with some difficulty, found Gilbert with his
neck stretched over a five-barred gate, snuffing up the
morning air.   The squire, however, was not remounted
without first having undergone a severe reprehension from
his master, who upbraided him with his cowardice, threatened

6

to chastise him on the spot, and declared that he would divorce his dastardly soul from his body should he ever be incommoded or affronted with another instance of his baseborn apprehension.

Though there was some risk in carrying on the altercation at this juncture, Timothy, having bound up his jaws, could not withstand the inclination he had to confute his master. He therefore, in a muttering accent, protested that if the knight would give him leave, he should prove that his honour had tied a knot with his tongue which he could not untie with all his teeth. "How, caitiff!" cried Sir Launcelot, "presume to contend with me in argument?"—"Your mouth is scarce shut," said the other, "since you declared that a man was not to be punished for madness, because it was a distemper. Now I will maintain that cowardice is a distemper as well as madness, for nobody would be afraid if he could help it."—"There is more logic in that remark," resumed the knight, "than I expected from your clod-pate, Crabshaw. But I must explain the difference between cowardice and madness. Cowardice, though sometimes the effect of natural imbecility, is generally a prejudice of education, or bad habit contracted from misinformation, or misapprehension, and may certainly be cured by experience and the exercise of reason. But this remedy cannot be applied in madness, which is a privation or disorder of reason itself."

"So is cowardice, as I'm a living soul," exclaimed the squire. "Don't you say a man is frightened out of his senses? For my peart, measter, I can neither see nor hear, much less argufy, when I'm in such a quandary. Wherefore I do believe, odds bodikins! that cowardice and madness are both distempers, and differ no more than the hot and cold fits of an ague. When it teakes your honour, you're all heat, and fire, and fury, Lord bless us! but when it catches poor Tim he's cold and dead-hearted, he sheakes and shivers like an aspen leaf, that he does."—"In that case," answered the knight, "I shall not punish you for the distemper which you cannot help, but for engaging in a service exposed to perils when you knew your own infirmity ; in the same manner as a man deserves punishment who enlists himself for a soldier while he labours under any secret disease."—" At that rate," said the squire, " my bread is like to be rarely buttered o' both sides, i'faith. But, I hope, as by the blessing of God I have run mad, so I shall in good time grow valiant, under your honour's precept and example."

By this time a very disagreeable night was succeeded by a fair bright morning, and a market-town appeared at the distance of three or four miles, when Crabshaw, having no longer the fear of hobgoblins before his eyes, and being moreover cheered by the sight of a place where he hoped to meet with comfortable entertainment, began to talk big, to expatiate on the folly of being afraid, and finally set all danger at defiance ; when all of a sudden he was presented with an opportunity of putting in practice those new-adopted maxims. In an opening between two lanes they perceived a gentleman's coach stopped by two highwaymen on horseback, one of whom advanced to reconnoitre and keep the coast clear, while the other exacted contribution from the travellers in the coach. He who acted as sentinel, no sooner saw our adventurer appearing from the lane than he rode up with a pistol in his hand, and ordered him to halt on pain of immediate death.

To this peremptory mandate the knight made no other reply than charging him with such impetuosity that he was unhorsed in a twinkling, and lay sprawling on the ground, seemingly sore bruised with his fall. Sir Launcelot, commanding Timothy to alight and secure the prisoner, couched his lance, and rode full speed at the other highwayman, who was not a little disturbed at sight of such an apparition. Nevertheless, he fired his pistol without effect, and, clapping spurs to his horse, fled away at full gallop. The knight pursued him with all the speed that Bronzomarte could exert ; but the robber, being mounted on a swift hunter, kept him at a distance, and, after a chase of several miles, escaped through a wood so entangled with coppice, that Sir Launcelot thought proper to desist. He then, for the first time, recollected the situation in which he had left the other thief, and, remembering to have heard a female shriek, as he passed by the coach window, resolved to return with all expedition, that he might make a proffer of his service to the lady, according to the obligation of knight-errantry. But he had lost his way, and after an hour's ride, during which he traversed many a field, and circled divers hedges, he found himself in the market-town aforementioned. Here the first object that presented itself to his eyes was Crabshaw, on foot, surrounded by a mob, tearing his hair, stamping with his feet, and roaring out in manifest distraction, " Show me the mayor ! for the love of God, show me the mayor !— O Gilbert, Gilbert ! a murrain take thee, Gilbert ! sure thou wast foaled for my destruction ! "

From these exclamations, and the antique dress of the squire, the people, not without reason, concluded that the poor soul had lost his wits, and the beadle was just going to secure him when the knight interposed, and at once attracted the whole attention of the populace. Timothy, seeing his master, fell down on his knees, crying, " The thief has run away with Gilbert—you may pound me into a peast, as the saying is. But now I'se as mad as your worship, I an't afeard of the divil and all his works." Sir Launcelot desiring the beadle would forbear, was instantly obeyed by that officer, who had no inclination to put the authority of his place in competition with the power of such a figure, armed at all points, mounted on a fiery steed, and ready for the combat. He ordered Crabshaw to attend him to the next inn, where he alighted ; then, taking him into a separate apartment, demanded an explanation of the unconnected words he had uttered.

The squire was in such agitation that, with infinite difficulty, and by dint of a thousand different questions, his master learned the adventure to this effect. Crabshaw, acccording to Sir Launcelot's command, had alighted from his horse, and drawn his cutlass, in hope of intimidating the discomfited robber into a tame surrender, though he did not at all relish the nature of the service. But the thief was neither so much hurt nor so tame as Timothy had imagined. He started on his feet with his pistol still in his hand, and presenting it to the squire, swore with dreadful imprecations that he would blow his brains out in an instant. Crabshaw, unwilling to hazard the trial of this experiment, turned his back and fled with great precipitation ; while the robber, whose horse had run away, mounted Gilbert, and rode off across the country. It was at this period that two footmen belonging to the coach, who had stayed behind to take their morning's whet at the inn where they lodged, came up to the assistance of the ladies, armed with blunderbusses, and the carriage proceeded, leaving Timothy alone in distraction and despair. He knew not which way to turn, and was afraid of remaining on the spot, lest the robbers should come back and revenge themselves upon him for the disappointment they had undergone. In this distress, the first thought that occurred was to make the best of his way to the town and demand the assistance of the civil magistrate towards the retrieval of what he had lost ; a design which he executed in such a manner as justly entailed upon him the imputation of lunacy.

While Timothy stood fronting the window, and answering the interrogations of his master, he suddenly exclaimed, " Bodikins ! there's Gilbert ! " and sprang into the street with incredible agility. There finding his strayed companion brought back by one of the footmen who attended the coach, he imprinted a kiss on his forehead, and, hanging about his neck, with the tears in his eyes, hailed his return with the following salutation : " Art thou come back, my darling ? Ah, Gilbert, Gilbert ! a pize upon thee ! thou hadst like to have been a dear Gilbert to me ! How couldst thou break the heart of thy old friend who has known thee from a colt ? Seven years next grass have I fed thee and bred thee, provided thee with sweet hay, delicate corn, and fresh litter, that thou mought lie warm, dry, and comfortable. Han't I currycombed thy carcass till it was as sleek as a sloe, and cherished thee as the apple of mine eye ? for all that thou hast played me a hundred dog's tricks—biting, and kicking, and plunging, as if the devil was in thy body ; and now thou couldst run away with a thief, and leave me to be flayed alive by measter. What canst thou say for thyself, thou cruel, hard-hearted, un-Christian tuoad ? " To this tender expostulation, which afforded much entertainment to the boys, Gilbert answered not one word, but seemed altogether insensible to the caresses of Timothy, who forthwith led him into the stable. On the whole, he seems to have been an unsocial animal, for it does not appear that he ever contracted any degree of intimacy even with Bronzomarte, during the whole course of their acquaintance and fellowship. On the contrary, he has been more than once known to signify his aversion, by throwing out behind, and other eruptive marks of contempt for that elegant charger, who excelled him as much in personal merit as his rider Timothy was outshone by his all-accomplished master.

While the squire accommodated Gilbert in the stable, the knight sent for the footman who had brought him back, and, having presented him with a liberal acknowledgment, desired to know in what manner the horse had been retrieved.

The stranger satisfied him in this particular, by giving him to understand that the highwayman, perceiving himself pursued across the country, plied Gilbert so severely with whip and spur that the animal resented the usage, and being besides, perhaps, a little struck with remorse for having left his old friend Crabshaw, suddenly halted, and stood stock still, notwithstanding all the stripes and tortures he underwent, or, if he moved at all, it was in a retrograde direction. The thief, seeing all his endeavours ineffectual, and himself in danger of being overtaken, wisely quitted his acquisition, and fled into the bosom of a neighbouring wood.

Then the knight inquired about the situation of the lady in the coach, and offered himself as her guard and conductor, but was told that she was already safely lodged in the house of a gentleman at some distance from the road. He likewise learned that she was a person disordered in her senses, under the care and tuition of a widow lady, her relation, and that in a day or two they should pursue their journey northward to the place of her habitation.

After the footman had been some time dismissed, the knight recollected that he had forgotten to ask the name of the person to whom he belonged, and began to be uneasy at this omission, which indeed was more interesting than he could imagine. For an explanation of this nature would, in all likelihood, have led to a discovery that the lady in the coach was no other than Miss Aurelia Darnel, who seeing him unexpectedly in such an equipage and attitude, as he passed the coach, for his helmet was off, had screamed with surprise and terror and fainted away. Nevertheless, when she recovered from her swoon she concealed the real cause of her agitation, and none of her attendants were acquainted with the person of Sir Launcelot.

The circumstances of the disorder under which she was said to labour shall be revealed in due course. In the meantime, our adventurer, though unaccountably affected, never dreamed of such an occurrence; but being very much fatigued, resolved to indemnify himself for the loss of last night's repose; and this happened to be one of the few things in which Crabshaw felt an ambition to follow his master's example.

CHAPTER IX

Which may serve to show that true Patriotism is of no Party.

THE knight had not enjoyed his repose above two hours when he was disturbed by such a variety of noises as might have discomposed a brain of the firmest texture. The rumbling of carriages and the rattling of horses' feet on the pavement, was intermingled with loud shouts, and the noise of fiddle, French horn, and bagpipe. A loud peal was heard ringing in the church tower, at some distance, while the inn resounded with clamour, confusion, and uproar.

Sir Launcelot, being thus alarmed, started from his bed, and running to the window, beheld a cavalcade of persons well mounted and distinguished by blue cockades. They were generally attired like jockeys, with gold-laced hats and buckskin breeches, and one of them bore a standard of blue silk, inscribed in white letters, LIBERTY AND THE LANDED INTEREST. He who rode at their head was a jolly figure, of a florid complexion and round belly, seemingly turned of fifty, and, in all appearance, of a choleric disposition. As they approached the market-place they waved their hats, huzzaed, and cried aloud, No FOREIGN CONNECTIONS !—OLD ENGLAND FOR EVER ! This acclamation, however, was not so loud or universal but that our adventurer could distinctly hear a counter-cry from the populace of, No SLAVERY !—No POPISH PRETENDER ! an insinuation so ill relished by the cavaliers, that they began to ply their horsewhips among the multitude, and were, in their turn, saluted with a discharge or volley of stones, dirt, and dead cats, in consequence of which some teeth were demolished, and many surtouts defiled.

Our adventurer's attention was soon called off from this scene, to contemplate another procession of people on foot, adorned with bunches of orange ribbons, attended by a regular band of music, playing *God save great George our King*, and headed by a thin swarthy personage, of a sallow aspect, and large goggling eyes, arched over with two thick semicircles of hair, or rather bristles, jet black, and frousy. His apparel was very gorgeous, though his address was very awkward ; he was accompanied by the mayor, recorder, and heads of the corporation, in their formalities. His ensigns were known by the inscription, *Liberty of Conscience, and the Protestant Succession ;* and the people saluted him as he passed with repeated cheers, that seemed to prognosticate success. He had particularly ingratiated himself with the good women, who lined the street, and sent forth many ejaculatory petitions in his favour.

Sir Launcelot immediately comprehended the meaning of this solemnity. He perceived it was the prelude to the election of a member to represent the county in Parliament, and he was seized with an eager desire to know the names and characters of the competitors.

In order to gratify this desire, he made repeated application to the bell-rope that depended from the ceiling of his apartment, but this produced nothing except the repetition of the words, "Coming, sir," which echoed from three or four different corners of the house. The waiters were so distracted by a variety of calls that they stood motionless, in the state of the schoolman's ass between two bundles of hay, incapable of determining where they should first offer their attendance.

Our knight's patience was almost exhausted, when Crab-shaw entered the room, in a very strange equipage. One half of his face appeared close shaved, and the other covered with lather, while the blood trickled in two rivulets from his nose upon a barber's cloth that was tucked under his chin; he looked grim with indignation, and under his left arm carried his cutlass, unsheathed. Where he had acquired so much of the profession of knight-errantry we shall not pretend to determine, but certain it is, he fell on his knees before Sir Launcelot, crying, with an accent of grief and distraction, " In the name of St. George for England, I beg a boon, Sir Knight, and thy compliance I demand, before the peacock and the ladies."

Sir Launcelot, astonished at this address, replied in a lofty strain, " Valiant squire, thy boon is granted, provided it doth not contravene the laws of the land, and the constitution of chivalry."—" Then I crave leave," answered Crab-shaw, " to challenge and defy to mortal combat that caitiff barber who hath left me in this piteous condition; and I vow by the peacock that I will not shave my beard until I have shaved his head from his shoulde s. So may I thrive in the occupation of an arrant squire."

Before his master had time to inquire into particulars they were joined by a decent man in boots, who was likewise a traveller, and had seen the rise and progress of Timothy's disaster. He gave the knight to understand that Crabshaw had sent for a barber, and already undergone one half of the operation, when the operator received the long-expected message from both the gentlemen who stood candidates at the election. The double summons was no sooner intimated to him than he threw down his basin, and retired with precipitation, leaving the squire in the suds. Timothy, incensed at this desertion, followed him with equal celerity into the street, where he collared the shaver, and insisted upon being entirely trimmed, on pain of the bastinado. The other, finding himself thus arrested, and having no time to spare for altercation, lifted up his fist and discharged it upon the snout of Crabshaw with such force that the unfortunate aggressor was fain to bite the ground, while the victor hastened away, in hope of touching the double wages of corruption.

The knight being informed of these circumstances told Timothy with a smile that he should have liberty to defy the barber ; but, in the meantime, he ordered him to saddle Bronzomarte, and prepare for immediate service. While the squire was thus employed, his master engaged in a conversation with the stranger, who happened to be a London dealer travelling for orders, and was well acquainted with the particulars which our adventurer wanted to know.

It was from this communicative tradesman he learned that the competitors were Sir Valentine Quickset and Mr. Isaac Vanderpelft ; the first a mere fox-hunter, who depended for success in his election upon his interest among the high-flying gentry ; the other a stock-jobber and contractor of foreign extract, not without a mixture of Hebrew blood, immensely rich, who was countenanced by his Grace of——, and supposed to have distributed large sums in securing a majority of votes among the yeomanry of the county, possessed of small freeholds, and copyholders, a great number of which last resided in this borough. He said these were generally dissenters and weavers ; and that the mayor, who was himself a manufacturer, had received a very considerable order for exportation, in consequence of which it was believed he would support Mr. Vanderpelft with all his influence and credit.

Sir Launcelot, roused at this intelligence, called for his armour, which, being buckled on in a hurry, he mounted his steed, attended by Crabshaw on Gilbert, and rode immediately into the midst of the multitude by which the hustings were surrounded, just as Sir Valentine Quickset began to harangue the people from an occasional theatre, formed of a plank supported by the upper board of the public stocks, and an inferior rib of a wooden cage pitched also for the accommodation of petty delinquents.

Though the singular appearance of Sir Launcelot at first attracted the eyes of all the spectators, yet they did not fail to yield attention to the speech of his brother-knight, Sir Valentine, which ran in the following strain :—" Gentlemen vreeholders of this here county, I shan't pretend to meake a vine flourishing speech—I'm a plain-spoken man, as you all know. I hope I shall always speak my maind without vear or vavour, as the zaying is. 'Tis the way of the Quicksets —we are no upstarts, nor vorreigners, nor have we any Jewish blood in our veins ; we have lived in this here neighbourhood time out of mind, as you all know, and possess an estate of vive thousand clear, which we spend at whoam, among you, in old English hospitality. All my vorevathers have been Parliament men, and I can prove that ne'er a one o' um gave a zingle vote for the court since the Revolution. Vor my own peart, I value not the ministry three skips of a louse, as the zaying is—I ne'er knew but one minister that was an honest man, and vor all the rest, I care not if they were hanged as high as Haman, with a pox to 'un. I am, thank God, a vree-born, true-hearted Englishman, and a loyal, thof unworthy, son of the Church—vor all they have done vor H——r, I'd vain know what they have done vor the Church, with a vengeance—vor my own peart, I hate all vorreigners and vorreign measures, whereby this poor nation is broken-backed with a dismal load of debt, and the taxes rise so high that the poor cannot get bread. Gentlemen vreeholders of this county, I value no minister a vig's end, d'ye see ; if you will vavour me with your votes and interest, whereby I may be returned, I'll engage one half of my estate that I never cry yea to vour shillings in the pound, but will cross the ministry in everything, as in duty bound, and as

becomes an honest vreeholder in the ould interest—but, if
you sell your votes and your country for hire, you will be
detested in this here world, and damned in the next to all
eternity : so I leave every man to his own conscience."

This eloquent oration was received by his own friends
with loud peals of applause, which, however, did not discourage his competitor, who, confident of his own strength,
ascended the rostrum, or, in other words, an old cask, set
upright for the purpose. Having bowed all round to the
audience, with a smile of gentle condescension, he told them
how ambitious he was of the honour to represent this county
in Parliament, and how happy he found himself in the en-
couragement of his friends, who had so unanimously agreed
to support his pretensions. He said, over and above the
qualifications he possessed among them, he had fourscore
thousand pounds in his pocket, which he had acquired by
commerce, the support of the nation, under the present
happy establishment, in defence of which he was ready to
spend the last farthing. He owned himself a faithful subject
to His Majesty King George, sincerely attached to the
Protestant succession, in detestation and defiance of a popish,
an abjured, and outlawed Pretender, and declared that he
would exhaust his substance and his blood, if necessary,
in maintaining the principles of the glorious Revolution.
" This," cried he, " is the solid basis and foundation upon
which I stand."

These last words had scarce proceeded from his mouth,
when the head of the barrel or puncheon on which he stood,
being frail and infirm, gave way, so that down he went with
a crash, and in a twinkling disappeared from the eyes of
the astonished beholders. The fox-hunters, perceiving his
disaster, exclaimed, in the phrase and accent of the chase,
" Stole away ! stole away ! " and with hideous vociferation
joined in the sylvan chorus which the hunters halloo when
the hounds are at fault.

The disaster of Mr. Vanderpelft was soon repaired by the
assiduity of his friends, who disengaged him from the barrel
in a trice, hoisted him on the shoulders of four strong weavers,

and, resenting the unmannerly exultation of their antagonists, began to form themselves in order of battle.

An obstinate fray would have undoubtedly ensued, had not their mutual indignation given way to their curiosity, at the motion of our knight, who had advanced into the middle between the two fronts, and waving his hand as a signal for them to give attention addressed himself to them, with graceful demeanour, in these words :—" Countrymen, friends, and fellow-citizens, you are this day assembled to determine a point of the utmost consequence to yourselves and your posterity—a point that ought to be determined by far other weapons than brutal force and factious clamour. You, the freemen of England, are the basis of that excellent constitution which hath long flourished the object of envy and admiration. To you belongs the inestimable privilege of choosing a delegate properly qualified to represent you in the High Court of Parliament. This is your birthright, inherited from your ancestors, obtained by their courage, and sealed with their blood. It is not only your birthright, which you should maintain in defiance of all danger, but also a sacred trust, to be executed with the most scrupulous care and fidelity. The person whom you trust ought not only to be endued with the most inflexible integrity, but should likewise possess a fund of knowledge that may enable him to act as a part of the legislature. He must be well acquainted with the history, the constitution, and the laws of his country ; he must understand the forms of business, the extent of the royal prerogative, the privilege of Parliament, the detail of government, the nature and regulation of the finances, the different branches of commerce, the politics that prevail, and the connections that subsist among the different powers of Europe ; for on all these subjects the deliberations of a House of Commons occasionally turn.

" But these great purposes will never be answered by electing an illiterate savage, scarce qualified, in point of understanding, to act as a country justice of peace, a man who has scarce ever travelled beyond the excursion of a fox-chase, whose conversation never rambles farther than his stable, his kennel, and the barnyard ; who rejects decorum as degeneracy, mistakes rusticity for independence, ascertains his courage by leaping over gates and ditches, and founds his triumph on feats of drinking ; who holds his estate by a factious tenure, professes himself the blind slave of a party, without knowing the principles that gave it birth, or the motives by which it is actuated, and thinks that all patriotism consists in railing indiscriminately at ministers, and obstinately opposing every measure of the administration. Such a man, with no evil intentions of his own, might be used as a dangerous tool in the hands of a desperate faction, by scattering the seeds of disaffection, embarrassing the wheels of government, and reducing the whole kingdom to anarchy."

Here the knight was interrupted by the shouts and acclamations of the Vanderpelfites, who cried aloud, " Hear him ! hear him ! long life to the iron-cased orator." This clamour subsiding, he prosecuted his harangue to the following effect :

" Such a man as I have described may be dangerous from ignorance, but is neither so mischievous, nor so detestable, as the wretch who knowingly betrays his trust, and sues to be the hireling and prostitute of a weak and worthless minister ; a sordid knave, without honour or principle, who belongs to no family whose example can reproach him with degeneracy, who has no country to command his respect, no friend to engage his affection, no religion to regulate his morals, no conscience to restrain his iniquity, and who worships no God but Mammon ; an insinuating miscreant, who undertakes for the dirtiest work of the vilest administration, who practises national usury, receiving by wholesale the rewards of venality, and distributing the wages of corruption by retail."

In this place our adventurer's speech was drowned in the acclamations of the fox-hunters, who now triumphed in their turn, and hoicksed the speaker, exclaiming, " Well opened, Jowler—to 'un, to 'un again, Sweetlips ! hey, Merry, Whitefoot ! " After a short interruption, he thus resumed his discourse :

"When such a caitiff presents himself to you, like the devil, with a temptation in his hand, avoid him as if he were in fact the devil—it is not the offering of disinterested love, for what should induce him, who has no affections, to love you, to whose person he is an utter stranger ? Alas ! it is not a benevolence, but a bribe. He wants to buy you at one market that he may sell you at another. Without doubt his intention is to make an advantage of his purchase, and this aim he cannot accomplish but by sacrificing, in some sort, your interest, your independency, to the wicked designs of a minister, as he can expect no gratification for the faithful discharge of his duty. But, even if he should not find an opportunity of selling you to advantage, the crime, the shame, the infamy, will still be the same in you, who, baser than the most abandoned prostitutes, have sold yourselves and your posterity for hire—for a paltry price, to be refunded with interest by some minister, who will indemnify himself out of your own pockets, for, after all, you are bought and sold with your own money—the miserable pittance you may now receive is no more than a pitcher full of water thrown in to moisten the sucker of that pump which will drain you to the bottom. Let me therefore advise and exhort you, my countrymen, to avoid the opposite extremes of the ignorant clown and the designing courtier, and choose a man of honesty, intelligence, and moderation, who will——"

The doctrine of moderation was a very unpopular subject in such an assembly, and, accordingly, they rejected it as one man. They began to think the stranger wanted to set up for himself—a supposition that could not fail to incense both sides equally, as they were both zealously engaged in their respective causes. The Whigs and the Tories joined against this intruder, who, being neither, was treated like a monster, or chimera in politics. They hissed, they hooted, and they hallooed ; they annoyed him with missiles of dirt, sticks, and stones ; they cursed, they threatened, and reviled, till, at length, his patience was exhausted.

"Ungrateful and abandoned miscreants ! " he cried, " I spoke to you as men and Christians—as free-born Britons and fellow-citizens ; but I perceive you are a pack of venal, infamous scoundrels, and I will treat you accordingly." So saying, he brandished his lance, and riding into the thickest of the concourse, laid about him with such dexterity and effect that the multitude was immediately dispersed, and he retired without further molestation.

The same good fortune did not attend Squire Crabshaw in his retreat. The ludicrous singularity of his features, and the half-mown crop of hair that bristled from one side of his countenance, invited some wags to make merry at his expense. One of them clapped a furze-bush under the tail of Gilbert, who, feeling himself thus stimulated *a posteriori*, kicked and plunged, and capered in such a manner, that Timothy could hardly keep the saddle. In this commotion he lost his cap and his periwig, while the rabble pelted him in such a manner that, before he could join his master, he looked like a pillar, or rather a pillory, of mud.

CHAPTER X

Which showeth that he who plays at Bowls will sometimes meet with Rubbers.

SIR LAUNCELOT, boiling with indignation at the venality and faction of the electors, whom he had harangued to so little purpose, retired with the most deliberate disdain towards one of the gates of the town, on the outside of which his curiosity was attracted by a concourse of people, in the midst of whom stood Mr. Ferret, mounted upon a stool, with a kind of satchel hanging round his neck, and a phial displayed in his right hand, while he held forth to the audience in a very vehement strain of elocution.

Crabshaw thought himself happily delivered when he reached the suburbs, and proceeded without halting ; but his master mingled with the crowd, and heard the orator express himself to this effect :

"Very likely you may undervalue me and my medicine, because I don't appear upon a stage of rotten boards, in a shabby velvet coat, and tie-periwig, with a foolish fellow in a motley coat, to make you laugh, by making wry faces ; but I scorn to use these dirty arts for engaging your attention. These paltry tricks, *ad captandum vulgus*, can have no effect but on idiots ; and if you are idiots, I don't desire you should be my customers. Take notice, I don't address you in the style of a mountebank, or a High German doctor ; and yet the kingdom is full of mountebanks, empirics, and quacks. We have quacks in religion, quacks in physic, quacks in law, quacks in politics, quacks in patriotism, quacks in government—High German quacks that have blistered, sweated, bled, and purged the nation into an atrophy. But this is not all ; they have not only evacuated her into a consumption, but they have intoxicated her brain, until she is become delirious ; she can no longer pursue her own interest, or, indeed, rightly distinguish it. Like the people of Nineveh, she can hardly tell her right hand from her left ; but, as a changeling, is dazzled and delighted by an *ignis fatuus*, a Will-o'-the-wisp, an exhalation from the vilest materials in nature, that leads her astray through Westphalian bogs and deserts, and will one day break her neck over some barren rocks, or leave her sticking in some H—n pit, or quagmire.

" For my part, if you have a mind to betray your country, I have no objection. In selling yourselves and your fellow-citizens, you only dispose of a pack of rascals who deserve to be sold. If you sell one another, why should not I sell this here Elixir of Long Life, which, if properly used, will protract your days till you shall have seen your country ruined. I shall not pretend to disturb your understandings, which are none of the strongest, with a hotchpotch of unintelligible terms, such as Aristotle's four principles of generation, unformed matter, privation, efficient, and final causes. Aristotle was a pedantic blockhead, and still more knave than fool. The same censure we may safely put on that wiseacre, Dioscorides, with his faculties of simples—his seminal, specific, and principal virtues ; and that crazy commentator, Galen, with his four elements, elementary

7

qualities, his eight complexions, his harmonies and discords. Nor shall I expatiate on the alkahest of that mad scoundrel, Paracelsus, with which he pretended to reduce flints into salt ; nor *archæus* or *spiritus rector* of that visionary Van Helmont, his simple, elementary water, his *gas*, ferments, and transmutations ; nor shall I enlarge upon the salt, sulphur, and oil, the *acidum vagum*, the mercury of metals, and the volatilised vitriol of other modern chemists, a pack of ignorant, conceited, knavish rascals, that puzzle your weak heads with such jargon, just as a Germanised m—r throws dust in your eyes, by lugging in and ringing the changes on the balance of power, the Protestant religion, and your allies on the continent ; acting like the juggler, who picks your pockets while he dazzles your eyes and amuses your fancy with twirling his fingers and reciting the gibberish of *hocus pocus ;* for, in fact, the balance of power is a mere chimera.   As for the Protestant religion, nobody gives himself any trouble about it ; and allies on the continent we have none, or, at least, none that would raise an hundred men to save us from perdition, unless we paid an extravagant price for their assistance.

" But, to return to this here Elixir of Long Life, I might embellish it with a great many high-sounding epithets ; but I disdain to follow the example of every illiterate vagabond, that, from idleness, turns quack, and advertises his nostrum in the public papers.   I am neither a felonious drysalter returned from exile, a hospital stump-turner, a decayed staymaker, a bankrupt printer, or insolvent debtor, released by Act of Parliament.   I do not pretend to administer medicines without the least tincture of letters, or suborn wretches to perjure themselves in false affidavits of cures that were never performed ; nor employ a set of led captains to harangue in my praise at all public places. I was bred regularly to the profession of chemistry, and have tried all the processes of alchemy ; and I may venture to say, that this here elixir is, in fact, the *chruseon pepuromenon ek puros*, the visible, glorious, spiritual body, from whence all other beings derive their existence, as proceeding from their father the sun, and their mother the moon; from the sun, as from a living and spiritual gold, which is mere fire; consequently, the common and universal first-created mover, from whence all movable things have their distinct and particular motions; and also from the moon, as from the wife of the sun, and the common mother of all sublunary things.

"And forasmuch as man is, and must be, the comprehensive end of all creatures, and the microcosm, he is counselled in the Revelation to buy gold that is thoroughly fired, or rather pure fire, that he may become rich and like the sun; as, on the contrary, he becomes poor, when he abuses the arsenical poison; so that, his silver, by the fire, must be calcined to a *caput mortuum*, which happens when he will hold and retain the menstruum, out of which he partly exists, for his own property, and doth not daily offer up the same in the fire of the sun, that the woman may be clothed with the sun, and become a sun, and thereby rule over the moon; that is to say, that he may get the moon under his feet. Now, this here elixir, sold for no more than sixpence a phial, contains the essence of the alkahest, the archæus, the catholicon, the menstruum, the sun, the moon, and, to sum up all in one word, is the true, genuine, unadulterated, unchangeable, immaculate, and specific *chruseon pepuromenon ek puros.*"

The audience were variously affected by this learned oration. Some of those who favoured the pretensions of the Whig candidate were of opinion that he ought to be punished for his presumption, in reflecting so scurrilously on ministers and measures. Of this sentiment was our adventurer, though he could not help admiring the courage of the orator, and owning within himself that he had mixed some melancholy truths with his scurrility.

Mr. Ferret would not have stood so long in his rostrum unmolested, had not he cunningly chosen his station immediately without the jurisdiction of the town, whose magistrates therefore could not take cognisance of his conduct; but application was made to the constable of the other parish, while our nostrum-monger proceeded in his speech, the conclusion of which produced such an effect upon his hearers, that his whole cargo was immediately exhausted. He had just stepped down from his stool, when the constable with his staff arrived, and took him under his guidance. Mr. Ferret, on this occasion, attempted to interest the people in his behalf, by exhorting them to vindicate the liberty of the subject against such an act of oppression ; but finding them deaf to the tropes and figures of his elocution, he addressed himself to our knight, reminding him of his duty to protect the helpless and the injured, and earnestly soliciting his interposition.

Sir Launcelot, without making the least reply to his entreaties, resolved to see the end of this adventure ; and, being joined by his squire, followed the prisoner at a distance, measuring back the ground he had travelled the day before, until he reached another small borough, where Ferret was housed in the common prison.

While he sat on horseback, deliberating on the next step he should take, he was accosted by the voice of Tom Clarke, who called, in a whimpering tone, through a window grated with iron, " For the love of God, Sir Launcelot, do, dear sir, be so good as to take the trouble to alight, and come upstairs ; I have something to communicate of consequence to the community in general, and you in particular. Pray do, dear Sir Knight. I beg a boon in the name of St. Michael and St. George for England."

Our adventurer, not a little surprised at this address, dismounted without hesitation, and, being admitted to the common jail, there found not only his old friend Tom, but also the uncle, sitting on a bench, with a woollen night-cap on his head, and a pair of spectacles on his nose, reading very earnestly in a book, which he afterwards understood was entitled, *The Life and Adventures of Valentine and Orson.* The captain no sooner saw his great pattern enter, than he rose, and received him with the salutation of, " What cheer, brother ? " and before the knight could answer, added these words : " You see how the land lies—here have Tom and I been fast ashore these four-and-twenty hours ; and this berth we have got by attempting to tow your galley, brother, from the enemy's harbour. Adds bobs ! if we had this here fellow w—eson for a consort, with all our tackle in order, brother, we'd soon show 'em the topsail, slip our cable, and down with their barricadoes. But, howsomever, it don't signify talking—patience is a good steam-anchor, and will hold, as the saying is—but, d—n my—as for the matter of my bolt-sprit.—Harkye, harkye, brother, d—ned hard to engage with three at a time, one upon my bow, one upon my quarter, and one right a-head, rubbing and drubbing, lying athwart hawse, raking fore and aft, battering and grappling, and lashing and clashing—adds heart, brother ; crash went the bolt-sprit—down came the round-top—up with the dead-lights—I saw nothing but the stars at noon, lost the helm of my seven senses, and down I broached upon my broadside."

As Mr. Clarke rightly conceived that his uncle would need an interpreter, he began to explain these hints, by giving a circumstantial detail of his own and the captain's disaster.

He told Sir Launcelot, that, notwithstanding all his persuasion and remonstrances, Captain Crowe insisted upon appearing in the character of a knight-errant ; and, with that view, had set out from the public-house on the morning that succeeded his vigil in the church. That upon the highway they had met with a coach, containing two ladies, one of whom seemed to be under great agitation ; for, as they passed, she struggled with the other, thrust out her head at the window, and said something which he could not distinctly hear. That Captain Crowe was struck with admiration of her unequalled beauty ; and he, Tom, no sooner informed him who she was, than he resolved to set her at liberty, on the supposition that she was under restraint, and in distress. That he accordingly unsheathed his cutlass, and, riding after the coach, commanded the driver to bring to, on pain of death. That one of the servants, believing the captain to be a highwayman, presented a blunderbuss, and, in all probability would have shot him on the spot, had not he, the nephew, rode up, and assured them the gentleman was *non compos*.   That, notwithstanding his intimation, all the three attacked him with the butt-ends of their horsewhips, while the coach drove on, and although he laid about him with great fury, at last brought him to the ground, by a stroke on the temple.   That Mr. Clarke himself then interposed in defence of his kinsman, and was also severely beaten.   That two of the servants, upon application to a justice of the peace, residing near the field of battle, had granted a warrant against the captain and his nephew, and, without examination, committed them as idle vagrants, after having seized their horses and their money, on pretence of their being suspected for highway-men.

"But, as there was no just cause of suspicion," added he, " I am of opinion, the justice is guilty of a trespass, and may be sued for *falsum imprisonamentum*, and consider-able damages obtained ; for you will please to observe, sir, no justice has a right to commit any person till after due examination ; besides, we were not committed for an assault and battery, *audita querela*, nor as wandering lunatics by the statute, who, to be sure, may be apprehended by a justice's warrant, and locked up and chained, if necessary, or to be sent to their last legal settlement ; but we were committed as vagrants and suspected highwaymen.   Now we do not fall under the description of vagrants ; nor did any circumstance appear to support the suspicion of robbery ; for, to constitute robbery, there must be something taken ; but here nothing was taken but blows, and they were upon compulsion.   Even an attempt to rob, without any taking, is not felony, but a misdemeanour.   To be sure, there is a taking in deed, and a taking in law.   But still the robber must be in possession of a thing stolen ; and we attempted to steal ourselves away.   My uncle, indeed, would have released the young lady *vi et armis*, had his strength been equal to his inclination ; and in so doing I would have willingly lent my assistance both from a desire to serve such a beautiful young creature, and also in regard to your honour, for I thought I heard her call upon your name."

"Ha! how! what! whose name? say, speak—Heaven and earth!" cried the knight, with marks of the most violent emotion. Clarke, terrified at his looks, replied, "I beg your pardon a thousand times; I did not say positively she did speak those words; but I apprehended she did speak them. Words, which may be taken or interpreted by law in a general or common sense, ought not to receive a strained or unusual construction; and ambiguous words——"

"Speak, or be dumb for ever!" exclaimed Sir Launcelot, in a terrific tone, laying his hand on his sword. "What young lady, ha? What name did she call upon?"—Clarke, falling on his knees, answered, not without stammering, "Miss Aurelia Darnel; to the best of my recollection, she called upon Sir Launcelot Greaves."—"Sacred powers!" cried our adventurer, "which way did the carriage proceed?"

When Tom told him that the coach quitted the post-road, and struck away to the right at full speed, Sir Launcelot was seized with a pensive fit; his head sank upon his breast, and he mused in silence for several minutes with the most melancholy expression on his countenance; then recollecting himself, he assumed a more composed and cheerful air, and asked several questions with respect to the arms on the coach, and the liveries worn by the servants? It was in the course of this interrogation, that he discovered he had actually conversed with one of the footmen, who had brought back Crabshaw's horse. A circumstance that filled him with anxiety and chagrin, as he had omitted to inquire the name of his master, and the place to which the coach was travelling; though, in all probability, had he made these inquiries, he would have received very little satisfaction, there being reason to think the servants were enjoined secrecy.

The knight, in order to meditate on this unexpected adventure, sat down by his old friend, and entered into a reverie, which lasted about a quarter of an hour, and might have continued longer had it not been interrupted by the voice of Crabshaw, who bawled aloud, "Look to it, my masters—as you brew you must drink—this shall be a dear day's work to some of you; for my part, I say nothing ;— the braying ass eats little grass—one barber shaves not so close, but another finds a few stubble—you wanted to catch a capon, and you've stole a cat—he that takes up his lodgings in a stable must be contented to lie upon litter."

The knight, desirous of knowing the cause that prompted Timothy to apothegmatise in this manner, looked through the grate, and perceived the squire fairly set in the stocks, surrounded by a mob of people. When he called to him, and asked the reason of this disgraceful restraint, Crabshaw replied, "There's no cake, but there's another of the same make—who never climbed, never fell—after clouds comes clear weather. 'Tis all along of your honour, I've met with this preferment; no deservings of my own, but the interest of my master. Sir knight, if you will slay the justice, hang the constable, release your squire, and burn the town, your name will be famous in story; but, if you are content, I am thankful. Two hours are soon spent in such good company; in the meantime, look to 'un, jailer, there's a frog in the stocks."

Sir Launcelot, incensed at this affront offered to his servant, advanced to the prison door, but found it fast locked; and when he called to the turnkey, he was given to understand, that he himself was prisoner. Enraged at this intimation, he demanded at whose suit, and was answered through the wicket, "At the suit of the King, in whose name I will hold you fast, with God's assistance."

The knight's looks now began to lighten; he rolled his eyes around, and snatching up an oaken bench, which three ordinary men could scarce have lifted from the ground, he, in all likelihood, would have shattered the door in pieces had not he been restrained by the interposition of Mr. Clarke, who entreated him to have a little patience, assuring him he would suggest a plan that would avenge himself amply on the justice, without any breach of the peace. "I say the justice," added Tom, "because it must be his doing. He is a little petulant sort of a fellow, ignorant of the law, guilty of numberless irregularities, and if properly managed, may, for this here act of arbitrary power, be not only cast in a swingeing sum, but even turned out of the commission with disgrace."

This was a very seasonable hint, in consequence of which the bench was softly replaced, and Captain Crowe deposited the poker, with which he had armed himself, to second the efforts of Sir Launcelot. They now, for the first time, perceived that Ferret had disappeared ; and, upon inquiry, found that he was in fact the occasion of the knight's detention and the squire's disgrace.

CHAPTER XI

Description of a modern Magistrate.

BEFORE the knight would take any resolution for extricating himself from his present embarrassment, he desired to be better acquainted with the character and circumstances of the justice by whom he had been confined, and likewise to understand the meaning of his own detention. To be informed in this last particular, he renewed his dialogue with the turnkey, who told him through the grate, that Ferret no sooner perceived him in the jail without his offensive arms, which he had left below, than he desired to be carried before the justice, where he had given information against the knight, as a violator of the public peace, who strolled about the country with unlawful arms, rendering the highways unsafe, encroaching upon the freedom of elections, putting his majesty's liege subjects in fear of their lives, and, in all probability, harbouring more dangerous designs under an affected cloak of lunacy. Ferret, upon this information, had been released, and entertained as an evidence for the King ; and Crabshaw was put into the stocks, as an idle stroller.

Sir Launcelot, being satisfied in these particulars, addressed himself to his fellow-prisoners, and begged they would communicate what they knew respecting the worthy magistrate, who had been so premature in the execution of his office. This request was no sooner signified, than a crew of naked wretches crowded around him, and, like a congregation of rooks, opened their throats all at once, in accusation of Justice Gobble. The knight was moved at this scene, which he could not help comparing, in his own mind, to what would appear upon a much more awful occasion, when the cries of the widow and the orphan, the injured and oppressed, would be uttered at the tribunal of an unerring Judge, against the villainous and insolent authors of their calamity.

When he had, with some difficulty, quieted their clamours, and confined his interrogation to one person of a tolerably decent appearance, he learned that Justice Gobble, whose father was a tailor, had for some time served as a journeyman hosier in London, where he had picked up some law terms, by conversing with hackney writers and attorneys' clerks of the lowest order; that, upon the death of his master, he had insinuated himself into the good graces of the widow, who took him for her husband, so that he became a person of some consideration, and saved money apace; that his pride, increasing with his substance, was reinforced by the vanity of his wife, who persuaded him to retire from business, that they might live genteelly in the country; that his father dying, and leaving a couple of houses in this town, Mr. Gobble had come down with his lady to take possession, and liked the place so well, as to make a more considerable purchase in the neighbourhood; that a certain peer being indebted to him in the large way of his business, and either unable or unwilling to pay the money, had compounded the debt, by inserting his name in the commission; since which period his own insolence, and his wife's ostentation, had exceeded all bounds; that, in the execution of his authority, he had committed a thousand acts of cruelty and injustice against the poorer sort of people, who were unable to call him to a proper account; that his wife domineered with a more ridiculous, though less pernicious usurpation, among the females of the place; that, in a word, she was the subject of continual mirth, and he the object of universal detestation.

Our adventurer, though extremely well disposed to believe what was said to the prejudice of Gobble, would not give entire credit to this description, without first inquiring into the particulars of his conduct. He therefore asked the speaker, what was the cause of his particular complaint. " For my own part, sir," said he, " I lived in repute, and kept a shop in this here town, well furnished with a great variety of articles. All the people in the place were my customers ; but what I and many others chiefly depended upon, was the extraordinary sale at two annual customary fairs, to which all the country people in the neighbourhood resorted to lay out their money. I had employed all my stock, and even engaged my credit, to procure a large assortment of goods for the Lammas market ; but, having given my vote in the election of a vestry-clerk, contrary to the interest of Justice Gobble, he resolved to work my ruin. He suppressed the annual fairs, by which a great many people, especially publicans, earned the best part of their subsistence The country people resorted to another town. I was overstocked with a load of perishable commodities, and found myself deprived of the best part of my home customers, by the ill-nature and revenge of the justice, who employed all his influence among the common people, making use of threats and promises, to make them desert my shop, and give their custom to another person, whom he settled in the same business under my nose. Being thus disabled from making punctual payments, my commodities spoiling, and my wife breaking her heart, I grew negligent and careless, took to drinking, and my affairs went to wreck. Being one day in liquor, and provoked by the fleers and taunts of the man who had set up against me, I struck him at his own door ; upon which I was carried before the justice, who treated me with such insolence, that I became desperate, and not only abused him in the execution of his office, but also made an attempt to lay violent hands upon his person. You know, sir, when a man is both drunk and desperate, he cannot be

supposed to have any command of himself. I was sent hither
to jail. My creditors immediately seized my effects ; and
as they were not sufficient to discharge my debts, a statute of
bankruptcy was taken out against me ; so that here I must
lie, until they think proper to sign my certificate, or the
Parliament shall please to pass an Act for the relief of insolvent
debtors."

The next person who presented himself in the crowd of
accusers was a meagre figure, with a green apron, who told
the knight that he had kept a public-house in town for a
dozen years, and enjoyed a good trade, which was in a great
measure owing to a skittle-ground, in which the best people
of the place diverted themselves occasionally. That Justice
Gobble, being disobliged at his refusing to part with a gelding
which he had bred for his own use, first of all shut up the
skittle-ground ; but, finding the publican still kept his house
open, he took care that he should be deprived of his licence,
on pretence that the number of alehouses was too great,
and that this man had been bred to another employment.
The poor publican being thus deprived of his bread was
obliged to try the staymaking business, to which he had
served an apprenticeship ; but being very ill-qualified for
this profession, he soon fell to decay and contracted debts,
in consequence of which he was now in prison, where he
had no other support but what arose from the labour of his
wife, who had gone to service.

The next prisoner who preferred his complaint against
the unrighteous judge was a poacher, at whose practices
Justice Gobble had for some years connived, so as even to
screen him from punishment, in consideration of being
supplied with game gratis, till at length he was disappointed
by accident. His lady had invited guests to an entertainment,
and bespoke a hare, which the poacher undertook to furnish.
He laid his snares accordingly overnight, but they were
discovered, and taken away by the gamekeeper of the gentleman to whom the ground belonged. All the excuses the
poacher could make proved ineffectual in appeasing the
resentment of the justice and his wife at being thus dis-

concerted. Measures were taken to detect the delinquent in the exercise of his illicit occupation; he was committed to safe custody, and his wife, with five bantlings, was passed to her husband's settlement in a different part of the country.

A stout squat fellow, rattling with chains, had just taken up the ball of accusation, when Sir Launcelot was startled with the appearance of a woman, whose looks and equipage indicated the most piteous distress. She seemed to be turned of the middle age, was of a lofty carriage, tall, thin, weather-beaten, and wretchedly attired; her eyes were inflamed with weeping, and her looks displayed that wildness and peculiarity which denote distraction. Advancing to Sir Launcelot, she fell upon her knees, and, clasping her hands together, uttered the following rhapsody in the most vehement tone of affliction:

"Thrice potent, generous, and august emperor; here let my knees cleave to the earth, until thou shalt do me justice on that inhuman caitiff Gobble. Let him disgorge my substance which he hath devoured; let him restore to my widowed arms my child, my boy, the delight of my eyes, the prop of my life, the staff of my sustenance, whom he hath torn from my embrace, stolen, betrayed, sent into captivity, and murdered! Behold these bleeding wounds upon his lovely breast: see how they mangle his lifeless corse! Horror! give me my child, barbarians! his head shall lie upon his Suky's bosom—she will embalm him with her tears. Ha! plunge him in the deep!—shall my boy then float in a watery tomb? Justice, most mighty emperor! justice upon the villain who hath ruined us all! May Heaven's dreadful vengeance overtake him! may the keen storm of adversity strip him of all his leaves and fruit! may peace forsake his mind, and rest be banished from his pillow, so that all his days shall be filled with reproach and sorrow, and all his nights be haunted with horror and remorse! may he be stung by jealousy without cause, and maddened by revenge without the means of execution! may all his offspring be blighted and consumed, like the mildewed ears of corn, except one that shall grow up to curse his old age, and bring his hoary head with sorrow to the grave, as he himself has proved a curse to me and mine ! "

The rest of the prisoners, perceiving the knight extremely shocked at her misery and horrid imprecation, removed her by force from his presence, and conveyed her to another room ; while our adventurer underwent a violent agitation, and could not for some minutes compose himself so well as to inquire into the nature of this wretched creature's calamity.

The shopkeeper, of whom he demanded this satisfaction, gave him to understand that she was born a gentlewoman, and had been well educated ; that she married a curate, who did not long survive his nuptials, and afterwards became the wife of one Oakley, a farmer in opulent circumstances. That after twenty years' cohabitation with her husband, he sustained such losses by the distemper among the cattle, as he could not repair ; and that this reverse of fortune was supposed to have hastened his death. That the widow, being a woman of spirit, determined to keep up and manage the farm, with the assistance of an only son, a very promising youth, who was already contracted in marriage with the daughter of another wealthy farmer. Thus the mother had a prospect of retrieving the affairs of her family, when all her hopes were dashed and destroyed by a ridiculous pique which Mrs. Gobble conceived against the young farmer's sweetheart, Mrs. Susan Sedgemoor.

This young woman chancing to be at a country assembly, where the gravedigger of the parish acted as master of the ceremonies, was called out to dance before Miss Gobble, who happened to be there present also with her mother. The circumstance was construed into an unpardonable affront by the justice's lady, who abused the director in the most opprobrious terms for his insolence and ill manners ; and retiring in a storm of passion, vowed revenge against the saucy minx who had presumed to vie in gentility with Miss Gobble. The justice entered into her resentment. The gravedigger lost his place ; and Suky's lover, young Oakley, was pressed for a soldier. Before his mother could take any steps for his discharge, he was hurried away to the

East Indies, by the industry and contrivance of the justice.
Poor Suky wept and pined until she fell into a consumption.
The forlorn widow, being thus deprived of her son, was
overwhelmed with grief to such a degree, that she could no
longer manage her concerns. Everything went backwards;
she ran in arrears with her landlord; and the prospect of
bankruptcy aggravated her affliction, while it added to her
incapacity. In the midst of these disastrous circumstances,
news arrived that her son Greaves had lost his life in a sea
engagement with the enemy; and these tidings almost
instantly deprived her of reason. Then the landlord seized
for his rent, and she was arrested at the suit of Justice Gobble,
who had bought up one of her debts in order to distress her,
and now pretended that her madness was feigned.

When the name of Greaves was mentioned, our adventurer
started and changed colour; and, now the story was ended,
asked with marks of eager emotion, if the name of the woman's
first husband was not Wilford. When the prisoner answered
in the affirmative, he rose up, and striking his breast, " Good
heaven ! " cried he, " the very woman who watched over
my infancy, and even nourished me with her milk ! She
was my mother's humble friend. Alas ! poor Dorothy ! how
would your old mistress grieve to see her favourite in this
miserable condition." While he pronounced these words,
to the astonishment of the hearers, a tear stole softly down
each cheek. Then he desired to know if the poor lunatic
had any intervals of reason; and was given to understand
that she was always quiet, and generally supposed to have the
use of her senses, except when she was disturbed by some
extraordinary noise, or when any person touched upon her
misfortune, or mentioned the name of her oppressor, in all
which cases she started out into extravagance and frenzy.
They likewise imputed great part of the disorder to the
want of quiet, proper food, and necessaries, with which she
was but poorly supplied by the cold hand of chance charity.
Our adventurer was exceedingly affected by the distress
of this woman, whom he resolved to relieve; and in proportion as his commiseration was excited, his resentment

rose against the miscreant, who seemed to have insinuated himself into the commission of the peace on purpose to harass and oppress his fellow-creatures.

Thus animated, he entered into consultation with Mr. Thomas Clarke concerning the steps he should take, first for their deliverance, and then for prosecuting and punishing the justice. In result of this conference, the knight called aloud for the jailer, and demanded to see a copy of his commitment, that he might know the cause of his imprisonment, and offer bail; or, in case that he should be refused, move for a writ of Habeas Corpus. The jailer told him the copy of the writ should be forthcoming. But after he had waited some time, and repeated the demand before witnesses, it was not yet produced. Mr. Clarke then, in a solemn tone, gave the jailer to understand, that an officer refusing to deliver a true copy of the commitment warrant was liable to the forfeiture of one hundred pounds for the first offence, and for the second to a forfeiture of twice that sum, besides being disabled from executing his office.

Indeed, it was no easy matter to comply with Sir Launce-lot's demand; for no warrant had been granted, nor was it now in the power of the justice to remedy this defect, as Mr. Ferret had taken himself away privately, without having communicated the name and designation of the prisoner. A circumstance the more mortifying to the jailer, as he perceived the extraordinary respect which Mr. Clarke and the captain paid to the knight, and was now fully convinced that he would be dealt with according to law. Disordered with these reflections, he imparted them to the justice, who had in vain caused search to be made for Ferret, and was now extremely well inclined to set the knight and his friends at liberty, though he did not at all suspect the quality and importance of our adventurer. He could not, however, resist the temptation of displaying the authority of his office, and therefore ordered the prisoners to be brought before his tribunal, that, in the capacity of a magistrate, he might give them a severe reproof, and proper caution with respect to their future behaviour.

They were accordingly led through the street in procession, guarded by the constable and his gang, followed
by Crabshaw, who had by this time been released from the
stocks, and surrounded by a crowd of people, attracted by
curiosity. When they arrived at the justice's house, they
were detained for some time in the passage ; then a voice
was heard, commanding the constable to bring in the
prisoners, and they were introduced to the hall of audience,
where Mr. Gobble sat in judgment, with a crimson velvet
nightcap on his head ; and on his right hand appeared
his lady, puffed up with the pride and insolence of her
husband's office, fat, frousy, and not over-clean, well stricken
in years, without the least vestige of an agreeable feature,
having a rubicund nose, ferret eyes, and imperious aspect.
The justice himself was a little, affected, pert prig, who
endeavoured to solemnise his countenance by assuming an
air of consequence, in which pride, impudence, and folly
were strangely blended. He aspired at nothing so much
as the character of an able spokesman ; and took all opportunities of holding forth at vestry and quarter sessions,
as well as in the administration of his office in private. He
would not, therefore, let slip this occasion of exciting the
admiration of his hearers, and, in an authoritative tone,
thus addressed our adventurer :

"The laws of this land has provided—I says as how
provision is made by the laws of this here land, in reverence
to delinquems and malefactors, whereby the king's peace
is upholden by we magistrates, who represents his majesty's
person, better than in e'er a contagious nation under the
sun ; but, howsomever, that there king's peace, and this
here magistrate's authority cannot be adequably and iden-
tically upheld, if so be as how criminals escapes unpunished.
Now, friend, you must be confidentious in your own mind
as you are a notorious criminal, who have trespassed again
the laws on divers occasions and importunities ; if I had a
mind to exercise the rigour of the law, according to the
authority wherewith I am wested, you and your companions
in iniquity would be sewerely punished by the statue ; but

8

we magistrates has a power to litigate the sewerity of justice,
and so I am contented that you should be mercifully dealt
withal, and even dismissed."

To this harangue the knight replied, with a solemn and
deliberate accent, " If I understand your meaning aright,
I am accused of being a notorious criminal ; but nevertheless
you are contented to let me escape with impunity. If
I am a notorious criminal, it is the duty of you, as a magistrate, to bring me to condign punishment ; and if you allow
a criminal to escape unpunished, you are not only unworthy
of a place in the commission, but become accessory to his
guilt, and, to all intents and purposes, *socius criminis*. With
respect to your proffered mercy, I shall decline the favour ;
nor do I deserve any indulgence at your hands, for, depend
upon it, I shall show no mercy to you in the steps I intend
to take for bringing you to justice. I understand that you
have been long hackneyed in the ways of oppression, and I
have seen some living monuments of your inhumanity—of
that hereafter. I myself have been detained in prison, without cause assigned. I have been treated with indignity,
and insulted by jailers and constables ; led through the streets
like a felon, as a spectacle to the multitude ; obliged to
dance attendance in your passage, and afterwards branded
with the name of notorious criminal.—I now demand to see
the information in consequence of which I was detained in
prison, the copy of the warrant of commitment or detainer
and the face of the person by whom I was accused. I insist
upon a compliance with these demands, as the privileges of
a British subject ; and if it is refused, I shall seek redress
before a higher tribunal."

The justice seemed to be not a little disturbed at this
peremptory declaration ; which, however, had no other effect
upon his wife, but that of enraging her choler, and inflaming
her countenance. " Sirrah ! sirrah ! " cried she, " do you
dares to insult a worshipful magistrate on the bench ?—Can
you deny that you are a vagram, and a dilatory sort of a
person ? Han't the man with the satchel made an affidavy
of it ? If I was my husband, I'd lay you fast by the heels

for your resumption, and ferk you with a priminery into the
bargain, unless you could give a better account of yourself—
I would."

Gobble, encouraged by this fillip, resumed his petulance,
and proceeded in this manner :—" Hark ye, friend, I might,
as Mrs. Gobble very justly observes, trounce you for your
audacious behaviour ; but I scorn to take such advantages.
Howsomever, I shall make you give an account of yourself
and your companions ; for I believes as how you are in a
gang, and all in a story, and perhaps you may be found one
day in a cord.—What are you, friend ?   What is your station
and degree ? "—" I am a gentleman," replied the knight.—
" Ay, that is English for a sorry fellow," said the justice.
" Every idle vagabond, who has neither home nor habitation,
trade nor profession, designs himself a gentleman.   But I
must know how you live ? "—" Upon my means."—" What
are your means ? "—" My estate."—" Whence does it
arise ? "—" From inheritance."—" Your estate lies in brass,
and that you have inherited from nature ; but do you
inherit lands and tenements ? "—" Yes."—" But they are
neither here nor there, I doubt.   Come, come, friend, I
shall bring you about presently."   Here the examination
was interrupted by the arrival of Mr. Fillet the surgeon,
who chancing to pass, and seeing a crowd about the door,
went in to satisfy his curiosity.

CHAPTER XII

Which shows there are more Ways to kill a Dog than Hanging.

MR. FILLET no sooner appeared in the judgment-chamber
of Justice Gobble, than Captain Crowe, seizing him by the
hand, exclaimed, " Body o'me ! Doctor, thou'rt come up
in the nick of time to lend us a hand in putting about.—
We're a little in the stays here—but howsomever we've got
a good pilot, who knows the coast ; and can weather the
point, as the saying is. As for the enemy's vessel, she has

had a shot or two already athwart her forefoot; the next, I do suppose, will strike the hull, and then you will see her taken all aback." The doctor, who perfectly understood his dialect, assured him he might depend upon his assistance; and, advancing to the knight, accosted him in these words: "Sir Launcelot Greaves, your most humble servant—when I saw a crowd at the door, I little thought of finding you within, treated with such indignity—yet I can't help being pleased with an opportunity of proving the esteem and veneration I have for your person and character.—You will do me particular pleasure in commanding my best services."

Our adventurer thanked him for this instance of his friendship, which he told him he would use without hesitation; and desired he would procure immediate bail for him and his two friends, who had been imprisoned contrary to law, without any cause assigned.

During this short dialogue, the justice, who had heard of Sir Launcelot's family and fortune, though an utter stranger to his person, was seized with such pangs of terror and compunction, as a grovelling mind may be supposed to h ve felt in such circumstances; and they seemed to produce the same unsavoury effects that are so humorously delineated by the inimitable Hogarth, in his print of Felix on his tribunal, done in the Dutch style. Nevertheless, seeing Fillet retire to execute the knight's commands, he recollected himself so far as to tell the prisoners, there was no occasion to give themselves any farther trouble, for he would release them without bail or mainprise. Then discarding all the insolence from his features, and assuming an aspect of the most humble adulation, he begged the knight ten thousand pardons for the freedoms he had taken, which were entirely owing to his ignorance of Sir Launcelot's quality.

"Yes, I'll assure you, sir," said the wife, "my husband would have bit off his tongue rather than say black is the white of your eye, if so be he had known your capacity. Thank God, we have been used to deal with gentlefolks. and many's the good pound we have lost by them; but

what of that ? Sure we know how to behave to our betters.
Mr. Gobble, thanks be to God, can defy the whole world
to prove that he ever said an uncivil word, or did a rude
thing to a gentleman, knowing him to be a person of fortune.
Indeed, as to your poor gentry and riffraff, your tag-rag and
bob-tail, or such vulgar scoundrelly people, he has always
behaved like a magistrate, and treated them with the rigger
of authority."—" In other words," said the knight, " he
has tyrannised over the poor, and connived at the vices
of the rich. Your husband is little obliged to you for this
confession, woman."—"Woman ! " cried Mrs. Gobble,
empurpled with wrath, and fixing her hands on her sides
by way of defiance, " I scorn your words.—Marry come up !
woman, quotha ! no more a woman than your worship."
Then bursting into tears, " Husband," continued she, " if
you had the soul of a louse, you would not suffer me to be
abused at this rate ; you would not sit still on the bench,
and hear your spouse called such contemptible epitaphs.—
Who cares for his title and his knightship ? You and I,
husband, knew a tailor that was made a knight ; but thank
God, I have noblemen to stand by me with their privileges
and beroguetifs."

At this instant Mr. Fillet returned with his friend, a
practitioner in the law, who freely offered to join in bailing
our adventurer, and the other two prisoners, for any sum
that should be required. The justice, perceiving the affair
began to grow more and more serious, declared that he would
discharge the warrants and dismiss the prisoners.

Here Mr. Clarke interposing, observed, that against the
knight no warrant had been granted, nor any information
sworn to ; consequently, as the justice had not complied
with the form of proceeding directed by statute, the imprisonment was *coram non judice*, void. " Right, sir," said
the other lawyer ; " if a justice commits a felon for trial
without binding over the prosecutor to the assizes, he shall be
fined."—" And again," cried Clarke, " if a justice issues a
warrant for commitment, where there is no accusation,
action will lie against the justice."—" Moreover," replied

the stranger, "if a justice of peace is guilty of any misdemeanour in his office, information lies against him in
Banco Regis, where he shall be punished by fine and imprisonment."—"And, besides," resumed the accurate Tom, "the
same court will grant an information against a justice of
peace, on motion, for sending even a servant to the house
of correction or common jail without sufficient cause."—
"True!" exclaimed the other limb of the law, "and, for
contempt of the law, attachment may be had against justices
of peace in *Banco Regis*. A justice of the peace was fined a
thousand marks for corrupt practices."

With these words, advancing to Mr. Clarke, he shook
him by the hand, with the appellation of brother, saying,
"I doubt the justice has got into a cursed *hovel*." Mr.
Gobble himself seemed to be of the same opinion. He
changed colour several times during the remarks which the
lawyers had made ; and now, declaring that the gentlemen
were at liberty, begged, in the most humble phrase, that the
company would eat a bit of mutton with him, and after
dinner the affair might be amicably compromised.

To this proposal our adventurer replied, in a grave and
resolute tone, "If your acting in the commission as a justice
of the peace concerned my own particular only, perhaps I
should waive any further inquiry, and resent your insolence
no other way but by silent contempt. If I thought the
errors of your administration proceeded from a good intention, defeated by want of understanding, I should pity
your ignorance, and, in compassion, advise you to desist
from acting a part for which you are so ill qualified ; but
the preposterous conduct of such a man deeply affects the
interest of the community, especially that part of it which,
from its helpless situation, is the more entitled to your
protection and assistance. I am, moreover, convinced that
your misconduct is not so much the consequence of an
uninformed head, as the poisonous issue of a malignant
heart, devoid of humanity, inflamed with pride, and rankling
with revenge. The common prison of this little town is
filled with the miserable objects of your cruelty and op-

pression. Instead of protecting the helpless, restraining the
hands of violence, preserving the public tranquillity, and
acting as a father to the poor, according to the intent and
meaning of that institution of which you are an unworthy
member ; you have distressed the widow and the orphan,
given a loose to all the insolence of office, embroiled your
neighbours by fomenting suits and animosities, and played
the tyrant among the indigent and forlorn. You have
abused the authority with which you were invested, entailed
a reproach upon your office, and, instead of being revered
as a blessing, you are detested as a curse among your fellow-
creatures. This indeed is generally the case of low fellows,
who are thrust into the magistracy without sentiment,
education, or capacity.

"Among other instances of your iniquity, there is now
in prison an unhappy woman, infinitely your superior in the
advantages of birth, sense, and education, whom you have,
even without provocation, persecuted to ruin and distraction,
after having illegally and inhumanly kidnapped her only
child, and exposed him to a violent death in a foreign land.
Ah, caitiff ! if you were to forego all the comforts of life,
distribute your means among the poor, and do the severest
penance that ever priestcraft prescribed for the rest of your
days, you could not atone for the ruin of that hapless family ;
a family through whose sides you cruelly and perfidiously
stabbed the heart of an innocent young woman, to gratify
the pride and diabolical malice of that wretched low-bred
woman, who now sits at your right hand as the associate
of power and presumption. Oh ! if such a despicable
reptile shall annoy mankind with impunity, if such a contemptible miscreant shall have it in his power to do such
deeds of inhumanity and oppression, what avails the law ?
Where is our admired constitution, the freedom, the security
of the subject, the boasted humanity of the British nation !
Sacred Heaven ! if there was no human institution to take
cognisance of such atrocious crimes, I would listen to the dictates of eternal justice, and, arming myself with the right of
nature, exterminate such villains from the face of the earth !"

These last words he pronounced in such a strain, while his eyes lightened with indignation, that Gobble and his wife underwent the most violent agitation ; the constable's teeth chattered in his head, the jailer trembled, and the whole audience was overwhelmed with consternation.

After a short pause, Sir Launcelot proceeded in a milder strain : " Thank Heaven, the laws of this country have exempted me from the disagreeable task of such an execution. To them we shall have immediate recourse, in three separate actions, against you for false imprisonment ; and any other person who has been injured by your arbitrary and wicked proceedings, in me shall find a warm protector, until you shall be expunged from the commission with disgrace, and have made such retaliation as your circumstances will allow for the wrongs you have done the community."

In order to complete the mortification and terror of the justice, the lawyer, whose name was Fenton, declared that, to his certain knowledge, these actions would be reinforced with divers prosecutions for corrupt practices, which had lain dormant until some person of courage and influence should take the lead against Justice Gobble, who was the more dreaded, as he acted under the patronage of Lord Sharpington. By this time fear had deprived the justice and his helpmate of the faculty of speech. They were indeed almost petrified with dismay, and made no effort to speak, when Mr. Fillet, in the rear of the knight, as he retired with his company, took his leave of them in these words : " And now, Mr. Justice, to dinner with what appetite you may."

Our adventurer, though warmly invited to Mr. Fenton's house, repaired to a public inn, where he thought he should be more at his ease, fully determined to punish and depose Gobble from his magistracy, to effect a general jail-delivery of all the debtors whom he had found in confinement, and in particular to rescue poor Mrs. Oakley from the miserable circumstances in which she was involved.

In the meantime he insisted upon entertaining his friends at dinner, during which many sallies of sea-wit and good humour passed between Captain Crowe and Dr. Fillet, which last had just returned from a neighbouring village, whither he was summoned to fish a man's yard-arm, which had snapped in the slings. Their enjoyment, however, was suddenly interrupted by a loud scream from the kitchen, whither Sir Launcelot immediately sprang, with equal eagerness and agility. There he saw the landlady, who was a woman in years, embracing a man dressed in a sailor's jacket, while she exclaimed, " It is thy own flesh and blood, so sure as I'm a living soul.—Ah! poor Greaves, poor Greaves, many a poor heart has grieved for thee!" To this salutation the youth replied, " I'm sorry for that, mistress.—How does poor mother? how does Suky Sedgemoor?"

The good woman of the house could not help shedding tears at these interrogations; while Sir Launcelot, interposing, said, not without emotion, " I perceive you are the son of Mrs. Oakley.—Your mother is in a bad state of health, but in me you will find a real parent." Perceiving that the young man eyed him with astonishment, he gave him to understand that his name was Launcelot Greaves.

Oakley no sooner heard these words pronounced, than he fell upon his knees, and seizing the knight's hand, kissed it eagerly, crying, " God for ever bless your honour, I am your name-son, sure enough—but what of that? I can earn my bread without being beholden to any man."

When the knight raised him up, he turned to the woman of the house, saying, " I want to see mother. I'm afraid as how times are hard with her; and I have saved some money for her use." This instance of filial duty brought tears into the eyes of our adventurer, who assured him his mother should be carefully attended, and want for nothing; but that it would be very improper to see her at present, as the surprise might shock her too much, considering that she believed him dead. " Ey, indeed," cried the landlady, " we were all of the same opinion, being as the report went, that poor Greaves Oakley was killed in battle."—" Lord, mistress," said Oakley, " there wan't a word of truth in it, I'll assure you.—What, d'ye think I'd tell a lie about the matter ? Hurt I was, to be sure, but that don't signify ; we gave 'em as good as they brought, and so parted.—Well, if so be I can't see mother, I'll go and have some chat with Suky.—What d'ye look so glum for ? she an't married, is she ? "—" No, no," replied the woman, " not married, but almost heart-broken. Since thou wast gone she has done nothing but sighed, and wept, and pined herself into a decay. I'm afraid thou hast come too late to save her life."

Oakley's heart was not proof against this information. Bursting into tears, he exclaimed, " O my dear, sweet, gentle Suky ! Have I then lived to be the death of her whom I loved more than the whole world ? " He would have gone instantly to her father's house, but was restrained by the knight and his company, who had now joined him in the kitchen.

The young man was seated at table, and gave them to understand, that the ship to which he belonged having arrived in England, he was indulged with a month's leave to see his relations ; and that he had received about fifty pounds in wages and prize-money. After dinner, just as they began to deliberate upon the measures to be taken against Gobble, that gentleman arrived at the inn, and humbly craved admittance. Mr. Fillet, struck with a sudden idea, retired into another apartment with the young farmer ; while the justice, being admitted to the company, declared that he came to propose terms of accommodation. He accordingly offered to ask pardon of Sir Launcelot in the public papers, and pay fifty pounds to the poor of the parish, as an atonement for his misbehaviour, provided the knight and his friends would grant him a general release. Our adventurer told him, he would willingly waive all personal concessions ; but, as the case concerned the community, he insisted upon his leaving off acting in the commission, and making satisfaction to the parties he had injured and oppressed. This declaration introduced a discussion, in the course of which the justice's petulance began to revive ; when Fillet, entering the room, told them he had a reconciling measure to propose, if Mr. Gobble would for a few minutes withdraw.

He rose up immediately, and was shown into the room which Fillet had prepared for his reception. While he sat musing on this untoward adventure, so big with disgrace and disappointment, young Oakley, according to the instructions he had received, appeared all at once before him, pointing to a ghastly wound, which the doctor had painted on his forehead. The apparition no sooner presented itself to the eyes of Gobble, than, taking it for granted it was the spirit of the young farmer whose death he had occasioned, he roared aloud, "Lord have mercy upon us!" and fell insensible on the floor. There being found by the company, to whom Fillet had communicated his contrivance, he was conveyed to bed, where he lay some time before he recovered the perfect use of his senses. Then he earnestly desired to see the knight, and assured him he was ready to comply with his terms, inasmuch as he believed he had not long to live. Advantage was immediately taken of this salutary disposition. He bound himself not to act as a justice of the peace, in any part of Great Britain, under the penalty of five thousand pounds. He burnt Mrs. Oakley's note; paid the debts of the shopkeeper; undertook to compound those of the publican, and to settle him again in business; and, finally, discharged them all from prison, paying the dues out of his own pocket. These steps being taken with peculiar eagerness, he was removed to his own house, where he assured his wife he had seen a vision that prognosticated his death; and had immediate recourse to the curate of the parish for spiritual consolation.

The most interesting part of the task that now remained was to make the widow Oakley acquainted with her good fortune, in such a manner as might least disturb her spirits, already but too much discomposed. For this purpose they chose the landlady, who, after having received proper directions how to regulate her conduct, visited her in person that same evening. Finding her quite calm, and her reflection quite restored, she began with exhorting her to put her trust in Providence, which would never forsake the cause of the injured widow and fatherless. She promised to assist and befriend her on all occasions, as far as her abilities would reach. She gradually turned the conversation upon the family of the Greaves ; and by degrees informed her, that Sir Launcelot, having learned her situation, was determined to extricate her from all her troubles. Perceiving her astonished, and deeply affected at this intimation, she artfully shifted the discourse, recommended resignation to the divine will, and observed, that this circumstance seemed to be an earnest of further happiness.

"Oh ! I'm incapable of receiving more ! " cried the disconsolate widow, with streaming eyes.—"Yet I ought not to be surprised at any blessing that flows from that quarter. The family of Greaves were always virtuous, humane, and benevolent. This young gentleman's mother was my dear lady and benefactress :—he himself was suckled at these breasts. Oh ! he was the sweetest, comeliest, best-conditioned babe !—I loved not my own Greaves with greater affection—but he, alas ! is now no more ! " "Have patience, good neighbour," said the landlady of the White Hart, "that is more than you have any right to affirm—all that you know of the matter is by common report, and common report is commonly false ; besides, I can tell you I have seen a list of the men that were killed in Admiral P——'s ship, when he fought the French in the East Indies, and your son was not in the number." To this intimation she replied, after a considerable pause, "Don't, my good neighbour, don't feed me with false hope.—My poor Greaves too certainly perished in a foreign land—yet he is happy ;—had he lived to see me in this condition, grief would soon have put a period to his days." "I tell you then," cried the visitant, "he is not dead. I have seen a letter that mentions his being well since the battle. You shall come along with me—you are no longer a prisoner, but shall live at my house comfortably, till your affairs are settled to your wish." The poor widow followed her in silent astonishment, and was immediately accommodated with necessaries.

Next morning her hostess proceeded with her in the same

cautious manner, until she was assured that her son had returned. Being duly prepared, she was blessed with a sight of poor Greaves, and fainted away in his arms. We shall not dwell upon this tender scene, because it is but of a secondary concern in the history of our knight-errant. Let it suffice to say, their mutual happiness was unspeakable. She was afterwards visited by Sir Launcelot, whom she no sooner beheld, than springing forwards with all the eagerness of maternal affection, she clasped him to her breast, crying, " My dear child ! my Launcelot ! my pride ! my darling ! my kind benefactor ! This is not the first time I have hugged you in these arms ! Oh ! you are the very image of Sir Everhard in his youth ; but you have got the eyes, the complexion, the sweetness, and complacency of my dear and ever-honoured lady." This was not in the strain of hireling praise, but the genuine tribute of esteem and admiration. As such, it could not but be agreeable to our hero, who undertook to procure Oakley's discharge, and settle him in a comfortable farm on his own estate.

In the meantime Greaves went with a heavy heart to the house of Farmer Sedgemoor, where he found Suky, who had been prepared for his reception, in a transport of joy, though very weak, and greatly emaciated. Nevertheless, the return of her sweetheart had such a happy effect on her constitution, that in a few weeks her health was perfectly restored.

This adventure of our knight was crowned with every happy circumstance that could give pleasure to a generous mind. The prisoners were released, and reinstated in their former occupations. The justice performed his articles from fear, and afterwards turned over a new leaf from remorse. Young Oakley was married to Suky, with whom he received a considerable portion. The new-married couple found a farm ready stocked for them on the knight's estate, and the mother enjoyed a happy retreat in the character of housekeeper at Greavesbury Hall.

CHAPTER XIII

In which our Knight is tantalised with a transient Glimpse
of Felicity.

THE success of our adventurer, which we have particularised
in the last chapter, could not fail of enhancing his character,
not only among those who knew him, but also among the
people of the town to whom he was not an utter stranger.
The populace surrounded the house, and testified their
approbation in loud huzzas. Captain Crowe was more than
ever inspired with veneration for his admired patron, and
more than ever determined to pursue his footsteps in the
road of chivalry. Fillet and his friend the lawyer could
not help conceiving an affection, and even a profound esteem
for the exalted virtue, the person, and accomplishments of
the knight, dashed as they were with a mixture of extravagance and insanity. Even Sir Launcelot himself was
elevated to an extraordinary degree of self-complacency
on the fortunate issue of his adventure, and became more
and more persuaded that a knight-errant's profession might
be exercised, even in England, to the advantage of the
community. The only person of the company who seemed
unanimated with the general satisfaction was Mr. Thomas
Clarke. He had, not without good reason, laid it down as
a maxim, that knight-errantry and madness were synonymous
terms ; and that madness, though exhibited in the most
advantageous and agreeable light, could not change its
nature, but must continue a perversion of sense to the end
of the chapter. He perceived the additional impression
which the brain of his uncle had sustained, from the happy
manner in which the benevolence of Sir Launcelot had so
lately operated ; and began to fear it would be in a little
time quite necessary to have recourse to a commission of
lunacy, which might not only disgrace the family of the
Crowes, but also tend to invalidate the settlement which
the captain had already made in favour of our young lawyer.

Perplexed with these cogitations, Mr. Clarke appealed

to our adventurer's own reflection. He expatiated upon the bad consequences that would attend his uncle's perseverance in the execution of a scheme so foreign to his faculties; and entreated him, for the love of God, to divert him from his purpose, either by arguments or authority; as, of all mankind, the knight alone had gained such an ascendency over his spirits, that he would listen to his exhortations with respect and submission.

Our adventurer was not so mad, but that he saw and owned the rationality of these remarks. He readily undertook to employ all his influence with Crowe, to dissuade him from his extravagant design; and seized the first opportunity of being alone with the captain to signify his sentiments on this subject. "Captain Crowe," said he, "you are then determined to proceed in the course of knight-errantry?" —"I am," replied the seaman, "with God's help, d'ye see, and the assistance of wind and weather."—"What dost thou talk of wind and weather?" cried the knight, in an elevated tone of affected transport. "Without the help of Heaven, indeed, we are all vanity, imbecility, weakness, and wretchedness; but if thou art resolved to embrace the life of an errant, let me not hear thee so much as whisper a doubt, a wish, a hope, or sentiment with respect to any other obstacle, which wind or weather, fire or water, sword or famine, danger or disappointment, may throw in the way of thy career. When the duty of thy profession calls, thou must singly rush upon innumerable hosts of armed men. Thou must storm the breach in the mouth of batteries loaded with death and destruction, while, every step thou movest, thou art exposed to the horrible explosion of subterranean mines, which, being sprung, will whirl thee aloft in air, a mangled corpse, to feed the fowls of heaven. Thou must leap into the abyss of dreadful caves and caverns, replete with poisonous toads and hissing serpents; thou must plunge into seas of burning sulphur; thou must launch upon the ocean in a crazy bark, when the foaming billows roll mountains high—when the lightning flashes, the thunder roars, and the howling tempest blows, as if it would commix the

jarring elements of air and water, earth and fire, and reduce
all nature to the original anarchy of chaos. Thus involved,
thou must turn thy prow full against the fury of the storm,
and stem the boisterous surge to thy destined port, though
at the distance of a thousand leagues. Thou must——"

"Avast, avast, brother," exclaimed the impatient
Crowe, "you've got into the high latitudes, d'ye see. If so
be as you spank it away at that rate, adad, I can't continue
in tow—we must cast off the rope, or 'ware timbers. As for
your 'osts and breeches, and hurling aloft, d'ye see—your
caves and caverns, whistling tuods and serpents, burning
brimstone and foaming billows, we must take our hap—I
value 'em not a rotten ratline; but as for sailing in the
wind's eye, brother, you must give me leave—no offence,
I hope—I pretend to be a thorough-bred seaman, d'ye see
—and I'll be d—ned if you, or e'er an arrant that broke
biscuit, ever sailed in a three-mast vessel with[in] five points
of the wind, allowing for variation and lee-way. No, no,
brother, none of your tricks upon travellers—I an't now to
learn my compass."—"Tricks!" cried the knight, starting
up, and laying his hand on the pummel of his sword; "what!
suspect my honour?"

Crowe, supposing him to be really incensed, interrupted
him with great earnestness, saying, "Nay, don't—what apize!
—adds-buntlines!—I didn't go to give you the lie, brother,
smite my limbs; I only said as how to sail in the wind's eye
was impossible."—"And I say unto thee," resumed the
knight, "nothing is impossible to a true knight-errant,
inspired and animated by love."—"And I say unto thee,"
hallooed Crowe, "if so be as how love pretends to turn his
hawse-holes to the wind, he's no seaman, d'ye see, but a
snotty-nosed lubberly boy, that knows not a cat from a
capstan—a don't."

"He that does not believe that love is an infallible pilot
must not embark upon the voyage of chivalry, for, next to
the protection of Heaven, it is from love that the knight
derives all his prowess and glory. The bare name of his
mistress invigorates his arm; the remembrance of her beauty

infuses into his breast the most heroic sentiments of courage, while the idea of her chastity hedges him round like a charm, and renders him invulnerable to the sword of his antagonist. A knight without a mistress is a mere nonentity, or, at least, a monster in nature—a pilot without a compass, a ship without rudder, and must be driven to and fro upon the waves of discomfiture and disgrace."

"An that be all," replied the sailor, "I told you before as how I've got a sweetheart, as true a hearted girl as ever swung in canvas. What thof she may have started a hoop in rolling, that signifies nothing; I'll warrant her tight as a nutshell."

"She must, in your opinion, be a paragon either of beauty or virtue. Now, as you have given up the last, you must uphold her charms unequalled, and her person without a parallel."—"I do, I do uphold she will sail upon a parallel as well as e'er a frigate that was rigged to the northward of fifty."

"At that rate she must rival the attractions of her whom I adore; but that I say is impossible. The perfections of my Aurelia are altogether supernatural; and as two suns cannot shine together in the same sphere with equal splendour, so I affirm, and will prove with my body, that your mistress, in comparison with mine, is as a glow-worm to the meridian sun, a rushlight to the full moon, or a stale mackerel's eye to a pearl of orient."—"Harkee, brother, you might give good words, however. An we once fall a-jawing, d'ye see, I can heave out as much bilgewater as another; and since you besmear my sweetheart Besselia, I can as well bedaub your mistress Aurelia, whom I value no more than old junk, pork slush, or stinking stock-fish."

"Enough, enough!—such blasphemy shall not pass un-chastised. In consideration of our having fed from the same table, and maintained together a friendly, though short intercourse, I will not demand the combat before you are duly prepared. Proceed to the first great town, where you can be furnished with horse and harnessing, with arms offensive and defensive; provide a trusty squire, assume a

9

motto and device, declare yourself a son of chivalry, and proclaim the excellence of her who rules your heart. I shall fetch a compass ; and wheresoever we may chance to meet, let us engage with equal arms in mortal combat, that shall decide and determine this dispute."

So saying, our adventurer stalked with great solemnity into another apartment ; while Crowe, being sufficiently irritated, snapped his fingers in token of defiance. Honest Crowe thought himself scurvily used by a man whom he had cultivated with such humility and veneration ; and, after an incoherent ejaculation of sea oaths, went in quest of his nephew, in order to make him acquainted with this unlucky transaction.

In the meantime, Sir Launcelot, having ordered supper, retired into his own chamber, and gave a loose to the most tender emotions of his heart. He recollected all the fond ideas which had been excited in the course of his correspondence with the charming Aurelia. He remembered, with horror, the cruel letter he had received from that young lady, containing a formal renunciation of his attachment, so unsuitable to the whole tenor of her character and conduct. He revolved the late adventure of the coach, and the declaration of Mr. Clarke, with equal eagerness and astonishment ; and was seized with the most ardent desire of unravelling a mystery so interesting to the predominant passion of his heart. All these mingled considerations produced a kind of ferment in the economy of his mind, which subsided into a profound reverie, compounded of hope and perplexity.

From this trance he was waked by the arrival of his squire, who entered the room with the blood trickling over his nose, and stood before him without speaking. When the knight asked whose livery was that he wore ? he replied, " 'Tis your honour's own livery ; I received it on your account, and hope as you will quit the score." Then he proceeded to inform his master, that two officers of the army having come into the kitchen, insisted upon having for their supper the victuals which Sir Launcelot had bespoken ; and that he,

the squire, objecting to the proposal, one of them had seized
the poker, and basted him with his own blood ; that when
he told them he belonged to a knight-errant, and threatened
them with the vengeance of his master, they cursed and
abused him, calling him Sancho Panza, and such dog's
names ; and bade him tell his master, Don Quicksot, that,
if he made any noise, they would confine him to his cage
and lie with his mistress, Dulcinea. " To be sure, sir,"
said he, " they thought you as great a nincompoop as your
squire—trim-tram, like master, like man ; but I hope as
how you will give them a Rowland for their Oliver."

"Miscreant ! " cried the knight, " you have provoked
the gentlemen with your impertinence, and they have
chastised you as you deserve. I tell thee, Crabshaw, they
have saved me the trouble of punishing thee with my own
hands ; and well it is for thee, sinner as thou art, that they
themselves have performed the office, for, had they complained to me of thy insolence and rusticity, by Heaven !
I would have made thee an example to all the impudent
squires upon the face of the earth. Hence, then ! avaunt,
caitiff ! let his majesty's officers, who perhaps are fatigued
with hard duty in the service of their country, comfort themselves with the supper which was intended for me, and leave
me undisturbed to my own meditations."

Timothy did not require a repetition of this command,
which he forthwith obeyed, growling within himself, that
thenceforward he should let every cuckold wear his own
horns ; but he could not help entertaining some doubts
with respect to the courage of his master, who, he supposed,
was one of those hectors who have their fighting days, but
are not at all times equally prepared for the combat.

The knight, having taken a slight repast, retired to his
repose, and had for some time enjoyed a very agreeable
slumber, when he was startled by a knocking at his chamber
door. " I beg your honour's pardon," said the landlady,
" but there are two uncivil persons in the kitchen who have
well-nigh turned my whole house topsy-turvy. Not content
with laying violent hands on your honour's supper, they

want to be rude to two young ladies who are just arrived, and have called for a post-chaise to go on. They are afraid to open their chamber door to get out, and the young lawyer is like to be murdered for taking the ladies' part."

Sir Launcelot, though he refused to take notice of the insult which had been offered to himself, no sooner heard of the distress of the ladies than he started up, huddled on his clothes, and girding his sword to his loins, advanced with a deliberate pace to the kitchen, where he perceived Thomas Clarke warmly engaged in altercation with a couple of young men dressed in regimentals, who, with a peculiar air of arrogance and ferocity, treated him with great insolence and contempt. Tom was endeavouring to persuade them, that, in the constitution of England, the military was always subservient to the civil power, and that their behaviour to a couple of helpless young women was not only unbecoming gentlemen, but expressly contrary to the law, inasmuch as they might be sued for an assault on an action of damages.

To this remonstrance the two heroes in red replied by a volley of dreadful oaths, intermingled with threats, which put the lawyer in some pain for his ears.

While one thus endeavoured to intimidate honest Tom Clarke, the other thundered at the door of the apartment to which the ladies had retired, demanding admittance, but received no other answer than a loud shriek. Our adventurer advancing to this uncivil champion, accosted him thus, in a grave and solemn tone : " Assuredly I could not have believed, except upon the evidence of my own senses, that persons who have the appearance of gentlemen, and bear his majesty's honourable commission in the army, could behave so wide of the decorum due to society, of a proper respect to the laws, of that humanity which we owe to our fellow-creatures, and that delicate regard for the fair sex which ought to prevail in the breast of every gentleman, and which in particular dignifies the character of a soldier. To whom shall that weaker, though more amiable part of the creation, fly for protection, if they are insulted and outraged by those whose more immediate duty it is to afford them security and defence from injury and violence ?   What right have you, or any man upon earth, to excite riot in a public inn, which may be deemed a temple sacred to hospitality ; to disturb the quiet of your fellow-guests, some of them perhaps exhausted by fatigue, some of them invaded by distemper ; to interrupt the king's lieges in their course of journeying upon their lawful occasions ?   Above all, what motive but wanton barbarity could prompt you to violate the apartment, and terrify the tender hearts of two helpless young ladies, travelling, no doubt, upon some cruel emergency, which compels them, unattended, to encounter in the night the dangers of the highway ? "

" Heark ye, Don Bethlem," said the captain, strutting up, and cocking his hat in the face of our adventurer, " you may be as mad as ever a straw-crowned monarch in Moorfields, for aught I care, but d—n me ! don't you be saucy, otherwise I shall dub your worship with a good stick across your shoulders."—" How ! petulant boy," cried the knight, " since you are so ignorant of urbanity, I will give you a lesson that you shall not easily forget." So saying, he unsheathed his sword, and called upon the soldier to draw in his defence.

The reader may have seen the physiognomy of a stock-holder at Jonathan's when the rebels were at Derby, or the features of a bard when accosted by a bailiff, or the countenance of an alderman when his banker stops payment ; if he has seen either of these phenomena, he may conceive the appearance that was now exhibited by the visage of the ferocious captain, when the naked sword of Sir Launcelot glanced before his eyes ; far from attempting to produce his own, which was of unconscionable length, he stood motionless as a statue, staring with the most ghastly look of terror and astonishment. His companion, who partook of his panic, seeing matters brought to a very serious crisis, interposed with a crest-fallen countenance, assuring Sir Launcelot they had no intention to quarrel, and what they had done was entirely for the sake of the frolic.

" By such frolics," cried the knight, " you become nuisances to society, bring yourselves into contempt, and disgrace the corps to which you belong. I now perceive the truth of the observation, that cruelty always resides with cowardice. My contempt is changed into compassion, and as you are probably of good families, I must insist upon this young man's drawing his sword, and acquitting himself in such a manner as may screen him from the most infamous censure which an officer can undergo."—" Lack-a-day, sir," said the other, " we are no officers, but prentices to two London haberdashers, travellers for orders ; Captain is a good travelling name, and we have dressed ourselves like officers to procure more respect upon the road."

The knight said he was very glad, for the honour of the service, to find they were impostors, though they deserved to be chastised for arrogating to themselves an honourable character which they had not spirit to sustain.

These words were scarce pronounced, when Mr. Clarke approaching one of the bravadoes, who had threatened to crop his ears, bestowed such a benediction on his jaw, as he could not receive without immediate humiliation ; while Timothy Crabshaw, smarting from his broken head and his want of supper, saluted the other with a Yorkshire hug, that laid him across the body of his companion. In a word, the two pseudo-officers were very roughly handled, for their presumption in pretending to act characters for which they were so ill qualified.

While Clarke and Crabshaw were thus laudably employed, the two young ladies passed through the kitchen so suddenly, that the knight had only a transient glimpse of their backs, and they disappeared before he could possibly make a tender of his services. The truth is, they dreaded nothing so much as their being discovered, and took the first opporunity of gliding into the chaise, which had been for some time waiting in the passage.

Mr. Clarke was much more disconcerted than our adventurer by their sudden escape. He ran with great eagerness to the door, and, perceiving they were flown, returned to Sir Launcelot, saying, " Lord bless my soul, sir, didn't

you see who it was?" "Ha! how!" exclaimed the
knight, reddening with alarm, "who was it?" "One of
them," replied the lawyer, "was Dolly, our old landlady's
daughter at the Black Lion. I knew her when first she
'lighted, notwithstanding her being neatly dressed in a
green joseph, which, I'll assure you, sir, becomes her remarkably well.—I'd never desire to see a prettier creature.
As for the other, she's a very genteel woman, but whether
old or young, ugly or handsome, I can't pretend to say,
for she was masked. I had just time to salute Dolly, and
ask a few questions; but all she could tell me was, that the
masked lady's name was Miss Meadows; and that she, Dolly,
was hired as her waiting-woman."

When the name of Meadows was mentioned, Sir Launcelot,
whose spirits had been in violent commotion, became suddenly calm and serene, and he began to communicate to
Clarke the dialogue which had passed between him and
Captain Crowe, when the hostess, addressing herself to our
errant, "Well," said she, "I have had the honour to accommodate many ladies of the first fashion at the White Hart,
both young and old, proud and lowly, ordinary and handsome; but such a miracle as Miss Meadows I never yet did
see.—Lord, let me never thrive but I think she is of something more than a human creature!—Oh! had your honour
but set eyes on her, you would have said it was a vision from
heaven, a cherubim of beauty. For my part, I can hardly
think it was anything but a dream—then so meek, so mild,
so good-natured and generous! I say, blessed is the young
woman who tends upon such a heavenly creature—and,
poor dear young lady! she seems to be under grief and
afflicton, for the tears stole down her lovely cheeks, and looked
for all the world like orient pearl."   ₄

Sir Launcelot listened attentively to the description,
which reminded him of his dear Aurelia, and, sighing
bitterly, withdrew to his own apartment.

CHAPTER XIV

Which shows that a Man cannot always sip, when the Cup
is at his Lip.

THOSE who have felt the doubts, the jealousies, the resent-
ments, the humiliations, the hopes, the despair, the impatience, and, in a word, the infinite disquiets of love,
will be able to conceive the sea of agitation on which our
adventurer was tossed all night long, without repose or
intermission. Sometimes he resolved to employ all his
industry and address in discovering the place in which
Aurelia was sequestered, that he might rescue her from the
supposed restraint to which she had been subjected. But
when his heart beat high with the anticipation of this
exploit, he was suddenly invaded, and all his ardour checked,
by the remembrance of that fatal letter, written and signed
by her own hand, which had divorced him from all hope,
and first unsettled his understanding. The emotions waked
by this remembrance were so strong that he leaped from
the bed, and the fire being still burning in the chimney,
lighted a candle, that he might once more banquet his
spleen by reading the original billet, which, together with
the ring he had received from Miss Darnel's mother, he
kept in a small box, carefully deposited within his portmanteau. This being instantly unlocked, he unfolded the
paper, and recited the contents in these words :

"SIR,—Obliged as I am by the passion you profess, and
eagerness with which you endeavour to give me the most
convincing proof of your regard, I feel some reluctance in
making you acquainted with a circumstance, which, in all
probability, you will not learn without some disquiet. But
the affair is become so interesting, I am compelled to tell
you, that however agreeable your proposals may have been
to those whom I thought it my duty to please by every
reasonable concession, and howsoever you may have been
flattered by the seeming complacency with which I have

heard your addresses, I now find it absolutely necessary to speak in a decisive strain, to assure you, that, without sacrificing my own peace, I cannot admit a continuation of your correspondence ; and that your regard for me will be best shown by your desisting from a pursuit which is altogether inconsistent with the happiness of

"AURELIA DARNEL."

Having pronounced aloud the words that composed this dismission, he hastily replaced the cruel scroll, and being too well acquainted with the hand to harbour the least doubt of its being genuine, threw himself into his bed in a transport of despair, mingled with resentment, during the predominancy of which he determined to proceed in the career of adventure, and endeavour to forget the unkindness of his mistress amidst the avocations of knight-errantry.

Such was the resolution that governed his thoughts, when he rose in the morning, ordered Crabshaw to saddle Bronzo-marte, and demanded a bill of his expense. Before these orders could be executed, the good woman of the house entering his apartment told him, with marks of concern, that the poor young lady, Miss Meadows, had dropped her pocket-book in the next chamber, where it was found by the hostess, who now presented it unopened.

Our knight having called in Mrs. Oakley and her son as witnesses, unfolded the book without reading one syllable of the contents, and found in it five bank-notes, amounting to two hundred and thirty pounds. Perceiving at once the loss of this treasure might be attended with the most em-barrassing consequences to the owner, and reflecting that this was a case which demanded the immediate interposition and assistance of chivalry, he declared that he himself would convey it safely into the hands of Miss Meadows ; and desired to know the road she had pursued, that he might set out in quest of her without a moment's delay. It was not without some difficulty that this information was obtained from the postboy, who had been enjoined to secrecy by the lady, and even gratified with a handsome reward for his promised discretion. The same method was used to make him disgorge his trust ; he undertook to conduct Sir Launcelot, who hired a post-chaise for despatch, and immediately departed, after having directed his squire to follow his track with the horses.

Yet, whatever haste he made, it is absolutely necessary, for the reader's satisfaction, that we should outstrip the chaise, and visit the ladies before his arrival. We shall therefore, without circumlocution, premise, that Miss Meadows was no other than that paragon of beauty and goodness, the all-accomplished Miss Aurelia Darnel. She had, with that meekness of resignation peculiar to herself, for some years submitted to every species of oppression which her uncle's tyranny of disposition could plan, and his unlimited power of guardianship execute, till at length it rose to such a pitch of despotism as she could not endure. He had projected a match between his niece and one Philip Sycamore, Esq., a young man who possessed a pretty considerable estate in the north country ; who liked Aurelia's person, but was enamoured of her fortune, and had offered to purchase Anthony's interest and alliance with certain concessions, which could not but be agreeable to a man of loose principles, who would have found it a difficult task to settle the accounts of his wardship.

According to the present estimate of matrimonial felicity, Sycamore might have found admittance as a future son-in-law to any private family of the kingdom. He was by birth a gentleman, tall, straight, and muscular, with a fair, sleek, unmeaning face, that promised more simplicity than ill-nature. His education had not been neglected, and he inherited an estate of five thousand a year. Miss Darnel, however, had penetration enough to discover and despise him, as a strange composition of rapacity and profusion, absurdity and good sense, bashfulness and impudence, self-conceit and diffidence, awkwardness and ostentation, insolence and good-nature, rashness and timidity. He was continually surrounded and preyed upon by certain vermin called Led Captains and Buffoons, who showed him in leading-strings like a sucking giant, rifled his pockets without ceremony, ridiculed him to his face, traduced his character, and exposed him in a thousand ludicrous attitudes for the diversion of the public; while at the same time he knew their knavery, saw their drift, detested their morals, and despised their understanding. He was so infatuated by indolence of thought, and communication with folly, that he would have rather suffered himself to be led into a ditch with company, than be at the pains of going over a bridge alone, and involved himself in a thousand difficulties, the natural consequences of an error in the first concoction, which, though he plainly saw it, he had not resolution enough to avoid.

Such was the character of Squire Sycamore, who professed himself the rival of Sir Launcelot Greaves in the good graces of Miss Aurelia Darnel. He had in this pursuit persevered with more constancy and fortitude than he ever exerted in any other instance. Being generally needy from extravagance, he was stimulated by his wants, and animated by his vanity, which was artfully instigated by his followers, who hoped to share the spoils of his success. These motives were reinforced by the incessant and eager exhortations of Anthony Darnel, who seeing his ward in the last year of her minority, thought there was no time to be lost in securing his own indemnification, and snatching his niece for ever from the hopes of Sir Launcelot, whom he now hated with redoubled animosity. Finding Aurelia deaf to all his remonstrances, proof against ill usage, and resolutely averse to the proposed union with Sycamore, he endeavoured to detach her thoughts from Sir Launcelot, by forging tales to the prejudice of his constancy and moral character; and, finally, by recapitulating the proofs and instances of his distraction, which he particularised with the most malicious exaggerations.

In spite of all his arts, he found it impracticable to surmount her objections to the proposed alliance, and therefore changed his battery. Instead of transferring her to the arms of his friend, he resolved to detain her in his own power by a legal claim, which would invest him with the uncontrolled management of her affairs. This was a charge of lunacy, in consequence of which he hoped to obtain a commission, to secure a jury to his wish, and be appointed sole committee of her person, as well as steward on her estate, of which he would then be heir-apparent.

As the first steps towards the execution of this honest scheme, he had subjected Aurelia to the superintendency and direction of an old duenna, who had been formerly the procuress of his pleasures, and hired a new set of servants, who were given to understand, at their first admission, that the young lady was disordered in her brain.

An impression of this nature is easily preserved among servants, when the master of the family thinks his interest is concerned in supporting the imposture. The melancholy produced from her confinement, and the vivacity of her resentment under ill usage, were, by the address of Anthony, and the prepossession of his domestics, perverted into the effects of insanity ; and the same interpretation was strained upon her most indifferent words and actions.

The tidings of Miss Darnel's disorder was carefully circulated in whispers, and soon reached the ears of Mr. Sycamore, who was not at all pleased with the information. From his knowledge of Anthony's disposition, he suspected the truth of the report ; and, unwilling to see such a prize ravished as it were from his grasp, he, with the advice and assistance of his myrmidons, resolved to set the captive at liberty, in full hope of turning the adventure to his own advantage ; for he argued in this manner :—"If she is in fact *compos mentis*, her gratitude will operate in my behalf, and even prudence will advise her to embrace the proffered asylum from the villainy of her uncle. If she is really disordered, it will be no great difficulty to deceive her into marriage, and then I become her trustee of course."

The plan was well conceived, but Sycamore had not discretion enough to keep his own counsel. From weakness and vanity, he blabbed the design, which in a little time was communicated to Anthony Darnel, and he took his precautions accordingly. Being infirm in his own person and consequently unfit for opposing the violence of some desperadoes, whom he knew to be the satellites of Sycamore, he prepared a private retreat for his ward at the house of an old gentleman, the companion of his youth, whom he had imposed upon with the fiction of her being disordered in her understanding, and amused with a story of a dangerous design upon her person. Thus cautioned and instructed, the gentleman had gone with his own coach and servants to receive Aurelia and her governante at a third house, to which she had been privately removed from her uncle's habitation ; and in this journey it was that she had been so accidentally protected from the violence of the robbers by the interposition and prowess of our adventurer.

As he did not wear his helmet in that exploit, she recognised his features as he passed the coach, and, struck with the apparition, shrieked aloud. She had been assured by her guardian that his design was to convey her to her own house ; but perceiving in the sequel that the carriage struck off upon a different road, and finding herself in the hands of strangers, she began to dread a much more disagreeable fate, and conceived doubts and ideas that filled her tender heart with horror and affliction. When she expostulated with the duenna, she was treated like a changeling, admonished to be quiet, and reminded that she was under the direction of those who would manage her with a tender regard to her own welfare, and the honour of her family. When she addressed herself to the old gentleman, who was not much subject to the emotions of humanity, and besides firmly persuaded that she was deprived of her reason, he made no answer, but laid his finger on his mouth by way of enjoining silence.

This mysterious behaviour aggravated the fears of the poor hapless young lady ; and her terrors waxed so strong, that when she saw Tom Clarke, whose face she knew, she called aloud for assistance, and even pronounced the name of his patron Sir Launcelot Greaves, which she imagined might stimulate him the more to attempt something for her deliverance.

The reader has already been informed in what manner the

endeavours of Tom and his uncle miscarried. Miss Darnel's
new keeper having in the course of his journey halted for
refreshment at the Black Lion, of which being landlord,
he believed the good woman and her family were entirely
devoted to his will and pleasure, Aurelia found an opportunity
of speaking in private to Dolly, who had a very prepossessing
appearance. She conveyed a purse of money into the hands
of this young woman, telling her, while the tears trickled
down her cheeks, that she was a young lady of fortune, in
danger, as she apprehended, of assassination. This hint,
which she communicated in a whisper while the governante
stood at the other end of the room, was sufficient to interest
the compassionate Dolly in her behalf. As soon as the coach
departed, she made her mother acquainted with the transaction, and as they naturally concluded that the young lady
expected their assistance, they resolved to approve themselves
worthy of her confidence.

Dolly having enlisted in their design a trusty countryman,
one of her own professed admirers, they set out together
for the house of the gentleman in which the fair prisoner
was confined, and waited for her in secret at the end of a
pleasant park, in which th y naturally concluded she might
be indulged with the privilege of taking the air. The
event justified their conception ; on the very first day of
their watch they saw her approach, accompanied by her
duenna. Dolly and her attendant immediately tied their
horses to a stake, and retired into a thicket, which Aurelia
did not fail to enter. Dolly forthwith appeared, and,
taking her by the hand, led her to the horses, one of which
she mounted in the utmost hurry and trepidation, while the
countryman bound the duenna with a cord prepared for the
purpose, gagged her mouth, and tied her to a tree, where
he left her to her own meditations. Then he mounted
before Dolly, and through unfrequented paths conducted
his charge to an inn on the post-road, where a chaise was
ready for their reception.

As he refused to proceed farther, lest his absence from
his own home should create suspicion, Aurelia rewarded him

liberally, but would not part with her faithful Dolly, who indeed had no inclination to be discharged ; such an affection and attachment had she already acquired for the amiable fugitive, though she knew neither her story nor her true name. Aurelia thought proper to conceal both, and assumed the fictitious appellation of Meadows, until she should be better acquainted with the disposition and discretion of her new attendant.

The first resolution she could take, in the present flutter of her spirits, was to make the best of her way to London, where she thought she might find an asylum in the house of a female relation, married to an eminent physician, known by the name of Kawdle. In the execution of this hasty resolve, she travelled at a violent rate, from stage to stage, in a carriage drawn by four horses, without halting for necessary refreshment or repose, until she judged herself out of danger of being overtaken. As she appeared overwhelmed with grief and consternation, the good-natured Dolly endeavoured to alleviate her distress with diverting discourse, and, among other less interesting stories, entertained her with the adventures of Sir Launcelot and Captain Crowe, which she had seen and heard recited while they remained at the Black Lion ; nor did she fail to introduce Mr. Thomas Clarke in her narrative, with such a favourable representation of his person and character, as plainly discovered that her own heart had received a rude shock from the irresistible force of his qualifications.

The history of Sir Launcelot Greaves was a theme which effectually fixed the attention of Aurelia, distracted as her ideas must have been by the circumstances of her present situation. The particulars of his conduct since the correspondence between him and her had ceased, she heard with equal concern and astonishment ; for, how far soever she deemed herself detached from all possibility of future connection with that young gentleman, she was not made of such indifferent stuff as to learn without emotion the calamitous disorder of an accomplished youth, whose extraordinary virtues she could not but **revere.**

As they had deviated from the post-road, taken precautions to conceal their route, and made such progress, that they were now within one day's journey of London, the careful and affectionate Dolly, seeing her dear lady quite exhausted with fatigue, used all her natural rhetoric, which was very powerful, mingled with tears that flowed from the heart, in persuading Aurelia to enjoy some repose; and so far she succeeded in the attempt, that for one night the toil of travelling was intermitted. This recess from incredible fatigue was a pause that afforded our adventurer time to overtake them before they reached the metropolis, that vast labyrinth, in which Aurelia might have been for ever lost to his inquiry.

It was in the afternoon of the day which succeeded his departure from the White Hart, that Sir Launcelot arrived at the inn, where Miss Aurelia Darnel had bespoken a dish of tea, and a post-chaise for the next stage. He had by inquiry chased her a considerable way, without ever dreaming who the person really was whom he thus pursued, and now he desired to speak with her attendant. Dolly was not a little surprised to see Sir Launcelot Greaves, of whose character she had conceived a very sublime idea from the narrative of Mr. Thomas Clarke; but she was still more surprised when he gave her to understand that he had charged himself with a pocket-book, containing the bank-notes which Miss Meadows had dropped in the house where they had been threatened with insult. Miss Darnel had not yet discovered her disaster, when her attendant, running into the apartment, presented the prize which she had received from our adventurer, with his compliments to Miss Meadows, implying a request to be admitted into her presence, that he might make a personal tender of his best services.

It is not to be supposed that the amiable Aurelia heard unmoved such a message from a person, whom her maid discovered to be the identical Sir Launcelot Greaves, whose story she had so lately related; but as the ensuing scene requires fresh attention in the reader, we shall defer it till another opportunity, when his spirits shall be recruited from the fatigue of this chapter.

CHAPTER XV

Exhibiting an Interview, which, it is to be hoped, will
Interest the Curiosity of the Reader.

THE mind of the delicate Aurelia was strangely agitated
by the intelligence which she received with her pocket-book
from Dolly. Confounded as she was by the nature of her
situation, she at once perceived that she could not, with
any regard to the dictates of gratitude, refuse complying
with the request of Sir Launcelot; but, in the first hurry
of her emotion, she directed Dolly to beg, in her name, that
she might be excused for wearing a mask at the interview
which he desired, as she had particular reasons, which concerned her peace, for retaining that disguise. Our adventurer
submitted to this preliminary with a good grace, as he had
nothing in view but the injunction of his order, and the
duties of humanity; and he was admitted without further
preamble.

When he entered the room, he could not help being
struck with the presence of Aurelia. Her stature was improved since he had seen her; her shape was exquisitely
formed, and she received him with an air of dignity, which
impressed him with a very sublime idea of her person and
character. She was no less affected at the sight of our
adventurer, who, though cased in armour, appeared with his
head uncovered; and the exercise of travelling had thrown
such a glow of health and vivacity on his features, which were
naturally elegant and expressive, that we will venture to say,
there was not in all England a couple that excelled this
amiable pair in personal beauty and accomplishments. Aurelia
shone with all the fabled graces of nymph or goddess; and
to Sir Launcelot might be applied what the divine poet
Ariosto says of the Prince Zerbino:

> Natura il fece e poi ruppe la stampa.
> When Nature stamp'd him, she the die destroy'd.

Our adventurer having made his obeisance to this supposed
Miss Meadows, told her, with an air of pleasantry, that

10

although he thought himself highly honoured in being admitted to her presence, and allowed to pay his respects to her, as superior beings are adored, unseen ; yet his pleasure would receive a very considerable addition, if she would be pleased to withdraw that invidious veil, that he might have a glimpse of the divinity which it concealed. Aurelia immediately took off her mask, saying with a faltering accent, "I cannot be so ungrateful as to deny such a small favour to a gentleman who has laid me under the most important obligations."

The unexpected apparition of Miss Aurelia Darnel, beaming with all the emanations of ripened beauty, blushing with all the graces of the most lovely confusion, could not but produce a violent effect upon the mind of Sir Launcelot Greaves. He was, indeed, overwhelmed with a mingled transport of astonishment, admiration, affection, and awe. The colour vanished from his cheeks, and he stood gazing upon her, in silence, with the most emphatic expression of countenance.

Aurelia was infected by his disorder. She began to tremble, and the roses fluctuated on her face. "I cannot forget," said she, "that I owe my life to the courage and humanity of Sir Launcelot Greaves, and that he at the same time rescued from the most dreadful death a dear and venerable parent."—"Would to Heaven she still survived ! " cried our adventurer, with great emotion. "She was the friend of my youth, the kind patroness of my felicity ! My guardian angel forsook me when she expired ! Her last injunctions are deep engraven on my heart ! "

While he pronounced these words, she lifted her handkerchief to her fair eyes, and, after some pause, proceeded in a tremulous tone, "I hope, sir—I hope you have—I should be sorry—— Pardon me, sir, I cannot reflect upon such an interesting subject unmoved——" Here she fetched a deep sigh, that was accompanied by a flood of tears ; while the knight continued to bend his eyes upon her with the utmost eagerness of attention.

Having recollected herself a little, she endeavoured to

shift the conversation : "You have been abroad since I had the pleasure to see you—I hope you were agreeably amused in your travels."—"No, madam," said our hero, drooping his head; "I have been unfortunate." When she, with the most enchanting sweetness of benevolence, expressed her concern to hear he had been unhappy, and her hope that his misfortunes were not past remedy, he lifted up his eyes, and fixing them upon her again, with a look of tender dejection, "Cut off," said he, "from the possession of what my soul held most dear, I wished for death, and was visited by distraction. I have been abandoned by my reason—my youth is for ever blasted."

The tender heart of Aurelia could bear no more—her knees began to totter, the lustre vanished from her eyes, and she fainted in the arms of her attendant. Sir Launcelot, aroused by this circumstance, assisted Dolly in seating her mistress on a couch, where she soon recovered, and saw the knight on his knees before her. "I am still happy," said he, "in being able to move your compassion, though I have been held unworthy of your esteem."—"Do me justice," she replied; "my best esteem has been always inseparably connected with the character of Sir Launcelot Greaves." —"Is it possible ?" cried our hero; "then surely I have no reason to complain. If I have moved your compassion, and possess your esteem, I am but one degree short of supreme happiness—that, however, is a gigantic step. Oh, Miss Darnel ! when I remember that dear, that melancholy moment."—So saying, he gently touched her hand, in order to press it to his lips, and perceived on her finger the very individual ring which he had presented in her mother's presence, as an interchanged testimony of plighted faith. Starting at the well-known object, the sight of which conjured up a strange confusion of ideas, "This," said he, "was once the pledge of something still more cordial than esteem." Aurelia, blushing at this remark, while her eyes lightened with unusual vivacity, replied, in a severer tone, "Sir, you best know how it lost its original signification."— "By heaven ! I do not, madam !" exclaimed our adventurer.

"With me it was ever held a sacred idea throned within my heart, cherished with such fervency of regard, with such reverence of affection, as the devout anchorite more unreasonably pays to those sainted reliques that constitute the object of his adoration."—"And, like those reliques," answered Miss Darnel, "I have been insensible of my votary's devotion. A saint I must have been, or something more, to know the sentiments of your heart by inspiration."

"Did I forbear," said he, "to express, to repeat, to enforce the dictates of the purest passion that ever warmed the human breast, until I was denied access, and formally discarded by that cruel dismission?"—"I must beg your pardon, sir," cried Aurelia, interrupting him hastily, "I know not what you mean."—"That fatal sentence," said he, "if not pronounced by your own lips, at least written by your own fair hand, which drove me out an exile for ever from the paradise of your affection."—"I would not," she replied, "do Sir Launcelot Greaves the injury to suppose him capable of imposition ; but you talk of things to which I am an utter stranger. I have a right, sir, to demand of your honour, that you will not impute to me your breaking off a connection, which—I would—rather wish—had never——" "Heaven and earth ! what do I hear ? " cried our impatient knight ; "have I not the baleful letter to produce ? What else but Miss Darnel's explicit and express declaration could have destroyed the sweetest hope that ever cheered my soul ; could have obliged me to resign all claim to that felicity for which alone I wished to live ; could have filled my bosom with unutterable sorrow and despair ; could have even divested me of reason, and driven me from the society of men, a poor, forlorn, wandering lunatic, such as you see me now prostrate at your feet ; all the blossoms of my youth withered, all the honours of my family decayed ? "

Aurelia looking wistfully at her lover, "Sir," said she, "you overwhelm me with amazement and anxiety ! you are imposed upon, if you have received any such letter. You are deceived, if you thought Aurelia Darnel could be so insensible, ungrateful, and—inconstant."

This last word she pronounced with some hesitation, and a downcast look, while her face underwent a total suffusion, and the knight's heart began to palpitate with all the violence of emotion. He eagerly imprinted a kiss upon her hand, exclaiming, in interrupted phrase, " Can it be possible ?— Heaven grant—Sure this is no illusion !—Oh, madam !— shall I call you my Aurelia ? My heart is bursting with a thousand fond thoughts and presages. You shall see that dire paper which has been the source of all my woes—it is the constant companion of my travels—last night I nourished my chagrin with the perusal of its horrid contents."

Aurelia expressed great impatience to view the cruel forgery, for such she assured him it must be. But he could not gratify her desire, till the arrival of his servant with the portmanteau. In the meantime, tea was called. The lovers were seated. He looked and languished ; she flushed and faltered. All was doubt and delirium, fondness and flutter. Their mutual disorder communicated itself to the kind-hearted sympathising Dolly, who had been witness to the interview, and deeply affected at the disclosure of the scene. Unspeakable was her surprise, when she found her mistress, Miss Meadows, was no other than the celebrated Aurelia Darnel, whose eulogium she had heard so eloquently pro-nounced by her sweetheart, Mr. Thomas Clarke ; a discovery which still more endeared her lady to her affection. She had wept plentifully at the progress of their mutual explana-tion, and was now so disconcerted, that she scarce knew the meaning of the orders she had received. She set the kettle on the table, and placed the tea-board on the fire. Her confusion, by attracting the notice of her mistress, helped to relieve her from her own embarrassing situation. She, with her own delicate hands, rectified the mistake of Dolly, who still continued to sob, and said, " Yau may think, my Leady Darnel, as haw I'aive yeaten hool-cheese ; but it y'an't soa. I'se think, vor mai peart, as how I'aive bean bewitched."

Sir Launcelot could not help smiling at the simplicity of Dolly, whose goodness of heart and attachment Aurelia did not fail to extol, as soon as her back was turned. It was in consequence of this commendation, that, the next time she entered the room, our adventurer, for the first time, considered her face, and seemed to be struck with her features. He asked her some questions, which she could not answer to his satisfaction ; applauded her regard for her lady, and assured her of his friendship and protection. He now begged to know the cause that obliged his Aurelia to travel at such a rate, and in such an equipage ; and she informed him of those particulars which we have already communicated to our reader.

Sir Launcelot glowed with resentment, when he understood how his dear Aurelia had been oppressed by her perfidious and cruel guardian. He bit his nether lip, rolled his eyes around, started from his seat, and striding across the room, " I remember," said he, " the dying words of her who now is a saint in heaven : ' That violent man, my brother-in-law, who is Aurelia's sole guardian, will thwart her wishes with every obstacle that brutal resentment and implacable malice can contrive.' What followed, it would ill-become me to repeat. But she concluded with these words : ' The rest we must leave to the dispensations of Providence.' Was it not Providence that sent me hither to guard and protect the injured Aurelia ? " Then turning to Miss Darnel, whose eyes streamed with tears, he added, " Yes, divine creature ! Heaven, careful of your safety, and in compassion to my sufferings, hath guided me hither, in this mysterious manner, that I might defend you from violence, and enjoy this transition from madness to deliberation, from despair to felicity."

So saying, he approached this amiable mourner, this fragrant flower of beauty, glittering with the dew-drops of the morning ; this sweetest, and gentlest, loveliest ornament of human nature. He gazed upon her with looks of love ineffable ; he sat down by her ; he pressed her soft hand in his, he began to fear that all he saw was the flattering vision of a distempered brain ; he looked and sighed, and, turning up his eyes to heaven, breathed, in broken murmurs,

the chaste raptures of his soul. The tenderness of this communication was too painful to be long endured. Aurelia
industriously interposed other subjects of discourse, that
his attention might not be dangerously overcharged, and
the afternoon passed insensibly away.

Though he had determined, in his own mind, never more
to quit this idol of his soul, they had not yet concerted any
plan of conduct, when their happiness was all at once interrupted by a repetition of cries, denoting horror ; and a
servant coming in, said he believed some rogues were murder-
ing a traveller on the highway. The supposition of such
distress operated like gunpowder on the disposition of our
adventurer, who, without considering the situation of Aurelia,
and indeed without seeing, or being capable to think on her
or any other subject for the time being, ran directly to the
stable, and, mounting the first horse which he found saddled,
issued out in the twilight, having no other weapon but his
sword.

He rode full speed to the spot whence the cries seemed
to proceed ; but they sounded more remote as he advanced.
Nevertheless, he followed them to a considerable distance
from the road, over fields, ditches, and hedges, and at last
came so near, that he could plainly distinguish the voice of
his own squire, Timothy Crabshaw, bellowing for mercy,
with hideous vociferation. Stimulated by this recognition,
he redoubled his career in the dark, till at length his horse
plunged into a hole, the nature of which he could not
comprehend ; but he found it impracticable to disengage
him. It was with some difficulty that he himself clambered
over a ruined wall, and regained the open ground. Here he
groped about, in the utmost impatience of anxiety, ignorant
of the place, mad with vexation for the fate of his unfortunate
squire, and between whiles invaded with a pang of concern
for Aurelia, left among strangers, unguarded, and alarmed.

In the midst of this emotion, he bethought himself of
hallooing aloud, that, in case he should be in the neighbourhood of any inhabited place, he might be heard and assisted.
He accordingly practised this expedient, which was not

altogether without effect ; for he was immediately answered
by an old friend, no other than his own steed Bronzomarte,
who, hearing his master's voice, neighed strenuously at a
small distance. The knight, being well acquainted with the
sound, heard it with astonishment, and, advancing in the
right direction, found his noble charger fastened to a tree.
He forthwith untied and mounted him ; then, laying the
reins upon his neck, allowed him to choose his own path,
in which he began to travel with equal steadiness and expedition. They had not proceeded far, when the knight's
ears were again saluted by the cries of Crabshaw ; which
Bronzomarte no sooner heard, than he pricked up his ears,
neighed, and quickened his pace, as if he had been sensible
of the squire's distress, and hastened to his relief.   Sir
Launcelot, notwithstanding his own disquiet, could not help
observing and admiring this generous sensibility of his horse.
He began to think himself some hero of romance, mounted
upon a winged steed, inspired with reason, directed by some
humane enchanter, who pitied virtue in distress.   All circumstances considered, it is no wonder that the commotion
in the mind of our adventurer produced some such delirium.
All night he continued the chase ; the voice, which was
repeated at intervals, still retreating before him, till the
morning began to appear in the east, when, by divers piteous
groans, he was directed to the corner of a wood, where he
beheld his miserable squire stretched upon the grass, and
Gilbert feeding by him altogether unconcerned, the helmet
and the lance suspended at the saddle-bow, and the portmanteau safely fixed upon the crupper.

The knight, riding up to Crabshaw, with equal surprise
and concern, asked what had brought him there ? and
Timothy, after some pause, during which he surveyed his
master with a rueful aspect, answered, " The devil."—" One
would imagine, indeed, you had some such conveyance,"
said Sir Launcelot.   " I have followed your cries since last
evening, I know not how nor whither, and never could come
up with you till this moment. But say, what damage have
you sustained, that you lie in that wretched posture, and

groan so dismally ? "—" I can't guess," replied the squire, " if it bean't that mai hoole carcass is drilled into oilet hools, and my flesh pinched into a jelly."—" How ! wherefore ! " cried the knight ; " who were the miscreants that treated you in such a barbarous manner ? Do you know the ruffians ? "—" I know nothing at all," answered the peevish squire, " but that I was tormented by vive houndred and vifty thousand legions of devils, and there's an end oon't."—" Well, you must have a little patience, Crabshaw— there's a salve for every sore."—" Yaw mought as well tell ma, for every zow there's a zirreverence."—" For a man in your condition, methinks you talk very much at your ease— try if you can get up and mount Gilbert, that you may be conveyed to some place where you can have proper assistance. So—well done—cheerly ! "

Timothy actually made an effort to rise, but fell down again, and uttered a dismal yell. Then his master exhorted him to take advantage of a park wall, by which he lay, and raise himself gradually upon it. Crabshaw, eyeing him askance, said, by way of reproach, for his not alighting and assisting him in person, " Thatch your house with t—d and you'll have more teachers than reachers."—Having pronounced this inelegant adage, he made shift to stand upon his legs ; and now, the knight lending a hand, was mounted upon Gilbert, though not without a world of ohs ! and ahs ! and other ejaculations of pain and impatience.

As they jogged on together, our adventurer endeavoured to learn the particulars of the disaster which had befallen the squire ; but all the information he could obtain amounted to a very imperfect sketch of the adventure. By dint of a thousand interrogations, he understood that Crabshaw had been, in the preceding evening, encountered by three persons on horseback, with Venetian masks on their faces, which he mistook for their natural features, and was terrified accordingly. That they not only presented pistols to his breast, and led his horse out of the highway ; but pricked him with goads, and pinched him, from time to time, till he screamed with the torture. That he was led through unfrequented places across the country, sometimes at an easy trot, sometimes at full gallop, and tormented all night by those hideous demons, who vanished at daybreak, and left him lying on the spot where he was found by his master.

This was a mystery which our hero could by no means unriddle. It was the more unaccountable, as the squire . .iot been robbed of his money, horses, and baggage. He was even disposed to believe that Crabshaw's brain was disordered, and the whole account he had given no more than a mere chimera. This opinion, however, he could no longer retain, when he arrived at an inn on the post-road, and found, upon examination, that Timothy's lower extremities were covered with blood, and all the rest of his body speckled with livid marks of contusion. But he was still more chagrined when the landlord informed him, that he was thirty miles distant from the place where he had left Aurelia, and that his way lay through cross-roads, which were almost impassable at that season of the year. Alarmed at this intelligence, he gave directions that his squire should be immediately conveyed to bed in a comfortable chamber, as he complained more and more, and, indeed, was seized with a fever, occasioned by the fatigue, the pain, and terror he had undergone. A neighbouring apothecary being called, and giving it as his opinion that he could not for some days be in a condition to travel, his master deposited a sum of money in his hands, desiring he might be properly attended till he should hear further. Then mounting Bronzomarte, he set out with a guide for the place he had left, not without a thousand fears and perplexities, arising from the reflection of having left the jewel of his heart with such precipitation.

CHAPTER XVI

Which, it is to be hoped, the Reader will find an agreeable Medley of Mirth and Madness, Sense and Absurdity.

It was not without reason that our adventurer afflicted himself ; his fears were but too prophetic. When he

alighted at the inn, which he had left so abruptly the preceding evening, he ran directly to the apartment where he
had been so happy in Aurelia's company; but her he saw
not—all was solitary. Turning to the woman of the house,
who had followed him into the room, " Where is the lady ? "
cried he, in a tone of impatience. Mine hostess screwing
up her features into a very demure aspect, said she saw so
many ladies she could not pretend to know who he meant.
" I tell thee, woman," exclaimed the knight, in a louder
accent, " thou never sawest such another—I mean that
miracle of beauty——" " Very like," replied the dame, as
she retired to the room door. " Husband, here's one as
axes concerning a miracle of beauty ; hi, hi, hi! Can you
give him any information about this miracle of beauty ?
Oh la ! hi, hi, hi ! "

Instead of answering this question, the innkeeper advancing, and surveying Sir Launcelot, " Friend," said he,
" you are the person that carried off my horse out of the
stable."—" Tell me not of a horse—where is the young
lady ? "—" Now, I will tell you of the horse, and I'll make
you find him too before you and I part."—" Wretched
animal ! how dar'st thou dally with my impatience ?
Speak, or despair—what is become of Miss Meadows ?   Say,
did she leave this place of her own accord, or was she—hah !
speak—answer, or by the powers above——" " I'll answer
you flat—she you call Miss Meadows is in very good hands—
so you may make yourself easy on that score." " Sacred
Heaven ! explain your meaning, miscreant, or I'll make you
a dreadful example to all the insolent publicans of the realm."
So saying, he seized him with one hand and dashed him on
the floor, set one foot on his belly, and kept him trembling
in that prostrate attitude. The ostler and waiter flying to
the assistance of their master, our adventurer unsheathed
his sword, declaring he would dismiss their souls from their
bodies, and exterminate the whole family from the face of
the earth, if they would not immediately give him the
satisfaction he required.

The hostess being by this time terrified almost out of her

senses fell on her knees before him, begging he would spare
their lives, and promising to declare the whole truth. He
would not, however, remove his foot from the body of her
husband, until she told him, that in less than half an hour
after he had sallied out upon the supposed robbers, two
chaises arrived, each drawn by four horses; that two men
armed with pistols alighted from one of them, laid violent
hands upon the young lady; and, notwithstanding her
struggling and shrieking, forced her into the other carriage
in which was an infirm gentleman, who called himself her
guardian; that the maid was left to the care of a third servant
to follow with a third chaise, which was got ready with all
possible despatch, while the other two proceeded at full speed
on the road to London. It was by this communicative
lacquey the people of the house were informed that the old
gentleman his master was Squire Darnel, the young lady
his niece and ward, and our adventurer a needy sharper
who wanted to make a prey of her fortune.

The knight, fired even almost to frenzy by this intimation,
spurned the carcass of his host; and, his eye gleaming terror,
rushed into the yard, in order to mount Bronzomarte, and
pursue the ravisher, when he was diverted from his purpose
by a new incident.

One of the postillions, who had driven the chaise in which
Dolly was conveyed, happened to arrive at that instant;
when, seeing our hero, he ran up to him cap in hand, and,
presenting a letter, accosted him in these words: " Please
your noble honour, if your honour be Sir Launcelot Greaves
of the West Riding, here's a letter from a gentlewoman, that
I promised to deliver into your honour's own hands."

The knight, snatching the letter with the utmost avidity,
broke it up, and found the contents couched in these terms:

" HONOURED SIR,—The man az gi'en me leave to lat yaw
knaw my dear leady is going to Loondon with her unkle
Squaire Darnel. Be not conzarned, honoured sir, vor I'se
take it on mai laife to let yaw knaw wheare we be zettled,
if zobe I can vind where you loadge in Loondon. The man

zays yaw may put it in the pooblic prints. I houp the bareheir will be honest enuff to deliver this scrowl; and that your honour will pardon
          "Your   umbil   servant   to   command,
                              "DOROTHY COWSLIP."

"*P.S.*—Please my kaind sarvice to laayer Clarke. Squire Darnel's man is very civil vor sartain; but I'ave no thoughts on him I'll assure yaw. Marry hap, worse ware may have a better chap, as the zaying goes."

Nothing could be more seasonable than the delivery of this billet, which he had no sooner perused than his reflection returned, and he entered into a serious deliberation with his own heart. He considered that Aurelia was by this time far beyond a possibility of being overtaken, and that by a precipitate pursuit he should only expose his own infirmities. He confided in the attachment of his mistress, and in the fidelity of her maid, who would find opportunities of communicating her sentiments by means of this lacquey, of whom he perceived by the letter she had already made a conquest. He therefore resolved to bridle his impatience, to proceed leisurely to London, and, instead of taking any rash step which might induce Anthony Darnel to remove his niece from that city, remain in seeming quiet until she should be settled, and her guardian returned to the country. Aurelia had mentioned to him the name of Doctor Kawdle, and from him he expected in due time to receive the most interesting information.

These reflections had an instantaneous effect upon our hero, whose rage immediately subsided, and whose visage gradually resumed its natural cast of courtesy and good-humour. He forthwith gratified the postillion with such a remuneration as sent him dancing into the kitchen, where he did not fail to extol the generosity and immense fortune of Sir Launcelot Greaves.

Our adventurer's next step was to see Bronzomarte properly accommodated; then he ordered a refreshment for himself and retired into an apartment, where mine host with his wife and all the servants waited on him to beseech his honour to forgive their impertinence, which was owing to their ignorance of his honour's quality, and the false information they had received from the gentleman's servant. He had too much magnanimity to retain the least resentment against such inconsiderable objects. He not only pardoned them without hesitation, but assured the landlord he would be accountable for the horse, which, however, was that same evening brought home by a countryman, who had found him pounded, as it were, within the walls of a ruined cottage. As the knight had been greatly fatigued without enjoying any rest for eight-and-forty hours, he resolved to indulge himself with one night's repose, and then return to the place where he had left his squire indisposed ; for by this time even his concern for Timothy had recurred.

On a candid scrutiny of his own heart, he found himself much less unhappy than he had been before his interview with Aurelia ; for, instead of being as formerly tormented with the pangs of despairing love, which had actually unsettled his understanding, he was now happily convinced that he had inspired the tender breast of Aurelia with mutual affection ; and, though she was invidiously snatched from his embrace in the midst of such endearments as had wound up his soul to esctasy and transport, he did not doubt of being able to rescue her from the power of an inhuman kinsman, whose guardianship would soon of course expire ; and in the meantime he rested with the most perfect dependence on her constancy and virtue.

As he next day crossed the country, ruminating on the disaster that had befallen his squire, and could now compare circumstances coolly, he easily comprehended the whole scheme of that adventure, which was no other than an artifice of Anthony Darnel and his emissaries to draw him from the inn, where he proposed to execute his design upon the innocent Aurelia. He took it for granted that the uncle, having been made acquainted with his niece's elopement, had followed her track by the help of such information as he received, from one stage to another; and that, receiving more particulars at the White Hart touching Sir Launcelot, he had formed the scheme in which Crabshaw was an involuntary instrument towards the seduction of his master.

Amusing himself with these and other cogitations, our hero in the afternoon reached the place of his destination, and, entering the inn where Timothy had been left at sick quarters, chanced to meet the apothecary retiring precipitately in a very unsavoury pickle from the chamber of his patient. When he inquired about the health of his squire, this retainer to medicine, wiping himself all the while with ı napkin, answered in manifest confusion, that he apprehended him to be in a very dangerous way from an inflammation of the *piamater*, which had produced a most furious delirium. Then he proceeded to explain, in technical terms, the method of cure he had followed; and concluded with telling him the poor squire's brain was so outrageously disordered, that he had rejected all administration, and just thrown a urinal in his face.

The knight's humanity being alarmed at this intelligence ıe resolved that Crabshaw should have the benefit of further advice, and asked if there was not a physician in the place? The apothecary, after some interjections of hesitation, owned there was a doctor in the village, an odd sort of a humourist; but he believed he had not much to do in the way of his profession, and was not much used to the forms of prescription. He was counted a scholar, to be sure, but as to his medical capacity—he would not take upon him to say. "No matter," cried Sir Launcelot, "he may strike out some lucky thought for the benefit of the patient, and I desire you will call him instantly."

While the apothecary was absent on this service, our adventurer took it in his head to question the landlord about the character of this physician, which had been so unfavourably represented, and received the following information:

"For my peart, measter, I knows nothing amiss of the doctor—he's a quiet sort of an inoffensive man; uses my house sometimes, and pays for what he has, like the rest of my customers. They says he deals very little in physic stuff, but cures his patients with fasting and water-gruel, whereby he can't expect the 'pothecary to be his friend. You knows, master, one must live, and let live, as the saying is. I must say, he, for the value of three guineas, set up my wife's constitution in such a manner, that I have saved within these two years, I believe, forty pounds in 'pothecary's bills. But what of that ? Every man must eat, thof at another's expense ; and I should be in a deadly hole myself if all my customers should take it in their heads to drink nothing but water-gruel, because it is good for the constitution. Thank God, I have as good a constitution as e'er a man in England, but for all that, I and my whole family bleed and purge, and take a diet-drink twice a year, by way of serving the 'pothecary, who is a very honest man, and a very good neighbour."

Their conversation was interrupted by the return of the apothecary with the doctor, who had very little of the faculty in his appearance. He was dressed remarkably plain, seemed to be turned of fifty, had a careless air, and a sarcastical turn in his countenance. Before he entered the sick man's chamber, he asked some questions concerning the disease ; and when the apothecary, pointing to his own head, said, " It lies all here," the doctor, turning to Sir Launcelot, replied, " If that be all there's nothing in it."

Upon a more particular inquiry about the symptoms, he was told that the blood was seemingly viscous, and salt upon the tongue ; the urine remarkably acrosaline, and the fæces atrabilious and fœtid. When the doctor said he would engage to find the same phenomena in every healthy man of the three kingdoms, the apothecary added, that the patient was manifestly comatous, and moreover afflicted with griping pains and borborygmata. " A f—t for your borborygmata," cried the physician ; " what has been done ? " To this question he replied, that venesection had been three times performed ; that a vesicatory had been applied *inter scapulas* ; that the patient had taken occasionally of a cathartic apozem, and between whiles, alexipharmic boluses and neutral draughts.—" Neutral, indeed," said the doctor ; " so neutral, that I'll be crucified if ever they declare either for the patient or the disease." So saying, he brushed into Crabshaw's chamber, followed by our adventurer, who was almost suffocated at his first entrance. The day was close ; the window-shutters were fastened ; a huge fire blazed in the chimney ; thick harateen curtains were close drawn round the bed, where the wretched squire lay extended under an enormous load of blankets. The nurse, who had all the exteriors of a bawd given to drink, sat stewing in this apartment like a damned soul in some infernal bagnio ; but rising when the company entered, made her curtsies with great decorum.—" Well," said the doctor, " how does your patient, nurse ? "— " Blessed be God for it, I hope in a fair way. To be sure his apozem has had a blessed effect—five-and-twenty stools since three o'clock in the morning. But then, a'would not suffer the blisters to be put upon his thighs. Good lack ! a'has been mortally obstropolous, and out of his senses all this blessed day."—" You lie," cried the squire, " I an't out of my seven senses, thof I'm half mad with vexation."

The doctor having withdrawn the curtain, the hapless squire appeared very pale and ghastly ; and having surveyed his master with a rueful aspect, addressed him in these words : " Sir Knight, I beg a boon. Be pleased to tie a stone about the neck of the apothecary, and a halter about the neck of the nurse, and throw the one into the next river, and the other over the next tree, and in so doing you will do a charitable deed to your fellow-creatures ; for he and she do the devil's work in partnership, and have sent many a score of their betters home to him before their time."— " Oh, he begins to talk sensibly."—" Have a good heart," said the physician. " What is your disorder ? "—" Physic." —" What do you chiefly complain of ? "—" The doctor."— " Does your head ache ? "—" Yea, with impertinence."— " Have you a pain in your back ? "—" Yes, where the blister

lies."—" Are you sick at stomach ? "—" Yes, with hunger."
—" Do you feel any shiverings ? "—" Always at sight of
the apothecary."—" Do you perceive any load in your
bowels ? "—" I would the apothecary's conscience was as
clear."—" Are you thirsty ? "—" Not thirsty enough to
drink barley-water."—" Be pleased to look into his fauces,"
said the apothecary ; " he has got a rough tongue, and a
very foul mouth, I'll assure you."—" I have known that the
case with some limbs of the faculty, where they stood more
in need of correction than of physic.—Well, my honest
friend, since you have already undergone the proper purga-
tions in due form, and say you have no other disease than the
doctor, we will set you on your legs again without further
question. Here, nurse, open that window, and throw
these phials into the street. Now lower the curtain, without
shutting the casement, that the man may not be stifled
in his own steam. In the next place, take off two-thirds
of these coals, and one-third of these blankets.—How dost
fecl now, my heart ? "—" I should feel heart-whole, if so be
as yow would throw the noorse a'ter the bottles, and the
'pothecary a'ter the noorse, and oorder me a pound of
chops for my dinner, for I be so hoongry, I could eat a horse
behind the saddle."

The apothecary, seeing what passed, retired of his own
accord, holding up his hands in sign of astonishment. The
nurse was dismissed in the same breath. Crabshaw rose,
dressed himself without assistance, and made a hearty meal
on the first eatable that presented itself to view. The
knight passed the evening with the physician, who, from his
first appearance, concluded he was mad ; but, in the course
of the conversation, found means to resign that opinion
without adopting any other in lieu of it, and parted with him
under all the impatience of curiosity. The knight, on his
part, was very well entertained with the witty sarcasms and
erudition of the doctor, who appeared to be a sort of cynic
philosopher tinctured with misanthropy, and at open war
with the whole body of apothecaries, whom however it
was by no means his interest to disoblige.

Next day, Crabshaw, being to all appearance perfectly recovered, our adventurer reckoned with the apothecary, paid the landlord, and set out on his return for the London road, resolving to lay aside his armour at some distance from the metropolis ; for, ever since his interview with Aurelia, his fondness for chivalry had been gradually abating. As the torrent of his despair had disordered the current of his sober reflection, so now, as that despair subsided, his thoughts began to flow deliberately in their ancient channel. All day long he regaled his imagination with plans of connubial happiness, formed on the possession of the incomparable Aurelia ; determined to wait with patience, until the law should supersede the authority of her guardian, rather than adopt any violent expedient which might hazard the interest of his passion.

He had for some time travelled in the turnpike road, when his reverie was suddenly interrupted by a confused noise ; and when he lifted up his eyes he beheld at a little distance a rabble of men and women, variously armed with flails, pitchforks, poles, and muskets, acting offensively against a strange figure on horseback, who, with a kind of lance, laid about him with incredible fury. Our adventurer was not so totally abandoned by the spirit of chivalry, to see without emotion a single knight in danger of being overpowered by such a multitude of adversaries. Without staying to put on his helmet, he ordered Crabshaw to follow him in the charge against those plebeians. Then couching his lance, and giving Bronzomarte the spur, he began his career with such impetuosity as overturned all that happened to be in his way ; and intimidated the rabble to such a degree, that they retired before him like a flock of sheep, the greater part of them believing he was the devil *in propria persona*. He came in the very nick of time to save the life of the other errant. against whom three loaded muskets were actually levelled, at the very instant that our adventurer began his charge. The unknown knight was so sensible of the seasonable interposition, that, riding up to our hero, " Brother," said he, " this is the second time you have holp me off, when I was bump ashore.—Bess Mizzen, I must say, is no more than a leaky bum-boat, in comparison of the glorious galley you want to man. I desire that henceforth we may cruise in the same latitudes, brother ; and I'll be d—ned if I don't stand by you as long as I have a stick standing, or can carry a rag of canvas."

By this address our knight recognised the novice Captain Crowe, who had found means to accommodate himself with a very strange suit of armour. By way of helmet, he wore one of the caps used by the light horse, with straps buckled under his chin, and contrived in such a manner as to conceal his whole visage, except the eyes. Instead of cuirass, mail, greaves, and other pieces of complete armour, he was cased in a postillion's leathern jerkin, covered with thin plates of tinned iron. His buckler was a pot-lid, his lance a hop-pole shod with iron, and a basket-hilt broad-sword, like that of Hudibras, depended by a broad buff belt, that girded his middle. His feet were defended by jack-boots, and his hands by the gloves of a trooper. Sir Launcelot would not lose time in examining particulars, as he perceived some mischief had been done, and that the enemy had rallied at a distance ; he therefore commanded Crowe to follow him, and rode off with great expedition ; but he did not perceive his squire was taken prisoner, nor did the captain recollect that his nephew, Tom Clarke, had been disabled and secured in the beginning of the fray. The truth is, the poor captain had been so belaboured about the pate, that it was a wonder he remembered his own name.

CHAPTER XVII

Containing Adventures of Chivalry equally new and surprising.

THE knight Sir Launcelot, and the novice Crowe, retreated with equal order and expedition to the distance of half a league from the field of battle, where the former, halting, proposed to make a lodgment in a very decent house of entertainment, distinguished by the sign of St. George of Cappadocia encountering the dragon, an achievement in which temporal and spiritual chivalry were happily reconciled. Two such figures alighting at the inn gate did not pass through the yard unnoticed and unadmired by the guests and attendants, some of whom fairly took to their heels, on the supposition that these outlandish creatures were the avant-couriers or heralds of a French invasion. The fears and doubts, however, of those who ventured to stay were soon dispelled, when our hero accosted them in the English tongue, and with the most courteous demeanour desired to be shown into an apartment.

Had Captain Crowe been spokesman, perhaps their suspicions would not have so quickly subsided, for he was, in reality, a very extraordinary novice, not only in chivalry, but also in his external appearance, and particularly in those dialects of the English language which are used by the terrestrial animals of this kingdom. He desired the ostler to take his horse in tow, and bring him to his moorings in a safe riding. He ordered the waiter, who showed them into a parlour, to bear a hand, ship his oars, mind his helm, and bring alongside a short allowance of brandy or grog, that he might cant a slug into his bread-room, for there was such a heaving and pitching, that he believed he should shift his ballast. The fellow understood no part of this address but the word *brandy*, at mention of which he disappeared. Then Crowe, throwing himself into an elbow chair, "Stop my hawse-holes," cried he, "I can't think what's the matter, brother ; but, egad, my head sings and simmers like a pot of chowder. My eyesight yaws to and again, d'ye see ; then there's such a walloping and whushing in my hold—smite me—Lord have mercy upon us. Here, you swab, ne'er mind the glass, hand me the noggin."

The latter part of this address was directed to the waiter, who had returned with a quartern of brandy, which Crowe, snatching eagerly, started into his bread-room at one cant. Indeed, there was no time to be lost, inasmuch as he seemed to be on the verge of fainting away when he swallowed this cordial, by which he was instantaneously revived.

He then desired the servant to unbuckle the straps of his helmet, but this was a task which the drawer could not perform, even though assisted with the good offices of Sir Launcelot, for the head and jaws were so much swelled with the discipline they had undergone, that the straps and buckles lay buried, as it were, in pits formed by the tume-faction of the adjacent parts.

Fortunately for the novice, a neighbouring surgeon passed by the door on horseback, a circumstance which the waiter, who saw him from the window, no sooner disclosed, than the knight had recourse to his assistance. This practitioner having viewed the whole figure, and more particularly the head of Crowe, in silent wonder, proceeded to feel his pulse, and then declared, that as the inflammation was very great, and going on with violence to its *acme*, it would be necessary to begin with copious phlebotomy, and then to empty the intestinal canal. So saying, he began to strip the arm of the captain, who, perceiving his aim, "Avast, brother," cried he, "you go the wrong way to work; you may as well rummage the afterhold when the damage is in the forecastle; I shall right again when my jaws are unhooped."

With these words he drew a clasp-knife from his pocket, and, advancing to a glass, applied it so vigorously to the leathern straps of his headpiece, that the gordian knot was cut, without any other damage to his face than a moderate scarification, which, added to the tumefaction of features naturally strong, and a whole week's growth of a very bushy beard, produced on the whole a most hideous caricatura. After all, there was a necessity for the administration of the surgeon, who found divers contusions on different parts of the skull, which even the tin cap had not been able to protect from the weapons of the rustics.

These being shaved and dressed *secundum artem*, and the operator dismissed with a proper acknowledgment, our knight detached one of the post-boys to the field of action for intelligence concerning Mr. Clarke and squire Timothy, and, in the interim, desired to know the particulars of Crowe's adventures since he parted from him at the White Hart.

A connected relation, in plain English, was what he had little reason to expect from the novice, who, nevertheless, exerted his faculties to the uttermost for his satisfaction. He gave him to understand, that in steering his course to Birmingham, where he thought of fitting himself with tackle, he had fallen in, by accident, at a public-house, with an itinerant tinker, in the very act of mending a kettle; that, seeing him do his business like an able workman, he had applied to him for advice, and the tinker, after having considered the subject, had undertaken to make him such a suit of armour as neither sword nor lance should penetrate; that they adjourned to the next town, where the leather coat, the plates of tinned iron, the lance, and the broadsword, were purchased, together with a copper saucepan, which the artist was now at work upon in converting it to a shield; but in the meantime, the captain, being impatient to begin his career of chivalry, had accommodated himself with a pot-lid, and taken to the highway, notwithstanding all the entreaties, tears, and remonstrances of his nephew, Tom Clarke, who could not however be prevailed upon to leave him in the dangerous voyage he had undertaken.

That this being but the second day of his journey, he descried five or six men on horseback bearing up full in his teeth, upon which he threw his sails aback, and prepared for action; that he hailed them at a considerable distance, and bade them bring to; when they came alongside, notwithstanding his hail, he ordered them to clew up their courses, and furl their topsails, otherwise he would be foul of their quarters; that, hearing this salute, they luffed all at once, till their cloth shook in the wind; then he hallooed in a loud voice, that his sweetheart, Besselia Mizzen, wore the broad pendant of beauty, to which they must strike their topsails on pain of being sent to the bottom; that, after having eyed him for some time with astonishment, they clapped on all their sails, some of them running under

his stern, and others athwart his forefoot, and got clear off ;
that, not satisfied with running ahead, they all of a sudden
tacked about, and one of them boarding him on the lee-
quarter, gave him such a drubbing about his upper works,
that the lights danced in his lanterns ; that he returned the
salute with his hop-pole so effectually that his aggressor
broached to in the twinkling of a handspike, and then he
was engaged with all the rest of the enemy, except one,
who sheered off, and soon returned with a mosquito fleet
of small craft, who had done him considerable damage, and,
in all probability, would have made prize of him, hadn't
he been brought off by the knight's gallantry. He said,
that in the beginning of the conflict Tom Clarke rode up to
the foremost of the enemy, as he did suppose in order to
prevent hostilities, but before he got up to him near enough
to hold discourse, he was pooped with a sea that almost sent
him to the bottom, and then towed off he knew not whither.

Crowe had scarce finished his narration, which consisted
of broken hints and unconnected explosions of sea terms,
when a gentleman of the neighbourhood, who acted in the
commission of the peace, arrived at the gate, attended by
a constable, who had in custody the bodies of Thomas
Clarke and Timothy Crabshaw, surrounded by five men on
horseback, and an innumerable posse of men, women, and
children, on foot. The captain, who always kept a good
lookout, no sooner descried this cavalcade and procession,
than he gave notice to Sir Launcelot, and advised that they
should crowd away with all the cloth they could carry.
Our adventurer was of another opinion, and determined, at
any rate, to procure the enlargement of the prisoners.

The justice, ordering his attendants to stay without the
gate, sent his compliments to Sir Launcelot Greaves, and
desired to speak with him for a few minutes. He was immediately admitted, and could not help staring at sight of
Crowe, who, by this time, had no remains of the human
physiognomy, so much was the swelling increased and the
skin discoloured. The gentleman, whose name was Mr.
Elmy, having made a polite apology for the liberty he had

taken, proceeded to unfold his business. He said, information had been lodged with him, as a justice of the peace, against two armed men on horseback, who had stopped five farmers on the king's highway, put them in fear and danger of their lives, and even assaulted, maimed, and wounded divers persons, contrary to the king's peace, and in violation of the statute ; that, by the description, he supposed the knight and his companion to be the persons against whom the complaint had been lodged ; and, understanding his quality from Mr. Clarke, whom he had known in London, he was come to wait upon him, and, if possible, effect an accommodation.

Our adventurer having thanked him for the polite and obliging manner in which he proceeded, frankly told him the whole story, as it had been just related by the captain ; and Mr. Elmy had no reason to doubt the truth of the narrative, as it confirmed every circumstance which Clarke had before reported. Indeed, Tom had been very communicative to this gentleman, and made him acquainted with the whole history of Sir Launcelot Greaves, as well as with the whimsical resolution of his uncle, Captain Crowe. Mr. Elmy now told the knight, that the persons whom the captain had stopped were farmers, returning from a neighbouring market, a set of people naturally boorish, and at that time elevated with ale to an uncommon pitch of insolence ; that one of them, in particular, called Prickle, was the most quarrelsome fellow in the whole county ; and so litigious, that he had maintained above thirty law-suits, in eight-and-twenty of which he had been condemned in costs. He said the others might be easily influenced in the way of admonition ; but there was no way of dealing with Prickle, except by the form and authority of the law. He therefore proposed to hear evidence in a judicial capacity, and his clerk being in attendance, the court was immediately opened in the knight's apartment.

By this time Mr. Clarke had made such good use of his time in explaining the law to his audience, and displaying the great wealth and unbounded liberality of Sir Launcelot

Greaves, that he had actually brought over to his sentiments the constable and the commonalty, tag-rag, and bob-tail, and even staggered the majority of the farmers, who, at first, had breathed nothing but defiance and revenge. Farmer Stake being first called to the bar, and sworn touching the identity of Sir Launcelot Greaves and Captain Crowe, declared that the said Crowe had stopped him on the king's highway and put him in bodily fear, that he afterwards saw the said Crowe with a pole or weapon, value threepence, breaking the king's peace by committing assault and battery against the heads and shoulders of his majesty's liege subjects, Geoffrey Prickle, Hodge Dolt, Richard Bumpkin, Mary Fang, Catherine Rubble, and Margery Litter, and that he saw Sir Launcelot Greaves, baronet, aiding, assisting, and comforting the said Crowe, contrary to the king's peace, and against the form of the statute.

Being asked if the defendant, when he stopped them, demanded their money, or threatened violence, he answered he could not say, inasmuch as the defendant spoke in an unknown language. Being interrogated if the defendant did not allow them to pass without using any violence, and if they did not pass unmolested, the deponent replied in the affirmative. Being required to tell for what reason they returned, and if the defendant Crowe was not assaulted before he began to use his weapon, the deponent made no answer. The depositions of Farmers Bumpkin and Muggins, as well as of Madge Litter and Mary Fang, were taken to much the same purpose, and his worship earnestly exhorted them to an accommodation, observing, that they themselves were in fact the aggressors, and that Captain Crowe had done no more than exerted himself in his own defence.

They were all pretty well disposed to follow his advice, except Farmer Prickle, who, entering the court with a bloody handkerchief about his head, declared that the law should determine it at next 'size, and in the meantime insisted that the defendants should find immediate bail, or go to prison, or be set in the stocks. He affirmed that they had been guilty of an *affray*, in appearing with armour and

weapons not usually worn, to the terror of others, which is
in itself a breach of the peace; but that they had, moreover,
with force of arms, that is to say, with swords, staves, and
other warlike instruments, by turns, made an assault and
affray, to the terror and disturbance of him and divers subjects of our lord the King, then and there being, and to the
evil and pernicious example of the liege people of the said
lord the King, and against the peace of our said lord the
King, his crown and dignity.

The peasant had purchased a few law terms at a considerable expense, and he thought he had a right to turn his
knowledge to the annoyance of all his neighbours. Mr.
Elmy, finding him obstinately deaf to all proposals of accommodation, held the defendants to very moderate bail, the
landlord and the curate of the parish freely offering themselves as sureties. Mr. Clarke, with Timothy Crabshaw,
against whom nothing appeared, were now set at liberty,
when the former, advancing to his worship, gave information
against Geoffrey Prickle, and declared upon oath that he had
seen him assault Captain Crowe without any provocation;
and when he, the deponent, interposed to prevent further
mischief, the said Prickle had likewise assaulted and wounded
him, the deponent, and detained him for some time in false
imprisonment, without warrant or authority.

In consequence of this information, which was corroborated
by divers evidences, selected from the mob at the gate, the
tables were turned upon Farmer Prickle, who was given to
understand that he must either find bail, or be forthwith
imprisoned. This *honest* boor, who was in opulent circumstances, had made such popular use of the benefits he
possessed, that there was not a housekeeeper in the parish
who would not have rejoiced to see him hanged. His
dealings and connections, however, were such that none of
the other four would have refused to bail him, had not
Clarke given them to understand that, if they did, he would
make them all principals and parties, and have two separate
actions against each. Prickle happened to be at variance
with the innkeeper, and the curate durst not disoblige the

vicar, who at that very time was suing the farmer for the
small tithes. He offered to deposit a sum equal to the
recognisance of the knight's bail ; but this was rejected, as
an expedient contrary to the practice of the courts. He
sent for the attorney of the village, to whom he had been a
good customer ; but the lawyer was hunting evidence in
another county. The exciseman presented himself as a
surety ; but he, not being a housekeeper, was not accepted.
Divers cottagers, who depended on Farmer Prickle, were
successively refused, because they could not prove that they
had paid scot and lot, and parish taxes.

The farmer, finding himself thus forlorn, and in imminent
danger of visiting the inside of a prison, was seized with a
paroxysm of rage, during which he inveighed against the
bench, reviled the two adventurers errant, declared that
he believed, and would lay a wager of twenty guineas, that
he had more money in his pocket than e'er a man in the
company ; and in the space of a quarter of an hour swore
forty oaths, which the justice did not fail to number. " Before we proceed to other matters," said Mr. Elmy, " I order
you to pay forty shillings for the oaths you have sworn,
otherwise I will cause you to be set in the stocks without
further ceremony."

Prickle, throwing down a couple of guineas, with two
execrations more to make up the sum, declared that he could
afford to pay for swearing as well as e'er a justice in the
county, and repeated his challenge of the wager, which our
adventurer now accepted, protesting, at the same time, that
it was not a step taken from any motive of pride, but entirely
with a view to punish an insolent plebeian, who could not
otherwise be chastised without a breach of the peace. Twenty
guineas being deposited on each side in the hands of Mr.
Elmy, Prickle, with equal confidence and despatch, produced
a canvas bag, containing two hundred and seventy pounds,
which, being spread upon the table, made a very formidable
show, that dazzled the eyes of the beholders, and induced
many of them to believe he had ensured his conquest.

Our adventurer, asking if he had anything further to offer,

and being answered in the negative, drew forth, with great deliberation, a pocket-book, in which there was a considerable parcel of bank-notes, from which he selected three of one hundred pounds each, and exhibited them upon the table, to the astonishment of all present. Prickle, mad with his overthrow and loss, said it might be necessary to make him prove the notes were honestly come by; and Sir Launcelot started up, in order to take vengeance upon him for this insult, but was withheld by the arms and remonstrances of Mr. Elmy, who assured him that Prickle desired nothing so much as another broken head, to lay the foundation of a new prosecution.

The knight, calmed by this interposition, turned to the audience, saying, with the most affable deportment, "Good people, do not imagine that I intend to pocket the spoils of such a contemptible rascal. I shall beg the favour of this worthy gentleman to take up these twenty guineas, and distribute them as he shall think proper among the poor of the parish; but, by this benefaction, I do not hold myself acquitted for the share I had in the bruises some of you have received in this unlucky fray, and therefore I give the other twenty guineas to be divided among the sufferers, to each according to the damage he or she shall appear to have sustained, and I shall consider it as an additional obligation if Mr. Elmy will likewise superintend this retribution."

At the close of this address, the whole yard and gateway rang with acclamation, while honest Crowe, whose generosity was not inferior even to that of the accomplished Greaves, pulled out his purse, and declared that, as he had begun the engagement, he would at least go share and share alike in new caulking their seams, and repairing their timbers. The knight, rather than enter into a dispute with his novice, told him he considered the twenty guineas as given by them both in conjunction, and that they would confer together on that subject hereafter.

This point being adjusted, Mr. Elmy assumed all the solemnity of the magistrate, and addressed himself to Prickle in these words: "Farmer Prickle, I am both sorry and ashamed to see a man of your years and circumstances so little respected that you cannot find sufficient bail for forty pounds, a sure testimony that you have neither cultivated the friendship, nor deserved the goodwill, of your neighbours. I have heard of your quarrels and your riots, your insolence and litigious disposition, and often wished for an opportunity of giving you a proper taste of the law's correction. That opportunity now offers ; you have, in the hearing of all these people, poured forth a torrent of abuse against me, both in the character of a gentleman and of a magistrate. Your abusing me personally perhaps I should have overlooked with the contempt it deserves, but I should ill vindicate the dignity of my office as a magistrate by suffering you to insult the bench with impunity. I shall therefore imprison you for contempt, and you shall remain in jail until you can find bail on the other prosecutions."

Prickle, the first transports of his anger having subsided, began to be pricked with the thorns of compunction. He was indeed extremely mortified at the prospect of being sent to jail so disgracefully. His countenance fell ; and, after a hard internal struggle, while the clerk was employed in writing the mittimus, he said he hoped his worship would not send him to prison. He begged pardon of him, and our adventurers, for having abused them in his passion ; and observed that, as he had received a broken head, and paid two-and-twenty guineas for his folly, he could not be said to have escaped altogether without punishment, even if the plaintiff should agree to exchange releases.

Sir Launcelot, seeing this stubborn rustic effectually humbled, became an advocate in his favour with Mr. Elmy and Tom Clarke, who forgave him at his request, and a mutual release being executed, the farmer was permitted to depart. The populace were regaled at our adventurer's expense, and the men, women, and children who had been wounded or bruised in the battle, to the number of ten or a dozen, were desired to wait upon Mr. Elmy in the morning, to receive the knight's bounty. The justice was prevailed upon to spend the evening with Sir Launcelot and his two companions, for whom supper was bespoken; but the first thing the cook prepared was a poultice for Crowe's head, which was now enlarged to a monstrous exhibition. Our knight, who was all kindness and complacency, shook Mr. Clarke by the hand, expressing his satisfaction at meeting with his old friends again, and told him softly that he had compliments for him from Mrs. Dolly Cowslip, who now lived with his Aurelia.

Clarke was confounded at this intelligence, and, after some hesitation, " Lord bless my soul ! " cried he, " I'll be shot, then, if the pretended Miss Meadows wa'n't the same as Miss Darnel ! " He then declared himself extremely glad that poor Dolly had got into such an agreeable situation, passed many warm encomiums on her goodness of heart and virtuous inclinations, and concluded with appealing to the knight, whether she did not look very pretty in her green joseph. In the meantime he procured a plaster for his own head, and helped to apply the poultice to that of his uncle, who was sent to bed betimes with a moderate dose of sack-whey, to promote perspiration. The other three passed the evening to their mutual satisfaction ; and the justice, in particular, grew enamoured of the knight's character, dashed as it was with extravagance.

Let us now leave them to the enjoyment of a sober and rational conversation, and give some account of other guests, who arrived late in the evening, and here fixed their night quarters. But as we have already trespassed on the reader's patience, we shall give him a short respite, until the next chapter makes its appearance.

CHAPTER XVIII

In which the Rays of Chivalry shine with renovated Lustre.

Our hero little dreamed that he had a formidable rival in the person of the knight, who arrived about eleven, at the sign of the St. George, and, by the noise he made, gave

intimation of his importance. This was no other than
Squire Sycamore, who, having received advice that Miss
Aurelia Darnel had eloped from the place of her retreat,
immediately took the field in quest of that lovely fugitive ;
hoping that, should he have the good fortune to find her in
present distress, his good offices would not be rejected.
He had followed the chaise so close, that, immediately after
our adventurer's departure, he alighted at the inn, from
whence Aurelia had been conveyed ; and there he learned
the particulars which we have related above.

Mr. Sycamore had a great deal of the childish romantic
in his disposition, and, in the course of his amours, is said
to have always taken more pleasure in the pursuit than in
the final possession. He had heard of Sir Launcelot's
extravagance, by which he was in some measure infected,
and he dropped an insinuation, that he could eclipse his
rival, even in his own lunatic sphere. This hint was not
lost upon his companion, counsellor, and buffoon, the
facetious Davy Dawdle, who had some humour, and a great
deal of mischief, in his composition. He looked upon his
patron as a fool, and his patron knew him to be both
knave and fool ; yet, the two characters suited each other
so well, that they could hardly exist asunder. Davy was
an artful sycophant, but he did not flatter in the usual way ;
on the contrary, he behaved *en cavalier*, and treated Sycamore, on whose bounty he subsisted, with the most sarcastic
familiarity. Nevertheless, he seasoned his freedom with
certain qualifying ingredients, that subdued the bitterness
of it, and was now become so necessary to the squire, that
he had no idea of enjoyment with which Dawdle was not
somehow or other connected.

There had been a warm dispute betwixt them about the
scheme of contesting the prize with Sir Launcelot in the
lists of chivalry. Sycamore had insinuated, that if he had
a mind to play the fool, he could wear armour, wield a
lance, and manage a charger, as well as Sir Launcelot Greaves.
Dawdle, snatching the hint, " I had, some time ago," said
he, " contrived a scheme for you, which I was afraid you

had not address enough to execute. It would be no difficult matter, in imitation of the bac⸺ .'⸺r, Sampson Carrasco, to go in quest of Greaves, as a knight-errant, defy him as a rival, and establish a compact, by which the vanquished should obey the injunctions of the victor."—"That is my very idea," cried Sycamore.—"Your idea!" replied the other; "had you ever an idea of your own conception?" Thus the dispute began, and was maintained with great vehemence, until other arguments failing, the squire offered to lay a wager of twenty guineas. To this proposal, Dawdle answered by the interjection *pish!* which inflamed Sycamore to a repetition of the defiance. "You are in the right," said Dawdle, "to use such an argument as you know is by me unanswerable. A wager of twenty guineas will at any time overthrow and confute all the logic of the most able syllogist, who has not got a shilling in his pocket."

Sycamore looked very grave at this declaration, and, after a short pause, said, "I wonder, Dawdle, what you do with all your money?"—"I am surprised you should give yourself that trouble—I never ask what you do with yours."—"You have no occasion to ask; you know pretty well how it goes."—"What, do you upbraid me with your favours?—'tis mighty well, Sycamore."—"Nay, Dawdle, I did not intend to affront."—"Z—s! affront! what d'ye mean?"—"I'll assure you, Davy, you don't know me, if you think I could be so ungenerous as to—a—to——"—"I always thought, whatever faults or foibles you might have, Sycamore, that you was not deficient in generosity,—though to be sure it is often very absurdly displayed."—"Ay, that's one of my greatest foibles; I can't refuse even a scoundrel, when I think he is in want.—Here, Dawdle, take that note."—"Not I, sir,—what d'ye mean?—what right have I to your notes?"—"Nay, but Dawdle—come."—"By no means; it looks like the abuse of good-nature; all the world knows you're good-natured to a fault."—"Come, dear Davy, you shall—you must oblige me."—Thus urged, Dawdle accepted the banknote with great reluctance, and restored the idea to the right owner.

A suit of armour being brought from the garret or armoury of his ancestors, he gave orders for having the pieces scoured and furbished up ; and his heart dilated with joy, when he reflected upon the superb figure he should make when cased in complete steel, and armed at all points for the combat.

When he was fitted with the other parts, Dawdle insisted on buckling on his helmet, which weighed fifteen pounds ; and, the headpiece being adjusted, made such a clatter about his ears with a cudgel that his eyes had almost started from their sockets. His voice was lost within the vizor, and his friend affected not to understand his meaning when he made signs with his gauntlets, and endeavoured to close with him, that he might wrest the cudgel from his hand. At length he desisted, saying, " I'll warrant the helmet sound by its ringing " ; and taking it off, found the squire in a cold sweat. He would have achieved his first exploit on the spot, had his strength permitted him to assault Dawdle ; but what with want of air, and the discipline he had undergone, he had well-nigh swooned away ; and before he retrieved the use of his members, he was appeased by the apologies of his companion, who protested he meant nothing more than to try if the helmet was free of cracks, and whether or not it would prove a good protection for the head it covered.

His excuses were accepted ; the armour was packed up, and next morning Mr. Sycamore set out from his own house, accompanied by Dawdle, who undertook to perform the part of his squire at the approaching combat. He was also attended by a servant on horseback, who had charge of the armour, and another who blowed the trumpet. They no sooner understood that our hero was housed at the George, than the trumpeter sounded a charge, which alarmed Sir Launcelot and his company, and disturbed honest Captain Crowe in the middle of his first sleep. Their next step was to pen a challenge, which, when the stranger departed, was by the trumpeter delivered with great ceremony into the hands of Sir Launcelot, who read it in these words :—
" To the knight of the Crescent, greeting. Whereas I am

informed you have the presumption to lay claim to the heart of the peerless Aurelia Darnel, I give you notice that I can admit no rivalship in the affection of that paragon of beauty; and I expect that you will either resign your pretensions, or make it appear in single combat, according to the law of arms and the institutions of chivalry, that you are worthy to dispute her favour with him of the Griffin.— POLYDORE."

Our adventurer was not a little surprised at this address, which however he pocketed in silence, and began to reflect, not without mortification, that he was treated as a lunatic by some person, who wanted to amuse himself with the infirmities of his fellow-creatures. Mr. Thomas Clarke, who saw the ceremony with which the letter was delivered, and the emotions with which it was read, hied him to the kitchen for intelligence, and there learned that the stranger was Squire Sycamore. He forthwith comprehended the nature of the billet, and, in the apprehension that bloodshed would ensue, resolved to alarm his uncle, that he might assist in keeping the peace. He accordingly entered the apartment of the captain, who had been waked by the trumpet, and now peevishly asked the meaning of that d—ned piping, as if all hands were called upon deck? Clarke having imparted what he knew of the transaction, together with his own conjectures, the captain said, he did not suppose as how they would engage by candle-light; and that, for his own part, he should turn out in the larboard watch, long enough before any signals could be hove out for forming the line.

With this assurance the lawyer retired to his nest, where he did not fail to dream of Mrs. Dolly Cowslip, while Sir Launcelot passed the night awake, in ruminating on the strange challenge he had received. He had got notice that the sender was Mr. Sycamore, and hesitated with himself whether he should not punish him for his impertinence; but when he reflected on the nature of the dispute, and the serious consequences it might produce, he resolved to decline the combat, as a trial of right and merit founded upon absurdity. Even in his maddest hours, he never adopted those maxims of knight-errantry which related to challenges. He always perceived the folly and wickedness of defying a man to mortal fight, because he did not like the colour of his beard, or the complexion of his mistress; or of deciding by homicide whether he or his rival deserved the preference, when it was the lady's prerogative to determine which should be the happy lover. It was his opinion that chivalry was a useful institution while confined to its original purposes of protecting the innocent, assisting the friendless, and bringing the guilty to condign punishment. But he could not conceive how these laws should be answered by violating every suggestion of reason, and every precept of humanity.

Captain Crowe did not examine the matter so philosophically. He took it for granted that in the morning the two knights would come to action, and slept sound on that supposition. But he rose before it was day, resolved to be somehow concerned in the fray; and understanding that the stranger had a companion, set him down immediately for his own antagonist. So impatient was he to establish this secondary contest, that by daybreak he entered the chamber of Dawdle, to which he was directed by the waiter, and roused him with a hilloah, that might have been heard at the distance of half a league. Dawdle, startled by this terrific sound, sprang out of bed, and stood upright on the floor, before he opened his eyes upon the object by which he had been so dreadfully alarmed. But when he beheld the head of Crowe, so swelled and swathed, so livid, hideous, and grisly, with a broadsword by his side, and a case of pistols in his girdle, he believed it was the apparition of some murdered man; his hair bristled up, his teeth chattered, and his knees knocked; he would have prayed, but his tongue denied its office. Crowe seeing his perturbation, " Mayhap, friend," said he, " you take me for a buccaneer; but I am no such person.—My name is Captain Crowe.—I come not for your silver nor your gold, your rigging nor your stowage; but hearing as how your friend intends to bring my friend Sir Launcelot Greaves to action, d'ye see, I desire in the way of friendship, that, while they are engaged, you and I, as their seconds, may lie board and board for a few glasses to divert one another, d'ye see." Dawdle, hearing this request, began to retrieve his faculties, and throwing himself into the attitude of Hamlet when the ghost appears, exclaimed in theatrical accent:

> Angels and ministers of grace defend us!
> Art thou a spirit of grace, or goblin damn'd?

As he seemed to bend his eye on vacancy, the captain began to think that he really saw something preternatural, and stared wildly round. Then addressing himself to the terrified Dawdle, "D—n'd," said he, "for what should I be d—n'd? If you are afeard of goblins, brother, put your trust in the Lord, and He'll prove a sheet-anchor to you." The other having by this time recollected himself perfectly, continued notwithstanding to spout tragedy, and, in the words of Macbeth, pronounced:

> What man dare, I dare:
> Approach thou like the rugged Russian bear,
> The arm'd rhinoceros, or Hyrcanian tiger;
> Take any shape but that, and my firm nerves
> Shall never tremble.

"'Ware names, Jack," cried the impatient mariner, "if so be as how you'll bear a hand and rig yourself, and take a short trip with me into the offing, we'll overhaul this here affair in the turning of a capstan."

At this juncture they were joined by Mr. Sycamore in his night-gown and slippers. Disturbed by Crowe's first salute, he sprang up, and now expressed no small astonishment at first sight of the novice's countenance. After having gazed alternately at him and Dawdle, "Who have we got here?" said he; "raw head and bloody bones?" When his friend, slipping on his clothes, gave him to understand that this was a friend of Sir Launcelot Greaves, and explained the purport of his errand, he treated him with more civility. He assured him that he should have the pleasure to break a spear with Mr. Dawdle ; and signified his surprise that Sir Launcelot had made no answer to his letter. It being by this time clear daylight, and Crowe extremely interested in this affair, he broke without ceremony into the knight's chamber, and told him abruptly that the enemy had brought to, and waited for his coming up, in order to begin the action. " I've hailed his consort," said he, " a shambling, chattering fellow. He took me first for a hobgoblin, then called me names, a tiger, a wrynoseo'-ross, and a Persian bear ; but egad, if I come athwart him, I'll make him look like the bear and ragged staff before we part—I wool."

This intimation was not received with that alacrity which the captain expected to find in our adventurer, who told him in a peremptory tone, that he had no design to come to action, and desired to be left to his repose. Crowe forthwith retired crestfallen, and muttered something, which was never distinctly heard.

About eight in the morning Mr. Dawdle brought him a formal message from the Knight of the Griffin, desiring he would appoint the lists, and give security of the field. To which request he made answer in a very composed and solemn accent, " If the person who sent you thinks I have injured him, let him without disguise or any such ridiculous ceremony, explain the nature of the wrong ; and then I shall give such satisfaction as may suit my conscience and my character. If he hath bestowed his affection upon any particular object, and looks upon me as a favourite rival, I shall not wrong the lady so much as to take any step that may prejudice her choice, especially a step that contradicts my own reason as much as it would outrage the laws of my country. If he who calls himself Knight of the Griffin is really desirous of treading in the paths of true chivalry, he will not want opportunities of signalising his valour in the cause of virtue. Should he, notwithstanding this declaration, offer violence to me in the course of my occasions, he will always find me in a posture of defence. Or, should he persist in repeating his importunities, I shall without cere-

mony chastise the messenger." His declining the combat
was interpreted into fear by Mr. Sycamore, who now became
more insolent and ferocious, on the supposition of our knight's
timidity. Sir Launcelot meanwhile went to breakfast with
his friends, and, having put on his armour, ordered the
horses to be brought forth. Then he paid the bill, and
walking deliberately to the gate, in presence of Squire
Sycamore and his attendants, vaulted at one spring into
the saddle of Bronzomarte, whose neighing and curveting
proclaimed the joy he felt in being mounted by his accomplished master.

Though the Knight of the Griffin did not think proper
to insult his rival personally, his friend Dawdle did not fail
to crack some jokes on the figure and horsemanship of Crowe,
who again declared he should be glad to fall in with him
upon the voyage. Nor did Mr. Clarke's black patch and
rueful countenance pass unnoticed and unridiculed. As
for Timothy Crabshaw, he beheld his brother squire with
the contempt of a veteran, and Gilbert paid him his compliments with his heels at parting. But when our adventurer
and his retinue were clear of the inn, Mr. Sycamore ordered
his trumpeter to sound a retreat, by way of triumph over
his antagonist.

Perhaps he would have contented himself with this kind
of victory, had not Dawdle further inflamed his envy and
ambition by launching out in praise of Sir Launcelot. He
observed that his countenance was open and manly; his
joints strong knit, and his form unexceptionable; that he
trod like Hercules, and vaulted into the saddle like a winged
Mercury. Nay, he even hinted it was lucky for Sycamore
that the Knight of the Crescent happened to be so pacifically
disposed. His patron sickened at these praises, and took
fire at the last observation. He affected to undervalue
personal beauty, though the opinion of the world had been
favourable to himself in that particular. He said he was
at least two inches taller than Greaves, and as to shape and
air, he would make no comparisons; but with respect to
riding, he was sure he had a better seat than Sir Launcelot,

and would wager five hundred to fifty guineas that he would
unhorse him at the first encounter. " There is no occasion
for laying wagers," replied Mr. Dawdle ; " the doubt may
be determined in half an hour. Sir Launcelot is not a man
to avoid you at full gallop." Sycamore, after some hesitation, declared he would follow and provoke him to battle,
on condition that Dawdle would engage Crowe ; and this
condition was accepted. For, though Davy had no stomach
to the trial, he could not readily find an excuse for declining
it. Besides, he had discovered the captain to be a very bad
horseman, and resolved to eke out his own scanty valour
with a border of ingenuity. The servants were immediately
ordered to unpack the armour, and, in a little time, Mr.
Sycamore made a very formidable appearance. But the
scene that followed is too important to be huddled in at the
end of a chapter, and therefore we shall reserve it for a more
conspicuous place in these memoirs.

CHAPTER XIX

Containing the Achievements of the Knights of the Griffin and Crescent.

MR. SYCAMORE, alias the Knight of the Griffin, so denominated from a griffin painted on his shield, being armed at
all points, and his friend Dawdle provided with a certain
implement, which he flattered himself would ensure a victory
over the novice Crowe, they set out from the George, with
their attendants, in all the elevation of hope, and pranced
along the highway that led toward London, that being the
road which our adventurer pursued. As they were extremely
well mounted, and proceeded at a round pace, they, in less
than two hours, came up with Sir Launcelot and his company ; and Sycamore sent another formal defiance to the
knight by his trumpeter, Dawdle having, for good reasons,
declined that office.

Our adventurer hearing himself thus addressed, and seeing

his rival, who had passed him, posted to obstruct his progress, armed *cap-à-pie*, with his lance in the rest, determined to give the satisfaction that was required, and desired that the regulations of the combat might be established. The Knight of the Griffin proposed that the vanquished party should resign all pretensions to Miss Aurelia Darnel, in favour of the victor ; that, while the principals were engaged, his friend Dawdle should run a tilt with Captain Crowe ; that Squire Crabshaw and Mr. Sycamore's servant should keep themselves in readiness to assist their respective masters occasionally, according to the law of arms ; and that Mr. Clarke should observe the motions of the trumpeter, whose province was to sound the charge to battle.

Our knight agreed to these regulations, notwithstanding the earnest and pathetic remonstrances of the young lawyer, who, with tears in his eyes, conjured all the combatants, in their turns, to refrain from an action that might be attended with bloodshed and murder; and was contrary to the laws both of God and man. In vain he endeavoured to move them by tears and entreaties, by threatening them with prosecutions in this world, and pains and penalties in the next. They persisted in their resolution, and his uncle would have begun hostilities on his carcass, had he not been prevented by Sir Launcelot, who exhorted Clarke to retire from the field, that he might not be involved in the consequences of the combat. He relished this advice so well, that he had actually moved off to some distance ; but his apprehensions and concern for his friends co-operating with an insatiable curiosity, detained him in sight of the engagement.

The two knights having fairly divided the ground, and the same precautions being taken by the seconds on another part of the field, Sycamore began to be invaded with some scruples, which were probably engendered by the martial appearance and well-known character of his antagonist. The confidence which he derived from the reluctance of Sir Launcelot now vanished, because it plainly appeared that the knight's backwardness was not owing to personal timidity, and he foresaw that the prosecution of this joke might be attended with very serious consequences to his own life and reputation. He therefore desired a parley, in which he observed his affection for Miss Darnel was of such a delicate nature, that, should the discomfiture of his rival contribute to make her unhappy, his victory must render him the most miserable wretch upon earth. He proposed, therefore, that her sentiments and choice should be ascertained before they proceeded to extremity.

Sir Launcelot declared that he was much more afraid of combating Aurelia's inclination than of opposing the Knight of the Griffin in arms, and that if he had the least reason to think Mr. Sycamore, or any other person, was distinguished by her preference, he would instantly give up his suit as desperate. At the same time he observed that Sycamore had proceeded too far to retract ; that he had insulted a gentleman, and not only challenged, but even pursued him, and blocked up his passage in the public highway—outrages which he (Sir Launcelot) would not suffer to pass unpunished. Accordingly, he insisted on the combat, on pain of treating Sycamore as a craven and a recreant. This declaration was reinforced by Dawdle, who told him that, should he now decline the engagement, all the world would look upon him as an infamous poltroon.

These two observations gave a necessary fillip to the courage of the challenger. The parties took their stations. The trumpet sounded to charge, and the combatants began their career with great impetuosity. Whether the gleam of Sir Launcelot's arms affrighted Mr. Sycamore's steed, or some other object had an unlucky effect on his eyesight, certain it is he started at about midway, and gave his rider such a violent shake as discomposed his attitude, and disabled him from using his lance to the best advantage. Had our hero continued his career, with his lance couched, in all probability Sycamore's armour would have proved but a bad defence to his carcass ; but Sir Launcelot, perceiving his rival's spear unrested, had just time to throw up the point of his own, when the two horses closed with such a shock that Sycamore, already wavering in the saddle, was over-thrown, and his armour crashed around him as he fell.

The victor, seeing him lie without motion, alighted im-mediately and began to unbuckle his helmet, in which office he was assisted by the trumpeter. When the headpiece was removed, the hapless Knight of the Griffin appeared in the pale livery of death, though he was only in a swoon, from which he soon recovered by the effect of the fresh air, and the aspersion of cold water, brought from a small pool in the neighbourhood. When he recognised his conqueror doing the offices of humanity about his person, he closed his eyes from vexation, told Sir Launcelot that his was the fortune of the day, though he himself owed his mischance to the fault of his own horse, and observed that this ridiculous affair would not have happened but for the mischievous instigation of that scoundrel Dawdle, on whose ribs he threatened to revenge this mishap.

Perhaps Captain Crowe might have saved him the trouble, had the wag honourably adhered to the institutions of chivalry in his conflict with our novice.   But on this occasion his ingenuity was more commendable than his courage.   He had provided at the inn a blown bladder, in which several smooth pebbles were enclosed, and this he slyly fixed on the head of his pole when the captain obeyed the signal of battle. Instead of bearing the brunt of the encounter, he turned out of the straight line, so as to avoid the lance of his antag-onist, and rattled his bladder with such effect that Crowe's horse, pricking up his ears, took to his heels, and fled across some ploughed land with such precipitation, that the rider was obliged to quit his spear and lay fast hold on the mane, that he might not be thrown out of the saddle.   Dawdle, who was much better mounted, seeing his condition, rode up to the unfortunate novice and belaboured his shoulders without fear of retaliation.

Mr. Clarke, seeing his kinsman so roughly handled, forgot his fears and flew to his assistance, but before he came up the aggressor had retired ; and now perceiving that fortune had declared against his friend and patron, very honourably abandoned him in his distress, and went off at full speed for London.

Nor was Timothy Crabshaw without his share in the noble achievements of this propitious day. He had by this time imbibed such a tincture of errantry that he firmly believed himself and his master equally invincible, and this belief operating upon a perverse disposition, rendered him as quarrelsome in his sphere as his master was mild and forbearing. As he sat on horseback, in the place assigned to him and Sycamore's lacquey, he managed Gilbert in such a manner as to invade with his heels the posteriors of the other's horse, and this insult produced some altercation which ended in mutual assault. The footman handled the butt-end of his horsewhip with great dexterity about the head of Crabshaw, who declared afterwards that it sung and simmered like a kettle of cod-fish; but the squire, who understood the nature of long lashes, as having been a carter from his infancy, found means to twine his thong about the neck of his antagonist, and pull him off his horse half strangled, at the very instant his master was thrown by Sir Launcelot Greaves.

Having thus obtained the victory, he did not much regard the punctilios of chivalry, but, taking it for granted he had a right to make the most of his advantage, resolved to carry off the *spolia opima*. Alighting with great agility, " Brother," cried he, " I think as haw yawrs bean't a butcher's horse, a doan't carry calves well—I'se make yaw knaw your churning days, I wool—what, yaw look as if yaw was crow-trodden, you do—now, you shall pay the score you have been running on my pate, you shall, brother."

So saying, he rifled his pockets, stripped him of his hat and coat, and took possession of his master's portmanteau. But he did not long enjoy his plunder. For the lacquey complaining to Sir Launcelot of his having been despoiled, the knight commanded his squire to refund, not without menaces of subjecting him to the severest chastisement for his injustice and rapacity. Timothy represented, with great vehemence, that he had won the spoils in fair battle, at the

expense of his head and shoulders, which he immediately
uncovered, to prove his allegation. But his remonstrance
having no effect upon his master, "Wounds!" cried he,
"an I mun gee thee back the pig, I'se gee thee back the poke
also; I'm a drubbing still in thy debt."

With these words, he made a most furious attack upon
the plaintiff with his horsewhip, and, before the knight could
interpose, repaid the lacquey with interest. As an appur-
tenance to Sycamore and Dawdle, he ran the risk of another
assault from the novice Crowe, who was so transported with
rage at the disagreeable trick which had been played upon
him by his fugitive antagonist, that he could not for some
time pronounce an articulate sound, but a few broken interjections, the meaning of which could not be ascertained.
Snatching up his pole, he ran towards the place where Mr.
Sycamore sat on the grass, supported by the trumpeter, and
would have finished what our adventurer had left undone,
if the Knight of the Crescent, with admirable dexterity,
had not warded off the blow which he aimed at the Knight
of the Griffin, and signified his displeasure in a resolute tone.
Then he collared the lacquey, who was just disengaged from
the chastising hand of Crabshaw, and swinging his lance with
his other hand, encountered the squire's ribs by accident.

Timothy was not slow in returning the salutation with
the weapon which he still wielded. Mr. Clarke running
up to the assistance of his uncle, was opposed by the lacquey,
who seemed extremely desirous of seeing the enemy revenge
his quarrel, by falling foul of one another. Clarke, thus
impeded, commenced hostilities against the footman, while
Crowe grappled with Crabshaw; a battle-royal ensued,
and was maintained with great vigour, and some bloodshed
on all sides, until the authority of Sir Launcelot, reinforced
by some weighty remonstrances applied to the squire, put
an end to the conflict. Crabshaw immediately desisted,
and ran roaring to communicate his grievances to Gilbert,
who seemed to sympathise very little with his distress. The
lacquey took to his heels; Mr. Clarke wiped his bloody nose,
declaring he had a good mind to put the aggressor in the

Crown Office; and Captain Crowe continued to ejaculate unconnected oaths; which, however, seemed to imply that he was almost sick of his new profession. " D—n my eyes, if you call this—start my timbers, brother—look ye, d'ye see—a lousy, lubberly, cowardly son of a—among the breakers, d'ye see—lost my steerage way—split my binnacle ; hawl away—Oh ! d—n all arrantry—give me a tight vessel, d'ye see, brother—mayhap you mayn't—snatch my—sea-room and a spanking gale—odds heart, I'll hold a whole year's—smite my limbs ; it don't signify talking."

Our hero consoled the novice for his disaster, by observing that if he had got some blows he had lost no honour. At the same time he observed, that it was very difficult, if not impossible, for a man to succeed in the paths of chivalry, who had passed the better part of his days in other occupations ; and hinted that, as the cause which had engaged him in this way of life no longer existed, he was determined to relinquish a profession which, in a peculiar manner, exposed him to the most disagreeable incidents. Crowe chewed the cud upon this insinuation, while the other personages of the drama were employed in catching the horses, which had given their riders the slip. As for Mr. Sycamore, he was so bruised by his fall, that it was necessary to procure a litter for conveying him to the next town, and the servant was despatched for this convenience, Sir Launcelot staying with him until it arrived.

When he was safely deposited in the carriage, our hero took leave of him in these terms : " I shall not insist upon your submitting to the terms you yourself proposed before this rencontre. I give you free leave to use all your advantages, in an honourable way, for promoting your suit with the young lady of whom you profess yourself enamoured. Should you have recourse to sinister practices, you will find Sir Launcelot Greaves ready to demand an account of your conduct, not in the character of a lunatic knight-errant, but as a plain English gentleman, jealous of his honour, and resolute in his purpose."

To this address Mr. Sycamore made no reply, but with a

Clump had left a letter for Dolly, informing her that his master, Squire Darnel, was to set out early in the morning for Yorkshire; but he could give no account of her lady, who had the day before been conveyed, he knew not whither, in a hackney-coach, attended by her uncle and an ill-looking fellow, who had much the appearance of a bailiff or turnkey, so that he feared she was in trouble.

Sir Launcelot was deeply affected by this intimation. His apprehension was even roused by a suspicion that a man of Darnel's violent temper and unprincipled heart might have practised upon the life of his lovely niece; but, upon recollection, he could not suppose that he had recourse to such infamous expedients, knowing, as he did, that an account of her would be demanded at his hands, and that it would be easily proved he had conveyed her from the lodging in which she resided.

His first fears now gave way to another suggestion, that Anthony, in order to intimidate her into a compliance with his proposals, had trumped up a spurious claim against her, and, by virtue of a writ, confined her in some prison or spunging-house. Possessed with this idea, he desired Mr. Clarke to search the sheriff's office in the morning, that he might know whether any such writ had been granted; and he himself resolved to make a tour of the great prisons belonging to the metropolis, to inquire if perchance she might not be confined under a borrowed name. Finally, he determined, if possible, to apprise her of his place of abode, by a paragraph in all the daily papers signifying that Sir Launcelot Greaves had arrived at his house near Golden Square.

All these resolutions were punctually executed. No such writ had been taken out in the sheriff's office; and therefore our hero set out on his jail expedition, accompanied by Mr. Clarke, who had contracted some acquaintance with the commanding officers in these garrisons, in the course of his clerkship and practice as an attorney. The first day they spent in prosecuting their inquiry through the Gate House, Fleet, and Marshalsea; the next day they allotted to the King's Bench, where they understood there was a great

variety of prisoners.   There they proposed to make a minute
scrutiny, by the help of Mr. Norton, the deputy-marshal,
who was Mr. Clarke's intimate friend, and had nothing at all
of the jailer, either in his appearance or in his disposition,
which was remarkably humane and benevolent towards all
his fellow-creatures.

The knight having bespoken dinner at a tavern in the
Borough, was, together with Captain Crowe, conducted
to the prison of the King's Bench, which is situated in
St. George's Fields, about a mile from the end of Westminster
Bridge, and appears like a neat little regular town, consisting
of one street, surrounded by a very high wall, including an
open piece of ground, which may be termed a garden, where
the prisoners take the air and amuse themselves with a variety
of diversions.   Except the entrance, where the turnkeys keep
watch and ward, there is nothing in the place that looks like
a jail, or bears the least colour of restraint.   The street is
crowded with passengers.   Tradesmen of all kinds here
exercise their different professions.   Hawkers of all sorts are
admitted to call and vend their wares as in any open street
of London.   Here are butchers' stands, chandlers' shops, a
surgery, a tap-house, well frequented, and a public kitchen,
in which provisions are dressed for all the prisoners gratis,
at the expense of the publican.   Here the voice of misery
never complains ; and, indeed, little else is to be heard but
the sounds of mirth and jollity.   At the farther end of the
street, on the right hand, is a little paved court, leading to
a separate building, consisting of twelve large apartments,
called state rooms, well furnished and fitted up for the
reception of the better sort of Crown prisoners ; and, on
the other side of the street, facing a separate division of
ground, called the common side, is a range of rooms occupied
by prisoners of the lowest order, who share the profits of a
begging-box, and are maintained by this practice, and some
established funds of charity.   We ought also to observe that
the jail is provided with a neat chapel, in which a clergyman,
in consideration of a certain salary, performs divine service
every Sunday.

Our adventurer, having searched the books, and perused the description of all the female prisoners who had been for some weeks admitted into the jail, obtained not the least intelligence of his concealed charmer, but resolved to alleviate his disappointment by the gratification of his curiosity.

Under the auspices of Mr. Norton he made a tour of the prison, and, in particular, visited the kitchen, where he saw a number of spits loaded with a variety of provision, consisting of butchers' meat, poultry, and game. He could not help expressing his astonishment, with uplifted hands, and congratulating himself in secret upon his being a member of that community which had provided such a comfortable asylum for the unfortunate. His ejaculation was interrupted by a tumultuous noise in the street; and Mr. Norton declaring he was sent for to the lodge, consigned our hero to the care of one Mr. Felton, a prisoner of a very decent appearance, who paid his compliments with a good grace, and invited the company to repose themselves in his apartment, which was large, commodious, and well furnished. When Sir Launcelot asked the cause of that uproar, he told him that it was the prelude to a boxing-match between two of the prisoners, to be decided in the ground or garden of the place.

Captain Crowe expressing an eager curiosity to see the battle, Mr. Felton assured him there would be no sport, as the combatants were both reckoned dunghills; "but in half an hour," said he, "there will be a battle of some consequence between two of the demagogues of the place, Dr. Crabclaw and Mr. Tapley, the first a physician and the other a brewer. You must know, gentlemen, that this imcrocosm, or republic in miniature, is, like the great world, split into factions. Crabclaw is the leader of one party, and the other is headed by Tapley; both are men of warm and impetuous tempers, and their intrigues have embroiled the whole place, insomuch that it was dangerous to walk the street on account of the continual skirmishes of their partisans. At length some of the more sedate inhabitants, having met and deliberated upon some remedy for these growing disorders, proposed that the dispute should be at once decided by single combat between the two chiefs, who readily agreed to the proposal. The match was accordingly made for five guineas, and this very day and hour appointed for the trial, on which considerable sums of money are depending. As for Mr. Norton, it is not proper that he should be present, or seem to countenance such violent proceedings, which, however, it is necessary to connive at, as convenient vents for the evaporation of those humours which, being confined, might accumulate and break out with greater fury in conspiracy and rebellion."

The knight owned he could not conceive by what means such a number of licentious people, amounting, with their dependants, to above five hundred, were restrained within the bounds of any tolerable discipline, or prevented from making their escape, which they might at any time accomplish, either by stealth or open violence, as it could not be supposed that one or two turnkeys, continually employed in opening and shutting the door, could resist the efforts of a whole multitude.

" Your wonder, good sir," said Mr. Felton, " will vanish when you consider it is hardly possible that the multitude should co-operate in the execution of such a scheme, and that the keeper perfectly well understands the maxim *divide et impera*. Many prisoners are restrained by the dictates of gratitude towards the deputy-marshal, whose friendship and good offices they have experienced ; some no doubt are actuated by motives of discretion. One party is an effectual check upon the other ; and I am firmly persuaded that there are not ten prisoners within the place that would make their escape if the doors were laid open. This is a step which no man would take, unless his fortune was altogether desperate, because it would oblige him to leave his country for life, and expose him to the most imminent risk of being retaken and treated with the utmost severity. The majority of the prisoners live in the most lively hope of being released by the assistance of their friends, the compassion of their creditors, or the favour of the legislature. Some who are cut off from all these proposals are become naturalised to the place, knowing they cannot subsist in any other situation. I myself am one of these. After having resigned all my effects for the benefit of my creditors, I have been detained these nine years in prison, because one person refuses to sign my certificate. I have long outlived all my friends from whom I could expect the least countenance or favour. I am grown old in confinement, and lay my account with ending my days in jail, as the mercy of the legislature in favour of insolvent debtors is never extended to uncertified bankrupts taken in execution. By dint of industry and the most rigid economy, I make shift to live independent in this retreat. To this scene my faculty of subsisting, as well as my body, is peculiarly confined. Had I an opportunity to escape, where should I go ? All my views of fortune have been long blasted. I have no friends nor connections in the world. I must, therefore, starve in some sequestered corner, or be recapti-vated and confined for ever to close prison, deprived of the indulgences which I now enjoy."

Here the conversation was broken off by another uproar, which was the signal to battle between the doctor and his antagonist. The company immediately adjourned to the field, where the combatants were already undressed, and the stakes deposited. The doctor seemed of the middle age and middle stature, active and alert, with an atrabilarious aspect, and a mixture of rage and disdain expressed in his counte-nance. The brewer was large, raw-boned, and round as a butt of beer, but very fat, unwieldy, short-winded, and phlegmatic. Our adventurer was not a little surprised when he beheld, in the character of seconds, a male and female stripped naked from the waist upwards, the latter ranging on the side of the physician ; but the commencement of the battle prevented his demanding of his guide an explanation of this phenomenon. The doctor retiring some paces back-wards, threw himself into the attitude of a battering-ram, and rushed upon his antagonist with great impetuosity, foreseeing that, should he have the good fortune to overturn him in the first assault, it would not be an easy task to raise

him up again, and put him in a capacity of offence. But
the momentum of Crabclaw's head, and the concomitant
efforts of his knuckles, had no effect upon the ribs of Tapley,
who stood firm as the Acroceraunian promontory; and
stepping forward with his projected fist, something smaller
and softer than a sledge-hammer, struck the phyiscian to
the ground.

In a trice, however, by the assistance of his female second,
he was on his legs again, and, grappling with his antagonist,
endeavoured to tip him a fall, but instead of accomplishing
his purpose, he received a cross-buttock, and the brewer
throwing himself upon him as he fell, had well-nigh smothered
him on the spot. The amazon flew to his assistance, and
Tapley showing no inclination to get up, she smote him on
the temple till he roared. The male second hastening to
the relief of his principal, made application to the eyes of
the female, which were immediately surrounded with black
circles, and she returned the salute with a blow which brought
a double stream of blood from his nostrils, greeting him at
the same time with the opprobrious appellation of a lousy
son of a b—h. A combat more furious than the first would
now have ensued, had not Felton interposed with an air of
authority, and insisted on the man's leaving the field, an
injunction which he forthwith obeyed, saying, " Well,
damme, Felton, you're my friend and commander; I'll
obey your order—but the b—h will be foul of me before
we sleep." Then Felton advancing to his opponent,
" Madam," said he, " I'm very sorry to see a lady of your
rank and qualifications expose yourself in this manner. For
God's sake behave with a little more decorum, if not for the
sake of your own family, at least for the credit of your sex in
general."—" Hark ye, Felton," said she, " decorum is
founded upon a delicacy of sentiment and deportment
which cannot consist with the disgraces of a jail and the
miseries of indigence. But I see the dispute is now terminated, and the money is to be drunk; if you'll dine with
us you shall be welcome; if not, you may die in your sobriety
and be d—ned."

By this time the doctor had given out, and allowed the brewer to be the better man ; yet he would not honour the festival with his presence, but retired to his chamber, exceedingly mortified at his defeat. Our hero was reconducted to Mr. Felton's apartment, where he sat some time without opening his mouth, so astonished he was at what he had seen and heard. " I perceive, sir," said the prisoner, "you are surprised at the manner in which I accosted that unhappy woman, and perhaps you will be more surprised when you hear that within these eighteen months she was actually a person of fashion, and her opponent, who, by the bye, is her husband, universally respected as a man of honour and a brave officer."—" I am, indeed," cried our hero, " overwhelmed with amazement and concern, as well as stimulated by an eager curiosity to know the fatal causes which have produced such a reverse of character and fortune. But I will rein my curiosity till the afternoon, if you will favour me with your company at a tavern in the neighbourhood, where I have bespoken dinner, a favour which I hope Mr. Norton will have no objection to your granting, as he himself is to be of the party." The prisoner thanked him for his kind invitation, and they adjourned immediately to the place, taking up the deputy-marshal in their passage through the lodge or entrance of the prison.

CHAPTER XXI

Containing further Anecdotes relating to the Children of Wretchedness.

DINNER being cheerfully discussed, and our adventurer expressing an eager desire to know the history of the male and female who had acted as squires or seconds to the champions of the King's Bench, Felton gratified his curiosity to this effect :

" All that I know of Captain Clewline, previous to his commitment, is, that he was a commander of a sloop of war, and bore the reputation of a gallant officer ; that he married the daughter of a rich merchant in the city of London, against the inclination and without the knowledge of her father, who renounced her for this act of disobedience ; that the captain consoled himself for the rigour of the parent with the possession of the lady, who was not only remarkably beautiful in person, but highly accomplished in her mind, and amiable in her disposition. Such, a few months ago, were those two persons whom you saw acting in such a vulgar capacity. When they first entered the prison they were undoubtedly the handsomest couple mine eyes ever beheld, and their appearance won universal respect even from the most brutal inhabitants of the jail.

" The captain, having unwarily involved himself as a security for a man to whom he had lain under obligations, became liable for a considerable sum, and his own father-in-law being the sole creditor of the bankrupt, took this opportunity of wreaking vengeance upon him for having espoused his daughter. He watched an opportunity until the captain had actually stepped into the post-chaise with his lady for Portsmouth, where his ship lay, and caused him to be arrested in the most public and shameful manner. Mrs. Clewline had like to have sunk under the first transports of her grief and mortification ; but these subsiding, she had recourse to personal solicitation. She went with her only child in her arms, a lovely boy, to her father's door, and, being denied admittance, kneeled down in the street, imploring his compassion in the most pathetic strain ; but this hard-hearted citizen, instead of recognising his child, and taking the poor mourner to his bosom, insulted her from the window with the most bitter reproach, saying, among other shocking expressions, ' Strumpet, take yourself away with your brat, otherwise I shall send for the beadle, and have you to Bridewell.'

" The unfortunate lady was cut to the heart by this usage, and fainted in the street, from whence she was conveyed to a public-house by the charity of some passengers. She afterwards attempted to soften the barbarity of her father by repeated letters, and by interesting some of his friends to intercede with him in her behalf; but all her endeavours proving ineffectual, she accompanied her husband to the prison of the King's Bench, where she must have felt, in the severest manner, the fatal reverse of circumstance to which she was exposed.

" The captain being disabled from going to sea was superseded, and he saw all his hopes blasted in the midst of an active war, at a time when he had the fairest prospects of fame and fortune. He saw himself reduced to extreme poverty, cooped up with the tender partner of his heart in a wretched hovel, amidst the refuse of mankind, and on the brink of wanting the common necessaries of life. The mind of man is ever ingenious in finding resources. He comforted his lady with vain hopes of having friends who would effect his deliverance, and repeated assurances of this kind so long, that he at length began to think they were not altogether void of foundation.

" Mrs. Clewline, from a principle of duty, recollected all her fortitude, that she might not only bear her fate with patience, but even contribute to alleviate the woes of her husband, whom her affection had ruined. She affected to believe the suggestions of his pretended hope; she interchanged with him assurances of better fortune; her appearance exhibited a calm, while her heart was torn with anguish. She assisted him in writing letters to former friends, the last consolation of the wretched prisoner; she delivered these letters with her own hand, and underwent a thousand mortifying repulses, the most shocking circumstances of which she concealed from her husband. She performed all the menial offices in her own little family, which was maintained by pawning her apparel; and both the husband and wife, in some measure, sweetened their cares by prattling and toying with their charming little boy, on whom they doted with an enthusiasm of fondness. Yet even this pleasure was mingled with the most tender and melancholy regret. I have seen the mother hang over him, with the most affecting expression of this kind in her aspect, the tears contending with the smiles upon her countenance, while she exclaimed, ' Alas ! my poor prisoner, little did your mother once think she should be obliged to nurse you in a jail.' The captain's paternal love was dashed with impatience; he would snatch up the boy in a transport of grief, press him to his breast, devour him as it were with kisses, throw up his eyes to heaven in the most emphatic silence, then convey the child hastily to his mother's arms, pull his hat over his eyes, stalk out into the common walk, and, finding himself alone, break out into tears and lamentation.

" Ah ! little did this unhappy couple know what further griefs awaited them ! The smallpox broke out in the prison, and poor Tommy Clewline was infected. As the eruption appeared unfavourable, you may conceive the consternation with which they were overwhelmed. Their distress was rendered inconceivable by indigence; for by this time they were so destitute, that they could neither pay for common attendance, nor procure proper advice. I did on that occasion what I thought my duty towards my fellow-creatures. I wrote to a physician of my acquaintance, who was humane enough to visit the poor little patient; I engaged a careful woman-prisoner as a nurse, and Mr. Norton supplied them with money and necessaries. These helps were barely sufficient to preserve them from the horrors of despair, when they saw their little darling panting under the rage of a loathsome pestilential malady, during the excessive heat of the dog-days, and struggling for breath in the noxious atmosphere of a confined cabin, where they scarce had room to turn on the most necessary occasions. The eager curiosity with which the mother eyed the doctor's looks as often as he visited the boy, the terror and trepidation of the father, while he desired to know his opinion; in a word, the whole tenor of their distress baffled all description.

" At length the physician, for the sake of his own character, was obliged to be explicit; and, returning with the captain to the common walk, told him, in my hearing, that the child could not possibly recover. This sentence seemed to have petrified the unfortunate parent, who stood motionless, and seemingly bereft of sense. I led him to my apart-

ment, where he sat a full hour in that state of stupefaction;
then he began to groan hideously, a shower of tears burst
from his eyes, he threw himself on the floor, and uttered
the most piteous lamentation that ever was heard. Meanwhile, Mrs. Norton being made acquainted with the doctor's
prognostic, visited Mrs. Clewline, and invited her to the
lodge. Her prophetic fears immediately took the alarm.
'What!' cried she, starting up with a frantic wildness
in her looks, 'then our case is desperate—I shall lose my dear
Tommy!—the poor prisoner will be released by the hand of
Heaven!—Death will convey him to the cold grave!' The
dying innocent hearing this exclamation, pronounced these
words, 'Tommy won't leave you, my dear mamma; if
death comes to take Tommy, papa shall drive him away with
his sword." This address deprived the wretched mother
of all resignation to the will of Providence. She tore her
hair, dashed herself on the pavement, shrieked aloud, and
was carried off in a deplorable state of distraction.

"That same evening the lovely babe expired, and the
father grew frantic. He made an attempt on his own life;
and, being with difficulty restrained, his agitation sank into
a kind of sullen insensibility, which seemed to absorb all
sentiment, and gradually vulgarised his faculty of thinking.
In order to dissipate the violence of his sorrow, he continually
shifted the scene from one company to another, contracted
abundance of low connections, and drowned his cares in
repeated intoxication. The unhappy lady underwent a
long series of hysterical fits and other complaints, which
seemed to have a fatal effect on her brain as well as constitution. Cordials were administered to keep up her spirits;
and she found it necessary to protract the use of them to
blunt the edge of grief, by overwhelming reflection, and
remove the sense of uneasiness arising from a disorder in her
stomach. In a word, she became an habitual dram-drinker;
and this practice exposed her to such communication as
debauched her reason, and perverted her sense of decorum
and propriety. She and her husband gave a loose to vulgar
excess, in which they were enabled to indulge by the charity

and interest of some friends, who obtained half-pay for the captain.

" They are now metamorphosed into the shocking creatures you have seen; he into a riotous plebeian, and she into a ragged trull. They are both drunk every day, quarrel and fight one with another, and often insult their fellow-prisoners. Yet they are not wholly abandoned by virtue and humanity. The captain is scrupulously honest in all his dealings, and pays off his debts punctually every quarter, as soon as he receives his half-pay. Every prisoner in distress is welcome to share his money while it lasts; and his wife never fails, while it is in her power, to relieve the wretched; so that their generosity, even in this miserable disguise, is universally respected by their neighbours. Sometimes the recollection of their former rank comes over them like a qualm, which they dispel with brandy, and then humorously rally one another on their mutual degeneracy. She often stops me in the walk, and, pointing to the captain, says, ' My husband, though he is become a blackguard jail-bird, must be allowed to be a handsome fellow still.'—On the other hand, he will frequently desire me to take notice of his rib, as she chances to pass.—' Mind that draggle-tailed drunken drab,' he will say; ' what an antidote it is—yet, for all that, Felton, she was a fine woman when I married her. Poor Bess, I have been the ruin of her, that is certain, and deserve to be d—ned for bringing her to this pass.'

" Thus they accommodate themselves to each other's infirmities, and pass their time not without some taste of plebeian enjoyment—but, name their child, they never fail to burst into tears, and still feel a return of the most poignant sorrow."

Sir Launcelot Greaves did not hear this story unmoved. Tom Clarke's cheeks were bedewed with the drops of sympathy, while, with much sobbing, he declared his opinion, that an action should lie against the lady's father.

Captain Crowe having listened to the story with uncommon attention, expressed his concern that an honest seaman should be so taken in stays; but he imputed all his calamities to the wife. " For why ? " said he; " a seafaring man may have a sweetheart in every port ; but he should steer clear of a wife, as he would avoid a quicksand. —You see, brother, how this here Clewline lags astern in the wake of a snivelling b—h ; otherwise he would never make a weft in his ensign for the loss of a child—odds heart ! he could have done no more if he had sprung a top-mast, or started a timber."

The knight declaring that he would take another view of the prison in the afternoon, Mr. Felton insisted upon his doing him the honour to drink a dish of tea in his apartment, and Sir Launcelot accepted his invitation. Thither they accordingly repaired, after having made another circuit of the jail, and the tea-things were produced by Mrs. Felton, when she was summoned to the door, and in a few minutes returning, communicated something in a whisper to her husband. He changed colour and repaired to the staircase, where he was heard to talk aloud in an angry tone.

When he came back, he told the company he had been teased by a very importunate beggar. Addressing himself to our adventurer, " You took notice," says he, " of a fine lady flaunting about our walk in all the frippery of the fashion. She was lately a gay young widow that made a great figure at the court-end of the town ; she distinguished herself by her splendid equipage, her rich liveries, her brilliant assemblies, her numerous routs, and her elegant taste in dress and furniture. She is nearly related to some of the best families in England, and, it must be owned, mistress of many fine accomplishments. But being deficient in true delicacy, she endeavoured to hide that defect by affectation. She pretended to a thousand antipathies which did not belong to her nature. A breast of veal threw her into mortal agonies ; if she saw a spider, she screamed ; and at sight of a mouse she fainted away. She could not, without horror, behold an entire joint of meat, and nothing but fricassees and other made dishes were seen upon her table. She caused all her floors to be lined with green

baize, that she might trip along them with more ease and
pleasure. Her footmen wore clogs, which were deposited
in the hall, and both they and her chairmen were laid under
the strongest injunctions to avoid porter and tobacco. Her
jointure amounted to eight hundred pounds per annum,
and she made shift to spend four times that sum. At length
it was mortgaged for nearly the entire value; but, far from
retrenching, she seemed to increase in extravagance, until
her effects were taken in execution, and her person here
deposited in safe custody.

" When one considers the abrupt transition she underwent
from her spacious apartments to a hovel scarce eight feet
square, from sumptuous furniture to bare benches, from
magnificence to meanness, from affluence to extreme poverty,
one would imagine she must have been totally overwhelmed
by such a sudden gush of misery. But this was not the
case. She has, in fact, no delicate feelings. She forthwith
accommodated herself to the exigency of her fortune; yet
she still affects to keep state amidst the miseries of a jail,
and this affectation is truly ridiculous. She lies a-bed till
two o'clock in the afternoon. She maintains a female
attendant for the sole purpose of dressing her person. Her
cabin is the least cleanly in the whole prison; she has learned
to eat bread and cheese and drink porter, but she always
appears once a day dressed in the pink of the fashion. She
has found means to run in debt at the chandler's shop, the
baker's, and the tap-house, though there is nothing got in
this place but with ready money. She has even borrowed
small sums from divers prisoners, who were themselves on
the brink of starving. She takes pleasure in being surrounded
with duns, observing, that by such people a person of fashion
is to be distinguished. She writes circular letters to her
former friends and acquaintance, and by this method has
raised pretty considerable contributions; for she writes in
a most elegant and irresistible style. About a fortnight ago
she received a supply of twenty guineas; when, instead of
paying her little jail-debts, or withdrawing any part of her
apparel from pawn, she laid out the whole sum in a fashion-

able suit and laces, and next day borrowed of me a shilling to purchase a neck of mutton for her dinner. She seems to think her rank in life entitles her to this kind of assistance. She talks very pompously of her family and connections, by whom however she has been long renounced. She has no sympathy nor compassion for the distresses of her fellow-creatures, but she is perfectly well-bred; she bears a repulse the best of any woman I ever knew, and her temper has never been once ruffled since her arrival at the King's Bench. She now entreated me to lend her half a guinea, for which she said she had the most pressing occasion, and promised upon her honour it should be repaid to-morrow; but I lent a deaf ear to her request, and told her in plain terms that her honour was already bankrupt."

Sir Launcelot, thrusting his hand mechanically into his pocket, pulled out a couple of guineas, and desired Felton to accommodate her with that trifle in his own name; but he declined the proposal, and refused to touch the money. "God forbid," said he, "that I should attempt to thwart your charitable intention; but this, my good sir, is no object —she has many resources. Neither should we number the clamorous beggar among those who really feel distress; he is generally gorged with bounty misapplied. The liberal hand of charity should be extended to modest want that pines in silence, encountering cold, nakedness, and hunger, and every species of distress. Here you may find the wretch of keen sensations blasted by accident in the blossom of his fortune, shivering in the solitary recess of indigence, dis-daining to beg, and even ashamed to let his misery be known Here you may see the parent who has known happier times, surrounded by his tender offspring, naked and forlorn, demanding food, which his circumstances cannot afford

"That man of decent appearance and melancholy aspect, who lifted his hat as you passed him in the yard, is a person of unblemished character. He was a reputable tradesman in the city, and failed through inevitable losses. A com-mission of bankruptcy was taken out against him by his sole creditor, a Quaker, who refused to sign his certificate. He has lived three years in prison, with a wife and five small children. In a little time after his commitment, he had friends who offered to pay ten shillings in the pound of what he owed, and to give security for paying the remainder in three years by instalments. The honest Quaker did not charge the bankrupt with any dishonest practices, but he rejected the proposal with the most mortifying indifference, declaring that he did not want his money. The mother repaired to his house, and, kneeling before him with her five lovely children, implored mercy with tears and exclamations. He stood this scene unmoved, and even seemed to enjoy the prospect, wearing the looks of complacency, while his heart was steeled with rancour. 'Woman,' said he, 'these be hopeful babes, if they were duly nurtured. Go thy ways in peace; I have taken my resolution.' Her friends maintained the family for some time, but it is not in human charity to persevere; some of them died, some of them grew unfortunate, some of them fell off, and now the poor man is reduced to the extremity of indigence, from whence he has no prospect of being retrieved. The fourth part of what you would have bestowed upon the lady would make this poor man and his family sing with joy."

He had scarce pronounced these words, when our hero desired the man might be called, and in a few minutes he entered the apartment with a low obeisance. "Mr. Coleby," said the knight, "I have heard how cruelly you have been used by your creditor, and beg you will accept this trifling present, if it can be of any service to you in your distress." So saying, he put five guineas into his hand. The poor man was so confounded at such an unlooked-for acquisition, that he stood motionless and silent, unable to thank the donor, and Mr. Felton conveyed him to the door, observing that his heart was too full for utterance. But in a little time his wife, bursting into the room with her five children, looked around, and going up to Sir Launcelot without any direction, exclaimed, "This is the angel sent by Providence to succour me and my poor innocents." Then falling at his feet, she pressed his hand and bathed it with her tears. He raised her up with that complacency which was natural to his disposition. He kissed all her children, who were remarkably handsome and neatly kept, though in homely apparel ; and, giving her his direction, assured her she might always apply to him in her distress.

After her departure he produced a bank-note of twenty pounds, and would have deposited it in the hands of Mr. Felton, to be distributed in charities among the objects of the place ; but he desired it might be left with Mr. Norton, who was the proper person for managing his benevolence, and he promised to assist the deputy with his advice in laying it out.

CHAPTER XXII

In which Captain Crowe is sublimed into the Regions of Astrology.

THREE whole days had our adventurer prosecuted his inquiry about the amiable Aurelia, whom he sought in every place of public and of private entertainment or resort, without obtaining the least satisfactory intelligence, when he received one evening, from the hands of a porter, who instantly vanished, the following billet :

" If you would learn the particulars of Miss Darnel's fate, fail not to be in the fields by the Foundling Hospital, precisely at seven o'clock this evening, when you shall be met by a person who will give you the satisfaction you desire, together with his reason for addressing you in this mysterious manner."

Had this intimation concerned any other subject, perhaps the knight would have deliberated with himself in what manner he should take a hint so darkly communicated. But his eagerness to retrieve the jewel he had lost divested him of all his caution ; the time of assignation was already at hand, and neither the captain nor his nephew could be found to accompany him, had he been disposed to make use of their attendance. He therefore, after a moment's hesitation, repaired to the place appointed, in the utmost agitation and anxiety, lest the hour should be elapsed before his arrival.

Crowe was one of those defective spirits who cannot subsist for any length of time on their own bottoms. He wanted a familiar prop, upon which he could disburden his cares, his doubts, and his humours; a humble friend who would endure his caprices, and with whom he could communicate, free of all reserve and restraint. Though he loved his nephew's person, and admired his parts, he considered him often as a little petulant jackanapes, who presumed upon his superior understanding; and as for Sir Launcelot, there was something in his character that overawed the seaman, and kept him at a disagreeable distance. He had, in this dilemma, cast his eyes upon Timothy Crabshaw, and admitted him to a considerable share of familiarity and fellowship. These companions had been employed in smoking a social pipe at an alehouse in the neighbourhood, when the knight made his excursion; and returning to the house about supper-time, found Mr. Clarke in waiting.

The young lawyer was alarmed when he heard the hour of ten without seeing our adventurer, who had been used to be extremely regular in his economy, and the captain and he supped in profound silence. Finding, upon inquiry among the servants, that the knight went out abruptly, in consequence of having received a billet, Tom began to be visited with the apprehension of a duel, and sat the best part of the night by his uncle, sweating with the expectation of seeing our hero brought home a breathless corpse. But no tidings of him arriving, he, about two in the morning, repaired to his own lodging, resolved to publish a description of Sir Launcelot in the newspapers if he should not appear next day.

Crowe did not pass the time without uneasiness. He was extremely concerned at the thought of some mischief having befallen his friend and patron, and he was terrified with the apprehensions that, in case Sir Launcelot was murdered, his spirit might come and give him notice of his fate. Now he had an insuperable aversion to all correspondence with the dead, and taking it for granted that the spirit of his departed friend could not appear to him except when he should be alone, and a-bed in the dark, he determined to pass the remainder of the night without going to bed. For this purpose, his first care was to visit the garret, in which Timothy Crabshaw lay fast asleep, snoring with his mouth wide open. Him the captain with difficulty roused, by dint of promising to regale him with a bowl of rum punch in the kitchen, where the fire, which had been extinguished, was soon rekindled. The ingredients were fetched from a public-house in the neighbourhood, for the captain was too proud to use his interest in the knight's family, especially at these hours, when all the rest of the servants had retired to their repose, and he and Timothy drank together until daybreak, the conversation turning upon hobgoblins, and God's revenge against murder.

The cookmaid lay in a little apartment contiguous to the kitchen, and whether disturbed by these horrible tales of apparitions, or titillated by the savoury steams that issued from the punch-bowl, she made a virtue of necessity, or appetite, and dressing herself in the dark, suddenly appeared before them, to the no small perturbation of both. Timothy, in particular, was so startled that, in his endeavours to make a hasty retreat towards the chimney-corner, he overturned the table ; the liquor was spilt, but the bowl was saved by falling on a heap of ashes. Mrs. Cook having reprimanded him for his foolish fear, declared she had got up betimes in order to scour her saucepans, and the captain proposed to have the bowl replenished if materials could be procured. This difficulty was overcome by Crabshaw, and they sat down with their new associate to discuss the second edition.

The knight's sudden disappearing being brought upon the carpet, their female companion gave it as her opinion that nothing would be so likely to bring this affair to light as going to a cunning man, whom she had lately consulted about a silver spoon that was mislaid, and who told her all the things that she ever did, and ever would happen to her through the whole course of her life.

Her two companions pricked up their ears at this intelligence, and Crowe asked if the spoon had been found. She answered in the affirmative, and said the cunning man described to a hair the person that should be her true lover and her wedded husband; that he was a seafaring man; that he was pretty well stricken in years—a little passionate or so; and that he went with his fingers clinched like, as it were. The captain began to sweat at this description, and mechanically thrust his hands into his pockets, while Crabshaw, pointing to him, told her he believed she had got the right sow by the ear. Crowe grumbled, that mayhap for all that he should not be brought up by such a grappling neither. Then he asked if this cunning man dealt with the devil, declaring, in that case, he would keep clear of him; for why? because he must have sold himself to Old Scratch, and being a servant of the devil, how could he be a good subject to his majesty? Mrs. Cook assured him the conjurer was a good Christian, and that he gained all his knowledge by conversing with the stars and planets. Thus satisfied, the two friends resolved to consult him as soon as it should be light, and being directed to the place of his habitation, set out for it by seven in the morning.

They found the house forsaken, and had already reached the end of the lane in their return, when they were accosted by an old woman, who gave them to understand that if they had occasion for the advice of a fortune-teller, as she did suppose they had, from their stopping at the house where Dr. Grubble lived, she would conduct them to a person of much more eminence in that profession; at the same time she informed them that the said Grubble had been lately sent to Bridewell, a circumstance which, with all his art, he had not been able to foresee. The captain, without any scruple, put himself and his companion under convoy of this beldam, who, through many winding sand turnings, brought them to the door of a ruinous house, standing in a blind alley; which door having opened with a key drawn from her pocket, she introduced them into a parlour, where they saw no other furniture than a naked bench, and some frightful figures on the bare walls, drawn or rather scrawled with charcoal.

Here she left them locked in, until she should give the doctor notice of their arrival, and they amused themselves with deciphering these characters and hieroglyphics. The first figure that engaged their attention was that of a man hanging upon a gibbet, which both considered as an unfavourable omen, and each endeavoured to avert from his own person. Crabshaw observed that the figure so suspended was clothed in a sailor's jacket and trousers—a truth which the captain could not deny; but, on the other hand, he affirmed that the said figure exhibited the very nose and chin of Timothy, together with the hump on one shoulder. A warm dispute ensued, and being maintained with much acrimonious altercation, might have dissolved the new-cemented friendship of those two originals, had it not been interrupted by the old sibyl, who, coming into the parlour, intimated that the doctor waited for them above. She likewise told them that he never admitted more than one at a time. This hint occasioned a fresh contest. The captain insisted upon Crabshaw's making sail a-head, in order to look out afore; but Timothy persisted in refusing this honour, declaring he did not pretend to lead, but he would follow, as in duty bound. The old gentlewoman abridged the ceremony by leading out Crabshaw with one hand and locking up Crowe with the other.

The former was dragged upstairs like a bear to the stake, not without reluctance and terror, which did not at all abate at sight of the conjurer, with whom he was immediately shut up by his conductress, after she had told him in a whisper that he must deposit a shilling in a little black coffin, supported by a human skull and thigh-bones crossed, on a stool covered with black baize, that stood in one corner of the apartment. The squire, having made this offer with fear and trembling, ventured to survey the objects around him, which were very well calculated to augment his confusion. He saw divers skeletons hung by the head, the stuffed skin of a young alligator, a calf with two heads, and several snakes suspended from the ceiling, with the jaws of a shark, and a starved weasel. On another funeral table he beheld two spheres, between which lay a book open, exhibiting outlandish characters and mathematical diagrams. On one side stood an ink-standish with paper, and behind this desk appeared the conjurer himself, in sable vestments, his head so overshadowed with hair that, far from contemplating his features, Timothy could distinguish nothing but a long white beard, which, for aught he knew, might have belonged to a four-legged goat, as well as to a two-legged astrologer.

This apparition, which the squire did not eye without manifest discomposure, extending a white wand, made certain evolutions over the head of Timothy, and having muttered an ejaculation, commanded him, in a hollow tone, to come forward and declare his name. Crabshaw, thus adjured, advanced to the altar, and, whether from design or (which is more probable) from confusion, answered, "Samuel Crowe." The conjurer, taking up the pen, and making a few scratches on the paper, exclaimed in a terrific accent, "How! miscreant! attempt to impose upon the stars? You look more like a *crab* than a *crow*, and was born under the sign of Cancer." The squire, almost annihilated by this exclamation, fell upon his knees, crying, " I pray yaw, my lord conjurer's worship, pardon my ignorance, and down't go to baind me over to the Red Sea like—I'se a poor Yorkshire tyke, and would no more cheat the stars than I'd cheat my own vather, as the saying is—a must be a good hand at *trapping*, that catches the stars a *napping*—but as your honour's worship observed, my name is Tim Crabshaw, of the East Raiding, groom and squair to Sir Launcelot Greaves, baron, knaight, and arrant-knaight, who ran mad for a wench, as your worship's conjuration well knoweth. The person below is Captain Crowe, and we coom by Margery Cook's recommendation, to seek after my master, who is gone away, or made away, the Lord He knows how and where."

Here he was interrupted by the conjurer, who exhorted him to sit down and compose himself till he should cast a figure; then he scrawled the paper, and waving his wand, repeated abundance of gibberish concerning the number, the names, the houses, and revolutions of the planets, with their conjunctions, oppositions, signs, circles, cycles, trines, and trigons. When he perceived that this artifice had its proper effect in disturbing the brain of Crabshaw, he proceeded to tell him from the stars, that his name was Crabshaw, or Crabsclaw; that he was born in the East Riding of Yorkshire, of poor, yet honest parents, and had some skill in horses; and that he served a gentleman whose name began with the letter G—, which gentleman had run mad for love, and left his family; but whether he would return alive or dead, the stars had not yet determined.

Poor Timothy was thunderstruck to find the conjurer acquainted with all these circumstances, and begged to know if he might be so bauld as to ax a question or two about his own fortune. The astrologer pointing to the little coffin, our squire understood the hint, and deposited another shilling. The sage had recourse to his book, erected another scheme, performed once more his airy evolutions with the wand, and having recited another mystical preamble, expounded the book of fate in these words : " You shall neither die by war nor water, by hunger or by thirst, nor be brought to the grave by old age or distemper; but, let me see—ay, the stars will have it so—you shall be—exalted—hah !—ay, that is—hanged for horse-stealing."—" Oh, good my lord conjurer ! " roared the squire, " I'd as lief give forty shillings as be hanged."—" Peace, sirrah ! " cried the other ; " would you contradict or reverse the immutable decrees of fate ? Hanging is your destiny, and hanged you shall be—and comfort yourself with the reflection, that as you are not the first, so neither will you be the last to swing on Tyburn tree." This comfortable assurance composed the mind of Timothy, and in a great measure reconciled him to the prediction. He now proceeded in a whining tone to ask whether he should suffer for the first fact; whether it would be for a horse or a mare, and of what colour, that he might know when his hour was come. The conjurer gravely answered,

that he would steal a dappled gelding on a Wednesday,
be cast at the Old Bailey on Thursday, and suffer on a
Friday; and he strenuously recommended it to him to
appear in the cart with a nosegay in one hand, and *The Whole
Duty of Man* in the other. " But if in case it should be in
the winter," said the squire, " when a nosegay can't be had ? "
—" Why, then," replied the conjurer, " an orange will do
as well."

These material points being adjusted to the entire satisfaction of Timothy, he declared he would bestow another
shilling to know the fortune of an old companion, who truly
did not deserve so much at his hands, but he could not help
loving him better than e'er a friend he had in the world.
So saying, he dropped a third offering in the coffin, and
desired to know the fate of his horse Gilbert. The astrologer
having again consulted his art, pronounced that Gilbert
would die of the staggers, and his carcass be given to the
hounds; a sentence which made a much deeper impression
upon Crabshaw's mind, than did the prediction of his own
untimely and disgraceful fate. He shed a plenteous shower
of tears, and his grief broke forth in some passionate expressions of tenderness. At length he told the astrologer he
would go and send up the captain, who wanted to consult
him about Margery Cook, because as how she had informed
him that Dr. Grubble had described just such another man
as the captain for her true love; and he had no great stomach
to the match, if so be as the stars were not bent upon their
coming together.

Accordingly the squire, being dismissed by the conjurer,
descended to the parlour with a rueful length of face, which
being perceived by the captain, he demanded, " What
cheer, ho ? " with some signs of apprehension. Crabshaw
making no return to this salute, he asked if the conjurer
had taken an observation, and told him anything. Then
the other replied, he had told him more than he desired to
know. " Why, an that be the case," said the seaman, " I
have no occasion to go aloft this trip, brother."

This evasion would not serve his turn. Old Tisiphone was

at hand, and led him up growling into the hall of audience, which he did not examine without trepidation. Having been directed to the coffin, where he presented half a crown, in hope of rendering the fates more propitious, the usual ceremony was performed, and the doctor addressed him in these words: " Approach, Raven." The captain advancing, " You an't much mistaken, brother," said he, " heave your eye into the binnacle, and box your compass, you'll find I'm a Crowe, not a Raven, thof indeed they be both fowls of a feather, as the saying is."—" I know it," cried the conjurer, " thou art a northern crow—a sea-crow; not a crow of prey, but a crow to be preyed upon—a crow to be plucked—to be flayed—to be basted—to be broiled by Margery upon the gridiron of matrimony." The novice changing colour at this denunciation, " I do understand your signals, brother," said he, " and if it be set down in the log-book of fate that we must grapple, why then 'ware timbers. But as I know how the land lies, d'ye see, and the current of my inclination sets me off, I shall haul up close to the wind, and mayhap we shall clear Cape Margery. But howsomever, we shall leave that reef in the fore top-sail. —I was bound upon another voyage, d'ye see—to look and to see, and to know if so be as how I could pick up any intelligence along shore concerning my friend Sir Launcelot, who slipped his cable last night, and has lost company, d'ye see."

"What!" exclaimed the cunning man; " art thou a crow, and canst not smell carrion? If thou wouldst grieve for Greaves, behold his naked carcass lies unburied, to feed the kites, the crows, the gulls, the rooks, the ravens." —" What! broach'd to?"—" Dead as a boil'd lobster."— " Odd's heart, friend, these are the heaviest tidings I have heard these seven long years—there must have been deadly odds when he lowered his top-sails—smite my eyes! I had rather the *Mufti* had foundered at sea, with myself and all my generation on board—well fare thy soul, flower of the world! had honest Sam Crowe been within hail—but what signifies palavering?" Here the tears of unaffected

sorrow flowed plentifully down the furrows of the seaman's
cheeks ; then his grief giving way to his indignation, " Hark
ye, brother conjurer," said he, " you can spy foul weather
before it comes, d—n your eyes ! why did not you give us
warning of this here squall ? B—st my limbs ! I'll make
you give an account of this here d—ned, horrid, confounded,
murder, d'ye see—mayhap you yourself was concerned,
d'ye see.—For my own part, brother, I put my trust in
God, and steer by the compass, and I value not your paw-
wawing and your conjuration of a rope's end, d'ye see."

The conjurer was by no means pleased, either with the
matter or the manner of this address. He therefore began
to soothe the captain's choler, by representing that he did
not pretend to omniscience, which was the attribute of God
alone ; that human art was fallible and imperfect ; and all
that it could perform was to discover certain partial circumstances of any particular object to which its inquiries were
directed. That being questioned by the other man concerning the cause of his master's disappearing, he had
exercised his skill upon the subject, and found reason to
believe that Sir Launcelot was assassinated ; that he should
think himself happy in being the instrument of bringing
the murderers to justice, though he foresaw they would of
themselves save him that trouble ; for they would quarrel
about dividing the spoil, and one would give information
against the other.

The prospect of this satisfaction appeased the resentment,
and, in some measure, mitigated the grief of Captain Crowe,
who took his leave without much ceremony ; and, being
joined by Crabshaw, proceeded with a heavy heart to the
house of Sir Launcelot, where they found the domestics at
breakfast, without exhibiting the least symptom of concern
for their absent master. Crowe had been wise enough to
conceal from Crabshaw what he had learned of the knight's
fate. This fatal intelligence he reserved for the ear of his
nephew, Mr. Clarke, who did not fail to attend him in the
forenoon.

As for the squire, he did nothing but ruminate in rueful

silence upon the dappled gelding, the nosegay, and the predicted fate of Gilbert. Him he forthwith visited in the stable, and saluted with the kiss of peace. Then he bemoaned his fortune with tears, and by the sound of his own lamentation was lulled asleep among the litter.

CHAPTER XXIII

In which the Clouds that cover the Catastrophe begin to disperse.

WE must now leave Captain Crowe and his nephew Mr. Clarke arguing with great vehemence about the fatal intelligence obtained from the conjurer, and penetrate at once the veil that concealed our hero. Know then, reader, that Sir Launcelot Greaves, repairing to the place described in the billet which he had received, was accosted by a person muffled in a cloak, who began to amuse him with a feigned story of Aurelia, to which, while he listened with great attention, he found himself suddenly surrounded by armed men, who seized and pinioned down his arms, took away his sword, and conveyed him by force into a hackney-coach provided for the purpose. In vain he expostulated on this violence with three persons who accompanied him in the vehicle. He could not extort one word by way of reply ; and, from their gloomy aspects, he began to be apprehensive of assassination. Had the carriage passed through any frequented place, he would have endeavoured to alarm the inhabitants, but it was already clear of the town, and his conductors took care to avoid all villages and inhabited houses.

After having travelled about two miles, the coach stopped at a large iron gate, which being opened, our adventurer was led in silence through a spacious house into a tolerably decent apartment, which he understood was intended for his bed-chamber. In a few minutes after his arrival he was visited by a man of no very prepossessing appearance, who endeavouring to smooth his countenance, which was naturally stern, welcomed our adventurer to his house; exhorted him to be of good cheer, assuring him he should want for nothing, and desired to know what he would choose for supper.

Sir Launcelot, in answer to this civil address, begged he would explain the nature of his confinement, and the reasons for which his arms were tied like those of the worst malefactor. The other postponed till to-morrow the explanation he demanded, but in the meantime unbound his fetters, and, as he declined eating, left him alone to his repose. He took care, however, in retiring, to double lock the door of the room, whose windows were grated on the outside with iron.

The knight, being thus abandoned to his own meditations, began to ruminate on the present adventure with equal surprise and concern; but the more he revolved circumstances, the more was he perplexed in his conjectures. According to the state of the mind, a very subtle philosopher is often puzzled by a very plain proposition; and this was the case of our adventurer.—What made the strongest impression upon his mind was a notion that he was apprehended on suspicion of treasonable practices, by a warrant from the Secretary of State, in consequence of some false malicious information; and that his prison was no other than the house of a messenger, set apart for the accommodation of suspected persons. In this opinion he comforted himself by recollecting his own conscious innocence, and reflecting that he should be entitled to the privilege of *habeas corpus*, as the act including that inestimable jewel was happily not suspended at this time.

Consoled by this self-assurance, he quietly resigned himself to slumber; but before he fell asleep, he was very disagreeably undeceived in his conjecture. His ears were all at once saluted with a noise from the next room, conveyed in distinct bounces against the wainscot; then a hoarse voice exclaimed, " Bring up the artillery—let Brutandorf's brigade advance—detach my black hussars to ravage the country—let them be new booted—take particular care of the spur-leathers—make a desert of Lusatia—bombard the suburbs of Pera—go, tell my brother Henry to pass the Elbe at Meissen with forty battalions and fifty squadrons—so ho, you Major-General Donder, why don't you finish your second parallel ?—send hither the engineer Shittenback —I'll lay all the shoes in my shop, the breach will be practicable in four-and-twenty hours—don't tell me of your works ; you and your works be d—n'd."

" Assuredly," cried another voice from a different quarter, " he that thinks to be saved by works is in a state of utter reprobation—I myself was a profane weaver, and trusted to the rottenness of works—I kept my journeymen and 'prentices at constant work, and my heart was set upon the riches of this world, which was a wicked work—but now I have got a glimpse of the new light—I feel the operations of grace—I am of the new birth—I abhor good works—I detest all working but the working of the Spirit—avaunt, Satan—Oh ! how I thirst for communication with our sister Jolly."

" The communication is already open with the Marche," said the first, " but as for thee, thou caitiff, who hast presumed to disparage my works, I'll have thee rammed into a mortar with a double charge of powder, and thrown into the enemy's quarters."

This dialogue operated like a train upon many other inhabitants of the place ; one swore he was within three vibrations of finding the longitude, when this noise confounded his calculation ; a second, in broken English, complained he vas distorped in the moment of de proshection ; a third, in the character of His Holiness, denounced interdiction, excommunication, and anathemas ; and swore by St. Peter's keys, they should howl ten thousand years in purgatory, without the benefit of a single mass. A fourth began to halloo in all the vociferation of a fox-hunter in the chase, and in an instant the whole house was in an uproar.

The clamour, however, was of a short duration. The different chambers being opened successively, every individual was effectually silenced by the sound of one cabalistical word, which was no other than *Waistcoat*. A charm which at once cowed the King of P——, dispossessed the fanatic, dumbfounded the mathematician, dismayed the alchemist, deposed the Pope, and deprived the squire of all utterance.

Our adventurer was no longer in doubt concerning the place to which he had been conveyed ; and the more he reflected on his situation, the more he was overwhelmed with the most perplexing chagrin. He could not conceive by whose means he had been immured in a madhouse ; but he heartily repented of his knight-errantry, as a frolic which might have very serious consequences, with respect to his future life and fortune. After mature deliberation, he resolved to demean himself with the utmost circumspection, well knowing that every violent transport would be interpreted into an undeniable symptom of insanity. He was not without hope of being able to move his jailer by a due administration of that which is generally more efficacious than all the flowers of elocution ; but when he rose in the morning, he found his pockets had been carefully examined, and emptied of all his papers and cash.

The keeper entering, he inquired about these particulars, and was given to understand, that they were all safely deposited for his use, to be forthcoming at a proper season. But, at present, as he should want nothing, he had no occasion for money. The knight acquiesced in this declaration, and ate his breakfast in quiet.

About eleven, he received a visit from the physician, who contemplated his looks with great solemnity ; and having examined his pulse, shook his head, saying, " Well, sir, how d'ye do ?—come, don't be dejected—everything is for the best—you are in very good hands, sir, I assure you ; and I dare say will refuse nothing that may be thought conducive to the recovery of your health."

" Doctor," said our hero, " if it is not an improper question to ask, I should be glad to know your opinion of my disorder."—" Oh ! sir, as to that," replied the physician, " your disorder is a—kind of a—sir, 'tis very common in this country—a sort of a——"—" Do you think my distemper is madness, doctor ? "—" Oh Lord, sir—not absolute madness—no—not madness—you have heard, no doubt, of what is called a weakness of the nerves, sir—though that is a very inaccurate expression ; for this phrase, denoting a morbid excess of sensation, seems to imply that sensation itself is owing to the loose cohesion of those material particles which constitute the nervous substance, inasmuch as the quantity of every effect must be proportionable to its cause ; now you'll please to take notice, sir, if the case were really what these words seem to import, all bodies, whose particles do not cohere with too great a degree of proximity, would be nervous ; that is, endued with sensation. Sir, I shall order some cooling things to keep you in due temperature ; and you'll do very well—sir, your humble servant."

So saying, he retired, and our adventurer could not but think it was very hard that one man should not dare to ask the most ordinary question without being reputed mad, while another should talk nonsense by the hour, and yet be esteemed as an oracle.

The master of the house finding Sir Launcelot so tame and tractable, indulged him after dinner with a walk in a little private garden, under the eye of a servant, who followed him at a distance. Here he was saluted by a brother-prisoner, a man seemingly turned of thirty, tall and thin, with staring eyes, a hook-nose, and a face covered with pimples.

The usual compliments having passed, the stranger, without further ceremony, asked him if he would oblige him with a chew of tobacco, or could spare him a mouthful of any sort of cordial, declaring he had not tasted brandy since he came to the house. The knight assured him it was not in his power to comply with his request ; and began to ask some questions relating to the character of their landlord, which the stranger represented in very unfavourable colours. He described him as a ruffian, capable of undertaking the darkest scenes of villainy. He said his house was a repository of the most flagrant iniquities. That it contained fathers kidnapped by their children, wives confined by their husbands, gentlemen of fortune sequestered by their relations, and innocent persons immured by the malice of their adversaries. He affirmed this was his own case ; and asked if our hero had never heard of Dick Distich, the poet and satirist. " Ben Bullock and I," said he, " were confident against the world in arms—did you never see his ode to me beginning with ' Fair blooming youth ' ? We were sworn brothers, admired and praised, and quoted each other, sir. We denounced war against all the world, actors, authors, and critics ; and having drawn the sword, threw away the scabbard—we pushed through thick and thin, hacked and hewed helter skelter, and became as formidable to the writers of the age as the Bœotian band of Thebes. My friend Bullock, indeed, was once rolled in the kennel ; but soon

> He vig'rous rose, and from th' effluvia strong
> Imbib'd new life, and scour'd and stunk along.

Here is a satire, which I wrote in an alehouse when I was drunk—I can prove it by the evidence of the landlord and his wife ; I fancy you'll own I have some right to say with my friend Horace,

> Qui me commôrit, (melius non tangere clamo,)
> Flebit, et insignis tota cantabitur urbe."

The knight, having perused the papers, declared his opinion that the verses were tolerably good ; but at the same time observed that the author had reviled as ignorant dunces several persons who had written with reputation, and were generally allowed to have genius ; a circumstance that would detract more from his candour than could be allowed to his capacity.

" D—n their genius ! " cried the satirist, " a pack of impertinent rascals ! I tell you, sir, Ben Bullock and I had determined to crush all that were not of our own party. Besides, I said before, this piece was written in drink."— " Was you drunk too when it was printed and published ? "— " Yes, the printer shall make affidavit that I was never other- wise than drunk or maudlin, till my enemies, on pretence that my brain was turned, conveyed me to this infernal mansion——"

"They seem to have been your best friends," said the knight, "and have put the most tender interpretation on your conduct; for, waiving the plea of insanity, your character must stand as that of a man who hath some small share of genius, without an atom of integrity. Of all those whom Pope lashed in his Dunciad, there was not one who did not richly deserve the imputation of dulness, and every one of them had provoked the satirist by a personal attack. In this respect the English poet was much more honest than his French pattern Boileau, who stigmatised several men of acknowledged genius; such as Quinault, Perrault, and the celebrated Lulli; for which reason every man of a liberal turn must, in spite of all his poetical merit, despise him as a rancorous knave. If this disingenuous conduct cannot be forgiven in a writer of his superior genius, who will pardon it in you whose name is not half emerged from obscurity ? "

"Hark ye, friend," replied the bard, "keep your pardon and your counsel for those who ask it; or, if you will force them upon people, take one piece of advice in return. If you don't like your present situation, apply for a committee without delay. They'll find you too much of a fool to have the least tincture of madness ; and you'll be released without further scruple. In that case I shall rejoice in your deliverance ; you will be freed from confinement, and I shall be happily deprived of your conversation."

So saying, he flew off at a tangent, and our knight could not help smiling at the peculiar virulence of his disposition. Sir Launcelot then endeavoured to enter into conversation with his attendant, by asking how long Mr. Distich had resided in the house ; but he might as well have addressed himself to a Turkish mute. The fellow either pretended ignorance, or refused an answer to every question that was proposed. He would not even disclose the name of his landlord, nor inform him whereabouts the house was situated.

Finding himself agitated with impatience and indignation,

he returned to his apartment, and the door being locked upon him, began to review, not without horror, the particulars of his fate. " How little reason," said he to himself, " have we to boast of the blessings enjoyed by the British subject, if he holds them on such a precarious tenure ; if a man of rank and property may be thus kidnapped even in the midst of the capital ; if he may be seized by ruffians, insulted, robbed, and conveyed to such a prison as this, from which there seems to be no possibility of escape ! Should I be indulged with pen, ink, and paper, and appeal to my relations, or to the magistrates of my country, my letters would be intercepted by those who superintend my confinement. Should I try to alarm the neighbourhood, my cries would be neglected as those of some unhappy lunatic under necessary correction. Should I employ the force which Heaven has lent me, I might imbrue my hands in blood, and after all find it impossible to escape through a number of successive doors, locks, bolts, and sentinels. Should I endeavour to tamper with the servant, he might discover my design, and then I should be abridged of the little comfort I enjoy. People may inveigh against the Bastille in France, and the Inquisition in Portugal ; but I would ask, if either of these be in reality so dangerous or dreadful as a private madhouse in England, under the direction of a ruffian ? The Bastille is a state prison, the Inquisition is a spiritual tribunal ; but both are under the direction of Government. It seldom, if ever, happens that a man entirely innocent is confined in either ; or, if he should, he lays his account with a legal trial before established judges. But, in England, the most innocent person upon earth is liable to be immured for life under the pretext of lunacy, sequestered from his wife, children, and friends, robbed of his fortune, deprived even of necessaries, and subjected to the most brutal treatment from a low-bred barbarian, who raises an ample fortune on the misery of his fellow-creatures, and may, during his whole life, practise this horrid oppression, without question or control."

This uncomfortable reverie was interrupted by a very

unexpected sound that seemed to issue from the other side of a thick party-wall. It was a strain of vocal music, more plaintive than the widowed turtle's moan, more sweet and ravishing than Philomel's love-warbled song. Through his ear it instantly pierced into his heart, for at once he recognised it to be the voice of his adored Aurelia. Heavens! what was the agitation of his soul, when he made this discovery! how did every nerve quiver! how did his heart throb with the most violent emotion! he ran round the room in distraction, foaming like a lion in the toil—then he placed his ear close to the partition, and listened as if his whole soul was exerted in his sense of hearing. When the sound ceased to vibrate on his ear, he threw himself on the bed; he groaned with anguish, he exclaimed in broken accents, and in all probability his heart would have burst, had not the violence of his sorrow found vent in a flood of tears.

These first transports were succeeded by a fit of impatience, which had well-nigh deprived him of his senses in good earnest. His surprise at finding his lost Aurelia in such a place, the seeming impossibility of relieving her, and his unspeakable eagerness to contrive some scheme for profiting by the interesting discovery he had made, concurred in brewing up a second ecstasy, during which he acted a thousand extravagances, which it was well for him the attendants did not observe. Perhaps it was well for the servant that he did not enter while the paroxysm prevailed. Had this been the case, he might have met with the fate of Lichas, whom Hercules in his frenzy destroyed.

Before the cloth was laid for supper, he was calm enough to conceal the disorder of his mind. But he complained of the headache, and desired he might be next day visited by the physician, to whom he resolved to explain himself in such a manner, as should make an impression upon him, provided he was not altogether destitute of conscience and humanity.

CHAPTER XXIV

The Knot that puzzles human Wisdom, the hand of Fortune
sometimes will untie familiar as her Garter.

WHEN the doctor made his next appearance in Sir Launcelot's apartment, the knight addressed him in these words : " Sir, the practice of medicine is one of the most honourable professions exercised among the sons of men ; a profession which hath been revered at all periods, and in all nations, and even held sacred in the most polished ages of antiquity. The scope of it is to preserve the being, and confirm the health of our fellow-creatures ; of consequence, to sustain the blessings of society, and crown life with fruition. The character of a physician, therefore, not only supposes natural sagacity, and acquired erudition, but it also implies every delicacy of sentiment, every tenderness of nature, and every virtue of humanity. That these qualities are centred in you, doctor, I would willingly believe. But it will be sufficient for my purpose, that you are possessed of common integrity. To whose concern I am indebted for your visits, you best know. But if you understand the art of medicine, you must be sensible by this time, that, with respect to me, your prescriptions are altogether unnecessary.

" Come, sir, you cannot—you don't believe that my intellects are disordered. Yet, granting me to be really under the influence of that deplorable malady, no person has a right to treat me as a lunatic, or to sue out a commission, but my nearest kindred.—That you may not plead ignorance of my name and family, you shall understand that I am Sir Launcelot Greaves, of the county of York, Baronet ; and that my nearest relation is Sir Reginald Meadows, of Cheshire, the eldest son of my mother's sister—that gentleman, I am sure, had no concern in seducing me by false pretences under the clouds of night into the fields, where I was surprised, overpowered, and kidnapped by armed ruffians. Had he really believed me insane, he would have proceeded according to the dictates of honour, humanity, and the laws of his country. Situated as I am, I have a right, by making application to the Lord Chancellor, to be tried by a jury of honest men. But of that right I cannot avail myself, while I remain at the mercy of a brutal miscreant, in whose house I am enclosed, unless you contribute your assistance. Your assistance, therefore, I demand, as you are a gentleman, a Christian, and a fellow-subject, who, though every other motive should be overlooked, ought to interest himself in my case as a common concern, and concur with all your power towards the punishment of those who dare commit such outrages against the liberty of your country."

The doctor seemed to be a little disconcerted ; but, after some recollection, resumed his air of sufficiency and import-ance, and assured our adventurer he would do him all the service in his power ; but in the meantime advised him to take the potion he had prescribed.

The knight's eyes lightening with indignation, " I am now convinced," cried he, " that you are an accomplice in the villainy which has been practised upon me ; that you are a sordid wretch, without principle or feeling, a disgrace to the faculty, and a reproach to human nature—yes, sirrah, you are the most perfidious of all assassins—you are the hireling minister of the worst of all villains ; who, from motives even baser than malice, envy, and revenge, rob the innocent of all the comforts of life, brand them with the imputation of madness, the most cruel species of slander, and wantonly protract their misery, by leaving them in the most shocking confinement, a prey to reflections infinitely more bitter than death—but I will be calm—do me justice at your peril. I demand the protection of the legislature— if I am refused—remember a day of reckoning will come —you and the rest of the miscreants who have combined against me must, in order to cloak your treachery, have recourse to murder,—an expedient which I believe you very capable of embracing—or a man of my rank and character cannot be much longer concealed. Tremble, caitiff, at the thoughts of my release—in the meantime, be gone, lest my just resentment impel me to dash your brains out upon that marble—away——"

The honest doctor was not so firmly persuaded of his patient's lunacy as to reject his advice, which he made what haste he could to follow, when an unexpected accident intervened.

That this may be properly introduced we must return to the knight's brace of trusty friends, Captain Crowe and lawyer Clarke, whom we left in sorrowful deliberation upon the fate of their patron. Clarke's genius being rather more fruitful in resources than that of the seaman, he suggested an advertisement, which was accordingly inserted in the daily papers, importing that, "Whereas a gentleman of considerable rank and fortune had suddenly disappeared on such a night, from his house near Golden Square, in consequence of a letter delivered to him by a porter; and there is great reason to believe some violence hath been offered to his life; any person capable of giving such information as may tend to clear up this dark transaction, shall, by applying to Mr. Thomas Clarke, attorney, at his lodgings in Upper Brook Street, receive proper security for the reward of one hundred guineas, to be paid to him upon his making the discovery required."

The porter who delivered the letter appeared accordingly, but could give no other information, except that it was put into his hand with a shilling, by a man muffled up in a greatcoat, who stopped him for the purpose, in his passing through Queen Street. It was necessary that the advertisement should produce an effect upon another person, who was no other than the hackney-coachman who drove our hero to the place of his imprisonment. This fellow had been enjoined secrecy; and, indeed, bribed to hold his tongue, by a considerable gratification, which, it was supposed, would have been effectual, as the man was a master coachman in good circumstances, and well known to the keeper of the madhouse, by whom he had been employed on former occasions of the same nature. Perhaps his fidelity to his employer, reinforced by the hope of many future jobs of that kind, might have been proof against the offer of fifty pounds; but double that sum was a temptation he could not resist. He no sooner read the intimation in the *Daily Advertiser*, over his morning's pot at an alehouse, than he entered into consultation with his own thoughts; and, having no reason to doubt that this was the very fare he had conveyed, he resolved to earn the reward, and abstain from all such adventures in time coming. He had the precaution, however, to take an attorney along with him to Mr. Clarke, who entered into a conditional bond; and, with the assistance of his uncle, deposited the money, to be forthcoming when the conditions should be fulfilled. These previous measures being taken, the coachman declared what he knew, and discovered the house in which Sir Launcelot had been immured. He, moreover, accompanied our two adherents to a judge's chamber, where he made oath to the truth of his information; and a warrant was immediately granted to search the house of Bernard Shackle, and set at liberty Sir Launcelot Greaves, if there found.

Fortified with this authority, they engaged a constable, with a formidable posse, and, embarking them in coaches, repaired with all possible expedition to the house of Mr. Shackle, who did not think proper to dispute their claim, but admitted them, though not without betraying evident symptoms of consternation. One of the servants directing them, by his master's order, to Sir Launcelot's apartment, they hurried upstairs in a body, occasioning such a noise as did not fail to alarm the physician, who had just opened the door to retire, when he perceived their irruption. Captain Crowe conjecturing he was guilty from the confusion that appeared in his countenance, made no scruple of seizing him by the collar as he endeavoured to retreat; while the tender-hearted Tom Clarke, running up to the knight, with his eyes brimful of joy and affection, forgot all the forms of distant respect, and throwing his arms round his neck blubbered in his bosom.

Our hero did not receive this proof of attachment unmoved. He strained him in his embrace, honoured him

with the title of his deliverer, and asked him by what miracle
he had discovered the place of his confinement. The
lawyer began to unfold the various steps he had taken with
equal minuteness and self-complacency, when Crowe, dragging the doctor still by the collar, shook his old friend by
the hand, protesting he was never so overjoyed since he got
clear of a Sallee rover on the coast of Barbary ; and that
two glasses ago he would have started all the money he had
in the world in the hold of any man who would have shown
Sir Launcelot safe at his moorings. The knight having
made a proper return to this sincere manifestation of goodwill, desired him to dismiss that worthless fellow, meaning
the doctor ; who, finding himself released, withdrew with
some precipitation.

Then our adventurer, attended by his friends, walked
off with a deliberate pace to the outward gate, which he
found open, and getting into one of the coaches, was entertained by the way to his own house with a detail of every
measure which had been pursued for his release.

In his own parlour he found Mrs. Dolly Cowslip, who
had been waiting with great fear and impatience for the
issue of Mr. Clarke's adventure. She now fell upon her
knees, and bathed the knight's hands with tears of joy ;
while the face of this young woman, recalling the idea of
her mistress, roused his heart to strong emotions, and
stimulated his mind to the immediate achievement he had
already planned. As for Mr. Crabshaw, he was not the last
to signify his satisfaction at his master's return. After having
kissed the hem of his garment, he retired to the stable,
where he communicated these tidings to his friend Gilbert,
whom he saddled and bridled ; the same office he performed
for Bronzomarte ; then putting on his squire-like attire
and accoutrements, he mounted one, and led the other
to the knight's door, before which he paraded, uttering,
from time to time, repeated shouts, to the no small entertainment of the populace, until he received orders to house
his companions. Thus commanded, he led them back to
their stalls, resumed his livery, and rejoined his fellow-

servants, who were resolved to celebrate the day with banquets and rejoicings.

Their master's heart was not sufficiently at ease to share in their festivity. He held a consultation with his friends in the parlour, whom he acquainted with the reasons he had to believe Miss Darnel was confined in the same house which had been his prison; a circumstance which filled them with equal pleasure and astonishment. Dolly in particular, weeping plentifully, conjured him to deliver her dear lady without delay. Nothing now remained but to concert the plan for her deliverance. As Aurelia had informed Dolly of her connection with Mrs. Kawdle, at whose house she proposed to lodge, before she was overtaken on the road by her uncle, this particular was now imparted to the council, and struck a light which seemed to point out the direct way to Miss Darnel's enlargement.

Our hero, accompanied by Mrs. Cowslip and Tom Clarke, set out immediately for the house of Dr. Kawdle, who happened to be abroad, but his wife received them with great courtesy. She was a well-bred, sensible, genteel woman, and strongly attached to Aurelia by the ties of affection, as well as of consanguinity. She no sooner learned the situation of her cousin than she expressed the most impatient concern for her being set at liberty, and assured Sir Launcelot she would concur in any scheme he should propose for that purpose. There was no room for hesitation or choice; he attended her immediately to the judge, who, upon proper application, issued another search-warrant for Aurelia Darnel. The constable and his posse were again retained, and Sir Launcelot Greaves once more crossed the threshold of Mr. Bernard Shackle. Nor was the search-warrant the only implement of justice with which he had furnished himself for this visit. In going thither they agreed upon the method in which they should introduce themselves gradually to Miss Darnel, that her tender nature might not be too much shocked by their sudden appearance.

When they arrived at the house, therefore, and produced their credentials, in consequence of which a female attendant

was directed to show the lady's apartment, Mrs. Dolly first
entered the chamber of the accomplished Aurelia, who,
lifting up her eyes, screamed aloud, and flew into the arms
of her faithful Cowslip. Some minutes elapsed before
Dolly could make shift to exclaim, "Am coom to live and
daai with my beloved leady ! "—" Dear Dolly ! " cried
her mistress, " I cannot express the pleasure I have in seeing
you again. Good Heaven : what solitary hours of keen
affliction have I passed since we parted !—but, tell me,
how did you discover the place of my retreat ?—has my uncle
relented ?—do I owe your coming to his indulgence ? "

Dolly answered in the negative ; and by degrees gave
her to understand that her cousin, Mrs. Kawdle, was in the
next room ; that lady immediately appeared, and a very
tender scene of recognition passed between the two relations.
It was she who, in the course of conversation, perceiving
that Aurelia was perfectly composed, declared the happy
tidings of her approaching deliverance. When the other
eagerly insisted upon knowing to whose humanity and address
she was indebted for this happy turn of fortune, her cousin
declared the obligation was due to a young gentleman of
Yorkshire, called Sir Launcelot Greaves. At mention of
that name her face was overspread with a crimson glow,
and her eyes beamed redoubled splendour. " Cousin," said
she, with a sigh, " I know not what to say—that gentleman,
Sir Launcelot Greaves, was surely born—Lord bless me !
I tell you, cousin, he has been my guardian angel."

Mrs. Kawdle, who had maintained a correspondence with
her by letters, was no stranger to the former part of the
connection subsisting between those two lovers, and had
always favoured the pretensions of our hero, without being
acquainted with his person. She now observed with a
smile, that as Aurelia esteemed the knight her guardian
angel, and he adored her as a demi-deity, nature seemed
to have intended them for each other ; for such sublime
ideas exalted them both above the sphere of ordinary
mortals. She then ventured to intimate that he was in the
house, impatient to pay his respects in person. At this

declaration the colour vanished from her cheeks, which, however, soon underwent a total suffusion. Her heart panted, her bosom heaved, and her gentle frame was agitated by transports rather violent than unpleasing. She soon, however, recollected herself, and her native serenity returned, when, rising from her seat, she declared she would see him in the next apartment, where he stood in the most tumultuous suspense, waiting for permission to approach her person. Here she broke in upon him, arrayed in an elegant white undress, the emblem of her purity, beaming forth the emanations of amazing beauty, warmed and improved with a glow of gratitude and affection. His heart was too big for utterance; he ran towards her with rapture, and throwing himself at her feet, imprinted a most respectful, kiss upon her lily hand.—" This, divine Aurelia," cried he, " is a foretaste of that ineffable bliss which you was born to bestow !—Do I then live to see you smile again ? to see you restored to liberty, your mind at ease, and your health unimpaired ? "—" You have lived," said she, " to see my obligations to Sir Launcelot Greaves accumulated in such a manner, that a whole life spent in acknowledgment will scarce suffice to demonstrate a due sense of his goodness."— " You greatly overrate my services, which have been rather the duties of common humanity, than the efforts of a generous passion, too noble to be thus evinced ;—but let not my unseasonable transports detain you a moment longer on this detested scene. Give me leave to hand you into the coach, and commit you to the care of this good lady, attended by this honest young gentleman, who is my particular friend." So saying, he presented Mr. Thomas Clarke, who had the honour to salute the fair hand of the ever-amiable Aurelia.

The ladies being safely coached under the escort of the lawyer, Sir Launcelot assured them he should wait on them in the evening at the house of Dr. Kawdle, v hither they immediately directed their course. Our hero, who remained with the constable and his gang, inquired for Mr. Bernard Shackle, upon whose person he intended to serve a writ of conspiracy, over and above a prosecution for robbery, in consequence of his having disencumbered the knight of his money and other effects, on the first night of his confinement. Mr. Shackle had discretion enough to avoid this encounter, and even to anticipate the indictment for felony, by directing one of his servants to restore the cash and papers, which our adventurer accordingly received before he quitted the house.

In the prosecution of his search after Shackle, he chanced to enter the chamber of the bard, whom he found in dishabille writing at a table, with a bandage over one eye, and his head covered with a nightcap of baize. The knight, having made an apology for this intrusion, desired to know if he could be of any service to Mr. Distich, as he was now at liberty to use the little influence he had for the relief of his fellow-sufferers.—The poet having eyed him for some time askance, " I told you," said he, " your stay in this place would be of short duration.—I have sustained a small disaster on my left eye, from the hands of a rascally cordwainer, who pretends to believe himself the King of Prussia, and I am now in the very act of galling his majesty with keen iambics.—If you can help me to a roll of tobacco and a bottle of Geneva, so—if you are not so inclined, your humble servant, I shall share in the joy of your deliverance."

The knight declined gratifying him in these particulars, which he apprehended might be prejudicial to his health, but offered his assistance in redressing his grievances, provided he laboured under any cruel treatment or inconvenience. " I comprehend the full extent of your generosity," replied the satirist ; " you are willing to assist me in everything, except the only circumstances in which assistance is required —God b'w'ye. If you see Ben Bullock, tell him I wish he would not dedicate any more of his works to me. D—n the fellow, he has changed his note, and begins to snivel.—For my part, I stick to my former maxim, defy all the world, and will die hard, even if death should be preceded by damnation."

The knight, finding him incorrigible, left him to the

slender chance of being one day comforted by the dram bottle; but resolved, if possible, to set on foot an accurate inquiry into the economy and transactions of this private inquisition, that ample justice might be done in favour of every injured individual confined within its walls.

In the afternoon he did not fail to visit his Aurelia; and all the protestations of their mutual passion were once more interchanged. He now produced the letter which had caused such fatal disquiet in his bosom, and Miss Darnel no sooner eyed the paper, than she recollected it was a formal dismission, which she had intended and directed for Mr. Sycamore. This the uncle had intercepted, and cunningly enclosed in another cover, addressed to Sir Launcelot Greaves, who was now astonished beyond measure to see the mystery so easily unfolded. The joy that now diffused itself in the hearts of our lovers is more easily conceived than described; but, in order to give a stability to this mutual satisfaction, it was necessary that Aurelia should be secured from the tyranny of her uncle, whose power of guardianship would not otherwise expire for some months.

Dr. Kawdle and his lady having entered into their deliberations on the subject, it was agreed that Miss Darnel should have recourse to the protection of the Lord Chancellor; but such application was rendered unnecessary by the unexpected arrival of John Clump with the following letter to Mrs. Kawdle from the steward of Anthony Darnel, dated at Aurelia's house in the country:

"MADAM,—It hath pleased God to afflict Mr. Darnel with a severe stroke of the dead palsy.—He was taken ill yesterday, and now lies insensible, seemingly at the point of death. Among the papers in his pocket I found the enclosed, by which it appears that my honoured young lady, Miss Darnel, is confined in a private madhouse. I am afraid Mr. Darnel's fate is a just judgment of God upon him for his cruelty to that excellent person. I need not exhort you, madam to take, immediately upon the receipt of this, such measures as will be necessary for the enlargement of my poor young lady. In the meantime, I shall do the needful for the preservation of her property in this place, and send you an account of any further alteration that may happen ; being very respectfully, madam, your most obedient humble servant,

"RALPH MATTOCKS."

Clump had posted up to London with this intimation on the wings of love, and being covered with clay from the heels to the eyes upwards, he appeared in such an unfavourable light at Dr. Kawdle's door, that the footman refused him admittance. Nevertheless, he pushed him aside, and fought his way upstairs into the dining-room, where the company was not a little astonished at such an apparition. The fellow himself was no less amazed at seeing Aurelia and his own sweetheart Mrs. Dolly Cowslip. He forthwith fell upon his knees, and in silence held out the letter, which was taken by the doctor, and presented to his wife, according to the direction. She did not fail to communicate the contents, which were far from being unwelcome to the individuals who composed this little society. Mr. Clump was honoured with the approbation of his young lady, who commended him for his zeal and expedition ; bestowed upon him a handsome gratuity in the meantime, and desired to see him again when he should be properly refreshed after the fatigue he had undergone.

Mr. Thomas Clarke being consulted on this occasion, gave it as his opinion, that Miss Darnel should, without delay, choose another guardian for the few months that remained of her minority. The opinion was confirmed by the advice of some eminent lawyers, to whom immediate recourse was had ; and Dr. Kawdle being the person pitched upon for this office, the necessary forms were executed with all possible despatch.

The first use the doctor made of his guardianship was to sign a power, constituting Mr. Ralph Mattocks his attorney *pro tempore* for managing the estate of Miss Aurelia Darnel ;

and this was forwarded to the steward by the hands of Clump, who set out with it for the seat of Darnel Hill, though not without a heavy heart, occasioned by some intimation he had received concerning the connection between his dear Dolly and Mr. Clarke, the lawyer.

CHAPTER XXV

Which, it is hoped, will be, on more accounts than one, agreeable to the Reader.

Sir Launcelot, having vindicated the liberty, confirmed the safety, and secured the heart of his charming Aurelia, now found leisure to unravel the conspiracy which had been executed against his person ; and with that view commenced a lawsuit against the owner of the house where he and his mistress had been separately confined. Mr. Shackle was, notwithstanding all the submissions and atonement which he offered to make, either in private or in public, indicted on the statute of kidnapping, tried, convicted, punished by a severe fine and standing in the pillory. A judicial writ *ad inquirendum* being executed, the prisons of his inquisition were laid open, and several innocent captives enlarged.

In the course of Shackle's trial, it appeared that the knight's confinement was a scheme executed by his rival Mr. Sycamore, according to the device of his counsellor, Dawdle, who, by this contrivance, had reconciled himself to his patron, after having deserted him in the day of battle. Our hero was so incensed at this discovery of Sycamore's treachery and ingratitude, that he went in quest of him immediately, to take vengeance on his person, accompanied by Captain Crowe, who wanted to balance accounts with Mr. Dawdle. But those gentlemen had wisely avoided the impending storm, by retiring to the Continent, on pretence of travelling for improvement.

Sir Launcelot was not now so much of a knight-errant as to leave Aurelia to the care of Providence, and pursue the traitors to the farthest extremities of the earth. He

16

practised a much more easy, certain, and effectual method of revenge, by instituting a process against them, which, after writs of *capias*, *alias et pluries*, had been repeated, subjected them both to outlawry. Mr. Sycamore, and his friend, being thus deprived of the benefit of the law by their own neglect, would likewise have forfeited their goods and chattels to the king, had not they made such submissions as appeased the wrath of Sir Launcelot and Captain Crowe ; then they ventured to return, and, by dint of interest, obtained a reversal of the outlawry. But this grace they did not enjoy till long after our adventurer was happily established in life.

While the knight waited impatiently for the expiration of Aurelia's minority, and in the meantime consoled himself with the imperfect happiness arising from her conversation, and those indulgences which the most unblemished virtue could bestow, Captain Crowe projected another plan of vengeance against the conjurer, whose lying oracles had cost him such a world of vexation. The truth is, the captain began to be tired of idleness, and undertook this adventure to keep his hand in use. He imparted his design to Crabshaw, who had likewise suffered in spirit from the predictions of the said offender, and was extremely well disposed to assist in punishing the false prophet. He now took it for granted that he should not be hanged for stealing a horse ; and thought it very hard to pay so much money for a deceitful prophecy, which, in all likelihood, would never be fulfilled.

Actuated by these motives, they set out together for the house of consultation, but they found it shut up and abandoned ; and, upon inquiry in the neighbourhood, learned that the conjurer had moved his quarters that very day on which the captain had recourse to his art. This was actually the case. He knew the fate of Sir Launcelot would soon come to light, and he did not choose to wait the consequence. He had other motives for decamping. He had run a score at the public-house, which he had no mind to discharge, and wanted to disengage himself from his female associate, who knew too much of his affairs to be kept at a proper distance. All these purposes he had answered by retreating softly, without beat of drum, while his sibyl was abroad running down prey for his devouring. He had not, however, taken his measures so cunningly, but that this old hag discovered his new lodgings, and, in revenge, gave information to the publican. This creditor took out a writ accordingly, and the bailiff had just secured his person, as Captain Crowe and Timothy Crabshaw chanced to pass by the door in their way homewards, through an obscure street, near the Seven Dials.

The conjurer having no subterfuge left, but a great many particular reasons for avoiding an explanation with the justice, like the man between the devil and the deep sea, of two evils chose the least; and beckoning to the captain, called him by his name. Crowe, thus addressed, replied with a "Hilloah!" and looking towards the place from whence he was hailed, at once recognised the necromancer. Without farther hesitation, he sprang across the street, and, collaring Albumazar, exclaimed, "Aha! old boy, is the wind in that corner? I thought we should grapple one day—now will I bring you up by the head, though all the devils in hell were blowing abaft the beam."

The bailiff seeing his prisoner so roughly handled before, and at the same time assaulted behind by Crabshaw, who cried, "Show me a liar, and I'll show you a thief—who is to be hanged now?" I say, the bailiff, fearing he should lose the benefit of his job, began to put on his contentious face, and, declaring the doctor was his prisoner, swore he could not surrender him without a warrant from the Lord Chief Justice. The whole group adjourning into the parlour, the conjurer desired to know of Crowe whether Sir Launcelot was found. Being answered, "Ey, ey, safe enough to see you made fast in the bilboes, brother"; he told the captain he had something of consequence to communicate for his advantage; and proposed that Crowe and Crabshaw should bail the action, which lay only for a debt of three pounds.

Crowe stormed, and Crabshaw grinned at this modest

proposal; but when they understood that they could only be bound for his appearance, and reflected that they need not part with him until his body should be surrendered unto justice, they consented to give bail; and the bond being executed, conveyed him directly to the house of our adventurer.

The boisterous Crowe introduced him to Sir Launcelot with such an abrupt unconnected detail of his offence as the knight could not understand without Timothy's annotations. These were followed by some questions put to the conjurer, who, laying aside his black gown, and plucking off his white beard, exhibited to the astonished spectators the very individual countenance of the empirical politician Ferret, who had played our hero such a slippery trick after the electioneering adventure.

"I perceive," said he, "you are preparing to expostulate and upbraid me for having given a false information against you to the country justice. I look upon mankind to be in a state of nature; a truth which Hobbes has stumbled upon by accident. I think every man has a right to avail himself of his talents, even at the expense of his fellow-creatures; just as we see the fish, and other animals of the creation, devouring one another. I found the justice but one degree removed from idiotism, and knowing that he would commit some blunder in the execution of his office, which would lay him at your mercy, I contrived to make his folly the instrument of my escape—I was dismissed without being obliged to sign the information I had given; and you took ample vengeance for his tyranny and impertinence. I came to London, where my circumstances obliged me to live in disguise. In the character of a conjurer, I was consulted by your follower, Crowe, and your squire, Crabshaw. I did little or nothing but echo back the intelligence they brought me, except prognosticating that Crabshaw would be hanged; a prediction to which I found myself so irresistibly impelled, that I am persuaded it was the real effect of inspiration. I am now arrested for a paltry sum of money, and, moreover, liable to be sent to Bridewell as an impostor;

let those answer for my conduct whose cruelty and insolence have driven me to the necessity of using such subterfuges. I have been oppressed and persecuted by the Government for speaking truth; your omnipotent laws have reconciled contradictions. That which is acknowledged to be truth in fact, is construed falsehood in law; and great reason we have to boast of a constitution founded on the basis of absurdity. But, waiving these remarks, I own I am unwilling to be either imprisoned for debt, or punished for imposture. I know how far to depend upon generosity, and what is called benevolence—words to amuse the weak-minded; I build upon a surer bottom. I will bargain for your assistance. It is in my power to put twelve thousand pounds in the pocket of Samuel Crowe, that there sea-ruffian, who, by his goodwill, would hang me to the yard's arm——"

There he was interrupted by the seaman. "D—n your rat's eyes! none of your—hang thee! fish my top-masts! if the rope was fairly reeved, and the tackle sound, d'ye see——" Mr. Clarke, who was present, began to stare, while the knight assured Ferret, that if he was really able and willing to serve Captain Crowe in anything essential, he should be amply rewarded. In the meantime he discharged the debt, and assigned him an apartment in his own house. That same day Crowe, by the advice of Sir Launcelot and his nephew, entered into conditional articles with the cynic, to allow him the interest of fifteen hundred pounds for life, provided by this means the captain should obtain possession of the estate of Hobby Hole in Yorkshire, which had belonged to his grandfather, and of which he was heir of blood.

This bond being executed, Mr. Ferret discovered that he himself was the lawful husband of Bridget Maple, aunt to Samuel Crowe, by a clandestine marriage; which, however, he convinced them he could prove by undeniable evidence. This being the case, she, the said Bridget Maple, alias Ferret, was a *covert femme*, consequently could not transact any deed of alienation without his concurrence; *ergo*, the docking of the entail of the estate of Hobby Hole was illegal and of none effect. This was a very agreeable declaration to the whole company, who did not fail to congratulate Captain Crowe on the prospect of his being restored to his inheritance. Tom Clarke, in particular, protested, with tears in his eyes, that it gave him unspeakable joy ; and his tears trickled the faster, when Crowe, with an arch look, signified, that now he was pretty well victualled for life, he had some thoughts of embarking on the voyage of matrimony.

But that point of happiness to which, as the north pole, the course of these adventures hath been invariably directed, was still unattained ; we mean, the indissoluble union of the accomplished Sir Launcelot Greaves and the enchanting Miss Darnel. Our hero now discovered in his mistress a thousand charms, which hitherto he had no opportunity to contemplate. He found her beauty excelled by her good sense, and her virtue superior to both. He found her untainted by that giddiness, vanity, and affectation, which distinguish the fashionable females of the present age. He found her uninfected by the rage for diversion and dissipation, for noise, tumult, gewgaws, glitter, and extravagance. He found her not only raised by understanding and taste far above the amusement of little vulgar minds, but even exalted by uncommon genius and refined reflection, so as to relish the more sublime enjoyments of rational pleasure. He found her possessed of that vigour of mind which constitutes true fortitude, and vindicates the empire of reason. He found her heart incapable of disguise or dissimulation ; frank, generous, and open ; susceptible of the most tender impressions, glowing with a keen sense of honour, and melting with humanity. A youth of his sensibility could not fail of being deeply affected by such attractions. The nearer he approached the centre of happiness, the more did the velocity of his passion increase. Her uncle still remained insensible as it were in the arms of death. Time seemed to linger in its lapse, till the knight was inflamed to the most eager degree of impatience. He communicated his distress to Aurelia ; he pressed her with the most pathetic remonstrances to abridge the torture of his suspense. He interested

Mrs. Kawdle in his behalf; and, at length, his importunity succeeded. The banns of marriage were regularly published, and the ceremony was performed in the parish church, in the presence of Dr. Kawdle and his lady, Captain Crowe, Lawyer Clarke, and Mrs. Dolly Cowslip

The bride, instead of being disguised in tawdry stuffs of gold and silver, and sweating under a harness of diamonds, according to the elegant taste of the times, appeared in a negligee of plain blue satin, without any other jewels than her eyes, which far outshone all that ever was produced by the mines of Golconda. Her hair had no other extraneous ornament than a small sprig of artificial roses; but the dignity of her air, the elegance of her shape, the sweetness and sensibility of her countenance, added to such warmth of colouring, and such exquisite symmetry of features, as could not be excelled by human nature, attracted the eyes and excited the admiration of all the beholders. The effect they produced in the heart of Sir Launcelot was such a rapture as we cannot pretend to describe. He made his appearance on this occasion in a white coat and blue satin vest, both embroidered with silver; and all who saw him could not but own that he alone seemed worthy to possess the lady whom Heaven had destined for his consort. Captain Crowe had put on a blue suit of clothes strongly guarded with bars of broad gold-lace, in order to honour the nuptials of his friend. He wore upon his head a bag-wig, *à la pigeon*, made by an old acquaintance in Wapping; and to his side he had girded a huge plate-hilted sword, which he had bought of a recruiting sergeant. Mr. Clarke was dressed in pompadour, with gold buttons, and his lovely Dolly in a smart checked lutestring, a present from her mistress.

The whole company dined, by invitation, at the house of Dr. Kawdle; and here it was that the most deserving lovers on the face of the earth attained to the consummation of all earthly felicity. The captain and his nephew had a hint to retire in due time. Mrs. Kawdle conducted the amiable Aurelia, trembling, to the marriage-bed; our hero, glowing with a bridegroom's ardour, claimed the husband's privilege. Hymen lighted up his brightest torch at Virtue's lamp, and every star shed its happiest influence on their Heaven-directed union.

Instructions had been already despatched to prepare Greavesbury Hall for the reception of its new mistress, and for that place the new-married couple set out next morning, according to the plan which had been previously concerted. Sir Launcelot and Lady Greaves, accompanied by Mrs. Kawdle and attended by Dolly, travelled in their own coach, drawn by six dappled horses. Dr. Kawdle, with Captain Crowe, occupied the doctor's post-chariot, provided with four bays. Mr. Clarke had the honour to bestride the loins of Bronzomarte. Mr. Ferret was mounted upon an old hunter ; Crabshaw stuck close to his friend Gilbert ; and two other horsemen completed the retinue. There was not an aching heart in the whole cavalcade, except that of the young lawyer, which was by turns invaded with hot desires and chilling scruples. Though he was fond of Dolly to distraction, his regard to worldly reputation, and his attention to worldly interest, were continually raising up bars to a legal gratification of his love. His pride was startled at the thought of marrying the daughter of a poor country publican ; and he moreover dreaded the resentment of his uncle Crowe, should he take any step of this nature without his concurrence. Many a wishful look did he cast at Dolly, the tears standing in his eyes, and many a woful sigh did he utter.

Lady Greaves immediately perceived the situation of his heart, and, by questioning Mrs. Cowslip, discovered a mutual passion between these lovers. She consulted her dear knight on the subject, and he catechised the lawyer, who pleaded guilty. The captain being sounded as to his opinion, declared he would be steered in that, as well as every other course of life, by Sir Launcelot and his lady, whom he verily revered as being of an order superior to the ordinary race of mankind. This favourable response being obtained from the sailor, our hero took an opportunity on the road, one day after dinner, in presence of the whole company, to accost the lawyer in these words :—" My good friend Clarke, I have your happiness very much at heart—your father was an honest man, to whom my family had manifold obligations. I have had these many years a personal regard for yourself, derived from your own integrity of heart and goodness of disposition—I see you are affected, and shall be brief. Besides this regard I am indebted to your friendship for the liberty—what shall I say ?—for the inestimable happiness I now enjoy, in possessing the most excellent—— But I understand that significant glance of my Aurelia—I will not offend her delicacy.—The truth is, my obligation is very great, and it is time I should evince my gratitude.—If the stewardship of my estate is worth your acceptance, you shall have it immediately, together with the house and farm of Cockerton in my neighbourhood. I know you have a passion for Mrs. Dolly ; and believe she looks upon you with the eyes of tender prepossession—don't blush, Dolly. Besides your agreeable person, which all the world must approve, you can boast of virtue, fidelity, and friendship. Your attachment to Lady Greaves neither she nor I shall ever forget. If you are willing to unite your fate with Mr. Clarke, your mistress gives me leave to assure you she will stock the farm at her own expense, and we will celebrate the wedding at Greavesbury Hall——"

By this time the hearts of these grateful lovers had over-flowed. Dolly was sitting on her knees, bathing her lady's hand with her tears, and Mr. Clarke appeared in the same attitude by Sir Launcelot. The uncle, almost as affected as the nephew by the generosity of our adventurer, cried aloud, " I pray God that you and your glorious consort may have smooth seas and gentle gales whithersoever you are bound ; as for my kinsman Tom, I'll give him a thousand pounds to set him fairly afloat ; and if he prove not a faithful tender to you his benefactor, I hope he will founder in this world, and be damned in that which is to come." Nothing now was wanting to the completion of their happiness but the consent of Dolly's mother at the Black Lion, who they did not suppose could have any objection to such an advantageous match for her daughter ; but in this particular they were mistaken.

In the meantime they arrived at the village where the knight had exercised the duties of chivalry, and there he received the gratulation of Mr. Fillet and the attorney who had offered to bail him before Justice Gobble. Mutual civilities having passed, they gave him to understand that Gobble and his wife were turned Methodists. All the rest of the prisoners whom he had delivered came to testify their gratitude, and were hospitably entertained. Next day they halted at the Black Lion, where the good woman was overjoyed to see Dolly so happily preferred ; but when Sir Launcelot unfolded the proposed marriage, she interrupted him with a scream—" Christ Jesus forbid—marry and amen !—match with her own brother ! "

At this exclamation Dolly fainted ; her lover stood with his ears erect, and his mouth wide open ; Crowe stared, while the knight and his lady expressed equal surprise and concern. When Sir Launcelot entreated Mrs. Cowslip to explain this mystery, she told him, that about sixteen years ago, Mr. Clarke, senior, had brought Dolly, then an infant, to her house, when she and her late husband lived in another part of the country; and as she had then been lately delivered of a child which did not live, he hired her as a nurse to the little foundling. He owned she was a love-begotten babe, and from time to time paid handsomely for the board of Dolly, who he desired might pass for her own daughter. In his last illness, he assured her he had taken care to provide for the child ; but since his death she had received no account of any such provision. She moreover informed his honour, that Mr. Clarke had deposited in her hands a diamond ring, and a sealed paper, never to be opened without his order, until Dolly should be demanded in marriage by the man she should like, and not then, except in the presence of the clergyman of the parish. " Send for the clergyman this instant," cried our hero, reddening, and fixing his eyes on Dolly ; " I hope all will yet be well."

The vicar arriving, and being made acquainted with the

nature of the case, the landlady produced the paper ; which, being opened, appeared to be an authentic certificate, that the person commonly known by the name of Dorothy Cowslip was in fact Dorothy Greaves, daughter of Jonathan Greaves, Esq., by a young gentlewoman who had been some years deceased.

" The remaining part of the mystery I myself can unfold," exclaimed the knight, while he ran and embraced the astonished Dolly as his kinswoman. " Jonathan Greaves was my uncle, and died before he came of age, so that he could make no settlement on his child, the fruit of a private amour, founded on a promise of marriage, of which this ring was a token. Mr. Clarke, being his confidant, disposed of the child, and at length, finding his constitution decay, revealed the secret to my father, who in his will bequeathed one hundred pounds a year to this agreeable foundling ; but, as they both died while I was abroad, and some of the memorandums touching this transaction probably were mislaid, I never till now could discover where or how my pretty cousin was situated. I shall recompense the good woman for her care and fidelity, and take pleasure in bringing this affair to a happy issue."

The lovers were now overwhelmed with transports of joy and gratitude, and every countenance was lighted up with satisfaction. From this place to the habitation of Sir Launcelot, the bells were rung in every parish, and the corporation in their formalities congratulated him in every town through which he passed. About five miles from Greavesbury Hall he was met by above five thousand persons of both sexes and every age, dressed out in their gayest apparel, headed by Mr. Ralph Mattocks from Darnel Hill, and the rector from the knight's own parish. They were preceded by music of different kinds, ranged under a great variety of flags and ensigns ; and the women, as well as the men, bedizened with fancy knots and marriage favours. At the end of the avenue, a select bevy of comely virgins arrayed in white, and a separate band of choice youths distinguished by garlands of laurel and holly interweaved,

fell into the procession, and sang in chorus a rustic epithala-
mium composed by the curate.   At the gate they were
received by the venerable housekeeper, Mrs. Oakley, whose
features were so brightened by the occasion, that with the
first glance she made a conquest of the heart of Captain
Crowe ; and this connection was improved afterwards into
a legal conjunction.

Meanwhile the houses of Greavesbury Hall and Darnel
Hill were set open for the entertainment of all comers,
and both echoed with the sounds of festivity.   After the
ceremony of giving and receiving visits had been performed
by Sir Launcelot Greaves and his lady, Mr. Clarke was
honoured with the hand of the agreeable Miss Dolly Greaves ;
and the captain was put in possession of his paternal estate.
The perfect and uninterrupted felicity of the knight and his
endearing consort diffused itself through the whole adjacent
country, as far as their example and influence could extend.
They were admired, esteemed, and applauded by every
person of taste, sentiment, and benevolence ; at the same
time beloved, revered, and almost adored by the common
people, among whom they suffered not the merciless hand
of indigence or misery to seize one single sacrifice.

Ferret, at first, seemed to enjoy his easy circumstances ;
but the novelty of this situation soon wore off, and all his
misanthropy returned.   He could not bear to see his fellow-
creatures happy around him, and signified his disgust to
Sir Launcelot, declaring his intention of returning to the
metropolis, where he knew there would be always food
sufficient for the ravenous appetite of his spleen.   Before
he departed, the knight made him partake of his bounty,
though he could not make him taste of his happiness, which
soon received a considerable addition in the birth of a son,
destined to be the heir and representative of two worthy
families, whose mutual animosity the union of his parents
had so happily extinguished.

THE END

THE HISTORY AND
ADVENTURES OF AN ATOM

Nathaniel Peacock hears a Voice.

ATOM.

THE HISTORY AND
ADVENTURES OF AN ATOM

THE EDITOR'S DECLARATION

I, NATHANIEL PEACOCK, of the parish of St. Giles, haberdasher and author, solemnly declare, that on the third of
last August, sitting alone in my study, up three pair of
stairs, between the hours of eleven and twelve at night,
meditating upon the uncertainty of sublunary enjoyment,
I heard a shrill small voice, seemingly proceeding from my
own pericranium, call distinctly three times, " Nathaniel
Peacock, Nathaniel Peacock, Nathaniel.Peacock." Astonished, yea, even affrighted at this citation, I replied in a
faltering tone, " In the name of the Lord, what art thou ? "
Thus adjured, the voice answered and said, " I am an atom."
I was now thrown into a violent perturbation of spirit,
for I never could behold an atomy without fear and trembling, even when I knew it was no more than a composition
of dry bones ; but the conceit of being in presence of an
atomy, informed with spirit, that is, animated by a ghost
or goblin, increased my fears exceedingly. I durst not lift
up mine eyes, lest I should behold an apparition more dreadful than the handwriting on the wall. My knees knocked
together : my teeth chattered : mine hair bristled up so
as to raise a cotton night-cap from the scalp : my tongue

cleaved to the roof of my mouth : my temples were bedewed with a cold sweat. Verily, I was for a season
entranced.

At length, by the blessing of God, I recollected myself,
and cried aloud, "Avaunt, Satan, in the name of the Father,
Son, and Holy Ghost."—"White-livered caitiff!" said
the voice (with a peculiar tartness of pronunciation), "what
art thou afraid of, that thou shouldest thus tremble, and
diffuse around thee such an unsavoury odour ? What thou
hearest is within thee—is part of thyself. I am one of those
atoms, or constituent particles of matter, which can neither
be annihilated, divided, nor impaired : the different arrange-
ments of us atoms, compose all the variety of objects and
essences which nature exhibits, or art can obtain. Of the
same shade, substance, and quality are the component particles, that harden in rock, and flow in water ; that blacken
in the negro, and brighten in the diamond ; that exhale
from a rose, and steam from a dunghill. Even now, ten
millions of atoms were dispersed in air by that odoriferous
gale, which the commotion of thy fear produced ; and I
can foresee that one of them will be consolidated in a fibre
of the olfactory nerve, belonging to a celebrated beauty,
whose nostril is excoriated by the immoderate use of plain
Spanish. Know, Nathaniel, that we atoms are singly endued
with such efficacy of reason, as cannot be expected in an
aggregate body, where we crowd and squeeze, and em-
barrass one another ! Yet, those ideas which we singly
possess, we cannot communicate, except once in a thousand
years, and then only, when we fill a certain place in the
pineal gland of a human creature, the very station which
I now maintain in thine. For the benefit of you miserable
mortals, I am determined to promulgate the history of one
period, during which I underwent some strange revolutions
in the empire of Japan, and was conscious of some political
anecdotes, now to be divulged for the instruction of British
ministers. Take up the pen, therefore, and write what I
shall unfold."

By this time my first apprehension vanished ; but another

fear, almost as terrible, usurped its place. I began to think myself insane, and concluded that the voice was no other than the fantastic undulation of a disturbed brain. I therefore preferred an earnest orison at the throne of grace, that I might be restored to the fruition of my right understanding and judgment. "O incredulous wretch!" exclaimed the voice, "I will now convince thee that this is no phantasma or hideous dream. Answer me, dost thou know the meaning and derivation of the word atom?"—I replied, "No, verily."—"Then I will tell thee," said the voice; "thou shalt write it down without delay, and consult the curate of the parish on the same subject. If his explanation and mine agree, thou wilt then be firmly persuaded that I am an actual, independent existence; and that this address is not the vague delirium of a disordered brain. *Atomos* is a Greek word, signifying indivisible particle, derived from *alpha* privativa and *temno*, to cut."

I marvelled much at this injunction, which, however, I literally obeyed; and next morning sallied forth to visit the habitation of the curate: but in going thither, it was my hap to encounter a learned physician of my acquaintance, who hath read all the books that ever were published in any nation or language: to him I referred for the derivation of the word atom. He paused a little, threw up his eyes to heaven, stroked his chin with great solemnity, and hemming three times, "Greek, sir," said he, "is more familiar to me than my native tongue. I have conversed, sir, with Homer and Plato, Hesiod and Theophrastus, Herodotus, Thucydides, Hippocrates, Aretæus, Pindar, and Sophocles, and all the poets and historians of antiquity. Sir, my library cost me two thousand pounds. I have spent as much more in making experiments; and you must know that I have discovered certain chemical specifics, which I would not divulge for fifty times the sum. As for the word *atomos* or *atime*, it signifies a scoundrel, sir, or as it were, sir, a thing of no estimation. It is derived, sir, from *alpha* privativa, and *time*, honour. Hence we call a skeleton an atomy, because, sir, the bones are, as it were, dishonoured

17

by being stripped of their clothing, and exposed in their nakedness."

I was sorely vexed at this interpretation, and my apprehension of lunacy recurred : nevertheless, I proceeded in my way to the lodgings of the curate, and desired his explanation, which tallied exactly with what I had written. At my return to my own house, I ascended to my study, asked pardon of my internal monitor ; and taking pen, ink, and paper, sat down to write what it dictated in the following strain.

It was in the era of Foggien,* one thousand years ago, that fate determined I should exist in the empire of Japan, where I underwent a great number of vicissitudes, till, at length, I was enclosed in a grain of rice, eaten by a Dutch mariner at Firanco, and, becoming a particle of his body, brought to the Cape of Good Hope. There I was discharged in a scorbutic dysentery, taken up in a heap of soil to manure a garden, raised to vegetation in a salad, devoured by an English supercargo, assimilated to a certain organ of his body, which, at his return to London, being diseased in consequence of impure contact, I was again separated, with a considerable portion of putrified flesh, thrown upon a dunghill, gobbled up, and digested by a duck, of which duck your father, Ephraim Peacock, having eaten plentifully at a feast of cordwainers, I was mixed with his circulating juices, and finally fixed in the principal part of that animalcule, which, in process of time, expanded itself into thee, Nathaniel Peacock.

Having thus particularised my transmigrations since my conveyance from Japan, I shall return thither, and unfold some curious particulars of state-intrigue, carried on during the short period, the history of which I mean to record : I need not tell thee, that the empire of Japan consists of three large islands ; or that the people who inhabit them are such inconsistent, capricious animals, that one would imagine they were created for the purpose of ridicule.

* The history of Japan is divided into three different eras, of which Foggien is the most considerable.

Their minds are in continual agitation, like a shuttlecock tossed to and fro, in order to divert the demons of philosophy and folly. A Japanese, without the intervention of any visible motive, is, by turns, merry and pensive, superficial and profound, generous and illiberal, rash and circumspect, courageous and fearful, benevolent and cruel. They seem to have no fixed principle of action, no certain plan of conduct, no effectual rudder to steer them through the voyage of life; but to be hurried down the rapid tide of each revolving whim, or driven, the sport of every gust of passion that happens to blow. A Japanese will sing at a funeral, and sigh at a wedding; he will this hour talk ribaldry with a prostitute, and the next immerse himself in the study of metaphysics or theology. In favour of one stranger, he will exert all the virtues of hospitality; against another, he will exercise all the animosity of the most sordid prejudice; one minute sees him hazarding his all on the success of the most extravagant project; another beholds him hesitating in lending a few copans* to his friend on undeniable security. To-day, he is afraid of cutting his corns; to-morrow, he scruples not to cut his own throat. At one season, he will give half his fortune to the poor; at another, he will not bestow the smallest pittance to save his brother from indigence and distress. He is elated to insolence by the least gleam of success; he is dejected to despondence by the slightest turn of adverse fortune. One hour he doubts the best established truths; the next, he swallows the most improbable fiction. His praise and his censure are what a wise man would choose to avoid, as evils equally pernicious: the first is generally raised without foundation, and carried to such extravagance, as to expose the object to the ridicule of mankind; the last is often unprovoked, yet usually inflamed to all the rage of the most malignant persecution. He will extol above Alexander the Great, a petty officer who robs a hen-roost; and damn, to infamy, a general, for not performing impossibilities. The

* Copan is a gold coin used in Japan, value about forty-three shillings.

same man whom he yesterday flattered with the most fulsome
adulation, he will to-morrow revile with the most bitter
abuse; and at the turning of a straw, take into his bosom
the very person whom he has formerly defamed as the most
perfidious rascal.

The Japanese value themselves much upon their constitution, and are very clamorous about the words liberty and
property; yet, in fact, the only liberty they enjoy is to get
drunk whenever they please, to revile the Government, and
quarrel with one another. With respect to their property,
they are the tamest animals in the world; and, if properly
managed, undergo, without wincing, such impositions, as
no other nation in the world would bear. In this particular,
they may be compared to an ass, that will crouch under the
most unconscionable burden, provided you scratch his long
ears, and allow him to bray his belly-full. They are so
practicable, that they have suffered their pockets to be
drained, their veins to be emptied, and their credit to be
cracked, by the most bungling administrations, to gratify
the avarice, pride, and ambition of the most sordid and
contemptible sovereigns that ever sat upon the throne.

The methods used for accomplishing these purposes are
extremely simple. You have seen a dancing bear incensed
to a dangerous degree of rage, and all at once appeased by
firing a pistol over his nose. The Japanese, even in their
most ferocious moods, when they denounce vengeance
against the Cuboy, or minister, and even threaten the throne
itself, are easily softened into meekness and condescension.
A set of tall fellows, hired for the purpose, tickle them under
the noses with long straws, into a gentle convulsion, during
which they shut their eyes, and smile, and quietly suffer
their pockets to be turned inside out. Nay, what is still
more remarkable, the ministry is in possession of a pipe, or
rather bullock's horn, which being sounded to a particular
pitch, has such an effect on the ears and understanding of
the people, that they allow their pockets to be picked with
their eyes open, and are bribed to betray their own interests
with their own money, as easily as if the treasure had come

from the remotest corner of the globe. Notwithstanding these capricious peculiarities, the Japanese are become a wealthy and powerful people, partly from their insular situation, and partly from a spirit of commercial adventure, sustained by all the obstinacy of perseverance, and conducted by repeated flashes of good sense, which almost incessantly gleam through the chaos of their absurdities.

Japan was originally governed by monarchs who possessed an absolute power, and succeeded by hereditary right, under the title of Dairo. But in the beginning of the period Foggien, this emperor became a cypher, and the whole administration devolved into the hands of the prime minister, or Cuboy, who now exercises all the power and authority, leaving the trappings of royalty to the inactive Dairo. The prince who held the reins of government in the short period which I intend to record was not a lineal descendant of the ancient Dairos, the immediate succession having failed, but sprung from a collateral branch which was invited from a foreign country in the person of *Bupo*, in honour of whom the Japanese erected Fakku-basi,* or the temple of the white horse. So much were all his successors devoted to the culture of this idol, which, by the bye, was made of the vilest materials, that, in order to enrich his shrine, they impoverished the whole empire, yet still with the connivance, and by the influence of the Cuboy, who gratified this sordid passion or superstition of the Dairo with a view to prevent him from employing his attention on matters of greater consequence.

Nathaniel, you have heard of the transmigration of souls, a doctrine avowed by one Pythagoras, a philosopher of Crotona. This doctrine, though discarded and reprobated by Christians, is nevertheless sound, and orthodox, I affirm on the integrity of an atom. Further I shall not explain myself on this subject, though I might with safety set the convocation and the whole hierarchy at defiance, knowing as I do, that it is not in their power to make me bate one

* *Vide* Kempfer, lib. i.

particle of what I advance ; or, if they should endeavour to reach me through your organs, and even condemn you to the stake at Smithfield, verily, I say unto thee, I should be a gainer by the next remove.   I should shift my quarter from a very cold and empty tenement, which I now occupy in the brain of a poor haberdasher, to the nervous plexus situated at the mouth of the stomach of a fat alderman fed with venison and turtle.

But to return to Pythagoras, whom one of your wise countrymen denominated *Peter Gore, the wiseacre* of Croton, you must know that philosopher was a type, which had not been fully unveiled.   That he taught the metempsychosis, explained the nature and property of harmonies, demonstrated the motion of the earth, discovered the elements of geometry and arithmetic, enjoined his disciples silence, and abstained from eating anything that was ever informed by the breath of life ; are circumstances known to all the learned world : but his veneration for beans, which cost him his life, his golden thigh, his adventures in the character of a courtesan, his golden verses, his epithet of αὐτὸς ἔφα, the fable of his being born of a virgin, and his descent into hell, are mysteries in which some of the most important truths are concealed.—Between friends, honest Nathaniel, I myself constituted part of that sage's body ; and I could say a great deal—but there is a time for all things.—I shall only observe, that Philip Tessier had some reason for supposing Pythagoras to have been a monk ; and there are shrewd hints in Meyer's dissertation, *Utrum Pythagoras Judæus fuit, an monachus Carmelita.*

Waiving these intricate discussions for the present (though I cannot help disclosing that Pythagoras was actually circumcised), know, Peacock, that the metempsychosis, or, transmigration of souls, is the method which nature and fate constantly pursue, in animating the creatures produced on the face of the earth ; and this process, with some variation, is such as the eleusinian mysteries imported, and such as you have read in Dryden's translation of the sixth book of Virgil's *Æneid.*   The gods have provided a great magazine, or diversorium, to which the departed souls of all animals repair at their dismission from the body. Here they are bathed in the waters of oblivion until they retain no memory of the scenes through which they have passed ; but they still preserve their original crasis and capacity. From this repository, all new-created beings are supplied with souls ; and these souls transmigrate into different animals, according to the pleasure of the great disposer. For example, my good friend Nathaniel Peacock, your own soul has within these hundred years threaded a goat, a spider, and a bishop ; and its next stage will be the carcase of a brewer's horse.

In what manner we atoms come by these articles of intelligence, whether by intuition, or communication of ideas, it is not necessary that you should conceive. Suffice it to say, the gods were merry on the follies of mankind, and Mercury undertook to exhibit a mighty nation, ruled and governed by the meanest intellects that could be found in the repository of pre-existing spirits. He laid the scene in Japan, about the middle of the period Foggien, when that nation was at peace with all her neighbours. Into the mass, destined to sway the sceptre, he infused, at the very article of conception, the spirit, which in course of strangulation had been expelled *a posteriori* from a goose, killed on purpose to regale the appetite of the mother. The animalcule, thus inspired, was born, and succeeded to the throne, under the name of Got-hama-baba. His whole life and conversation was no other than a repetition of the humours he had displayed in his last character. He was rapacious, shallow, hot-headed, and perverse ; in point of understanding, just sufficient to appear in public without a slavering-bib ; imbued with no knowledge, illumined by no sentiment, and warmed with no affection ; except a blind attachment to the worship of Fakku-basi, which seemed indeed to be a disease in his constitution. His heart was meanly selfish, and his disposition altogether unprincely.

Of all his recreations, that which he delighted in most was, kicking the breech of his Cuboy, or prime minister, an exercise which he every day performed in private. It was therefore

necessary that a Cuboy should be found to undergo this
diurnal operation without repining. This was a circumstance foreseen and provided for by Mercury, who, a little
after the conception of Got-hama-baba, impregnated the
ovum of a future Cuboy, and implanted in it a changing soul,
which had successively passed through the bodies of an ass,
a dottrel, an apple-woman, and a cowboy. It was diverting
enough to see the rejoicings with which the birth of this
Quanbuku* was celebrated ; and still more so, to observe the
marks of fond admiration in the parents, as the soul of the
cowboy proceeded to expand itself in the young Cuboy.
This is a species of diversion we atoms often enjoy. We at
different times behold the same spirit hunted down in a hare,
and cried up in a Hector ; fawning in a prostitute, and
bribing in a minister ; breaking forth in a whistle at the
plough, and in a sermon from the pulpit ; impelling a hog to
the stye, and a counsellor to the cabinet ; prompting a
shoe-boy to filch, and a patriot to harangue ; squinting in
a goat, and smiling in a matron.

Tutors of all sorts were provided betimes for the young
Quanbuku, but his genius rejected all cultivation ; at least
the crops it produced were barren and ungrateful. He was
distinguished by the name of Fika-kaka, and caressed as the
heir of an immense fortune. Nay, he was really considered
as one of the most hopeful young Quanbukus in the empire
of Japan ; for his want of ideas was attended with a total
absence of pride, insolence, or any other disagreeable vice :
indeed, his character was founded upon negatives. He had
no understanding, no economy, no courage, no industry, no
steadiness, no discernment, no vigour, no retention. He
was reputed generous and good-humoured ; but was really
profuse, chicken-hearted, negligent, fickle, blundering, weak,
and leaky. All these qualifications were agitated by an
eagerness, haste, and impatience, that completed the most
ludicrous composition which human nature ever produced.
He appeared always in hurry and confusion, as if he had lost

* Quanbuku is a dignity of the first order in Japan.

his wits in the morning, and was in quest of them all day.—
Let me whisper a secret to you, my good friend Peacock.
All this bustle and trepidation proceeded from a hollowness
in the brain, forming a kind of eddy, in which his animal
spirits were hurried about in a perpetual twirl. Had it not
been for this *Lusus Naturæ*, the circulation would not have
been sufficient for the purposes of animal life. Had the
whole world been searched by the princes thereof, it would
not have produced another to have matched this half-witted
original, to whom the administration of a mighty empire
was wholly consigned. Notwithstanding all the care that
was taken of his education, Fika-kaka never could comprehend
any art or science, except that of dancing bare-headed among
the Bonzes at the great festival of Cambadoxi. The extent
of his knowledge in arithmetic went no farther than the
numeration of his ten fingers. In history, he had no idea
of what preceded a certain treaty with the Chinese, in the
reign of Queen Syko, who died within his own remembrance;
and was so ignorant of geography, that he did not know that
his native country was surrounded by the sea. No system
of morality could he ever understand ; and of the fourteen
sects of religion that are permitted in Japan, the only discipline he could imbibe was a superstitious devotion for
Fakku-basi, the temple of the white horse. This, indeed,
was neither the fruit of doctrine, nor the result of reason ;
but a real instinct, implanted in his nature for fulfilling the
ends of Providence. His person was extremely awkward ;
his eye vacant, though alarmed ; his speech thick and embarrassed ; his utterance ungraceful ; and his meaning
perplexed. With much difficulty he learned to write his
own name, and that of the Dairo ; and picked up a smattering
of the Chinese language, which was sometimes used at court.
In his youth, he freely conversed with women ; but, as he
advanced in age, he placed his chief felicity in the delights
of the table. He hired cooks from China at an enormous
expense, and drank huge quantities of the strong liquor
distilled from rice, which, by producing repeated intoxication, had an unlucky effect upon his brain, that was naturally

of a loose, flimsy texture. The immoderate use of this potation was likewise said to have greatly impaired his retentive faculty; inasmuch as he was subject, upon every extraordinary emotion of spirit, to an involuntary discharge from the last of the intestines.

Such was the character of Fika-kaka, entitled by his birth to a prodigious estate, as well as to the honours of Quanbuku, the first hereditary dignity in the empire. In consequence of his high station, he was connected with all the great men in Japan, and used to the court from his infancy. Here it was he became acquainted with young Got-hama-baba, his future sovereign; and their souls being congenial, they soon contracted an intimacy, which endured for life. They were like twin particles of matter, which having been divorced from one another by a most violent shock, had floated many thousand years in the ocean of the universe, till at length meeting by accident, and approaching within the spheres of each other's attraction, they rush together with an eager embrace, and continue united ever after.

The favour of the sovereign, added to the natural influence arising from a vast fortune and great alliances, did not fail to elevate Fika-kaka to the most eminent offices of the state, until, at length, he attained to the dignity of Cuboy, or chief minister, which virtually comprehends all the rest. Here then was the strangest phenomenon that ever appeared in the political world. A statesman without capacity or the smallest tincture of human learning; a secretary who could not write; a financier who did not understand the multiplication-table; and the treasurer of a vast empire, who never could balance accounts with his own butler.

He was no sooner, for the diversion of the goods promoted to the Cuboyship, than his vanity was pamperd, with all sorts of adulation. He was in magnificence extelled above the first Meckaddo, or line of emperors, to whom divine honours had been paid; equal in wisdom to Tensio-dai-sin, the first founder of the Japanese monarchy; braver than Whey-vang, of the dynasty of Chew; more learned than Jacko, the chief pontiff of Japan; more liberal than Shiwang-ti, who was possessed of the universal medicine ; and more religious than *Bupo,* alias *Kobot,* who, from a foreign country, brought with him, on a white horse, a book called *Kio,* containing the mysteries of his religion.

But, by none was he more cultivated than by the Bonzes, or clergy, especially those of the University Frenoxena,* so renowned for their learning, sermons, and oratory, who actually chose him their supreme director, and every morning adored him with a very singular rite of worship. This attachment was the more remarkable, as Fika-kaka was known to favour the sect of Nem-buds-ju, who distinguished themselves by the ceremony of circumcision. Some malicious people did not scruple to whisper about, that he himself had privately undergone the operation : but these, to my certain knowledge, were the suggestions of falsehood and slander. A slight scarification, indeed, it was once necessary to make, on account of his health ; but this was no ceremony of any religious worship. The truth was this. The Nem-buds-ju, being few in number, and generally hated by the whole nation, had recourse to the protection of Fika-kaka, which they obtained for a valuable consideration. Then a law was promulgated in their favour ; a step which was so far from exciting the jealousy of the Bonzes, that there were not above three, out of one hundred and fifty-nine thousand, that opened their lips in disapprobation of the measure. Such were the virtue and moderation of the Bonzes, and so loth were they to disoblige their great director Fika-kaka.

What rendered the knot of connection between the Dairo Got-hama-baba, and this Cuboy, altogether indissoluble, was a singular circumstance, which I shall now explain. Fika-kaka not only devoted himself entirely to the gratification of his master's prejudices and rapacity, even when they interfered the most with the interest and reputation of Japan ; but he also submitted personally to his capricious humours with the most placid resignation. He presented his posteriors

* Vide *Hist. Eccles. Japan,* vol. i.

to be kicked as regularly as the day revolved ; and presented them not barely with submission, but with all the appearance of fond desire ; and truly this diurnal exposure was attended with such delectation as he never enjoyed in any other attitude.

To explain this matter, I must tell thee, Peacock, that Fika-kaka was from his infancy afflicted with an itching of the podex, which the learned Dr. Woodward would have termed *immanis αἰδοίων pruritus*. That great naturalist would have imputed it to a redundancy of cholicky salts, got out of the stomach and guts into the blood, and thrown upon these parts, and he would have attempted to break their colluctations with oil, etc., but I, who know the real causes of this disorder, smile at these whims of philosophy.

Be that as it may, certain it is, all the most eminent physicians in Japan were consulted about this strange tickling and tingling, and among these the celebrated Fan-sey, whose spirit afterwards informed the body of Rabelais. This experienced leech, having prescribed a course of cathartics, balsamics, and sweeteners, on the supposition that the blood was tainted with a scorbutical itch ; at length found reason to believe that the disease was local. He therefore tried the method of gentle friction : for which purpose he used almost the very same substances which were many centuries after applied by Gargantua to his own posteriors ; such as a night-cap, a pillow-bier, a slipper, a poke, a pannier, a beaver, a hen, a cock, a chicken, a calf-skin, a hare-skin, a pigeon, a cormorant, a lawyer's bag, a lamprey, a coif, a lure, nay even a goose's neck, without finding that *volupté mirifique au trou de cul*, which was the portion of the son of Grangousier. In short, there was nothing that gave Fika-kaka such respite from this tormenting titillation as did smearing the parts with thick cream, which was afterwards licked up by the rough tongue of a boar-cat. But the administration of this remedy was once productive of a disagreeable incident. In the meantime, the distemper gaining ground became so troublesome, that the unfortunate

Quanbuku was incessantly in the fidgets, and ran about distracted, cackling like a hen in labour.

The source of all this misfortune was the juxtaposition of two atoms quarrelling for precedency, in this Cuboy's seat of honour. Their pressing and squeezing, and elbowing and jostling, though of no effect in discomposing one another, occasioned all this irritation and titillation in the posteriors of Fika-kaka.—What! dost thou mutter, Peacock? Dost thou presume to question my veracity? Now by the indivisible rotundity of an atom, I have a good mind, caitiff, to raise such a buzzing commotion in thy glandula pinealis, that thou shalt run distracted over the face of the earth, like Io, when she was stung by Juno's gad-fly! What! thou who hast been wrapped from the cradle in visions of mystery and revelation, swallowed impossibilities like lamb's wool, and digested doctrines harder than iron three times quenched in the Ebro! thou to demur at what I assert upon the evidence and faith of my own consciousness and consistency!— Oh! you capitulate; well, then beware of a relapse—you know a relapsed heretic finds no mercy.

I say, while Fika-kaka's podex was the scene of contention between two turbulent atoms, I had the honour to be posted immediately under the nail of the Dairo's great toe, which happened one day to itch more than usual for occupation. The Cuboy presenting himself at that instant, and turning his face from his master, Got-hama-baba performed the exercise with such uncommon vehemence, that first his slipper, and then his toe-nail flew off, after having made a small breach in the perineum of Fika-kaka. By the same effort I was divorced from the great toe of the sovereign, and lodged near the great gut of his minister, exactly in the interstice between the two hostile particles, which were thus in some measure restrained from wrangling: though it was not in my power to keep the peace entirely. Nevertheless, Fika-kaka's torture was immediately suspended; and he was even seized with an orgasm of pleasure, analogous to that which characterises the ecstasy of love.

Think not, however, Peacock, that I would adduce this

circumstance as a proof that pleasure and pain are mere relations, which can exist only as they are contrasted. No, pleasure and pain are simple, independent ideas, incapable of definition ; and this which Fika-kaka felt was an ecstasy compounded of positive pleasure ingrafted upon the removal of pain ; but whether this positive pleasure depended upon a particular centre of percussion hit upon by accident, or was the inseparable effect of a kicking and scratching conferred by a royal foot and toe, I shall not at present unfold : neither will I demonstrate the *modus operandi* on the nervous papillæ of Fika-kaka's breech, whether by irritation, relaxation, undulation, or vibration. Were these essential discoveries communicated, human philosophy would become too arrogant. It was but the other day that Newton made shift to dive into some subaltern laws of matter ; to explain the revolution of the planets, and analyse the composition of light ; and ever since, that reptile man has believed itself a demi-god—I hope to see the day when the petulant philosopher shall be driven back to his Categories, and the Organum Universale of Aristotle his οὐσία, his ὕλη, and his ὑποκείμενον.

But waiving these digressions, the pleasure which the Cuboy felt from the application of the Dairo's toe-nail was succeeded by a kind of tension or stiffness, which began to grow troublesome just as he reached his own palace, where the Bonzes were assembled to offer up their diurnal incense. Instinct, on this occasion, performed what could hardly have been expected from the most extraordinary talents. At sight of a grizzled beard belonging to one of those venerable doctors, he was struck with the idea of a powerful assuager ; and taking him into his cabinet, proposed that he should make oral application to the part affected. The proposal was embraced without hesitation, and the effect even transcended the hope of the Cuboy. The osculation itself was soft, warm, emollient, and comfortable ; but when the nervous papillæ were gently stroked, and as it were fondled by the long, elastic, peristaltic, abstersive fibres that composed this reverend verriculum, such a delectable titillation ensued, that Fika-kaka was quite in raptures.

That which he intended at first for a medicine he now converted into an article of luxury. All the Bonzes who enrolled themselves in the number of his dependants, whether old or young, black or fair, rough or smooth, were enjoined every day to perform this additional and posterior rite of worship, so productive of delight to the Cuboy, that he was every morning impatient to receive the Dairo's calcitration, or rather his pedestrian digitation ; after which he flew with all the eagerness of desire to the subsequent part of his entertainment.

The transports thus produced seemed to disarrange his whole nervous system, and produce an odd kind of revolution in his fancy ; for though he was naturally grave, and indeed overwhelmed with constitutional hebetude, he became, in consequence of this periodical tickling, the most giddy, pert buffoon in nature. All was grinning, giggling, laughing, and prating, except when his fears intervened ; then he started and stared, and cursed and prayed by turns. There was but one barber in the whole empire that would undertake to shave him, so ticklish and unsteady he was under the hands of the operator. He could not sit above one minute in the same attitude, or on the same seat ; but shifted about from couch to chair, from chair to stool, from stool to close-stool, with incessant rotation, and all the time gave audience to those who solicited his favour and protection. To all and several he promised his best offices and confirmed these promises with oaths and protestations. One he took by the hand ; another he hugged ; a third he kissed on both sides of the face ; with a fourth he whispered ; a fifth he honoured with a familiar horse-laugh. He never had courage to refuse even that which he could not possibly grant ; and at last his tongue actually forgot how to pro-nounce the negative particle ; but as in the English language two negatives amount to an affirmative, five hundred affirmatives in the mouth of Fika-kaka did not altogether destroy the efficacy of simple negation. A promise five hundred times repeated and at every repetition confirmed by oath, barely amounted to a computable chance of performance.

It must be allowed, however, he promoted a great number of Bonzes, and in this promotion he manifested an uncommon taste. They were preferred according to the colour of their beards. He found, by experience, that beards of different colours yielded him different degrees of pleasure in the friction we have described above; and the provision he made for each was in proportion to the satisfaction the candidate could afford. The sensation ensuing from the contact of a grey beard was soft and delicate, and agreeably demulcent, when the parts were unusually inflamed; a red, yellow, or brindled beard, was in request when the business was to thrill or tingle; but a black beard was of all others the most honoured by Fika-kaka, not only on account of its fleecy feel, equally spirited and balsamic, but also for another philosophical reason, which I shall now explain. You know, Peacock, that black colour absorbs the rays of light, and detains them as it were in a repository. Thus a black beard, like the back of a black cat, becomes a phosphorus in the dark, and emits sparkles upon friction. You must know that one of the gravest doctors of the Bonzes, who had a private request to make, desired an audience of Fika-kaka in his closet at night, and the taper falling down by accident, at that very instant when his beard was in contact with the Cuboy's seat of honour, the electrical snap was heard, and the part illuminated, to the astonishment of the spectators, who looked upon it as a prelude to the apotheosis of Fika-kaka. Being made acquainted with this phenomenon, the minister was exceeding elevated in his own mind. He rejoiced in it as a communication of divine efficacy, and raised the happy Bonze to the rank of Pontifex Maximus, or chief priest, in the temple of Fakku-basi. In the course of experiments, he found that all black beards were electrical in the same degree, and being ignorant of philosophy, ascribed it to some supernatural virtue, in consequence of which they were promoted as the holiest of the Bonzes. But you and

I know, that such a phosphorus is obtained from the most worthless and corrupted materials, such as rotten wood, putrified veal, and stinking whiting.

Fika-kaka, such as I described him, could not possibly act in the character of Cuboy, without the assistance of counsellors and subalterns, who understood the detail of government and the forms of business. He was accordingly surrounded by a number of satellites, who reflected his lustre in their several spheres of rotation; and though their immersions and emersions were apparently abrupt and irregular, formed a kind of luminous belt as pale and comfortless as the ring of Saturn, the most distant, cold, and baleful of all the planets.

The most remarkable of these subordinates, was Sti-phi-rum-poo, a man who, from a low plebeian origin, had raised himself to one of the first offices of the empire, to the dignity of *Quo*, or nobleman, and a considerable share of the Dairo's personal regard. He owed his whole success to his industry, assiduity, and circumspection. During the former part of his life, he studied the laws of Japan with such severity of application, that though unassisted by the least gleam of genius, and destitute of the smallest pretensions to talent, he made himself master of all the written ordinances, all the established customs, and forms of proceeding in the different tribunals of the empire. In the progress of his vocation, he became an advocate of some eminence, and even acquired reputation for polemical eloquence, though his manner was ever dry, laboured, and unpleasant. Being elevated to the station of a judge, he so far justified the interest by which he had been promoted, that his honesty was never called into question; and his sentences were generally allowed to be just and upright. He heard causes with the most painful attention, seemed to be indefatigable in his researches after truth; and though he was forbidding in his aspect, slow in deliberation, tedious in discussion, and cold in his address; yet I must own he was also unbiassed in his decisions. I mean, unbiassed by any consciousness of sinister motive: for a man may be biassed by the nature of his disposition, as well as by prejudices acquired, and yet not guilty of intentional partiality. Sti-phi-rum-poo was scrupulously just, according to his own ideas of justice, and consequently well qualified to decide in common controversies. But in delicate cases, which required an uncommon share of penetration—when the province of a supreme judge is to mitigate the severity, and sometimes even deviate from the dead letter of the common law, in favour of particular institutions, or of humanity in general—he had neither genius to enlighten his understanding, sentiment to elevate his mind, nor courage to surmount the petty inclosures of ordinary practice. He was accused of avarice and cruelty; but, in fact, these were not active passions in his heart. The conduct which seemed to justify these imputations was wholly owing to a total want of taste and generosity. The nature of his post furnished him with opportunities to accumulate riches; and as the narrowness of his mind admitted no ideas of elegance or refined pleasure, he knew not how to use his wealth so as to avoid the charge of a sordid disposition. His temper was not rapacious but attentive: he knew not the use of wealth, and therefore did not use it at all: but was in this particular neither better nor worse than a strong box for the convenience and advantage of his heir. The appearance of cruelty remarkable in his counsels, relating to some wretched insurgents who had been taken in open rebellion, and the rancorous pleasure he seemed to feel in pronouncing sentence of death by self-exenteration,* was in fact the gratification of a dastardly heart, which had never acknowledged the least impulse of any liberal sentiment. This being the case, mankind ought not to impute that to his guilt which was, in effect, the consequence of his infirmity. A man might, with equal justice, be punished for being purblind. Sti-phi-rum-poo was much more culpable for seeking to shine in a sphere for which nature never intended him; I mean for commencing statesman, and

* A gentleman capitally convicted in Japan is allowed the privilege of anticipating the common executioner by ripping out his own bowels.

intermeddling in the machine of government : yet even into this character he was forced, as it were, by the opinion and injunctions of Fika-kaka, who employed him at first in making speeches for the Dairo, which that prince used to pronounce in public, at certain seasons of the year. These speeches being tolerably well received by the populace, the Cuboy conceived an extraordinary opinion of his talents ; and thought him extremely well qualified to ease him of great part of the burthen of government. He found him very well disposed to engage heartily in his interests. Then he was admitted to the osculation *a posteriori* ; and though his beard was not black, but rather of a subfuscan hue, he managed it with such dexterity, that Fika-kaka declared the salute gave him unspeakable pleasure : while the bystanders protested that the contact produced not simply electrical sparks or scintillations, but even a perfect irradiation, which seemed altogether supernatural. From this moment Sti-phi-rum-poo was initiated in the mysteries of the cabinet, and even introduced to the person of the Dairo Got-hama-baba, whose pedestrian favours he shared with his new patron. It was observed, however, that even after his promotion and nobilitation, he still retained his original awkwardness, and never could acquire that graceful ease of attitude with which the Cuboy presented his parts averse to the contemplation of his sovereign. Indeed, this minister's body was so well moulded for the celebration of the rite, that one would have imagined nature had formed him expressly for that purpose, with his head and body projecting forwards, so as to form an angle of forty-five with the horizon, while the glutæi muscles swelled backwards, as if ambitious to meet half way the imperial encounter.

The third connection that strengthened this political band was Nin-kom-poo-po, commander of the *Fune*, or navy of Japan, who, if ever man was, might surely be termed the child of fortune. He was bred to the sea from his infancy, and, in the course of pacific service, rose to the command of a jonkh, when he was so lucky as to detect a crew of pirates employed on a desolate shore, in concealing a hoard of money which they had taken from the merchants of Corea. Nin-kom-poo-po falling in with them at night, attacked them unawares, and having obtained an easy victory, carried off the treasure. I cannot help being amused at the folly of you silly mortals, when I recollect the transports of the people, at the return of this fortunate officer, with a paltry mass of silver, parading in covered waggons, escorted by his crew in arms. The whole city of Meaco resounded with acclamations ; and Nin-kom-poo-po was extolled as the greatest hero that ever the empire of Japan produced, The Cuboy honoured him with five kisses in public ; accepted of the osculation in private, recommended him in the strongest terms to the Dairo, who promoted him to the rank of Sey-seo-gun, or general at sea. He professed himself an adherent to the Cuboy, entered into a strict alliance with Sti-phi-rum-poo, and the whole management of the *Fune* was consigned into his hands. With respect to his understanding, it was just sufficient to comprehend the duties of a common mariner, and to follow the ordinary route of the most sordid avarice. As to his heart, he might be said to be in a state of total apathy, without principle or passion ; for I cannot afford the name of passion to such a vile appetite as an insatiable thirst of lucre. He was, indeed, so cold and forbidding, that in Japan, the people distinguished him by a nickname equivalent to the English word Salamander ; not that he was inclined to live in fire, but that the coldness of his heart would have extinguished any fire it had approached. Some individuals imagined he had been begot upon a mermaid by a sailor of Kamtschatka ; but this was a mere fable. I can assure you, however, that when his lips were in contact with the Cuboy's posteriors, Fika-kaka's teeth were seen to chatter. The pride of this animal was equal to his frigidity. He affected to establish new regulations at the council where he presided : he treated his equals with insolence, and his superiors with contempt. Other people generally rejoice in obliging their fellow-creatures, when they can do it without prejudice to their own interest. Nin-kom-poo-po had a repulsive power in his disposition ; and seemed to take pleasure in denying a request. When this vain creature, selfish, inelegant, arrogant, and uncouth, appeared in all his trappings at the Dairo's court, upon a festival, he might have been justly compared unto a Lapland idol of ice, adorned with a profusion of brass leaf, and trinkets of pewter. In the direction of the *Fune*, he was provided with a certain number of assessors, counsellors or co-adjutors ; but these he never consulted, more than if they had been wooden images. He distributed his commands among his own dependants ; and left all the forms of the office to the care of the scribe, who thus became so necessary, that his influence sometimes had well-nigh interfered with that of the president : nay, they have been seen, like the electrical spheres of two bodies, repelling each other. Hence it was observed, that the office of the Sey-seo-gunsialty resembled the serpent called Amphisbæna, which, contrary to the formation of other animals in head and tail, has a head where the tail should be. Well indeed might they compare them to a serpent, in creeping, cunning, coldness, and venom ; but the comparison would have held with more propriety had nature produced a serpent, without ever a head at all.

The fourth who contributed his credit and capacity to this coalition, was Foksi-roku, a man who greatly surpassed them all in the science of politics, bold, subtle, interested, insinuating, ambitious, and indefatigable. An adventurer from his cradle ; a latitudinarian in principle, a libertine in morals, without the advantages of birth, fortune, character, or interest ; by his own natural sagacity, a close attention to the follies and foibles of mankind, a projecting spirit, an invincible assurance, and an obstinacy of perseverance, proof against all the shocks of disappointment and repulse ; he forced himself, as it were, into the scale of preferment ; and being found equally capable and compliant, rose to high offices of trust and profit, detested by the people, as one of the most desperate tools of a wicked administration ; and odious to his colleagues in the m——y, for his superior talents, his restless ambition, and the uncertainty of his attachment.

As interest prompted him, he hovered between the triumvirate we have described, and another knot of competitors for the ad——n, headed by the Quamba-cun-dono, a great Quo related to the Dairo, who had borne the supreme command in the army, and was styled Fatz-man,* κατ᾽ ἐξοχήν or by way of eminence. This accomplished prince was not only the greatest in his mind, but also the largest in his person, of all the subjects of Japan ; and whereas your Shakespeare makes Falstaff urge it as a plea in his own favour, that as he had more flesh, so likewise he had more frailty than other men ; I may justly convert the proposition in favour of Quamba-cun-dono, and affirm, that as he had more flesh, so he had more virtue than any other Japanese ; more bowels, more humanity, more beneficence, more affability. He was undoubtedly, for a Fatzman, the most courteous, the most gallant, the most elegant, generous, and munificent Quo, that ever adorned the court of Japan. So consummate in the art of war, that the whole world could not produce a general to match him, in foresight, vigilance, conduct, and ability. Indeed his intellects were so extraordinary and extensive, that he seemed to sentimentalise at every pore, and to have the faculty of thinking diffused all over his frame, even to his finger ends : or, as the Latins call it, *ad unguem* : nay, so wonderful was his organical conformation, that, in the opinion of many Japanese philosophers, his whole body was enveloped in a kind of poultice of brain, and that if he had lost his head in battle, the damage, with regard to his power of reflection, would have been scarce perceptible. After he had achieved many glorious exploits, in a war against the Chinese on the continent, he was sent with a strong army, to quell a dangerous insurrection, in the northern parts of Ximo, which is one of the Japanese islands. He accordingly by his valour crushed the rebellion ; and afterwards, by dint of clemency and discretion, extinguished the last embers of disaffection. When the insurgents were defeated, dispersed, and disarmed,

* *Vide* Kempfer, *Amœnitat. Japan.*

and a sufficient number selected for example, his humanity emerged, and took full possession of his breast. He considered them as wretched men misled by false principles of honour, and sympathised with their distress : he pitied them as men and fellow-citizens : he regarded them as useful fellow-subjects, who might be reclaimed, and reunited to the community. Instead of sending out the ministers of blood, rapine, and revenge, to ravage, burn, and destroy, without distinction of age, sex, or principle ; he extended the arms of mercy to all who would embrace that indulgence : he protected the lives and habitations of the helpless, and diminished the number of malcontents, much more effectually by his benevolence, than by his sword.

The southern Japanese had been terribly alarmed at this insurrection, and in the first transports of their deliverance, voluntarily taxed themselves with a considerable yearly tribute to the hero Quamba-cun-dono. In all probability, they would not have appeared so grateful, had they stayed to see the effects of his merciful disposition towards the vanquished rebels : for mercy is surely no attribute of the Japanese, considered as a people. Indeed, nothing could form a more striking contrast, than appeared in the northern and southern parts of the empire at this juncture. While the amiable Quamba-cun-dono was employed in the godlike office of gathering together, and cherishing under his wings the poor, dispersed, forlorn widows and orphans, whom the savage hand of war had deprived of parent, husband, home, and sustenance ; while he, in the north, gathered these miserable creatures, even as a hen gathereth her chickens ; Sti-phi-rum-poo and other judges in the south, were condemning such of their parents and husbands as survived the sword, to crucifixion, cauldrons of boiling oil, or exenteration : and the people were indulging their appetites, by feasting upon the viscera thus extracted. The liver of a Ximian was in such request at this period that if the market had been properly managed and supplied, this delicacy would have sold for two obans a pound, or about four pounds sterling. The troops in the north might have

provided at the rate of a thousand head per month, for the
demand of Meaco ; and though the other parts of the
carcase would not have sold at so high a price as the liver,
heart, harrigals, sweet-bread, and pope's eye ; yet the whole,
upon an average, would have fetched at the rate of three
hundred pounds a head ; especially if those animals, which
are but poorly fed in their own country, had been fattened
up, and kept upon hard meat for the slaughter. This new
branch of traffic would have produced about three hundred
and sixty thousand pounds annually : for the rebellion might
easily have been fomented from year to year ; and consequently it would have yielded a considerable addition to the
emperor's revenue, by a proper taxation.

The philosophers of Japan, were divided in their opinion,
concerning this new taste for Ximian flesh, which sprang
up among the Japanese. Some ascribed it to a principle
of hatred and revenge, agreeable to the common expression
of animosity among the multitude—" You dog, I'll have your
liver." Others imputed it to a notion analogous to the
vulgar conceit that the liver of a mad dog being eaten is a
preventive against madness ; ergo, the liver of a traitor is
an antidote against treason. A third sort derived this strange
appetite from the belief of the Americans, who imagine
they shall inherit all the virtues of the enemies they devour ;
and a fourth affirmed, that the demand for this dainty
arose from a very high and peculiar flavour in Ximian flesh,
which flavour was discovered by accident : moreover,
there were not wanting some who supposed this banquet
was a kind of sacrifice to the powers of sorcery ; as we find
that one of the ingredients of the charm, prepared in Shakespeare's cauldron was " the liver of blaspheming Jew ; "
and indeed it is not at all impossible, that the liver of a re-
bellious Ximian, might be altogether as effectual. I know
that Fika-kaka was stimulated by curiosity to try the experiment, and held divers consultations with his cooks on
this subject. They all declared in favour of the trial ;
and it was accordingly presented at the table, where the
Cuboy ate of it to such excess, as to produce a surfeit. He

underwent a severe evacuation both ways, attended with cold sweats and swoonings. In a word, his agony was so violent, that he ever after loathed the sight of Ximian flesh, whether dead or alive.

With the Fatzman Quamba-cun-dono was connected another Quo, called Gotto-mio, viceroy of Xicoco, one of the islands of Japan. If his understanding had been as large as his fortune, and his temper a little more tractable, he would have been a dangerous rival to the Cuboy. But if their brains had been weighed against each other, the nineteenth part of a grain would have turned either scale ; and as Fika-kaka had negative qualities, which supported and extended his personal influence, so Gotto-mio had positive powers, that defended him from all approaches of popularity. His pride was of the insolent order ; his temper extremely irascible ; and his avarice quite rapacious ; nay, he is said to have once declined the honour of a kicking from the Dairo. Conceited of his own talents, he affected to harangue in the council of twenty-eight ; but his ideas were embarrassed ; his language was mean ; and his elocution more discordant, than the braying of fifty asses. When Fika-kaka addressed himself to speech, an agreeable simper played upon the countenances of all the audience : but soon as Gotto-mio stood up, every spectator raised his thumbs to his ears, as it were instinctively. The Dairo, Got-hama-baba, by the advice of the Cuboy, sent him over to govern the people of Xicoco, and a more effectual method could not have been taken, to mortify his arrogance. His deportment was so insolent, his economy so sordid, and his government so arbitrary, that those islanders, who are remarkably ferocious and impatient, expressed their hatred and contempt of him on every occasion. His Quanbukuship, was hardly safe from outrage, in the midst of his guards ; and a cross was actually erected, for the execution of his favourite Kow-kin ; who escaped with some difficulty to the island of Niphon, whither also his patron soon followed him, attended by the curses of the people whom he had been sent to rule.

He who presided at the council of twenty-eight, was
called Soo-san-sin-o, an old, experienced, shrewd politician,
who conveyed more sense in one single sentence, than could
have been distilled from all the other brains in the council,
had they been macerated in one alembic. He was a man of
extensive learning and elegant taste. He saw through the
characters of his fellow-labourers in the ad——n. He
laughed at the folly of one faction, and detested the arrogance
and presumption of the other. In an assembly of sensible
men, his talents would have shone with superior lustre :
but at the council of twenty-eight, they were obscured
by the thick clouds of ignorance that enveloped his brethren.
The Dairo had a personal respe_t for him, and is said to have
conferred frequent favours on his posteriors in private.
He kicked the Cuboy often *ex officio*, as a husband thinks
it incumbent upon him to caress his wife : but he kicked
the president with pleasure, as a voluptuary embraces his
mistress. Soo-san-sin-o, conscious that he had no family
interest to support him in cabals among the people, and
careless of his country's fate, resolved to enjoy the comforts
of life in quiet. He laughed and quaffed, with his select
companions in private ; received his appointments thankfully,
and swam with the tide of politics, as it happened to flow.
It was pretty extraordinary, that the wisest man should be
the greatest cypher : but such was the will of the gods.

Besides these great luminaries, that enlightened the
cabinet of Japan, I shall have occasion, in the course of my
narrative, to describe many other stars of an inferior order.
At this board, there was as great a variety of characters,
as we find in the celebrated table of Cebes. Nay, indeed,
what was objected to the philosopher, might have been more
justly said of the Japanese councils. There was neither
invention, unity, nor design among them. They consisted
of mobs of sauntering, strolling, vagrant, and ridiculous
politicians. Their schemes were absurd, and their deliberations, like the sketches of anarchy. All was bellowing,
bleating, braying, grinning, grumbling, confusion, and
uproar. It was more like a dream of chaos than a picture

of human life. If the δαίμων or genius was wanting, it must be owned that Fika-kaka exactly answered Cebes' description Τύχη, or Fortune, blind and frantic, running about everywhere ; giving to some and taking from others, without rule or distinction ; while her emblem of the round stone fairly shows his *giddy* nature καλῶς μηνύε φύσιν αὐτῆς. Here, however, one might have seen many other figures of the painter's allegory ; such as Deception, tendering the cup of ignorance and error, opinions and appetites ; Disappointment and Anguish ; Debauchery, Profligacy, Gluttony, and Adulation ; Luxury, Fraud, Rapine, Perjury, and Sacrilege ; but not the least traces of the virtues, which are described in the group of true education, and in the grove of happiness.

The two factions, that divided the councils of Japan, though inveterate enemies to each other, heartily and cordially concurred in one particular, which was the worship established in the temple of Fakku-basi, or the White Horse. This was the orthodox faith in Japan, and was certainly founded, as St. Paul saith of the Christian religion, upon the evidence of things not seen. All the votaries of this superstition of Fakku-basi, subscribed and swore to the following creed : " I believe in the White Horse, that he descended from heaven, and sojourned in Jeddo, which is the land of promise. I believe in *Bupo* his apostle, who first declared to the children of Niphon, the glad tidings of the gospel of Fakku-basi. I believe that the White Horse was begot by a black mule, and brought forth by a green dragon ; that his head is of silver, and his hoofs are of brass : that he eats gold as provender, and discharges diamonds as dung ; that the Japanese are ordained and predestined to furnish him with food, and the people of Jeddo, to clear away his litter. I believe that the island of Niphon is joined to the continent of Jeddo ; and that whoever thinks otherwise shall be damned to all eternity. I believe that the smallest portion of matter may be practically divided, *ad infinitum* : that equal quantities, taken from equal quantities, an unequal quantity will remain : that two and two make seven : the sun rules the night, the stars the day : and the moon is made of green cheese. Finally, I believe, that a man cannot be saved, without devoting his goods, and his chattels, his children, relations, and friends, his senses and ideas, his soul and his body, to the religion of the White Horse, as it is prescribed in the ritual of Fakku-basi." These are the tenets, which the Japanese ministers swallowed as glib as the English clergy the thirty-nine articles.

Having thus characterised the chiefs, that disputed the administration, or in other words, the empire of Japan, I shall now proceed to a plain narration, of historical incidents, without pretending to philosophise like H——e, or dogmatise like S——tt. I shall only tell thee, Nathaniel, that Britain never gave birth but to two historians worthy of credit, and they were Taliessin and Geoffrey of Monmouth. I'll tell you another secret. The whole world has never been able to produce six good historians. Herodotus is fabulous even to a proverb ; Thucydides is perplexed, obscure, and unimportant ; Polybius is dry and inelegant ; Livy superficial ; and Tacitus a coxcomb. Guicciardini wants interest ; Davila digestion ; and Sarpi truth. In the whole catalogue of French historians, there is not one of tolerable authenticity.

In the year of the period Foggien, one hundred and fifty-four, the tranquillity of Japan was interrupted by the encroachments of the Chinese adventurers, who made descents upon certain islands, belonging to the Japanese, a great way to the southward of Xicoco. They even settled colonies, and built forts on some of them, while the two empires were at peace with each other. When the Japanese governors expostulated with the Chinese officers on this intrusion, they were treated with ridicule and contempt : then they had recourse to force of arms, and some skirmishes were fought with various success. When the tidings of these hostilities arrived at Meaco, the whole council of twenty-eight, was overwhelmed with fear and confusion. The Dairo kicked them all round, not from passion, but by way of giving an animating fillip to their deliberative faculties. The disputes had happened in the island of

Fatsissio : but there were only three members of the council who knew that Fatsissio was an island, although the commerce there carried on, was of the utmost importance to the empire of Japan.

They were as much in the dark, with respect to its situation. Fika-kaka, on the supposition that it adjoined to the coast of Corea, expressed his apprehension that the Chinese would invade it with a numerous army; and was so transported, when Foksi-roku assured him it was an island, at a vast distance from any continent, that he kissed him five times in the face of the whole council; and his royal master, Got-hama-baba, swore he should be indulged with a double portion of kicking, at his next private audience. The same counsellor proposed, that as the Fune, or navy of Japan, was much more numerous than the fleet of China, they should immediately avail themselves of this advantage. Quamba-cun-dono the Fatzman, was of opinion that war should be immediately declared, and an army transported to the continent. Stiphi-rum-poo thought it would be more expedient to sweep the seas of the Chinese trading vessels, without giving them any previous intimation; and to this opinion Admiral Nin-kom-poo-po subscribed, not only out of deference to the superior understanding of his sage ally, who undertook to prove it was not contrary to the law of nature and nations, to plunder the subjects of foreign powers, who trade on the faith of treaties; but also from his own inclination, which was much addicted to pillage without bloodshed. To him therefore the task was left of scouring the seas, and intercepting the succours which (they had received intelligence) were ready to sail from one of the ports of China, to the island of Fatsissio. In the meantime junks were provided, for transporting thither a body of Japanese troops, under the command of one Koan, an obscure officer, without conduct or experience, whom the Fatzman selected for this service; not that he supposed him possessed of superior merit, but because no leader of distinction cared to engage in such a disagreeable expedition.

Nin-kom-poo-po acted according to the justest ideas which had been formed of his understanding. He let loose his cruisers among the merchant ships of China, and the harbours of Japan were quickly filled with prizes and prisoners. The Chinese exclaimed against these proceedings, as the most perfidious acts of piracy ; and all the other powers of Asia beheld them with astonishment. But the consummate wisdom of the sea Sey-seo-gun, appeared most conspicuous in another stroke of generalship, which he now struck. Instead of blocking up in the Chinese harbour the succours destined to reinforce the enemy in Fatsissio, until they should be driven from their encroachments on that island, he very wisely sent a strong squadron of Fune, to cruise in the open sea, midway between China and Fatsissio, in the most tempestuous season of the year, when the fogs are so thick and so constant in that latitude, as to rival the darkness of a winter night ; and supported the feasibility of this scheme in council, by observing that the enemy would be thus decoyed from their harbour, and undoubtedly intercepted in their passage by the Japanese squadron. This plan was applauded as one of the most ingenious stratagems that ever was devised ; and Fika-kaka insisted upon kissing his posteriors, as the most honourable mark of his approbation.

Philosophers have observed, that the motives of actions are not to be estimated by events. Fortune did not altogether fulfil the expectations of the council. General Koan suffered himself and his army to be decoyed into the middle of a wood, where they stood like sheep in the shambles, to be slaughtered by an unseen enemy. The Chinese succours, perceiving their harbour open, set sail for Fatsissio, which they reached in safety by changing their course about one degree from the common route ; while the Japanese Fune continued cruising among the fogs, until the ships were shattered by storms, and the crews more than half destroyed by cold and distemper.

When the news of these disasters arrived, great commotion arose in the council. The Dairo Got-hama-baba fluttered, and clucked and cackled, and hissed like a goose disturbed in the act of incubation. Quamba-cun-dono shed bitter tears; the Cuboy snivelled and sobbed: Sti-phi-rum-poo groaned: Gotto-mio swore: but the sea Sey-seo-gun, Nin-kom-poo-po, underwent no alteration. He sat as the emblem of insensibility, fixed as the north star, and as cold as that luminary, sending forth emanations of frigidity. Fika-kaka, mistaking this congelation for fortitude, went round and embraced him where he sat, exclaiming, "My dear Day, Sey-seo-gun, what would you advise in this dilemma?" But the contact had almost cost him his life; for the touch of Nin-kom-poo-po, thus congealed, had the same effect as that of the fish called Torpor. The Cuboy's whole body was instantly benumbed; and if his friends had not instantly poured down his throat a considerable quantity of strong spirit, the circulation would have ceased. This is what philosophers call a generation of cold, which became so intense, that the mercury in a Japanese thermometer, constructed on the same principles which were afterwards adopted by Fahrenheit, and fixed in the apartment, imme-diately sank thirty degrees below the freezing point.

The first astonishment of the council was succeeded by critical remarks and argumentation. The Dairo consoled himself by observing that his troops made a very soldierly appearance, as they lay on the field in their new clothing, smart caps, and clean buskins; and that the enemy allowed they had never seen beards and whiskers in better order. He then declared, that should a war ensue with China, he would go abroad and expose himself, for the glory of Japan. Foksi-roku expressed his surprise, that a general should march his army through a wood, in an unknown country, without having it first reconnoitred: but the Fatzman assured him, that was a practice never admitted into the discipline of Japan. Gotto-mio swore the man was mad to stand with his men, like oxen in a stall, to be knocked on the head without using any means of defence. Why the devil (said he), did not he either retreat, or advance to close engagement, with the handful of Chinese who formed the ambuscade?

" I hope, my dear Quanbuku," replied the Fatzman, " that
the troops of Japan will always stand without flinching. I
should have been mortified beyond measure, had they retreated without seeing the face of the enemy : that would
have been a disgrace which never befell any troops formed
under my direction : and as for advancing, the ground would
not permit any manœuvre of that nature. They were
engaged in a *cul de sac*, where they could not form, either in
hollow square, front line, potence, column, or platoon. It
was the fortune of war, and they bore it like men—we shall
be more fortunate on another occasion." The president
Soo-san-sin-o took notice, that if there had been one spaniel
in the whole Japanese army, this disaster could not have
happened ; as the animal would have beat the bushes,
and discovered the ambuscade. He therefore proposed,
that if the war was to be prosecuted in Fatsissio, which is a
country overgrown with wood, a number of bloodhounds
might be provided and sent over, to run upon the foot in
the front and on the flanks of the army, when it should
be on its march through such impediments. Quamba-cun-
dono declared, that soldiers had much better die in the bed
of honour, than be saved and victorious by such an unmilitary
expedient ; that such a proposal was contrary to the rules
of war, and the scheme of enlisting dogs, so derogatory from
the dignity of the service, that if ever it should be embraced,
he would resign his command, and spend the remainder
of his life in retirement. This canine project was equally
disliked by the Dairo, who approved of the Fatzman's
objection, and sealed his approbation with a pedestrian
salute of such momentum, that the Fatzman could hardly
stand under the weight of the compliment. It was agreed
that new levies should be made, and a new squadron of
Fune equipped with all expedition ; and thus the assembly
broke up.

Fortune had not yet sufficiently humbled the pride of
Japan. That body of Chinese which defeated Koan, made
several conquests in Fatsissio, and seemed to be in a fair way
of reducing the whole island. Yet, the court of China,

not satisfied with this success, resolved to strike a blow, that should be equally humiliating to the Japanese, in another part of the world. Having by specious remonstrances already prepossessed all the neighbouring nations against the Government of Japan, as the patrons of perfidy and piracy; they fitted out an armament, which was intended to subdue the island of Motao, on the coast of Corea, which the Japanese had taken in a former war, and now occupied at a very great expense, as a place of the utmost importance to the commerce of the empire. Repeated advices of the enemy's design were sent from different parts to the m——y of Japan: but they seemed all overwhelmed by such a lethargy of infatuation, that no measures of prevention were concerted.

Such was the opinion of the people; but the truth is, they were fast asleep. The Japanese hold with the ancient Greeks and modern Americans, that dreams are from Heaven: and in any perplexing emergency, they, like the Indians, Jews, and natives of Madagascar, have recourse to dreaming as to an oracle. These dreams or divinations are preceded by certain religious rites analogous to the ceremony of the ephod, the urim, and the thummim The rites were religiously performed in the council of twenty-eight; and a deep sleep overpowered the Dairo and all his counsellors.

Got-hama-baba the emperor, who reposed his head upon the pillowy sides of Quamba-cun-dono, dreamed that he was sacrificing in the temple of Fakku-basi, and saw the deity of the White Horse devouring pearls by the bushel at one end, and voiding corruption by the ton at the other. The Fatzman dreamed that a great number of Chinese cooks were busy buttering his brains. Gotto-mio dreamed of lending money and borrowing sense. Sti-phi-rum-poo thought he had procured a new law for clapping padlocks upon the chastity of all the females in Japan under twenty, of which padlocks he himself kept the keys. Nin-kom-poo-po dreamed he was metamorphosed into a sea-lion, in pursuit of a shoal of golden gudgeons *One did laugh in's sleep, and one cried murder.* The first was Soo-san-sin-o, who had precisely the same vision that disturbed the imagination of the Cuboy. He thought he saw the face of a right reverend prelate of the Bonzes, united with and growing to the posteriors of the minister. Fika-kaka underwent the same disagreeable illusion, with this aggravating circumstance, that he already felt the teeth of the said Bonze. The president laughed aloud at the ridiculous phenomenon : the Cuboy exclaimed in the terror of being encumbered with such a monstrous appendage. It was not without some reason he cried, " Murder ! " Fok-si-roku, who happened to sleep on the next chair, dreamed of money-bags, places, and reversions ; and in the transport of his eagerness, laid fast hold of the trunk breeches of the Cuboy, including certain fundamentals, which he grasped so violently as to excite pain, and extort an exclamation from Fika-kaka, even in his sleep.

The council being at last waked by the clamours of the people, who surrounded the palace, and proclaimed that Motao was in danger of an invasion ; the sea Sey-seo-gun, Nin-kom-poo-po, was ordered to fit out a fleet of Fune for the relief of that island ; and directions were given that the commander of these Fune should, in his voyage, touch at the garrison of Foutao, and take on board from thence a certain number of troops, to reinforce the Japanese governor of the place that was in danger. Nin-kom-poo-po for this service chose the commander Bihn-goh, a man who had never signalised himself by an act of valour. He sent him out with a squadron of Fune ill-manned, wretchedly provided, and inferior in number to the fleet of China, which was by this time known to be assembled in order to support the invasion of the island of Motao. He sailed, nevertheless, on this expedition, and touched at the garrison of Foutao to take in the reinforcement : but the orders sent for this purpose from Nob-od-i, minister for the department of war, appeared so contradictory and absurd, that they could not possibly be obeyed ; so that Bihn-goh proceeded without the reinforcement towards Motao, the principal fortress of which was by this time invested. He had been accidentally joined by a few cruisers, which rendered him equal in strength to the Chinese squadron which he now descried. Both commanders seemed afraid of each other. The fleets, however, engaged ; but little damage was done to either.

They parted as if by consent. Bihn-goh made the best of his way back to Foutao, without making the least attempt to succour, or open a communication with Fi-de-ta-da, the governor of Matao, who, looking upon himself as abandoned by his country, surrendered his fortress, with the whole island, to the Chinese general. These disgraces happening on the back of the Fatsissian disasters, raised a prodigious ferment in Japan, and the ministry had almost sunk under the first fury of the people's resentment. They not only exclaimed against the folly of the administration, but they also accused them of treachery ; and seemed to think that the glory and advantage of the empire had been betrayed. What increased the commotion was the terror of an invasion, with which the Chinese threatened the islands of Japan. The terrors of Fika-kaka had already cost him two pair of trunk hose, which were defiled by sudden sallies or irruptions from the postern of his microcosm ; and these were attended with such noisome effluvia, that the Bonzes could not perform the barbal abstertion without marks of abhorrence. The emperor himself was seen to stop his nose, and turn away his head, when he approached him to perform the pedestrian exercise.

Here I intended to insert a dissertation on trousers or trunk breeches, called by the Greeks βράκαι and περίζωματα by the Latins *braccæ laxæ*, by the Spaniards *bragas anchas*, by the Italians *calzone largo*, by the French *haut de chausses*, by the Saxons *braccæ*, by the Swedes *brackor*, by the Irish *briechan*, by the Celtæ *brag*, and by the Japanese *bra-ak*. I could make some curious discoveries touching the analogy between the περίζωματα and ζώνιον γυναικεῖον, and point out the precise time at which the Grecian women began to wear the breeches. I would have demonstrated that

the *cingulum muliebre* was originally no other than the
wife's literally wearing the husband's trousers at certain
orgia, as a mark of dominion transferred *pro tempore* to the
female. I would have drawn a curious parallel between
the ζώνιον of the Greek, and the *shim* or middle cloth
worn by the black ladies in Guinea. I would have proved
that breeches were not first used to defend the central parts
from the injuries of the weather, inasmuch as they were
first worn by the Orientals in a warm climate ; as you may
see in Persius, *Braccatis illita medis—porticus.* I would
have shown that breeches were first brought from Asia to
the northern parts of Europe, by the Celtæ sprung from
the ancient Gomanaus : that trousers were worn in Scotland
long before the time of Pythagoras ; and indeed we are told
by Jamblychus, that Abaris, the famous Highland philosopher, contemporary, and personally acquainted with the
sage of Crotona, wore long trousers. I myself can attest
the truth of that description, as I well remember the person
and habits of that learned mountaineer. I would have
explained the reasons that compelled the posterity of those
mountaineers to abandon the breeches of their forefathers,
and expose their posteriors to the wind. I would have
convinced the English antiquaries that the inhabitants of
Yorkshire came originally from the Highlands of Scotland,
before the Scots had laid aside their breeches, and wore this
part of dress, long after their ancestors, as well as the southern
Britons, were unbreeched by the Romans. From this
distinction they acquired the name of *Brigantes, quasi
Bragantes* ; and hence came the verb to *brag*, or boast
contemptuously ; for the neighbours of the Brigantes
being at variance with that people, used by way of con-
tumelious defiance, when they saw any of them passing or
repassing, to clap their hands on their posteriors, and cry,
Brag-Brag. I would have drawn a learned comparison
between the shield of Ajax and the seven-fold breeches of
a Dutch skipper. Finally, I would have promulgated the
original use of trunk breeches, which would have led me into
a discussion of the rites of Cloacina, so differently worshipped

by the southern and northern inhabitants of this kingdom. These disquisitions would have unveiled the mysteries that now conceal the origin, migration, superstition, language, laws, and connections of different nations—*sed nunc non erit his locus*. I shall only observe, that Linschot and others are mistaken in deriving the Japanese from their neighbours the Chinese ; and that Dr. Kempfer is right in his conjecture, supposing them to have come from Media immediately after the confusion of Babel. It is no wonder, therefore, that being *Braccatorum filii*, they should retain the wide breeches of their progenitors.

Having dropped these hints concerning the origin of breeches, I shall now return to the great personage that turned me into this train of thinking. The council of twenty-eight being assembled in a great hurry, Fika-kaka sat about five seconds in silence, having in his countenance nearly the same expression which you have seen in the face and attitude of Felix on his tribunal, as represented by the facetious Hogarth, in his print done after the Dutch taste. After some pause he rose, and surveying every individual of the council through a long tube, he began a speech to this effect :

" Imperial Got-hama-baba, my ever glorious master ; and you, ye illustrious nobles of Japan, Quanbukus, Quos, Days, and Daygos, my fellows and colleagues in the work of administration ; it is well known to you all, and they are rascals that deny it, I have watched and fasted for the public weal.—By G—d I have deprived myself of two hours of my natural rest, every night for a week together.—Then I have been so hurried with state affairs, that I could not eat a comfortable meal in a whole fortnight : and what rend-dered this misfortune the greater, my chief cook had dressed an olio *à la Chine*. I say an olio, my lords, such an olio as never appeared before upon a table in Japan—by the Lord it cost me fifty obans ; and I had not time to taste a morsel. Well, then, I have watched that my fellow-subjects should sleep ; I have fasted that they should feed. I have not only watched and fasted, but I have prayed—no, not much of that—yes, by the Lord, I have prayed, as it were—I have ejaculated—I have danced and sung at the Matsuris, which, you know, are religious rites—I have headed the multitude, and treated all the raggamuffins in Japan. To be certain, I could not do too much for our most excellent and sublime emperor, an emperor unequalled in wisdom, and unrivalled in generosity. Were I to expatiate from the rising of the sun to the setting thereof, I should not speak half his praise.— O happy nation! O fortunate Japan! happy in such a Dairo to wield the sceptre; and, let me add (vanity apart), fortunate in such a Cuboy to conduct the administration. Such a prince! and such a minister!—aha! my noble friend Soo-san-sin-o, I see your Dayship smile—I know what you think, ha! ha! Very well, my lord, you may think what you please; but two such head-pieces—pardon, my royal master, my presumption in laying our heads together— you won't find again in the whole universe, ha! ha!—I'll be damn'd if you do, ha! ha! ha!"

The tumult without doors, was, by this time, increased to such a degree, that the Cuboy could utter nothing more *ab anteriori*; and the majority of the members sat aghast in silence. The Dairo declared he would throw his cap out of the window into the midst of the popu- lace, and challenge any single man of them to bring it up; but he was dissuaded from hazarding his sacred person in such a manner. Quamba-cun-dono proposed to let loose the guards among the multitude: but Fika-kaka protested he could never agree to an expedient so big with danger to the persons of all present. Sti-phi- rum-poo was of opinion that they should proceed according to law, and indict the leaders of the mob for a riot. Nin- kom-poo-po exhorted the Dairo and the whole council to take refuge on board the fleet. Gotto-mio sweated in silence: he trembled for his money-bags, and dreaded another encounter with the mob, by whom he had suffered severely in the flesh upon a former occasion. The president shrugged up his shoulders, and kept his eye fixed upon a postern or back door. In this general consternation, Foksi-roku stood up and offered a scheme which was immediately put in execution.

"The multitude, my lords," says he, "is a many-headed monster—it is a Cerberus that must have a sop : it is a wild beast, so ravenous that nothing but blood will appease its appetite : it is a whale that must have a barrel for its amusement ; it is a demon to which we must offer up human sacrifice. Now the question is, who is to be this sop, this barrel, this scape-goat ? Tremble not, illustrious Fika-kaka, be not afraid, your life is of too much consequence. But I perceive that the Cuboy is moved—an unsavoury odour assails my nostrils : brief let me be, Bihn-goh must be the victim, happy, if the sacrifice of his single life can appease the commotions of his country. To him let us impute the loss of Motao. Let us, in the meantime, soothe the rabble with solemn promises that national justice shall be done ; let us employ emissaries to mingle in all places of plebeian resort ; to puzzle, perplex, and prevaricate ; to exaggerate the misconduct of Bihn-goh ; to traduce his character with retrospective reproach ; strain circumstances to his prejudice ; inflame the resentment of the vulgar against that devoted officer ; and keep up the flame by feeding it with continual fuel."

The speech was heard with universal applause : Foksi-roku was kicked by the Dairo, and kissed by the Cuboy, in token of approbation. The populace were dispersed by means of fair promises. Bihn-goh was put under arrest, and kept as a malefactor in close prison. Agents were employed through the whole metropolis to vilify his character, and accuse him of cowardice and treachery. Authors were enlisted to defame him in public writings ; and mobs hired to hang and burn him in effigy. By these means the revenge of the people was artfully transferred, and their attention effectually diverted from the ministry, which was the first object of their indignation. At length, matters being duly prepared for the exhibition of such an extraordinary spectacle, Bihn-goh underwent a public trial, was unanimously found guilty, and unanimously declared innocent ; by the same mouths

condemned to death and recommended to mercy : but
mercy was incompatible with the designs of the ad——n.
The unfortunate Bihn-goh was crucified for cowardice, and
bore his fate with the most heroic courage. His behaviour
at his death was so inconsistent with the crime for which
he was doomed to die, that the emissaries of the Cuboy were
fain to propagate a report, that Bihn-goh had bribed a person
to represent him at his execution, and be crucified in his
stead.

This was a stratagem very well calculated for the meridian
of the Japanese populace ; and it would have satisfied them
entirely, had not their fears been concerned. But the
Chinese had for some time been threatening an invasion,
the terror of which kept the people of Japan in perpetual
agitation and disquiet. They neglected their business, and
ran about in distraction, inquiring news, listening to reports,
staring, whispering, whimpering, clamouring, neglecting
their food and renouncing their repose. The Dairo, who
believed the Tartars of Yesso (from whom he himself was
descended) had more valour, and skill, and honesty, than
was possessed by any other nation on earth, took a large body
of them into his pay, and brought them over to the island
of Niphon, for the defence of his Japanese dominions. The
truth is, he had a strong predilection for that people : he
had been nursed among them, and sucked it from the nipple.
His father had succeeded as heir to a paltry farm in that
country, and there he fitted up a cabin, which he preferred
to all the palaces of Meaco and Jeddo. The son received
the first rudiments of his education among these Tartars,
whose country had given birth to his progenitor Bupo. He
therefore loved their country ; he admired their manners,
because they were conformable to his own ; and he was in
particular captivated by the taste they showed in trimming
and curling their mustachios.

In full belief that the Yessites stood as high in the estimation of his Japanese subjects as in his own, he imported a
body of them into Niphon, where, at first they were received
as saviours and protectors ; but the apprehension of danger

no sooner vanished, than they were exposed to a thousand insults and mortifications arising from the natural prejudice to foreigners, which prevails among the people of Japan. They were reviled, calumniated, and maltreated in every different form, and by every class of people ; and when the severe season set in, the Japanese refused shelter from the extremities of the weather, to those very auxiliaries they had hired to defend everything that was dear to them, from the swords of an enemy whom they themselves durst not look in the face. In vain Fika-kaka employed a double band of artists to tickle their noses. They shut their eyes, indeed, as usual : but their eyes no sooner closed, than their mouths opened, and out flew the tropes and figures of obloquy and execration. They exclaimed that they had not bought, but caught the Tartar ; that they had hired the wolves to guard the sheep ; that they were simple beasts who could not defend themselves from the dog with their own horns ; but what could be expected from a flock which was led by such a pusillanimous bell-wether ? In a word, the Yessites were sent home in disgrace : but the ferment did not subside ; and the conduct of the administration was summoned before the venerable tribunal of the populace.

There was one Taycho who had raised himself to great consideration in this self-constituted college of the mob. He was distinguished by a loud voice, an unabashed countenance, a fluency of abuse, and an intrepidity of opposition to the measures of the Cuboy, who was far from being a favourite with the plebeians. Orator Taycho's eloquence was admirably suited to his audience ; he roared and he brayed, and he bellowed against the m——y : he threw out personal sarcasms against the Dairo himself. He inveighed against his partial attachment to the land of Yesso, which he had more than once manifested to the detriment of Japan ; he inflamed the national prejudices against foreigners : and as he professed an inviolable zeal for the commons of Japan, he became the first demagogue of the empire. The truth is, he generally happened to be on the right side. The partiality of the Dairo, the errors, absurdities, and corruption of the ministry, presented such a palpable mark as could not be missed by the arrows of his declamation. This Cerberus had been silenced more than once with a sop ; but whether his appetite was not satisfied to the full, or he was still stimulated by the turbulence of his disposition, which would not allow him to rest, he began to shake his chains anew, and open in the old cry : which was a species of music to the mob, as agreeable as the sound of a bagpipe to a mountaineer of North Britain, or the strum-strum to the swarthy natives of Angola. It was a strain which had the wonderful effect of effacing from the memory of his hearers every idea of his former fickleness and apostasy.

In order to weaken the effect of orator Taycho's harangues, the Cuboy had found means to intrude upon the councils of the mob, a native of Ximo called Muraclami, who had acquired some reputation for eloquence, as an advocate in the tribunals of Japan. He certainly possessed an uncommon share of penetration, with a silver tone of voice, and a great magazine of words and phrases, which flowed from him in a pleasing tide of elocution. He had withal the art of soothing, wheedling, insinuating, and misrepresenting with such a degree of plausibility, that his talents were admired even by the few who had sense enough to detect his sophistry. He had no idea of principle and no feeling of humanity. He had renounced the maxims of his family, after having turned them to the best account by execrating the rites of Fakku-basi or the White Horse, in private among malcontents, while he worshipped him in public with the appearance of enthusiastic devotion. When detected in this double dealing, he fairly owned to the Cuboy, that he cursed the White Horse in private for his private interest, but that he served him in public from inclination.

The Cuboy had just sense enough to perceive that he would always be true to his own interest ; and therefore he made it his interest to serve the m——y to the full extent of his faculties. Accordingly Muraclami fought a good battle with orator Taycho, in the occasional assemblies of the populace. But as it is much more easy to inflame than to allay, to accuse than to acquit, to asperse than to purify, to unveil truth than to varnish falsehood—in a word, to patronise a good cause than to support a bad one—the majesty of the mob snuffed up the excrementitious salts of Taycho's invectives, until their jugulars ached, while they rejected with signs of loathing the flowers of Muraclami's elocution; just as a citizen of Edinburgh stops his nose when he passes by the shop of a perfumer.

While the constitution of human nature remains unchanged, satire will be always better received than panegyric, in those popular harangues. The Athenians and Romans were better pleased with the Philippics of Demosthenes and Tully, than they would have been with all the praise those two orators could have culled from the stores of their eloquence. A man feels a secret satisfaction in seeing his neighbour treated as a rascal. If he be a knave himself (which ten to one is the case), he rejoices to see a character brought down to the level of his own, and a new member added to his society; if he be one degree removed from actual roguery (which is the case with nine-tenths of those who enjoy the reputation of virtue), he indulges himself with the Pharisaical consolation, of thanking God he is not like that publican.

But to return from this digression, Muraclami, though he could not with all his talents maintain any sort of competition with Taycho, in the opinion of the mob; he, nevertheless, took a more effectual method to weaken the force of his opposition. He pointed out to Fika-kaka the proper means for amending the errors of his administration: he proposed measures for prosecuting the war with vigour: he projected plans of conquest in Fatsissio: recommended active officers: forwarded expeditions, and infused such a spirit into the councils of Japan, as had not before appeared for some centuries.

But his patron was precluded from the benefit of these

measures, by the obstinate prejudice and precipitation of
the Dairo, who valued his Yessian farm above all the empire
of Japan. This precious morsel of inheritance bordered
upon the territories of a Tartar chief called Brut-an-tiffi,
a famous freebooter, who had inured his Kurd to bloodshed,
and enriched himself with rapine. Of all mankind he hated
most the Dairo, though his kinsman ; and sought a pretence
for seizing the farm, which in three days he could have made
his own. The Dairo Got-hama-baba was not ignorant
of his sentiments. He trembled for his cabin, when he considered its situation between hawk and buzzard ; exposed
on one side to the talons of Brut-an-tiffi, and open on the
other to the incursions of the Chinese, under whose auspices
the said Brut-an-tiffi had acted formerly as a zealous partisan.
He had, indeed, in a former quarrel exerted himself with
such activity and rancour, to thwart the politics of the
Dairo, and accumulate expenses on the subjects of Niphon,
that he was universally detested through the whole empire
of Japan as a lawless robber, deaf to every suggestion of
humanity, respecting no law, restricted by no treaty, scoffing
at all religion, goaded by ambition, instigated by cruelty,
and attended by rapine.

In order to protect the farm from such a dangerous
neighbour, Got-hama-baba, by an effort of sagacity peculiar
to himself, granted a large subsidy from the treasury of
Japan, to a remote nation of Mantchoux Tartars, on
condition that they should march to the assistance of his
farm, whenever it should be attacked. With the same
sanity of foresight, the Dutch might engage in a defensive
league with the Ottoman Porte, to screen them from the
attempts of the most Christian king, who is already on their
frontiers. Brut-an-tiffi knew his advantage, and was resolved
to enjoy it. He had formed a plan of usurpation, which
could not be executed without considerable sums of money.
He gave the Dairo to understand, he was perfectly sensible
how much the farm lay at his mercy : then proposed, that
Got-hama-baba should renounce his subsidiary treaty with
the Mantchoux ; pay a yearly tribute to him, Brut-an-tiffi,

in consideration of his forbearing to seize the farm ; and maintain an army to protect it on the other side from the irruptions of the Chinese.

Got-hama-baba, alarmed at this declaration, began by his emissaries to sound the inclinations of his Japanese subjects touching a continental war, for the preservation of the farm ; but he found them totally averse to his wise system of politics. Taycho, in particular, began to bawl and bellow among the mob, upon the absurdity of attempting to defend a remote cabin, which was not defensible ; upon the iniquity of ruining a mighty empire, for the sake of preserving a few barren acres, a naked common, a poor, pitiful, pelting farm, the interest of which, like Aaron's rod, had already, on many occasions, swallowed up all regard and consideration for the advantage of Japan. He inveighed against the shameful and senseless partiality of Got-hama-baba : he mingled menaces with his representations. He expatiated on the folly and pernicious tendency of a conti-nental war : he enlarged upon the independence of Japan, secure in her insular situation. He declared, that not a man should be sent to the continent, nor a subsidy granted to any greedy, mercenary, freebooting Tartar ; and threatened, that if any corrupt minister should dare to form such a connection he would hang it about his neck, like a millstone, to sink him to perdition. The bellows of Taycho's oratory blew up such a flame in the nation, that the Cuboy and all his partisans were afraid to whisper one syllable about the farm.

Meanwhile, Brut-an-tiffi, in order to quicken their deter-minations, withdrew the garrison he had in a town on the frontiers of China, and it was immediately occupied by the Chinese : an army of whom poured in like a deluge through this opening upon the lands adjoining to the farm. Got-hama-baba was now seized with a fit of temporary distraction. He foamed and raved, and cursed and swore in the Tartarian language : he declared he would challenge Brut-an-tiffi to single combat. He not only kicked but also cuffed the council of twenty-eight, and played at football with his

imperial tiara. Fika-kaka was dumfounded : Sti-phi-rum-
poo muttered something about a commission of lunacy :
Nin-kom-poo-po pronounced the words flat-bottomed
junks ; but his teeth chattered so much that his meaning
could not be understood. The Fatzman offered to cross
the sea and put himself at the head of a body of light horse,
to observe the motions of the enemy : and Gotto-mia
prayed fervently within himself, that God Almighty would
be pleased to annihilate that accursed farm, which had been
productive of such mischief to Japan. Nay, he even ventured
to exclaim, " Would to God, the farm was sunk in the
middle of the Tartarian ocean ! "—" Heaven forbid ! " cried
the president Soo-san-sin-o, " for in that case, Japan must
be at the expense of weighing it up again."

In the midst of this perplexity, they were suddenly
surprised at the apparition of Taycho's head nodding from
a window that overlooked their deliberations. At sight
of this horrid spectacle the council broke up. The Dairo
fled to the inmost recesses of the palace, and all his counsellors
vanished, except the unfortunate Fika-kaka, whose fear
had rendered him incapable of any sort of motion but one,
and that he instantly had to a very efficacious degree.
Taycho bolting in at the window, advanced to the Cuboy
without ceremony, and accosted him in these words : " It
depends upon the Cuboy, whether Taycho continues to
oppose his measures, or becomes his most obsequious servant.
Arise, illustrious Quanbuku, and cast your eyes upon the
steps by which I ascended." Accordingly Fika-kaka looked,
and saw a multitude of people who had accompanied their
orator into the court of the palace, and raised for him an
occasional stair of various implements. The first step was
made by an old fig-box, the second by a nightman's bucket,
the third by a cask of hempseed, the fourth by a tar-barrel,
the fifth by an empty kilderkin, the sixth by a keg, the seventh
by a bag of soot, the eighth by a fish-woman's basket, the
ninth by a rotten pack-saddle, and the tenth by a block of
hard wood from the island of Fatsissio. It was supported
on one side by a varnished lettered post, and on the other

by a crazy hogshead. The artificers who erected this climax, and now exulted over it with hideous clamour, consisted of grocers, scavengers, halter-makers, carpenters, draymen, distillers, chimney-sweepers, oysterwomen, ass drivers, aldermen, and dealers in waste paper. To make myself understood, I am obliged, Peacock, to make use of those terms and denominations which are known in this metropolis.

Fika-kaka, having considered this work with astonishment, and heard the populace declare upon oath, that they would exalt their orator above all competition, was again addressed by the invincible Taycho. " Your Quanbukuship perceives how bootless it will be to strive against the torrent. What need is there of many words ? Admit me to a share of the administration—I will commence your humble slave—I will protect the farm at the expense of Japan, while there is an oban left in the island of Niphon ; and I will muzzle these bears so effectually, that they shall not show their teeth, except in applauding our proceedings." An author who sees the apparition of a bailiff standing before him in his garret, and instead of being shown a *capias*, is presented with a bank-note ; an impatient lover stopped upon Bagshot heath by a person in a mask, who proves to be his sweetheart come to meet him in disguise, for the sake of the frolic ; a condemned criminal, who, on the morning of execution day, instead of being called upon by the finisher of the law, is visited by the sheriff with a free pardon ; could not be more agreeably surprised than was Fika-kaka at the demagogue's declaration. He flew into his embrace and wept aloud with joy, calling him his dear Taycho. He squeezed his hand, kissed him on both cheeks, and swore he should share the better half of all his power : then he laughed and snivelled by turns, lolled out his tongue, waddled about the chamber, wriggled and niggled and noddled. Finally, he undertook to prepare the Dairo for his reception, and it was agreed that the orator should wait on his new colleague next morning. This matter being settled to their mutual satisfaction, Taycho retreated through the window into the courtyard, and was convoyed home in triumph by that many-headed hydra, the mob, which shook its multi-tudinous tail, and brayed through every throat with hideous exultation.

The Cuboy, meanwhile, had another trial to undergo, a trial which he had not foreseen. Taycho was no sooner departed, than he hied him to the Dairo's cabinet, in order to communicate the happy success of his negotiation. But at certain periods, Got-hama-baba's resentment was more than a match for any other passion that belonged to his disposition, and now it was its turn to reign. The Dairo was made of very combustible materials, and these had been kindled up by the appearance of orator Taycho, who (he knew) had treated his person with indecent freedoms, and publicly vilified the worship of the White Horse. When Fika-kaka, therefore, told him he had made peace with the demagogue, the Dairo, instead of giving him the kick of approbation, turned his own back upon the Cuboy, and silenced him with a *boh!* Had Fika-kaka assailed him with the same syllogistical sophism which was used by the Stagyrite to Alexander in a passion, perhaps he might have listened to reason: Ἡ ὀργὴ οὐ πρὸς ἴσους, ἀλλὰ πρὸς τοὺς κρείττονας γίνεται, Σοὶ δὲ οὐδεὶς ἴσος—" Anger should be raised not by our equals, but by our superiors ; but you have no equal."—Certain it is, that Got-hama-baba had no equal ; but Fika-kaka was no more like Aristotle, than his master resembled Alexander. The Dairo remained deaf to all his remonstrances, tears, and entreaties, until he declared that there was no other way of saving the farm, but that of giving a *carte blanche* to Taycho. This argument seemed at once to dispel the clouds which had been compelled by his indignation : he consented to receive the orator in quality of minister, and next day was appointed for his introduction.

In the morning Taycho the Great repaired to the palace of the Cuboy, where he privately performed the ceremony of osculation *a posteriori*, sang a solemn palinodia on the subject of political system, repeated and signed the Buponian creed, embraced the religion of Fakku-basi, and adored the

White Horse with marks of unfeigned piety and contrition. Then he was conducted to the ante-chamber of the emperor, who could not, without great difficulty, so far master his personal dislike, as to appear before him with any degree of composure. He was brought forth by Fika-kaka like a tame bear to the stake, if that epithet of *tame* can be given with any propriety to an animal which nobody but his keeper dares approach. The orator, perceiving him advance, made a low obeisance, according to the custom of Japan, that is, by bending the body averse from the Dairo, and laying the right hand upon the left buttock ; and pronounced with an audible voice, " Behold, invincible Got-hama-baba, a sincere penitent come to make atonement for his virulent opposition to your government, for his atrocious insolence to your sacred person. I have calumniated your favourite farm, I have questioned your integrity, I have vilified your character, ridiculed your understanding, and despised your authority."—This recapitulation was so disagreeable to the Dairo, that he suddenly flew off at a tangent, and retreated growling to his den ; from whence he could by no means be lugged again by the Cuboy, until Taycho, exalting his voice, uttered these words : " But I will exalt your authority more than ever it was debased. I will extol your wisdom, and expatiate on your generosity ; I will glorify the White Horse, and sacrifice all the treasures of Japan, if needful, for the protection of the farm of Yesso." By these cabalistical sounds the wrath of Got-hama-baba was entirely appeased. He now returned with an air of gaiety, strutting, sideling, circling, fluttering, and cobbling like a turkey-cock in his pride, when he displays his feathers to the sun. Taycho hailed the omen ; and turning his face from the emperor, received such a salutation on the *os sacrum*, that the parts continued vibrating and tingling for several days.

An indenture tripartite was now drawn up and executed. Fika-kaka was continued treasurer, with his levees, his bonzes, and his places ; and orator Taycho undertook, in the character of chief scribe, to protect the farm of Yesso,

20

as well as to bridle and manage the blatant beast whose name was Legion. That a person of his kidney should have the presumption to undertake such an affair, is not at all surprising ; the wonder is, that his performance should even exceed his promise. The truth is, he promised more than he could have performed, had not certain unforeseen incidents, in which he had no concern, contributed towards the infatuation of the people.

The first trial to which he brought his ascendency over the mob, was his procuring from them a free gift, to enable the Dairo to arm his own private tenants in Yesso, together with some raggamuffin Tartars in the neighbourhood, for the defence of the farm. They winked so hard upon this first overt act of his apostasy, that he was fully persuaded they had resigned up all their senses to his direction ; and resolved to show them to all Europe, as a surprising instance of his art in monster-taming. This furious beast not only suffered itself to be bridled and saddled, but frisked and fawned, and purred and yelped, and crouched before the orator, licking his feet, and presenting its back to the burthens which he was pleased to impose. Immediately after this first essay, Quamba-cun-dono, the Fatzman, was sent over to assemble and command a body of light horse in Yesso, in order to keep an eye on the motions of the enemy ; and indeed this vigilant and sagacious commander conducted himself with such activity and discretion, that he soon brought the war in those parts to a point of termination.

Meanwhile, Brut-an-tiffi continuing to hover on the skirts of the farm, at the head of his myrmidons, and demanding of the Dairo a categorical answer to the hints he had given, Got-hama-baba underwent several successive fits of impatience and distraction. The Cuboy, instigated by his own partisans, and in particular by Muraclami, who hoped to see Taycho take some desperate step that would ruin his popularity : I say, the Cuboy thus stimulated, began to ply the orator with such pressing entreaties as he could no longer resist ; and now he exhibited such a specimen of his own power and the people's insanity, as transcends

the flight of ordinary faith. Without taking the least trouble
to scratch their long ears, tickle their noses, drench them
with mandragora or Geneva, or make the slightest apology
for his own turning tail to the principles which he had all
his life so strenuously inculcated, he crammed down their
throats an obligation to pay a yearly tribute to Brut-an-
tiffi, in consideration of his forbearing to seize the Dairo's
farm; a tribute which amounted to seven times the value
of the lands for the defence of which it was paid. When
I said *crammed*, I ought to have used another phrase.
The beast, far from showing any signs of loathing, closed
its eyes, opened its hideous jaws, and as it swallowed
the inglorious bond, wagged its tail in token of entire
satisfaction.

No fritter on Shrove Tuesday was ever more dexterously
turned, than were the hydra's brains by this mountebank
in patriotism, this juggler in politics, this cat in pan, or cake
in pan, or κατὰ πᾶν in principle. Some people gave out
that he dealt with a conjurer, and others scrupled not to
insinuate that he had sold himself to the evil spirit. But
there was no occasion for a conjurer to deceive those whom
the demon of folly had previously confounded; and as to
selling, he sold nothing but the interest of his country;
and of that he made a very bad bargain. Be that as it
may, the Japanese now viewed Brut-an-tiffi either through
a new perspective, or else surveyed him with organs entirely
metamorphosed.

Yesterday they detested him as a profligate ruffian lost to
all sense of honesty and shame, addicted to all manner of
vice, a scoffer at religion, particularly that of Fakku-basi,
the scourge of human nature, and the inveterate enemy
of Japan. To-day, they glorified him as an unblemished
hero, the protector of good faith, the mirror of honesty,
the pattern of every virtue, a saint in piety, a devout votary
to the White Horse, a friend to mankind, the fast ally and
the firmest prop of the Japanese empire. The farm of
Yesso which they had so long execrated as a putrid and
painful excrescence upon the breech of the country, which

would never be quiet until this cursed wart was either
exterminated or taken away; they now fondled as a
favourite mole, nay, and cherished as the apple of their eye.
One would have imagined that all the inconsistencies and
absurdities which characterise the Japanese nation had
taken their turns to reign, just as the interest of Taycho's
ambition required. When it was necessary for him to
establish new principles, at that very instant their levity
prompted them to renounce their former maxims. Just
as he had occasion to fascinate their senses, the demon of
caprice instigated them to shut their eyes, and hold out
their necks, that they might be led by the nose. At the very
nick of time, when he adopted the cause of Brut-an-tiffi,
in diametrical opposition to all his former professions, the
spirit of whim and singularity disposed them to kick against
the shins of common sense, deny the light of day at noon,
and receive in their bosoms as a dove, the man whom before
they had shunned as a serpent. Thus everything concurred
to establish for orator Taycho, a despotism of popularity ;
and that not planned by reason, or raised by art, but founded
on fatality and finished by accident. *Quos Jupiter vult
perdere prius dementat.*

Brut-an-tiffi being so amply gratified by the Japanese
for his promise of forbearance with respect to the farm of
Yesso, and determined at all events to make some new
acquisition, turned his eyes upon the domains of Pol-hassan-
akousti, another of his neighbours, who had formed a most
beautiful colony in this part of Tartary ; and rushed upon
it at a minute's warning. His resolution in this respect
was so suddenly taken, and quickly executed, that he had
not yet formed any excuse for this outrage, in order to save
appearances. Without giving himself the trouble to invent
a pretence, he drove old Pol-hassan-akousti out of his
residence ; compelled the domestics of that prince to
enter among his own banditti ; plundered his house, seized
the archives of his family, threatened to shoot the ancient
gentlewoman his wife, exacted heavy contributions from
the tenants ; then dispersed a manifesto in which he declared

himself the best friend of the said Akousti and his spouse, assuring him he would take care of his estate as a precious deposit to be restored to him in due season. In the meantime, he thought proper to sequester the rents, that they might not enable Pol-hassan to take any measures that should conduce to his own prejudice. As for the articles of meat, drink, clothing, and lodging, for him and his wife, and a large family of small children, he had nothing to do but depend upon Providence, until the present troubles should be appeased. His behaviour on this occasion, Peacock, puts me in mind of the Spaniard whom Philip II. employed to assassinate his own son Don Carlos. This compassionate Castilian, when the prince began to deplore his fate, twirled his mustachio, pronouncing with great gravity these words of comfort : " *Calla, calla, Senor, todo que se haze es por su bien* "—" I beg your highness won't make any noise; this is all for your own good "—or the politeness of Gibbet in the play called the Beaux Stratagem, to Mrs. Sullen, " Your jewels, madam, if you please—don't be under any uneasiness, madam—if you make any noise I shall blow your brains out. I have a particular regard for the ladies, madam."

But the possession of Pol-hassan's dominions was not the ultimate aim of Brut-an-tiffi. He had an eye to a fair and fertile province belonging to a Tartar princess of the house of Ostrog. He saw himself at the head of a numerous banditti trained to war, fleshed in carnage, and eager for rapine; his coffers were filled with the spoils he had gathered in his former freebooting expeditions ; and the incredible sums paid him as an annual tribute from Japan, added to his other advantages, rendered him one of the most formidable chiefs in all Tartary. Thus elated with the consciousness of his own strength, he resolved to make a sudden irruption into the dominions of Ostrog, at a season of the year when that house could not avail itself of the alliances they had formed with the other powers ; and he did not doubt but that, in a few weeks, he should be able to subdue the whole country belonging to the Amazonian princess. But I can

tell thee, Peacock, his views extended even farther than the
conquest of the Ostrog dominions. He even aspired at the
empire of Tartary, and had formed the design of deposing
the great Cham, who was intimately connected with the
princess of Ostrog. Inspired by these projects, he, at the
beginning of winter, suddenly poured like a deluge into one
of the provinces that owned this Amazon's sway; but he
had hardly gained the passes of the mountains, when he
found himself opposed by a numerous body of forces,
assembled under the command of a celebrated general,
who gave him battle without hesitation, and handled him
so roughly, that he was fain to retreat into the demesnes
of Pol-hassan, where he spent the greatest part of the
winter in exacting contributions and extending the reign
of desolation.

All the petty princes and states who held of the great
Cham, began to tremble for their dominions, and the
Cham himself was so much alarmed at the lawless proceedings
of Brut-an-tiffi, that he convoked a general assembly of all
the potentates who possessed fiefs in the empire, in order
to deliberate upon measures for restraining the ambition
of this ferocious freebooter. Among others, the Dairo
of Japan, as lord of the farm of Yesso, sent a deputy to this
convention, who, in his master's name, solemnly disclaimed
and professed his detestation of Brut-an-tiffi's proceedings,
which, indeed, were universally condemned. The truth
is, he at this period, dreaded the resentment of all the other
co-estates rather more than he feared the menaces of Brut-
an-tiffi; and, in particular, apprehended a sentence of
outlawry from the Cham, by which, at once, he would
have forfeited all legal title to his beloved farm. Brut-an-
tiffi on the other hand, began to raise a piteous clamour,
as if he meant to excite compassion. He declared himself
an injured prince, who had been a dupe to the honesty
and humanity of his own heart. He affirmed that the
Amazon of Ostrog had entered into a conspiracy against
him, with the Mantchoux Tartars, and Prince Akousti;
he published particulars of this dreadful conjuration, which

appeared to be no other than a defensive alliance formed
in the apprehension that he would fall upon some of them,
without any regard to treaty, as he had done on a former
occasion, when he seized one of the Amazon's best provinces.
He publicly taxed the Dairo of Japan with having prompted
him to commence hostilities, and hinted that the said Dairo
was to have shared his conquests. He openly entreated
his co-estates to interpose their influence towards the re-
establishment of peace in the empire: and gave them
privately to understand, that he would ravage their territories
without mercy, should they concur with the Cham in any
sentence to his prejudice.

As he had miscarried in his first attempt, and perceived
a terrible cloud gathering round him, in all probability he
would have been glad to compound matters at this juncture,
on condition of being left *in statu quo*; but this was a
condition not to be obtained. The Princess of Ostrog had
by this time formed such a confederacy as threatened him
with utter destruction. She had contracted an offensive
and defensive alliance with the Chinese, the Mantchoux,
and the Serednee Tartars; and each of these powers engaged
to furnish a separate army to humble the insolence of Brut-
an-tiffi. The majority of the Tartar fiefs agreed to raise
a body of forces to act against him as a disturber of the
public peace; the great Cham threatened him with a
degree of outlawry and rebellion; and the Amazon herself
opposed him at the head of a very numerous and warlike
tribe, which had always been considered as the most formidable in that part of Tartary. Thus powerfully sustained,
she resolved to enjoy her revenge; and at any rate retrieve the province which had been ravished from her by
Brut-an-tiffi, at a time when she was embarrassed with
other difficulties.

Brut-an-tiffi did not think himself so reduced as to purchase peace with such a sacrifice. The Mantchoux were
at a distance, naturally slow in their motions, and had
a very long march through a desert country, which they
would not attempt without having first provided prodigious

magazines. The Serednee were a divided people, among whom he had made shift to foment intestine divisions, that would impede the national operations of the war. The Japanese Fatzman formed a strong barrier between him and the Chinese ; the army furnished by the fiefs he despised as raw, undisciplined militia ; besides, their declaring against him afforded a specious pretence for laying their respective dominions under contribution. But he chiefly depended upon the coffers of Japan, which he firmly believed would hold out until all his enemies should be utterly exhausted.

As this freebooter was a principal character in the drama which I intend to rehearse, I shall sketch his portrait according to the information I received from a fellow-atom who once resided at his court, constituting part in one of the organs belonging to his first chamberlain. His stature was under the middle size ; his aspect mean and forbidding, with a certain expression which did not at all prepossess the spectator in favour of his morals. Had an accurate observer beheld him without any exterior distinctions, in the streets of the metropolis, he would have naturally clapped his hands to his pockets. Thou hast seen the character of Gibbet represented on the stage by a late comedian of expressive feature.

Nature sometimes makes a strange contrast between the interior workmanship and the exterior form ; but here the one reflected a true image of the other. His heart never felt an impression of tenderness : his notions of right and wrong did not refer to any idea of benevolence, but were founded entirely on the convenience of human commerce ; and there was nothing social in the turn of his disposition. By nature he was stern, insolent, and rapacious, uninfluenced by any motive of humanity : unawed by any precept of religion. With respect to religion, he took all opportunities of exposing it to ridicule and contempt. Liberty of con- science he allowed to such extent, as exceeded the bounds of decorum, and disgraced all legislation. He pardoned a criminal convicted of bestiality, and publicly declared that all modes of religion, and every species of amour, might be freely practised and prosecuted through all his dominions.

His capacity was of the middling mould, and he had taken some pains to cultivate his understanding. He had studied the Chinese language, which he spoke with fluency, and piqued himself upon his learning, which was but superficial. His temper was so capricious and inconstant, that it was impossible, even for those who knew him best, to foresee any one particular of his personal demeanour. The same individual he would caress and insult by turns, without the least apparent change of circumstance. He has been known to dismiss one of his favourites with particular marks of regard, and the most flattering professions of affection; and before he had time to pull off his buskins at his own house, he has been hurried on horseback by a detachment of cavalry, and conveyed to the frontiers. Thus harassed, without refreshment or repose, he was brought back by another party, and reconveyed to the presence of Brut-an-tiffi, who embraced him at meeting, and gently chid him for being so long absent. The fixed principles of this Tartar were these: insatiable rapacity, restless ambition, and an insuperable contempt for the Japanese nation. His maxims of government were entirely despotic. He considered his subjects as slaves to be occasionally sacrificed to the accomplishment of his capital designs; but in the meantime, he indulged them with the protection of equitable laws, and encouraged them to industry for his own emolument.

His virtues consisted of temperance, vigilance, activity, and perseverance. His folly chiefly appeared in childish vanity and self-conceit. He amused himself with riding, reviewing his troops, reading Chinese authors, playing on a musical instrument in use among the Tartars, trifling with buffoons, conversing with supposed wits, and reasoning with pretended philosophers: but he had no communication with the female sex; nor, indeed, was there any ease, comfort, or enjoyment to be derived from a participation of his pastime. His wits, philosophers, and buffoons, were composed of Chinese refugees, who soon discovered his weak side, and flattered his vanity to an incredible pitch of infatuation.

They persuaded him that he was an universal genius and invincible hero, a sage legislator, a sublime philosopher, a consummate politician, a divine poet, and an elegant historian. They wrote systems, compiled memoirs, and composed poems, which were published in his name ; nay, they contrived witticisms which he uttered as his own. They had, by means of commercial communication with the banks of the Ganges, procured the history of a western hero, called Raskalander, which, indeed, was no other than the memoirs of Alexander written by Quintus Curtius, translated from the Indian language, with an intermixture of Oriental fables. This they recommended, with many hyperbolical encomiums, to the perusal of Brut-an-tiffi, who became enamoured of the performance, and was fired with the ambition of rivalling, if not excelling, Raskalander, not only as a warrior, but likewise as a patron of taste and a protector of the liberal arts. As Alexander deposited Homer's *Iliad* in a precious casket, so Brut-an-tiffi procured a golden box for preserving this sophistication of Quintus Curtius. It was his constant companion : he affected to read it in public ; and to lay it under his pillow at night.

Thus pampered with adulation and intoxicated with dreams of conquest, he made no doubt of being able to establish a new empire in Tartary, which should entirely eclipse the kingdom of Tum-ming-qua, and raise a reputation that should infinitely transcend the fame of Yan, or any emperor that ever sat upon the throne of Thibet. He now took the field against the Amazon of the house of Ostrog ; penetrated into her dominions ; defeated one of her generals in a pitched battle ; and undertook the siege of one of her principal cities, in full confidence of seeing her kneeling at his gate before the end of the campaign. In the meantime, her scattered troops were rallied and reinforced by another old experienced commander, who being well acquainted with the genius of his adversary, pitched upon an advantageous situation, where he waited another attack. Brut-an-tiffi, flushed with his former victory, and firmly persuaded that no mortal power could withstand his prowess, gave him battle at a very great disadvantage. The consequence was natural. He lost great part of his army, was obliged to abandon the siege, and retreat with disgrace. A separate body, commanded by one of his ablest captains, met with the same fate in a neighbouring country; and a third detachment at the farthest extremity of his dominions, having attacked an army of the Mantchoux, was repulsed with great loss.

These were not all the mortifications to which he was exposed about this period. The Fatzman of Japan, who had formed an army for the defence of the farm of Yesso against the Chinese, met with a terrible disaster. Notwithstanding his being outnumbered by the enemy, he exhibited many proofs of uncommon activity and valour. At length they came to blows with him, and handled him so roughly, that he was fain to retreat from post to pillar, and leave the farm at their mercy. Had he pursued his route to the right, he might have found shelter in the dominions of Brut-an-tiffi, and this was his intention; but, instead of marching in a straight line he revolved to the right, like a planet round the sun, impelled as it were by a compound impulse, until he had described a regular semi-circle; and then he found himself with all his followers engaged in a sheep-pen, from whence there was no egress; for the enemy, who followed his steps, immediately blocked up the entrance. The unfortunate Fatzman being thus pounded, must have fallen a sacrifice to his centripetal force, had not he been delivered by the interposition of a neighbouring chief, who prevailed upon the Chinese general to let Quamba-cun-dono escape, provided his followers would lay down their arms, and return peaceably to their own habitations. This was a bitter pill, which the Fatzman was obliged to swallow, and is said to have cost him five stone of suet. He returned to Japan in obscurity; the Chinese general took possession of the farm in the name of his emperor; and all the damage which the tenants sustained was nothing more than a change of masters, which they had no cause to regret.

To the thinking part of the Japanese, nothing could be more agreeable than this event, by which they were at once delivered from a pernicious excrescence, which, like an ulcerated tumour, exhausted the juices of the body by which it was fed. Brut-an-tiffi considered the transaction in a different point of view. He foresaw that the Chinese forces would now be at liberty to join his enemies, the tribe of Ostrog, with whom the Chinese emperor was intimately connected; and that it would be next to impossible to withstand the joint efforts of the confederacy which he had brought upon his own head. He therefore raised a hideous clamour. He accused the Fatzman of misconduct, and insisted, not without a mixture of menaces, upon the Dairo's assembling his forces in the country of Yesso. The Dairo himself was inconsolable. He neglected his food, and refused to confer with his ministers. He dismissed the Fatzman from his service; he locked himself in his cabinet, and spent the hours in lamentation. "Oh, my dear farm of Yesso!" cried he, "shall I never more enjoy thy charms! Shall I never more regale my eye with thy beauteous prospects, thy hills of heath, thy meads of broom, and thy wastes of sand! Shall I never more eat thy black bread, drink thy brown beer, and feast upon thy delicate porkers! Shall I never more receive the homage of the sallow Yessites, with their meagre faces, ragged skirts, and wooden shoes! Shall I never more improve their huts and regulate their pigstyes! Oh, cruel Fate! In vain did I face thy mud-walled mansion with a new freestone front! In vain did I cultivate thy turnip-garden! In vain did I enclose a piece of ground at a great expense, and raise a crop of barley, the first that ever was seen in Yesso! In vain did I send over a breed of mules and black cattle for the purposes of husbandry! In vain did I supply you with all the implements of agriculture! In vain did I sow grass and grain for food, and plant trees, and furze and fern for shelter to the game, which could not otherwise subsist upon your

naked downs ! In vain did I furnish your houseless sides, and
fill your hungry bellies with the good things of Japan ! In
vain did I expend the treasures of my empire for thy meliora-
tion and defence ! In vain did I incur the execration of
my people, if I must now lose thee for ever ; if thou must
now fall into the hands of an insolent alien, who has no
affection for thy soil, and no regard for thy interest ! O
Quamba-cun-dono ! Quamba-cun-dono ! how hast thou
disappointed my hope ! I thought thou wast too ponderous
to flinch ; that thou wouldst have stood thy ground, fixed
as the temple of Fakku-basi, and larded the lean earth with
thy carcase, rather than leave my farm uncovered : but,
alas ! thou hast fled before the enemy like a partridge on
the mountains ; and suffered thyself at last to be taken in a
snare like a foolish dotterel ! "
    The Cuboy, who overheard this exclamation, attempted
to comfort him through the key-hole. He soothed, and
whined, and wheedled, and laughed, and wept all in a breath.
He exhorted the illustrious Got-hama-baba to bear this
misfortune with his wonted greatness of mind. He offered
to present his Imperial Majesty with lands in Japan that
should be equal in value to the farm he had lost : or, if that
should not be agreeable, to make good at the peace all the
damage that should be done to it by the enemy. Finally,
he cursed the farm, as the cause of his master's chagrin, and
fairly wished it at the devil. Here he was suddenly interrupted with a " Bub-ub-ub-boh ! my Lord Cuboy, your
grace talks like an apothecary. Go home to your own
palace, and direct your cooks ; and may your Bonzes kiss
your a— to your heart's content. I swear by the horns of
the Moon and the hoofs of the White Horse, that my foot
shall not touch your posteriors these three days."—Fika-kaka,
having received this severe check, craved pardon in a whimpering tone, for the liberty he had taken, and retired to
consult with Muraclami, who advised him to summon orator
Taycho to his assistance.
    This mob-driver being made acquainted with the passion
of the Dairo, and the cause of his distress, readily undertook

to make such a speech through the key-hole, as should effectually dispel the emperor's despondence ; and to this enterprise he was encouraged by the hyperbolical praises of Muraclami, who exhausted all the tropes of his own rhetoric in extolling the eloquence of Taycho. This triumvirate immediately adjourned to the door of the apartment in which Got-hama-baba was sequestered, where the orator, kneeling upon a cushion, with his mouth applied to the key-hole, opened the sluices of his elocution to this effect :

"Most gracious ! "—" Bo, bo, boh ! "—" Most illus-trious ! "—" Bo, boh ! "—" Most invincible Got-hama-baba ! "—" Boh ! "—" When the sun, that glorious lumin-ary, is obscured by envious clouds, all nature saddens, and seems to sympathise with his apparent distress. Your Imperial Majesty is the sun of our hemisphere, whose splendour illuminates our throne ; and whose genial warmth enlivens our hearts ; and shall we, your subjects, your slaves, the creatures of your nod—shall we, unmoved, behold your ever-glorious effulgence overcast ? No ! while the vital stream bedews our veins, while our souls retain the faculty of reason, and our tongues the power of speech, we shall not cease to embalm your sorrow with our tears ; we shall not cease to pour the overflowings of our affection— our filial tenderness, which will always be reciprocal with your parental care : these are the inexhaustible sources of the nation's happiness. They may be compared to the rivers Jodo and Jodo-gava, which derive their common origin from the vast lake of Ami. The one winds its silent course, calm, clear, and majestic, reflecting the groves and palaces that adorn its banks, and fertilising the delightful country through which it runs : the other gushes impetuous through a rugged channel, and less fertile soil ; yet serves to beautify a number of wild romantic scenes ; to fill a hundred aqueducts, and to turn a thousand mills : at length they join their streams below the imperial city of Meaco, and form a mighty flood devolving to the bay of Osaca, bearing on its spacious bosom the riches of Japan."—Here the orator paused for breath. The Cuboy clapped him on the back, whispering, "Super-excellent! Oh, charming simile! Another such will sink the Dairo's grief to the bottom of the sea : and his heart will float like a blown bladder upon the waves of Kugava." Muraclami was loud in his praise, while he squeezed an orange between the lips of Taycho : and Got-hama-baba seemed all attention. At length the orator resumed his subject. "Think not, august emperor, that the cause of your disquiet is unknown, or unlamented by your weeping servants. We have not only perceived your eclipse, but discovered the invidious body by whose interposition that eclipse is effected. The rapacious arms of the hostile Chinese have seized the farm of Yesso! "—"Oh, oh, oh!"—"That farm so cherished by your imperial favour : that farm which, in the north of Tartary, shone like a jewel in an Æthiop's ear—yes, that jewel hath been snatched by the savage hand of a Chinese freebooter. But dry your tears, my prince : that jewel shall detect his theft, and light us to revenge. It shall become a rock to crush him in his retreat : a net of iron to entangle his steps ; a fallen trunk, over which his feet shall stumble. It shall hang like a weight about his neck, and sink him to the lowest gulf of perdition. Be comforted, then, my liege! Your farm is rooted to the centre ; it can neither be concealed nor removed. Nay, should he hide it at the bottom of the ocean ; or place it among the constellations in the heavens ; your faithful Taycho would fish it up entire, or tear it headlong from the starry firmament. We will retrieve the farm of Yesso."—"But how, how, how, dear orator Taycho ?"—"The empire of Japan shall be mortgaged for the sake of that precious—that sacred spot, which produced the patriarch apostle Bupo, and resounded under the hoofs of the holy steed. Your people of Japan shall chant the litany of Fakku-basi. They shall institute crusades for the recovery of the farm ; they shall pour their treasures at your imperial feet ; they shall clamour for imposition ; they shall load themselves with tenfold burthens, desolate their country, and beggar their posterity in behalf of Yesso. With these funds, I could undertake even to overturn the councils of

Pekin. While the Tartar princes deal in the trade of blood, there will be no want of hands to cut away those noxious weeds which have taken root in the farm of Yesso : those vermin that have pressed upon her delightful blossoms ! Amidst such a variety of remedies, there can be no difficulty in choosing. Like a weary traveller, I will break a bough from the first pine that presents, and brush away those troublesome insects that gnaw the fruits of Yesso. Should not the mercenary bands of Tartary suffice to repel those insolent invaders, I will engage to chain this island to the continent : to build a bridge from shore to shore, that shall afford a passage more free and ample, than the road to Hell. Through this avenue, I will ride the mighty beast whose name is Legion. I have studied the art of war, my liege : I had once the honour to serve my country as Lance-presado, in the militia of Niphon. I will unpeople these realms, and overspread the land of Yesso, with the forces of Japan."

Got-hama-baba could no longer resist the energy of such expressions. He flew to the door of his cabinet, and embraced the orator in a transport of joy ; while Fika-kaka fell upon his neck, and wept aloud : and Muraclami kissed the hem of his garment.

You must know, Peacock, I had by this time changed my situation. I was discharged in the perspiratory vapour, from the perinæum of the Cuboy, and sucked into the lungs of Muraclami, through which I pervaded into the course of the circulation, and visited every part of his composition. I found the brain so full and compact, that there was not room for another particle of matter. But instead of a heart, he had a membranous sac, or hollow viscus, cold and callous, the habitation of sneaking caution, servile flattery, griping avarice, creeping malice, and treacherous deceit. Among these tenants it was my fate to dwell ; and there I discovered the motives by which the lawyer's conduct was influenced. He now secretly rejoiced at the presumption of Taycho, which he hoped had already prompted him to undertake more than he could perform ; in which case he would infallibly incur disgrace, either with the Dairo or the people.

It is not impossible but this hope might have been realised, had not fortune unexpectedly interposed, and operated as an auxiliary to the orator's presumption. Success began to dawn upon the arms of Japan in the island of Fatsissio ; and towards the end of the campaign, Brut-an-tiffi obtained two petty advantages in Tartary, against one body of Chinese, and another of the Ostrog. All these were magnified into astonishing victories, and ascribed to the wisdom and courage of Taycho, because during his ministry they were obtained ; though he neither knew why, nor wherefore : and was in this respect as innocent as his master, Got-hama-baba, and his colleague, Fika-kaka. He had penetration enough to perceive, however, that these events had intoxicated the rabble, and began to pervert their ideas. Success of any kind is apt to perturb the weak brain of a Japanese ; but the acquisition of any military trophy produces an actual delirium. The streets of Meaco were filled with multitudes who shouted, whooped, and hallooed. They made processions with flags and banners ; they illuminated their houses ; they extolled Ian-on-i, a provincial captain of Fatsissio, who had by accident repulsed a body of the enemy, and reduced an old barn which he had fortified. They magnified Brut-an-tiffi ; they deified orator Taycho ; they drank, they damned, they squabbled, and acted a thousand extravagances which I shall not pretend to enumerate or particularise. Taycho, who knew their trim, seized this opportunity to strike while the iron was hot. He forthwith mounted an old tub, which was his public rostrum, and waving his hand in an oratorial attitude, was immediately surrounded by the thronging populace. I have already given you a specimen of his manner, and therefore shall not repeat the tropes and figures of his harangue ; but only sketch out the plan of his address, and specify the chain of his argument alone. He assailed them in the way of paradox, which never fails to produce a wonderful effect upon a heated imagination and a shallow understanding.

Having in this exordium artfully fascinated their faculties,
like a juggler in Bartholomew Fair, by means of an assem-
blage of words without meaning or import, he proceeded to
demonstrate, that a wise and good man ought to discard his
maxims the moment he finds they are certainly established
on the foundation of eternal truth. That the people of
Japan ought to preserve the farm of Yesso, as the apple of
their eye, because nature had disjointed it from their empire ;
and the maintenance of it would involve them in all the
quarrels of Tartary ; that it was to be preserved at all
hazards, because it was not worth preserving ; that all the
power and opulence of Japan ought to be exerted and employed in its defence, because, by the nature of its situation,
it could not possibly be defended ; that Brut-an-tiffi was
the great protector of the religion of the Bonzes, because he
had never shown the least regard to any religion at all ; that
he was the fast friend of Japan, because he had more than
once acted as a rancorous enemy to this empire, and never
let slip the least opportunity of expressing his contempt for
the subjects of Niphon ; that he was an invincible hero,
because he had been thrice beaten, and once compelled to
raise a siege, in the course of two campaigns ; that he was a
prince of consummate honour, because he had, in the time
of profound peace, usurped the dominions, and ravaged the
countries of his neighbours, in defiance of common honesty,
in violation of the most solemn treaties ; that he was the
most honourable and important ally that the empire of Japan
could choose, because his alliance was to be purchased with
an enormous annual tribute, for which he was bound to
perform no earthly office of friendship or assistance, because
connection with him effectually deprived Japan of the
friendship of all other princes and states of Tartary, and
the utmost exertion of his power could never conduce, in the
smallest degree, to the interest or advantage of the Japanese
empire.

Such were the propositions orator Taycho undertook to
demonstrate ; and the success justified his undertaking.
After a weak mind had been duly prepared, and turned as it

were, by opening a sluice or torrent of high-sounding words, the greater the contradiction proposed, the stronger impression it makes, because it increases the puzzle, and lays fast hold on the admiration ; depositing the small proportion of reason with which it was before impregnated, like the vitriolic acid in the copper mines of Wicklow, into which, if you immerse iron, it immediately quits the copper which it had before dissolved, and unites with the other metal, to which it has a stronger attraction. Orator Taycho was not so well skilled in logic as to amuse his audience with definitions of concrete and abstract terms ; or expatiate upon the genus and the difference ; or state propositions by the subject, the predicate, or the copula ; or form syllogisms by mood or figure ; but he was perfectly well acquainted with all the equivocal or synonymous words in his own language, and could ring the changes on them with great dexterity. He knew perfectly well how to express the same ideas by words that literally implied opposition—for example, a valuable conquest or an invaluable conquest ; a shameful rascal or a shameful villain ; a hard head or a soft head ; a large conscience or no conscience ; immensely great or immensely little ; damned high or damned low ; damned bitter, damned sweet ; damned severe, damned insipid ; and damned fulsome. He knew how to invert the sense of words by changing the manner of pronunciation—*e.g.*, " You are a very pretty fellow ! " to signify, " You are a very dirty scoundrel."—" You have *always* spoken respectfully of the higher powers ! " to express, " You have often insulted your betters, and even your sovereign."—" You have *never* turned tail to the principles you professed ! " to declare, " You have acted the part of an infamous apostate." He was well aware that words alter their signification according to the circumstances of times, customs, and the difference of opinion. Thus the name of Jack, who used to turn the spit, and pull off his master's boots, was transferred to an iron machine, and a wooden instrument now substituted for these purposes ; thus a stand for the tea-kettle acquired the name of a footman ; and the words Canon and Ordinance, signifying originally a rule or law, were extended to a piece of artillery, which is counted the *ultima lex*, or *ultima ratio regum*.

In the same manner the words infidel, heresy, good man, and political orthodoxy, imply very different significations, among different classes of people. A Mussulman is an infidel at Rome, and a Christian is distinguished as an unbeliever at Constantinople. A Papist by Protestantism understands heresy; to a Turk the same idea is conveyed by the sect of Ali. The term *good man* at Edinburgh implies fanaticism; upon the Exchange of London it signifies cash; and in the general acceptation, benevolence. Political orthodoxy has different, nay, opposite definitions, at different places in the same kingdom; at O—— and C——; at the Cocoa Tree in Pall Mall; and at Garraway's in Exchange Alley Our orator was well acquainted with all the legerdemain of his own language, as well as with the nature of the beast he had to rule. He knew when to distract its weak brain with a tumult of incongruous and contradictory ideas; he knew when to overwhelm its feeble faculty of thinking, by pouring in a torrent of words without any ideas annexed. These throng in, like city milliners to a Mile End assembly, while it happens to be under the direction of a conductor without strength and authority. Those that have ideas annexed, may be compared to the females provided with partners, which, though they may crowd the place, do not absolutely destroy all regulation and decorum. But those that are uncoupled, press in promiscuously, with such impetuosity, and in such numbers, that the puny master of the ceremonies is unable to withstand the irruption; far less to distinguish their quality, or accommodate them with partners; thus they fall into the dance without order, and immediately anarchy ensues. Taycho having kept the monster's brain on a simmer, until, like the cow-heel in *Don Quixote*, it seemed to cry, *Comenme, Comenme*—" Come eat me, come eat me "—then told him in plain terms, that it was expedient they should part with their wives and their children, their souls and their bodies, their substance and

their senses, their blood and their suet, in order to defend
the indefensible farm of Yesso, and to support Brut-an-tiffi,
their insupportable ally. The hydra, rolling itself in the
dust, turned up its huge, unwieldy paunch, and wagged its
forky tail; then licked the feet of Taycho, and through all
its hoarse, discordant throats, began to bray applause. The
Dairo rejoiced in his success, the first-fruits of which consisted in their agreeing to maintain an army of twenty thousand Tartar mercenaries, who, reinforced by the flower of
the national troops of Japan, were sent over to defend the
farm of Yesso; and in their consenting to prolong the annual
tribute granted to Brut-an-tiffi, who, in return for this
condescension, accommodated the Dairo with one of his
freebooting captains to command the Yessite army. This
new general had seen some service, and was counted a good
officer: but it was not so much on account of his military
character that he obtained this command, as for his dexterity
in prolonging the war; his skill in exercising all the different
arts of peculation; and his attachment to Brut-an-tiffi, with
whom he had agreed to co-operate in milking the Japanese
cow.

This plan they executed with such effect, as could not
possibly result from address alone, unassisted by the infatuation of those whom they pillaged. Every article of contingent expense for draught-horses, waggons, postage, forage,
provision, and secret service, was swelled to such a degree
as did violence to common sense as well as common honesty.
The general had a fellow-feeling with all the contractors in
the army, who were connected with him in such a manner
as seemed to preclude all possibility of detection. In vain
some of the Japanese officers endeavoured to pry into this
mysterious commerce; in vain inspectors were appointed by
the Government of Japan. The first were removed on different pretences: the last were encountered by such disgraces
and discouragements, as in a little time compelled them to
resign the office they had undertaken. In a word, there
was not a private mercenary Tartar soldier in this army,
who did not cost the empire of Japan as much as any subaltern

officer of its own ; and the annual charge of this continental war, undertaken for the protection of the farm of Yesso, exceeded the whole expense of any former war which Japan had ever maintained on its own account, since the beginning of the empire : nay, it was attended with one circumstance which rendered it still more insupportable. The money expended in armaments and operations, equipped and prosecuted on the side of Japan, was all circulated within the empire ; so that it still remained useful to the community in general : but no instance could be produced, of a single copan that ever returned from the continent of Tartary ; therefore, all the sums sent thither, were clear loss to the subjects of Japan. Orator Taycho acted as a faithful ally to Brut-an-tiffi, by stretching the bass-strings of the mobile in such a manner as to be always in concert with the extravagance of the Tartar's demands, and the absurdity of the Dairo's predilection. Fika-kaka was astonished at this phenomena ; while Muraclami hoped in secret, that the orator's brain was disordered ; and that his insanity would soon stand confessed, even to the conviction of the people.— " If," said he to himself, " they are not altogether destitute of human reason, they must, of their own accord, perceive and comprehend this plain proposition : a cask of water that discharges *three* by one pipe, and receives no more than *two* by another, must infallibly be emptied at the long run. Japan discharges *three* millions of obans every year for the defence of that blessed farm, which, were it put up to sale, would not fetch one-sixth part of the sum ; and the annual balance of her trade with all the world brings in *two* millions : ergo, it runs out faster than it runs in, and the vessel at the long run must be empty." Muraclami was mistaken. He had studied philosophy only in profile. He had endeavoured to investigate the sense, but he had never fathomed the absurdities of human nature. All that Taycho had done for Yesso, amounted not to one-third of what was required for the annual expense of Japan while it maintained the war against China in different quarters of Asia. A former Cuboy (rest his soul !), finding it impossible to raise within the year the exorbitant supplies that were required to gratify the avarice and ambition of the Dairo, had contrived the method of funding, which hath been lately adopted with such remarkable success in this kingdom. You know, Peacock, this is no more than borrowing a certain sum on the credit of the nation, and laying a fresh tax upon the public, to defray the interest of every sum thus borrowed : an excellent expedient, when kept within due bounds, for securing the established government, multiplying the dependants of the m——y, and throwing all the money of the empire into the hands of the administration. But those loans were so often repeated, that the national debt had already swelled to an enormous burthen : such a variety of taxes was laid upon the subject, as grievously enhanced all the necessaries of life ; consequently, the poor were distressed, and the price of labour was raised to such a degree, that the Japanese manufactures were everywhere undersold by the Chinese traders, who employed their workmen at a more moderate expense.

Taycho, in this dilemma, was seized with a strange conceit. Alchemy was at that period become a favourite study in Japan. Some Bonzes having more learning and avarice than their brethren, applied themselves to the study of certain Chaldean manuscripts, which their ancestors had brought from Assyria ; and in these they found the substance of all that is contained in the works of Hermes Trismegistus, Geber, Zosymus, the Panapolite, Olympiodorus, Heliodorus, Agathodæmon, Morienus, Albertus Magnus, and, above all, your countryman Roger Bacon, who adopted Geber's opinion, that Mercury is the common basis, and sulphur the cement of all metals. By-the-bye, this same Friar Bacon was well acquainted with the composition of gunpowder, though the reputation arising from the discovery has been given to Swartz, who lived many years after that monk of Westminster. Whether the philosopher's stone, otherwise called the Gift Azoth, the fifth Essence, or the Alkahest ; which last Van Helmont pilfered from the tenth book of the Archidoxa, that treasure so long deposited in the occiput of

the renowned Aureolus, Philippus, Paracelsus, Theophrastus,
Bombast, De Hohenheim ; was ever really attained by
human adept I am not at liberty to disclose ; but certain it
is, the philosophers and alchemists of Japan, employed by
orator Taycho to transmute baser metals into gold, miscarried in all their experiments. The whole evaporated in
smoke, without leaving so much as the scrapings of a crucible
for a specific against the itch. Tickets made of a kind of
bamboo had been long used to reinforce the circulation of
Japan ; but these were of no use in Tartary ; the mercenaries
and allies of that country would receive nothing but gold
and silver, which, indeed, one would imagine they had a
particular method of decomposing or annihilating ; for, of
all the millions transported thither, not one copan was ever
known to revisit Japan. "It was a country (as Hamlet
says), from whose bourne no travelling copan e'er returned."
    As the war of Yesso, therefore, engrossed all the specie of
Niphon, and some currency was absolutely necessary to the
subsistence of the Japanese, the orator contrived a method
to save the expense of solid food. He composed a mess that
should fill their bellies, and, at the same time, protract the
intoxication of their brains, which it was so much their
interest to maintain. He put them upon a diet of yeast ;
where this did not agree with the stomach, he employed
his emissaries to blow up the patients *a posteriori*, as the dog
was blown up by the madman of Seville, recorded by Cervantes. The individuals thus inflated were seen swaggering
about the streets, smooth and round, sleek and jolly, with
leering eyes and florid complexion. Every one seemed to
have the *os magna sonaturum*. He strutted with an air of
importance. He broke wind, and broached new systems.
He declared as if by revelation, that the more debt the public
owed, the richer it became ; that food was not necessary to
the support of life ; nor an intercourse of the sexes required
for the propagation of the species. He expatiated on yeast,
as the nectar of the gods, that would sustain the animal
machine, fill the human mind with divine inspiration, and
confer immortality. From the efficacy of this specific, he

began to prophesy concerning the White Horse, and declared himself an apostle of Bupo. Thus they strolled through the island of Niphon, barking and preaching the gospel of Fakku-basi, and presenting their barm goblets to all who were in quest of political salvation. The people had been so well prepared for infatuation by the speeches of Taycho, and the tidings of success from Tartary, that every passenger greedily swallowed the drench, and in a little time the whole nation was converted; that is, they were totally freed from those troublesome and impertinent faculties of reason and reflection, which could have served no other purpose but to make them miserable under the burthens to which their backs were now subjected. They offered up all their gold and silver, their jewels, their furniture and apparel, at the shrine of Fakku-basi, singing psalms and hymns in praise of the White Horse. They put arms into the hands of their children, and drove them into Tartary, in order to fatten the land of Yesso with their blood. They grew fanatics in that cause, and worshipped Brut-an-tiffi, as the favourite prophet of the beautified Bupo. All was staggering, staring, incoherence, and contortion, exclamation and eructation.

Still, this was no more than a temporary delirium which might vanish as the intoxicating effects of the yeast subsided. Taycho, therefore, called in two reinforcements to the drench. He resolved to satiate their appetite for blood, and to amuse their infantine vanity with the gew-gaws of triumph. He equipped out one armament at a considerable expense to make a descent on the coast of China, and sent another at a much greater, to fight the enemy in Fatsissio. The commander of the first disembarked upon a desolate island, demolished an unfinished cottage, and brought away a few bunches of wild grapes. He afterwards hovered on the Chinese coast; but was deterred from landing by a very singular phenomenon. In surveying the shore, through spying-glasses, he perceived the whole beach instantaneously fortified, as it were, with parapets of sand, which had escaped the naked eye; and at one particular part, there appeared a body of giants with very hideous features, peeping, as it were, from behind those parapets : from which circumstances the Japanese general concluded there was a very formidable ambuscade, which he thought it would be madness to encounter, and even folly to ascertain. One would imagine he had seen Homer's account of the Cyclops, and did not think himself safe, even at the distance of some miles from the shore ; for he pressed the commander of the Fune to weigh anchor immediately, and retire to a place of more safety. I shall now, Peacock, let you into the whole secret. This great officer was deceived by the carelessness of the commissary, who, instead of perspectives, had furnished him with glasses peculiar to Japan, that magnified and multiplied objects at the same time. They are called Pho-beron-tia. The large parapets of sand were a couple of mole-hills ; and the gigantic faces of grim aspect were the posteriors of an old woman sacrificing *sub dio*, to the powers of digestion.

There was another circumstance which tended to the miscarriage of this favourite expedition. The principal design was against a trading town, situated on a navigable river ; and at the place where this river disembogued itself into the sea, there was a Chinese fort called Sarouf. The admiral of the Fune sent the second in command, whose name was Sel-uon, to lay this fort in ashes, that the embarkation might pass without let or molestation. A Chinese pilot offered to bring his junk within a cable-length of the walls ; but he trusted to the light of his own penetration. He ran his junk aground, and solemnly declared there was not water sufficient to float any vessel of force, within three miles of Sarouf. This discovery he had made by sounding, and it proved two very surprising paradoxes : first, that the Chinese junks drew little or no water, otherwise they could not have arrived at the town where they were laid up ; secondly, that the fort Sarouf was raised in a spot where it neither could offend, nor be offended. But the Sey-seo-gun, Sel-uon, was a mighty man for paradoxes. His superior ni command was a plain man, who did not understand these niceties : he therefore grumbled, and began to be trouble-some ; upon which, a council of war was held, and he being over-ruled by a majority of voices, the whole embarkation returned to Niphon *re infecta*. You have been told how the beast called Legion brayed, and bellowed, and kicked, when the fate of Bihn-goh's expedition was known ; it was disposed to be very unruly at the return of this armament : but Taycho lulled it with a double dose of his mandragora. It growled at the giants, the sand-hills, and the paradoxes of Sel-uon : then brayed aloud *Taycho for ever !* rolled itself up like a lubberly hydra, yawned, and fell fast asleep. The other armament equipped for the operations in Fatsissio did not arrive at the place of destination till the opportunity for action was lost.

The object was the reduction of a town and island be-longing to the Chinese ; but before the Fune with the troops arrived from Niphon, the enemy having received intimation of their design, had reinforced the garrison and harbour with a greater number of forces and Fune than the Japanese commander could bring against them. He there-fore wisely declined an enterprise which must have ended in his own disgrace and destruction. The Chinese were successful in other parts of Fatsissio. They demolished some forts, they defeated some parties, and massacred some people belonging to the colonies of Japan. Perhaps the tidings of these disasters would have roused the people of Niphon from the lethargy of intoxication in which they were overwhelmed, had not their delirium been kept up by some fascinating amulets from Tartary : these were no other than the bubbles which Brut-an-tiffi swelled into mighty victories over the Chinese and Ostrog ; though, in fact, he had been severely cudgelled, and more than once in very great danger of crucifixion. Taycho presented the monster with a bowl of blood, which he told it this invincible ally had drawn from its enemies the Chinese, and, at the same time, blowed the gay bubbles athwart its numerous eyes. The hydra lapped the gore with signs of infinite relish ; groaned and grunted to see the bubbles dance ;

exclaimed, " O rare Taycho ! " and relapsed into the arms of slumber. Thus passed the first campaign of Taycho's administration.

By this time Fika-kaka was fully convinced that the orator actually dealt with the devil, and had even sold him his soul for this power of working miracles on the understanding of the populace. He began to be invaded with fears that the same consideration would be demanded of him for the ease and pleasure he now enjoyed in partnership with that magician. He no longer heard himself scoffed, ridiculed, and reviled in the assemblies of the people. He no longer saw his measures thwarted, nor his person treated with disdain. He no longer racked his brains for pretences to extort money, nor trembled with terror when he used these pretences to the public. The mouth of the opposition was now glued to his own posteriors. Many a time and often, when he heard orator Taycho declaiming against him from his rostrum, he cursed him in his heart, and was known to ejaculate " Kiss my a—se, Taycho," but little did he think that the orator would one day stoop to his compliance. He now saw that insolent, foul-mouthed demagogue ministering with the utmost servility to his pleasure and ambition. He filled his bags with the treasures of Japan, as if by enchantment ; so that he could now gratify his own profuse temper without stint or control. He took upon himself the whole charge of the administration ; and left Fika-kaka to the full enjoyment of his own sensuality thus divested of all its thorns.

It was the contemplation of these circumstances which inspired the Cuboy with a belief that the devil was concerned in producing this astonishing calm of felicity ; and that his infernal highness would require of him some extraordinary sacrifice for the extraordinary favours he bestowed. He could not help suspecting the sincerity of Taycho's attachment, because it seemed altogether unnatural ; and if his soul was to be the sacrifice, he wished to treat with Satan as a principal. Full of this idea he had recourse to his Bonzes as the most likely persons to procure him such an interview with the prince of darkness, as should not be attended with immediate danger to his corporal parts : but, upon inquiry, he found there was not one conjurer among them all. Some of them made a merit of their ignorance ; pretending they could not in conscience give application to an art which must have led them into communication with demons : others insisted that there was no such a thing as the devil ; and this opinion seemed to be much relished by the Cuboy : the rest frankly owned they knew nothing at all of the matter. For my part, Peacock, I not only know there is a devil, but I likewise know that he has marked out nineteen-twentieths of the people of this metropolis for his prey. How now ! You shake, sirrah ! You have some reason, considering the experiments you have been trying in the way of sorcery ; turning the sieve and shears ; mumbling gibberish over a goose's liver stuck with pins ; pricking your thumbs, and writing mystical characters with your blood ; forming spells with sticks laid across ; reading prayers backwards ; and invoking the devil by the name, style, and title of *Sathan, Abrasaæ, Adonai*. I know what communication you had with goody Thrusk at Camberwell, who undertook for three shillings and fourpence to convey you on a broomstick to Norway, where the devil was to hold a conventicle ; but you boggled at crossing the sea, without such security for your person as the beldame could not give. I remember your poring over the treatise *De volucri arborea*, until you had well-nigh lost your wits ; and your intention to enrol yourself in the Rosicrusian Society, until your intrigue with the tripe-woman in Thieving Lane destroyed your pretensions to chastity. Then you cloaked your own wickedness with an affectation of scepticism, and declared there never was any such existence as devil, demon, spirit, or goblin ; nor any such art as magic, necromancy, sorcery, or witchcraft. O infidel ! hast thou never heard of the three divisions of magic into natural, artificial, and diabolical ? The first of these is no more than medicine, hence the same word Pharmacopola signified both a wiseacre and apothecary. To the second belong the glass sphere of Archimedes, the flying wooden pigeon of Archytus, the emperor Leo's singing birds of gold, Boetius the Consolator's flying birds of brass, hissing serpents of the same metal, and the famous speaking head of Albertus Magnus. The last, which we call diabolical, depends upon the evocation of spirits : such was the heart exercised by the magicians of Pharaoh, as well as by that conjurer recorded by Gasper Puecerus, who animated the dead carcase of a famous female harper in Bologna, in such a manner, that she played upon her instrument as well as ever she had done in her life, until another magician removing the charm, which had been placed in her armpits, the body fell down deprived of all motion.

It is by such means that conjurers cure distempers with charms and amulets ; that, according to St. Isidore, they confound the elements, disturb the understanding, slay without poison or any perceptible wound, call up devils, and learn from them how to torment their enemies. Magic was known even to the ancient Romans. Cato teaches us how to charm a dislocated bone, by repeating these mystical words, *Incipe, cantare in alto, S. F. motas danata dardaries, Astotaries, dic una parite dum coeunt, etc.* Besides, the virtues of ABRACADABRA are well known ; though the meaning of the word has puzzled some of the best critics of the last age : such as Wendelinus, Scaliger, Saumaise, and Father Kircher, not to mention the ancient physician Serenus Sammoniaus, who describes the disposition of these characters in hexameter verse. I might here launch out into a very learned dissertation to prove that this very Serenus formed the word ABRACADABRA from the Chinese word 'Αβρασάξ, a name by which Basilides, the Egyptian heretic, defined the Deity, as the letters of it imply 365, the number of days in the year. This is the word still fair and legible in one of the two talismans found in the seventeenth century, of which Baronius gives us the figure in the second volume of his *Annals.*

By-the-bye, Peacock, you must take notice, that the figure of St. George encountering the dragon, which is the symbol

of the order of the Garter, and at this day distinguishes so
many inns, taverns, and ale-houses in this kingdom, was no
other originally than the device of an abraxas or amulet
worn by the Basilidians, as a charm against infection : for,
by the man on horseback killing the dragon, was typified
the sun purifying the air, and dispersing the noxious vapours
from the earth. An abraxas marked with this device, is
exhibited by Montfaucon out of the collection of Sig.
Capello. This symbol, improved by the cross on the top
of the spear, was afterwards adopted by the Christian
crusards, as a badge of their religious warfare, as well as an
amulet to ensure victory ; the cross alluding to Constantine's
labarum, with the motto ἐν τούτῳ νίκα, " In this you shall
conquer." The figure on horseback they metamorphosed
into St. George, the same with George the Arian, who at
one time was reckoned a martyr, and maintained a place in
the Roman Martyrology, from which he and others were
erased by Pope Gelasius in the fifth century, because the
accounts of their martyrdom were written by heretics.
This very George, while he officiated as Bishop of Alexandria,
having ordered a temple of the god *Mythras* to be purified,
and converted into a Christian church, found in the said
temple this emblem of the sun, which the Persians adored
under the name of *Mythras ;* and with the addition of the
cross, metamorphosed it into a symbol of Christian warfare
against idolatry. It was on this occasion that the Pagans
rose against George, and murdered him with the utmost
barbarity ; and from this circumstance he became a saint
and martyr, and the amulet or abraxas became his badge
of distinction. The cross was considered a sure protection
in battle, that every sword-hilt was made in this form, and
every warrior, before he engaged, kissed it in token of devotion : hence the phrase, " I kiss your hilt," which is sometimes
used even at this day. With respect to the mystical words,
ABRACAΞ, IAΩ, ΔOYNAI, which are found upon those
amulets, and supposed to be of Hebrew extract, though of
Greek character in termination ; if thou wouldst know
their real signification, thou mayest consult the learned

De Croy, in his treatise concerning the genealogies of the *Gnostics*. Thou wilt find it at the end of St. Irenæus's works, published by Grabius at Oxford.

But, to return to magic, thou must have heard of the famous Albertus Magnus de Bolstadt, who indifferently exercised the professions of conjurer, bawd, and man-mid-wife; who forged the celebrated *Androides*, or brazen-head, which pronounced oracles, and solved questions of the utmost difficulty; nor can the fame of Henry Cornelius Agrippa have escaped thee: he who wrote the treatises *De occulta Philosophia*; and *De cæcis Ceremoniis*; who kept his demon secured with an enchanted iron collar, in the shape of a black dog; which black dog being dismissed in his last moments with these words, *Abi perdita bestia quæ me totum perdidisti*, plunged itself in the river Soame, and immediately disappeared. But what need of those profane instances to prove the existence of magicians who held communication with the devil? Don't we read in the Scripture of the magicians of Pharaoh and Manasses; of the witch of Endor; of Simon and Barjesus, magicians; and of that sorceress of whose body the apostle Paul dispossessed the devil? Have not the fathers mentioned magicians and sorcerers? Have not different councils denounced anathemas against them? Hath not the civil law decreed punishments to be inflicted upon those convicted of the black art? Have not all the tribunals in France, England, and particularly in Scotland, condemned many persons to the stake for sorceries, on the fullest evidence, nay, even on their own confession?

Thou thyself mayest almost remember the havoc that was made among the sorcerers in one of the English colonies in North America, by Dr. Encrease Mather and Dr. Cotton Mather, those luminaries of the New England Church, under the authority and auspices of Sir William Phipps, that flower of knighthood and mirror of governors, who, not contented with living witnesses, called in the assistance of spectral evidence, to the conviction of those diabolical delinquents. This was a hint, indeed, which he borrowed from the famous trial of Urban Grandier, canon of Loudun in France, who was duly convicted of magic, upon the depositions of the devils *Astaroth, Eusas, Celsus, Acaos, Cedon, Asmodeus, Alix, Zabulon, Nephthalim, Cham, Uriel,* and *Acbas.* I might likewise refer thee to King James's *History of Witchcraft,* wherein it appears, upon incontrovertible evidence, that the devil not only presided in person at the assemblies of those wise women, but even condescended to be facetious; and often diverted them by dancing and playing gambols with a lighted candle in his breech. I might bid thee recollect the authenticated account of the Earl of Gowry's conspiracy against the said king, in which appears the deposition of a certain person, certifying that the Earl of Gowry had studied the black art: that he wore an amulet about his person, of such efficacy, that although he was run several times through the body, not one drop of blood flowed from the wounds until those mystical characters were removed. Finally, I could fill whole volumes with undeniable facts to prove the existence of magic: but what I have said shall suffice. I must only repeat it again, that there was not one magician, conjurer, wizard, or witch, among all the Bonzes of Japan, whom the Cuboy consulted: a circumstance that astonished him the more, as divers of them, nowithstanding their beards, were shrewdly suspected to be old women; and till that time, an old woman with a beard upon her chin had been always considered as an agent of the devil.

It was the nature of Fika-kaka to be impatient and impetuous. Perceiving that none of his Bonzes had any communication with the devil, and that many of them doubted whether there was any such personage as the devil, he began to have some doubts about his own soul: "For if there is no devil," says he, "there is no soul to be damned; and it would be a reproach to the justice of Heaven to suppose that all souls are to be saved, considering what rascally stuff mankind are made of." This was an inference which gave him great disturbance; for he was one of those who would rather encounter eternal damnation,

22

than run any risk of being annihilated. He therefore
assembled all those among the Bonzes who had the reputation
of being great philosophers and metaphysicians, in order to
hear their opinions concerning the nature of the soul. The
first reverend sage who delivered himself on this mysterious
subject, having stroked his grey beard, and hemmed thrice
with great solemnity, declared that the soul was an animal ;
a second pronounced it to be the number *three*, or proportion ;
a third contended for the number *seven*, or harmony ; a
fourth defined the soul the *universe* ; a fifth affirmed it was a
mixture of elements ; a sixth asserted it was composed of
fire ; a seventh opined it was formed of *water* ; an eighth
called it an *essence* ; a ninth an *idea* ; a tenth stickled for
substance without extension ; an eleventh for *extension without
substance* ; a twelfth cried it was an *accident* ; a thirteenth
called it a *reflecting mirror* ; a fourteenth the *image reflected* ;
a fifteenth insisted upon its being a *tune* ; a sixteenth believed
it was the *instrument* that played the tune ; a seventeenth
undertook to prove it was *material* ; an eighteenth exclaimed
it was *immaterial* ; a nineteenth allowed it was *something* ;
and a twentieth swore it was *nothing*. By this time all the
individuals that composed this learned assembly spoke
together, with equal eagerness and vociferation. The
volubility with which a great number of abstruse and
unintelligible terms and definitions were pronounced and
repeated, not only resembled the confusion of Babel, but
they had just the same effect upon the brain of Fika-kaka,
as is generally produced in weak heads by looking steadfastly
at a mill-wheel or vortex, or any other object in continual
rotation. He grew giddy, ran three times round, and
dropped down in the midst of the Bonzes, deprived of sense
and motion.

When he recovered so far as to be able to reflect upon
what had happened, he was greatly disturbed with the
terror of annihilation, as he had heard nothing said
in the consultation which could give him any reason to
believe that there was such a thing as an immortal soul.
In this emergency he sent for his counsellor Muraclami,

and when that lawyer entered his chamber, exclaimed, "My dear Mura, as I have a soul to be saved !—a soul to be saved ! Ay, there's the rub !—the devil a soul have I ! Those Bonzes are good for nothing but to kiss my a—se ; a parcel of ignorant asses ! Pox on their philosophy ! Instead of demonstrating the immortality of the soul, they have plainly proved the soul is a chimera, a Will-o'-the-wisp, a bubble, a term, a word, a nothing ! My dear Mura ! prove but that I have a soul, and I shall be contented to be damned to all eternity ! "—" If that be the case," said the other, "your Quambukuship may set your heart at rest : for, if you proceed to govern this empire, in conjunction with Taycho, as you have begun, it will become a point of eternal justice to give you an immortal soul (if you have not one already), that you may undergo eternal punishment, according to your demerits." The Cuboy was much comforted by this assurance, and returned to his former occupations with redoubled ardour. He continued to confer benefices on his back friends the Bonzes ; to regulate the whole army of tax-gatherers ; to bribe the tribunes, the centurions, the decuriones, and all the inferior mob-drivers of the empire ; to hire those pipers who were best skilled in making the multitude dance, and find out the ablest artists to scratch their long ears, and tickle their noses.

These toils were sweetened by a variety of enjoyments. He possessed all the pomp of ostentation, the vanity of levees, the pride of power, the pleasure of adulation, the happiness of being kicked by his sovereign and kissed by his Bonzes, and, above all, the delights of the stomach and the close-stool, which recurred in perpetual succession, and which he seemed to enjoy with particular relish ; for, it must be observed, to the honour of Fika-kaka, that what he eagerly received at one end, he as liberally refunded at the other. But as the faculties of his mind were insufficient to digest the greatness of power which had fallen to his share, so were the organs of his body unable to concoct the enormous mass of aliments which he so greedily swallowed. He laboured under an indigestion of both; and the vague promises which went upwards, as well as the murmurs which passed the other way, were no other than eruptive crudities arising from the defects of his soul and body.

As for Taycho, he confined himself to the management of the war. He recalled the general-in-chief from Fatsissio, because he had not done that which he could not possibly do : but, instead of sending another on whose abilities he could depend, he allowed the direction of the armament to devolve upon the second in command, whose character he could not possibly know; because, indeed, he was too obscure to have any character at all. The fruits of his sagacity soon appeared. The new general, Abra-moria, having reconnoitred a post of the enemy, which was found too strong to be forced, attacked it without hesitation, and his troops were repulsed and routed with considerable slaughter. It was lucky for Taycho that the tidings of this disaster were qualified by the news of two other advantages which the arms of Japan had gained. A separate corps of troops, under Yaf-frai and Ya-loff, reduced a strong Chinese fortress in the neighbourhood of Fatsissio ; and a body of Japanese, headed by a factor called Ka-liff, obtained a considerable victory at Fla-soa, in the farther extremity of Tartary, where a trading company of Meaco possessed a commercial settlement. The hydra of Meaco began to shake its numerous heads and growl, when it heard of Abra-moria's defeat. At that instant, one of its leaders exclaimed, " Bless thy long ears ! It was not Taycho that recommended Abra-moria to this command. He was appointed by the Fatzman." This was true. It was likewise true, that Taycho had allowed him quietly to succeed to the command, without knowing anything of his abilities ; it was equally true that Taycho was an utter stranger to Yaf-frai and Ya-loff, who took the fortress, as well as to the factor Ka-liff, who obtained the victory at the farther end of Tartary. Nevertheless, the beast cried aloud, " Hang Abra-moria ! and a fig for the Fatzman. But let the praise of Taycho be magnified ! " It was Taycho that subdued the fortress in the isle Ka-frit-o. It was Taycho that defeated the enemy at Fla-sao. Yaf-frai has slain his thousands ; Ya-loff has slain his five thousands ; but Taycho had slain his ten thousands.

Taycho had credit not only for the success of the Japanese arms, but likewise for the victories of Brut-an-tiffi, who had lately been much beholden to fortune. I have already observed what a noise that Tartar made when the Fatzman of Japan found himself obliged to capitulate with the Chinese general. In consequence of that event, the war was already at an end with respect to the Japanese, on the continent of Tartary. The Emperor of China took possession of the farm of Yesso ; the peasants quietly submitted to their new masters ; and those very freebooting Tartar chiefs, who had sold their subjects as soldiers to serve under the Fatzman, had already agreed to send the very same mercenaries into the army of China. It was at this juncture that Brut-an-tiffi exalted his throat. In the preceding campaign he had fought with various success. One of his generals had given battle to the Mantchoux Tartars, and each side claimed the victory. Another of his leaders had been defeated and taken by the Ostrog. The Chinese had already advanced to the frontiers of Brut-an-tiffi's dominions. In this dilemma he exerted himself with equal activity and address : he repulsed the Chinese army with considerable loss ; and in the space of one month after this action, gained a victory over the general of the Ostrog. These advantages rendered him insufferably arrogant. He exclaimed against the Fatzman, he threatened the Dairo, and, as I have taken notice above, a new army was raised at the expense of Japan, to defend him from all future invasions of the Chinese.

Already the Tartar general, Bron-xi-tic, who was vested, at his desire, with the command of the mercenary army of Japan, had given a severe check to a strong body of the Chinese, and even threatened to carry the war into the empire of China ; and he was forced to retreat in his turn towards the farm of Yesso. But from nothing did orator

Taycho reap a fuller harvest of praise, than from the conquest of Tzin-khall, a settlement of the Chinese on the coast of Terra Australis ; which conquest was planned by a Banyan merchant of Meaco, who had traded on that coast and was particularly known to the king of the country.   This royal savage was uneasy at the neighbourhood of the Chinese, and conjured the merchant, whose name was Thum-Khumm-qua, to use his influence at the court of Meaco, that an armament should be equipped against the settlement of Tzin-khall, he himself solemnly promising to co-operate in the reduction of it with all his forces.   Thum-Khumm-qua, whose zeal for the good of his country got the better of all his prudential maxims, did not fail to present this object in the most interesting points of view.   He demonstrated to Taycho the importance of the settlement ; that it abounded with slaves, ivory, gold, and a precious gum which was not to be found in any other part of the world : a gum in great request all over Asia, and particularly among the Japanese, who were obliged to purchase it in time of war at second-hand from their enemies the Chinese, at an exorbitant price.   He demonstrated that the loss of this settlement would be a terrible wound to the Emperor of China, and proved that the conquest of it could be achieved at a very trifling expense. He did more. Though by the maxims of his sect he was restrained from engaging in any military enterprise, he offered to conduct the armament in person, in order the more effectually to keep the king of the country steady to his engagements. Though the scheme was in itself plausible and practicable, Mr. Orator Taycho shuffled and equivocated until the season for action was past. But Thum-Khumm-qua was indefatigable. He exhorted, he pressed, he remonstrated, he complained ; and besieged the orator's house in such a manner, that Taycho at length, in order to be rid of his importunity, granted his request. A small armament was fitted out ; the Banyan embarked in it, leaving his own private affairs in con-fusion ; and the settlement was reduced according to his prediction.

When the news of this conquest arrived at Meaco, the multifarious beast brayed hoarse applause, and the minister Taycho was magnified exceedingly. As for Thum-Khumm-qua, whose private fortune was consumed in the expedition, all the recompense he received was the consciousness of having served his country. In vain he reminded Taycho of his promises : in vain he recited the minister's own letters, in which he had given his word that the Banyan should be liberally rewarded, according to the importance of his services: Taycho was both deaf and blind to all his remonstrances and representations ; and, at last, fairly flung the door in his face.

Such was the candour and gratitude of the incomparable Taycho. The poor projector, Thum-Khumm-qua, found himself in a piteous case, while the whole nation resounded with joy for the conquest which his sagacity had planned, and his zeal carried into execution. He was not only abandoned by the minister Taycho, but also renounced by the whole sect of the Banyans, who looked upon him as a wicked apostate, because he had been concerned with those who fought with the arm of the flesh. It was lucky for him that he afterwards found favour with a subsequent minister, who had not adopted all the maxims of his pre-decessor, Taycho. The only measures which this egregious demagogue could hitherto properly call his own were these : his subsidiary treaty with Brut-an-tiffi ; his raising an im-mense army of mercenaries to act in Tartary for the benefit of that prince ; his exacting an incredible sum of money from the people of Japan ; and finally, two successive armaments which he had sent to annoy the sea-coast of China. I have already given an account of the first, the intent of which was frustrated by a mistake in the perspectives. The other was more fortunate in the beginning. Taycho had, by the force of his genius, discovered that nothing so effectually destroyed the oiled paper which the Chinese use in their windows, instead of glass, as the gold coin called oban, when discharged from a military engine at a proper distance. He found that the gold was more compact, more heavy,

more malleable, more manageable than any other metal
or substance that he knew : he therefore provided a great
quantity of obans, and a good body of slingers ; and these
being conveyed to the coast of China, in a squadron of
Fune, as none of the Chinese appeared to oppose these
hostilities, a select number of troops were employed to make
ducks and drakes with the obans, on the supposition that
this diversion would allure the enemy to the sea-side, where
they may be knocked on the head without further trouble :
but the care of their own safety got the better of their
curiosity on this occasion : and fifty thousand obans were
expended in this manner, without bringing one Chinese
from his lurking hole. Considerable damage was done to
the windows of the enemy. Then the forces were landed in
a village which they found deserted. Here they burned
some fishing boats, and from hence they carried off
some military machines, which were brought to Meaco,
and conveyed through the streets in procession, amidst
the acclamations of the hydra, who sang the praise of
Taycho.

Elevated by this triumph, the minister sent forth the same
armament a second time under a new general of his own
choosing, whose name was Hylib-bib, who had long entertained an opinion, that the inhabitants of China were not
beings of flesh and blood, but mere fantastic shadows, who
could neither offend nor be offended. Full of this opinion he
made a descent on the coast of that empire ; and to convince
his followers that his notion was right, he advanced some
leagues into the country, without having taken any precautions to secure a retreat, leaving the Fune at anchor
upon an open beach. Some people alleged that he depended upon the sagacity of an engineer recommended
to him by Taycho ; which engineer had such an excellent nose that he could smell a Chinese at the distance
of ten leagues : but it seems the scent failed him at this
juncture.

Perhaps the Chinese general had trailed rusty bacon and
other odoriferous substances to confound his sense of smelling.

Perhaps no dew had fallen over-night, and a strong breeze blew towards the enemy. Certain it is, Hylib-bib, in the evening, received repeated intelligence that he was within half a league of a Chinese general, at the head of a body of troops greatly superior in number to the Japanese forces which he himself commanded. He still believed it was all illusion; and when he heard the drums beat, declared it was no more than a ridiculous enchantment. He thought proper, however, to retreat towards the sea-side; but this he did with great deliberation, after having given the enemy fair notice by beat of drum. His motions were so slow, that he took seven hours to march three miles. When he reached the shore where the Fune were at anchor, he saw the whole body of the Chinese drawn up on a rising ground ready to begin the attack. He ordered his rear guard to face about, on the supposition that the phantoms would disappear as soon as they showed their faces; but finding himself mistaken, and perceiving some of his own people to drop, in consequence of missiles that came from the enemy, he very calmly embarked with his van, leaving his rear to amuse the Chinese, by whom they were, in less than five minutes, either massacred or taken. From this small disgrace the general deduced two important corollaries: first, that the Chinese were actually material beings capable of impulsion; and secondly, that his engineer's nose was not altogether infallible. The people of Meaco did not seem to relish the experiments by which these ideas were ascertained. The monster was heard to grunt in different streets of the metropolis; and these notes of discontent produced the usual effect in the bowels of Fika-kaka: but orator Taycho had his flowers of rhetoric and his bowl of mandragora in readiness. He assured them that Hylib-bib should be employed for the future in keeping sheep on the island of Xicoco, and the engineer be sent to hunt truffles on the mountains of Ximo. Then he tendered his dose, which the hydra swallowed with signs of pleasure; and lastly, he mounted upon its back, and rode in triumph under the windows of the astonished Cuboy, who, while he shifted his trousers, exclaimed in a rapture of joy, "All hail, Taycho, thou prince of monster-taming men! The Dairo shall kick thy posteriors, and I will kiss them in token of approbation and applause."

The time was now come when Fortune, which had hitherto smiled upon the Chinese arms, resolved to turn tail to that vainglorious nation; and precisely at the same instant, Taycho undertook to display his whole capacity in the management of the war. But before he assumed this province, it was necessary that he should establish a despotism in the council of twenty-eight, some members of which had still the presumption to offer their advice towards the administration of affairs. This council being assembled by the Dairo's order, to deliberate upon the objects of the next campaign, the president began by asking the opinion of Taycho, who was the youngest member; upon which the orator made no articulate reply, but cried "Ba-ba-ba-ba!" The Dairo exclaimed "Boh!" The Fatzman ejaculated the interjection "Pish!" The Cuboy sat in silent astonishment. Gotto-mio swore the man was dumb, and hinted something of lunacy. Foksi-rokhu shook his head; and Soo-san-sin-o shrugged up his shoulders. At length, Fika-kaka going round and kissing Taycho on the forehead, "My dear boy," cried he, "Gad's curse! what's the matter? Do but open the sluices of your eloquence once more, my dear orator; let us have one simile, one dear simile; and then I shall die contented. With respect to the operations of the campaign, don't you think——" Here he was interrupted with "Ka-ka-ka-ka!"—"Heigh-day!" cried the Cuboy. "Ba-ba-ba, ka-ka-ka! that's the language of children!"—"And children you shall be," exclaimed the orator. "Here is a twopenny trumpet for the amusement of the illustrious Got-hama-baba, a sword of gingerbread covered with gold leaf for the Fatzman, and a rattle for my Lord Cuboy. I have likewise, sugar-plums for the rest of the council."

So saying, he, without ceremony, advanced to the

Dairo, and tied a scarf round the eyes of his imperial majesty; then he produced a number of padlocks, and sealed up the lips of every Quo in council, before they could recollect themselves from their first astonishment. The assembly broke up abruptly; and the Dairo was conducted to his cabinet by the Fatzman and the Cuboy, which last endeavoured to divert the chagrin of his royal master by blowing the trumpet, and shaking the rattle in his ears; but Got-hama-baba could not be so easily appeased. He growled like an enraged bear at the indignity which had been offered to him, and kicked the Cuboy before, as well as behind. Mr. Orator Taycho was fain to come to an explanation. He assured the Dairo it was necessary that his imperial majesty should remain in the dark, and that the whole council should be muzzled for a season, otherwise he should not accomplish the great things he had projected, in favour of the farm of Yesso. He declared that while his majesty remained blindfold, he would enjoy all his other senses in greater perfection; that his ears would be every day regaled with the shouts of triumph, conveyed in notes of uncommon melody; and that the less quantity of animal spirits was expended in vision, the greater proportion would flow to his extremities; consequently, his pleasure would be more acute in his pedestrian exercitations upon the Cuboy, and others whom he delighted to honour. He, therefore, exhorted him to undergo a total privation of eyesight, which at best was a troublesome faculty, that exposed mankind to a great variety of disagreeable spectacles.

This was a proposal which the Dairo did not relish : on the contrary, he waxed exceedingly wroth, and told the orator, he would rather enjoy one transient glance of the farm of Yesso, than the most exquisite delights that could be procured for all the other senses. "To gratify your majesty with that ineffable pleasure," cried Taycho, "I have devoted myself, soul and body, and even reconciled contradictions. I have renounced all my former principles without forfeiting the influence which, by professing those principles, I had gained. I have obtained the most astonishing victories over common sense, and even refuted mathematical demonstration. The many-headed mob, which no former demagogue could ever tame, I have taught to fetch and to carry ; to dance to my pipe, to bray to my tune, to swallow what I present without murmuring, to lick my feet when I am angry, and kiss the rod when I think proper to chastise it. I have done more, my liege. I have prepared a drench for it, which, like Lethe, washes away the remembrance of what is past, and takes away all sense of its own condition. I have swept away all the money of the empire ; and persuaded the people not only to beggar themselves, but likewise to entail indigence upon the latest posterity ; and all for the sake of Yesso. It is by dint of these efforts, I have been able to subsidise Brut-an-tiffi, and raise an army of one hundred thousand men, to defend your imperial majesty's farm, which, were the entire property of it brought to market, would not fetch one third part of the sums which are now yearly expended in its defence. I shall strike but one great stroke in the country of Fatsissio, and then turn the whole stream of the war into the channel of Tartary, until the barren plains of Yesso are fertilised with human blood. In the meantime, I must insist upon your majesty's continuing in the dark, and amusing yourself in your cabinet, with the trumpet and other gewgaws, which I have provided for your diversion, otherwise I quit the reins of administration, and turn the monster out of my trammels ; in which case, like the dog that returns to its vomit, it will not fail to take up its former prejudices against Yesso, which I have with such pains obliged it to resign."—" Oh, my dear Taycho ! " cried the affrighted Dairo, " talk not of leaving me in such a dreadful dilemma. Rather than the dear farm should fall into the hands of the Chinese, I would be contented to be led about blindfold all the days of my life. Proceed in your own way. I invest you with full power and authority, not only to gag my whole council, but even to nail their ears to the pillory, should it be found necessary for the benefit of Yesso. In token of which delegation, present your posteriors, and I will bestow upon you a double portion of my favour." Taycho humbly thanked his imperial majesty for the great honour he intended him, but begged leave to decline the ceremony, on account of the hæmorrhoids which at that time gave him great disturbance.

The orator, having thus annihilated all opposition in the council of twenty-eight, repaired to his own house, in order to plan the operations of the next campaign. Though he had reinforced the army in Tartary with the flower of the Japanese soldiery, and destined a strong squadron of Fune, as usual, to parade on the coast of China ; he foresaw it would be necessary to amuse the people, with some new stroke on the side of Fatsissio, which indeed, was the original and the most natural scene of the war. He locked himself up in his closet : and consulting the map of Fatsissio, he found that the principal Chinese settlement of that island, was a fortified town called Quib-quab, to which there was access by two different avenues : one by a broad, rapid, navigable river, on the banks of which the town was situated : and the other by an inland route, over mountains, lakes, and dangerous torrents. He measured the map with his compass, and perceived that both routes were nearly of the same length : and therefore he resolved, that the forces in Fatsissio, being divided into two equal bodies, should approach the place, by the two different avenues, on the supposition that they would both arrive before the wall of Quib-quab, at the same instant of time. The conduct of the inland expedition was given to Yaf-frai, who now commanded in chief in Fatsissio ; and the rest of the troops were sent up the great river, under the auspices of Ya-loff, who had so eminently distinguished himself in the course of the preceding year.

Orator Taycho had received some articles of intelligence, which embarrassed him a little at first, but these difficulties soon vanished, before the vigour of his resolutions. He knew that not only the town of Quib-quab was fortified by art, but also, that the whole adjacent country was almost impregnable by nature : that one Chinese general blocked up the passes, with a strong body of forces, in the route which was to be followed by Yaf-frai; and that another commanded a separate corps in the neighbourhood of Quib-quab, equal, at least in number, to the detachment of Ya-loff, whom he might therefore either prevent from landing, or attack after he should be landed; or finally, should neither of these attempts succeed, he might reinforce the garrison of Quib-quab, so as to make it more numerous than the besieging army, which, according to the rules of war, ought to be ten times the number of the besieged.

On the other hand, in order to invalidate these objections, he reflected that fortune, which hath such a share in all military events, is inconstant and variable; that as the Chinese had been so long successful in Fatsissio, it was now their turn to be unfortunate. He reflected that the demon of folly was capricious, and that as it had so long possessed the rulers and generals of Japan, it was high time it should shift its quarters, and occupy the brains of the enemy; in which case they would quit their advantageous posts, and commit some blunder, that would lay them at the mercy of the Japanese. With respect to the reduction of Quib-quab, he had heard, indeed, that the besiegers ought to be ten times the number of the garrison besieged; but as every Japanese was equivalent to ten subjects of China, he thought the match was pretty equal. He reflected, that even if this expedition should not succeed, it would be of little consequence to his reputation, as he could plead at home, that he neither conceived the original plan, nor appointed any of the officers concerned in the execution. It is true, he might have reinforced the army in Fatsissio, so as to leave very little to fortune: but then he must have subtracted something from the strength of the operations in Tartary, which was now become the favourite scene of the war; or he must have altogether suspended the execution of another darling scheme, which was literally his own conception. There was an island in the great Indian Ocean, at a considerable distance from Fatsissio; and here the

Corbould fecit.

Mr. Orator Taycho in his Study.

ATOM.

Chinese had a strong settlement. Taycho was inflamed with the ambition of reducing this island, which was called Thin-quo ; and for this purpose he resolved to embark a body of forces which should co-operate with the squadron of Fune, destined to cruise in those latitudes. The only difficulty that remained, was to choose a general to direct this enterprise.

He perused a list of all the military officers in Japan ; and as they were all equal in point of reputation, he began to examine their names, in order to pitch upon that, which should appear to be the most significant : and in this particular, Taycho was a little superstitious. Not but that surnames, when properly bestowed, might be rendered very useful terms of distinction : but I must tell thee, Peacock, nothing can be more preposterously absurd than the practice of inheriting *cognomina*, which ought ever to be purely personal. I would ask thee, for example, what propriety there was in giving the name *Xenophon*, which signifies *one that speaks a foreign language*, to the celebrated Greek who distinguished himself not only as a consummate captain, but also as an elegant writer in his mother tongue ? What could be more ridiculous than to denominate the great philosopher of Crotona, *Pythagoras*, which implies a *stinking speech* ? Or what could be more misapplied than the name of the weeping philosopher *Heraclitus*, signifying *military glory* ? The inheritance of surnames among the Romans, produced still more ludicrous consequences. The best and noblest families in Rome derived their names from the coarsest employments, or else from the corporeal blemishes of their ancestors. The *Pisones* were millers ; the *Cicerones* and the *Lentuli* were so called from the *vetches* and the *lentils* which their forefathers dealt in ; the *Fabij* were so denominated from a dung-pit, in which the first of the family were begot by stealth in the way of fornication. A ploughman gave rise to the great family of the *Serrani*, the ladies of which always went without smocks ; the *Suilli*, the *Bubulci*, and the *Porci* were descended from a swineherd and a hog-butcher. What could be more disgraceful than to call the senator *Strabo, Squintum* ? or a fine lady of the house of *Pæti, Pigsnies* ? or to distinguish a matron of the *Limi,* by the appellation of *Sheep's-eye* ? What could be more dishonourable than to give the surname of *Snub-nose* to P. *Silius,* the proprætor, because his great, great, great-grandfather had a nose of that make ? Ovid, indeed, had a long nose, and therefore was justly denominated *Naso* : but why should Horace be called *Flaccus,* as if his ears had been stretched in the pillory ? I need not mention the *Burrbi, Nigri, Rufi, Aquilij,* and *Rutilij,* because we have the same foolish surnames in England ; and even the *Lappa,* for I myself know a very pretty miss called *Rough-head,* though in fact there is not a young lady in the Bills of Mortality who takes more pains to dress her hair to the best advantage. The famous dictator whom the deputies of Rome found at the plough, was known by the name of *Cincinnatus,* or *Ragged-head.* Now I leave you to judge how it would sound in these days, if a footman at the playhouse should call out, " *My Lady Ragged-head's coach. Room for my Lady Ragged-head.*" I am doubtful whether the English name of *Hale* does not come from the Roman cognomen *Hala,* which signified *stinking breath.* What need I mention the *Plauti, Panci, Valgi, Vari, Vatiæ,* and *Scauri,* the *Tuditanti,* the *Malici, Cenestellæ,* and *Leceæ* ; in other words, the *Splay-foots, Bandy-legs, Shamble-shins, Baker-knees, Club-foots, Hammer-heads, Chubby-cheeks, Bald-heads,* and *Letchers.* I shall not say a word of the *Butio* or *Buzzard,* that I may not be obliged to explain the meaning of the word *Triorchis,* from whence it takes its denomination ; yet all those were great families in Rome. But I cannot help taking notice of some of the same improprieties which have crept into the language and customs of this country.

Let us suppose, for example, a foreigner reading an English newspaper in these terms : " Last Tuesday the right honourable *Timothy Sillyman,* secretary of state for the southern department, gave a grand entertainment to the nobility and gentry at his house in *Knave's Acre.* The evening was concluded with a ball, which was opened by Sir *Samuel Hog* and Lady *Diana Rough-head*.—We hear there is purpose of marriage between Mr. Alderman *Small-cock* and Miss *Harriot Hair-stones*, a young lady of great fortune and superlative merit.—By the last mail from Germany we have certain advice of a complete victory which General *Coward* has obtained over the enemy. On this occasion the general displayed all the intrepidity of a renowned hero. By the same channel we are informed that Lieutenant *Little-fear* has been broke by a court-martial for cowardice.—We hear that *Edward West*, Esq., will be elected president of the directors of the *East India* Company for the ensuing year.— It is reported that Commodore *North* will be sent with a squadron into the *South Sea*. Captains *East* and *South* are appointed by the Lords of the Admiralty, commanders of two frigates to sail on the discovery of the *North-west* passage.—Yesterday morning Sir *John Summer*, Bart., lay dangerously ill at his house in *Spring Garden*: he is attended by Dr. *Winter*: but there is no hope of his recovery.— Saturday last *Philip Frost*, a dealer in *Gunpowder*, died at his house on *Snow Hill*, of a high fever caught by over-heating himself in walking for a wager from *No Man's Land* to the *World's End*.—Last week Mr. *John Fog*, teacher of astronomy in Rotherhithe, was married to the widow *Fairweather* of *Puddledock*.—We hear from Bath, that on Thursday last a duel was fought on Lansdown, by Captain *Sparrow* and *Richard Hawke*, Esq., in which the latter was mortally wounded.—Friday last ended the sessions at the Old Bailey, when the following persons received sentence of death: *Leonard Lamb*, for the murder of *Julius Wolf*; and *Henry Grave*, for robbing and assaulting Dr. *Death*, whereby the said *Death* was put in fear of his life. *Giles Gosling*, for defrauding *Simeon Fox* of four guineas and his watch, by subtle craft, was transported for seven years; and *David Drinkwater* was ordered to be set in the stocks, as an habitual drunkard. The trial of *Thomas Green*, whitster, at Fulham, for a rape on the body of *Flora White*, a mulatto, was put off till next sessions, on account of the absence of two material evidences, viz., *Sarah Brown*, clear-starcher, of *Pimlico*, and *Anthony Black*, scarlet-dyer, of *Wandsworth*."— I ask thee, Peacock, whether a sensible foreigner, who understood the literal meaning of these names, which are all truly British, would not think ye a nation of humorists, who delighted in cross-purposes and ludicrous singularity?

But, indeed, ye are not more absurd in this particular than some of your neighbours. I know a Frenchman of the name of *Bouvier*, which signifies *Cowkeeper*, pique himself upon his noblesse; and a general called *Valavoir*, is said to have lost his life by the whimsical impropriety of his surname, which signifies * *Go and see*. You may remember an Italian minister called *Grossa-testa*, or *Great-head*, though in fact he had scarce any head at all. That nation has, likewise, its *Sforzas*, *Malatestas*, *Boccanigras*, *Porcinas*, *Giudices*; its *Colonnas*, *Muratorios*, *Medicis*, and *Gozzi*; *Endeavours*, *Cuckle-heads*, *Black-muzzles*, *Hogs*, *Judges*, *Pillars*, *Masons*, *Leeches*, and *Chubby-chops*. Spain has its *Almohadas*, *Girones*, *Uteras*, *Urfinas*, and *Zapatas*; signifying *Cushions*, *Gores*, *Bullocks*, *Bears*, and *Slippers*. The Turks, in other respects sensible people, fall into the same extravagance, with respect to the inheritance of surnames. An Armenian merchant, to whom I once belonged at Aleppo, used to dine at the house of a cook whose name was *Clock-maker*; and the handsomest Ichoglan in the Bashaw's seraglio was surnamed *Crook-back*. If we may believe the historian *Buck*, there was the same impropriety in the same epithet bestowed upon Richard III. king of England, who, he says, was one of the best made men of the age in which he lived: but here I must contradict the said *Buck*, from my own knowledge. Richard had, undoubtedly, one shoulder higher than the other, and his left arm was a little shrunk and contracted:

---

* The general taking a solitary walk in the evening, was questioned by a sentinel, and answered " Va la voir." The soldier taking the words in the literal sense, repeated the challenge: he was answered in the same manner; and being affronted, fired on the general, who fell dead on the spot.

but notwithstanding the ungracious colours in which he has been drawn by the flatterers of the house of Lancaster, I can assure thee, Peacock, that Richard was a prince of a very agreeable aspect, and excelled in every personal accomplishment; neither was his heart a stranger to 'the softer passions of tenderness and pity. The very night that preceded the battle of Bosworth, in which he lost his life, he went in disguise to the house of a farmer in the neighbourhood, to visit an infant son there boarded, who was the fruit of an amour between him and a young lady of the first condition. Upon this occasion he embraced the child with all the marks of paternal affection, and doubtful of the issue of the approaching battle, shed a flood of tears at parting from him, after having recommended him to the particular care of his nurse, to whom he gave money and jewels to a considerable value. After the catastrophe of Richard this house was plundered, and the nurse with difficulty escaped to another part of the country; but as the enemies of Richard now prevailed, she never durst reveal the secret of the boy's birth, and he was bred up as her own son to the trade of brick-laying, in which character he lived and died at an advanced age in London. Moreover, it is but justice in me, who constituted part of one of Richard's yeomen of the guard, to assure thee that this prince was not so wicked and cruel as he has been represented. The only share he had in the death of his brother Clarence, was his forbearing to interpose in the behalf of that prince with their elder brother King Edward IV., who, in fact, was the greatest brute of the whole family: neither did he poison his own wife, nor employ assassins to murder his two nephews in the tower. Both the boys were given by Tyrrel in charge to a German Jew, with directions to breed them up as his own children, in a remote country; and the eldest died of a fever at Embden, and the other afterwards appeared as claimant of the English crown: all the world knows how he finished his career under the name of Perkin Warbeck.

So much for the abuse of surnames, in the investigation

of which I might have used thy own by way of illustration ;
for, if thou and all thy generation were put to the rack,
they would not be able to give any tolerable reason why
thou shouldst be called *Peacock* rather than *Crab-louse*.
But it is now high time to return to the thread of our
narration. Taycho, having considered the list of officers,
without finding one name which implied any active virtue,
resolved that the choice should depend upon accident.
He hustled them altogether in his cap, and putting in his
hand at random, drew forth that of Hob-nob ; a person who
had grown old in obscurity, without ever having found an
opportunity of being concerned in actual service. His
very name was utterly unknown to Fika-kaka ; and this
circumstance the orator considered as a lucky omen, for the
Cuboy had such a remarkable knack at finding out the
least qualified subjects, and overlooking merit, his new
colleague concluded (not without some shadow of reason)
that Hob-nob's being unknown to the prime minister was
a sort of negative presumption in favour of his character.
This officer was accordingly placed at the head of an armament, and sent against the island of Thin-quo, in the conquest
of which he was to be supported by a squadron of Fune
already in those latitudes under the command of the chief
He-Rhumn.

The voyage was performed without much loss : the
troops were landed without opposition. They had already
advanced towards a rising ground which commanded the
principal town of the island, and He-Rhumn had offered to
land and draw the artillery by the mariners of his squadron,
when Hob-nob had a dream which disconcerted all his
measures. He dreamed that he entertained all the islanders
in the temple of the White Horse ; and that his own grandmother did the honours of the table. Indeed, he could
not have performed a greater act of charity ; for they were
literally in danger of perishing by famine. Having consulted
his interpreter on this extraordinary dream, he was given
to understand that the omen was unlucky ; that if he persisted in his hostilities, he himself would be taken prisoner,

and offered up as a sacrifice to the idol of the place. While he ruminated on this unfavourable response, the principal inhabitants of the island assembled, in order to deliberate upon their own deplorable situation. They had neither troops, arms, fortifications, nor provisions, and despaired of supplies, as the fleet of Japan surrounded the island. In this emergency, they determined to submit without opposition, and appointed a deputation to go and make a tender of the island to General Hob-nob. This deputation, preceded by white flags of truce, the Japanese commander no sooner descried, than he thought upon the interpretation of his dream. He mistook the deputies with their white flags for the Bonzas of the idol to which he was to be sacrificed : and, being sorely troubled in mind, ordered the troops to be immediately embarked, notwithstanding the exhortations of He-Rhumn, and the remonstrances of Rha-rin-tumm, the second in command, who used a number of arguments to dissuade him from his purpose. The deputies seeing the enemy in motion made a halt, and after they were fairly on board, returned to the town, singing hymns in praise of the idol Fo, who, they imagined, had confounded the understanding of the Japanese general.

The attempt upon Thin-quo, having thus miscarried, Hob-nob declared he would return to Japan ; but was with great difficulty persuaded by the commander of the Fune and his own second, to make a descent upon another island belonging to the Chinese, called *Qua-chu*, where they assured him he would meet with no opposition. As he had no dream to deter him from this attempt, he suffered himself to be persuaded, and actually made good his landing : but the horror occasioned by the apparition of his grandmother had made such an impression upon his mind, as affected the constitution of his body. Before he was visited by another such vision he sickened and died ; and in consequence of his death, Rha-rin-tumm and He-Rhumn made a conquest of the island of Qua-chu, which was much more valuable than Thin-quo, the first and sole object of the expedition. When the first news of this second descent arrived in Japan,

the ministry were in the utmost confusion. Mr. Orator
Taycho did not scruple to declare that General Hob-nob
had misbehaved : first, in relinquishing Thin-quo, upon such
a frivolous pretence as the supposed apparition of an old
woman ; secondly, in attempting the conquest of another
place, which was not so much as mentioned in his instructions.
The truth is, the importance of Qua-chu was not known
to the cabinet of Japan.   Fika-kaka believed it was some
place on the continent of Tartary, and exclaimed in a violent
passion, " Rot the blockhead, Hob-nob ; he'll have an army
of Chinese on his back in a twinkling ! "   When the president
Soo-san-sin-o assured him that Qua-chu was a rich island at
an immense distance from the continent of Tartary, the
Cuboy insisted upon kissing his excellency's posteriors for
the agreeable information he had received.   In a few weeks
arrived the tidings of the island's being totally reduced by
Rha-rin-tumm and He-Rhumn.   Then the conquest was
published throughout the empire of Japan, with every
circumstance of exaggeration.   The blatant beast brayed
applause.   The rites of Fakku-basi were celebrated with
unusual solemnity, and hymns of triumph were sung to the
glory of the great Taycho.   Even the Cuboy arrogated
to himself some share of the honour gained by this expedition;
inasmuch as the general, Rha-rin-tumm, was the brother of
his friend Mr. Secretary *No-bo-dy*.   Fika-kaka gave a grand
entertainment at his palace, where he appeared crowned
with a garland of the *Tsikk-bura-siba*, or laurel of Japan ;
and ate so much of the soup of *Joniku*, or famous *Swallow's-
nest*, that he was for three days troubled with flatulencies
and indigestion.

In the midst of all this festivity, the emperor still growled
and grumbled about Yesso.   His new ally Brut-an-tiffi had
met with a variety of fortune, and even suffered some shocks,
which orator Taycho, with all his art, could not keep from
the knowledge of the Dairo.   He had been severely drubbed
by the Mantchoux, who had advanced for that purpose
even to his court-yard : but this was nothing in comparison
to another disaster, from which he had a hair's-breadth

escape. The Great Khan had employed one of his most wily and enterprising chiefs to seize Brut-an-tiffi by surprise, that he might be brought to justice, and executed as a felon and perturbator of the public peace. Kunt-than, who was the partisan pitched upon for this service, practised a thousand stratagems to decoy Brut-an-tiffi into a careless security : but he was still baffled by the vigilance of Yam-a-Kheit, a famous soldier of fortune, who had engaged in the service of the outlawed Tartar. At length the opportunity offered, when this captain was sent out to lay the country under contribution. Then Kunt-than marching solely in the dead of the night, caught Brut-an-tiffi napping. He might have slain him upon the spot, but his orders were to take him alive, that he might be made a public example ; accordingly, his sentinels being dispatched, he was pulled out of bed, and his hands were already tied with cords, like those of a common malefactor, when by his roaring and bellowing, he gave the alarm to Yam-a-Kheit, who chanced to be in the neighbourhood, returning from his excursion. He made all the haste he could, and came up in the very nick of time to save his master. He fell upon the party of Kunt-than with such fury, that they were fain to quit their prey ; then he cut the fetters of Brut-an-tiffi, who took to his heels and fled with incredible expedition, leaving his preserver in the midst of his enemies, by whom he was overpowered, struck from his horse, and trampled to death. The grateful Tartar not only deserted this brave captain in such extremity, but he also took care to asperse his memory, by insinuating that Yam-a-Kheit had undertaken to watch him while he took his repose, and had himself fallen asleep upon his post, by which neglect of duty the Ostrog had been enabled to penetrate into his quarters. 'Tis an ill wind that blows nobody good !—the same disaster that deprived him of a good officer, afforded him an opportunity to shift the blame of neglect from his own shoulders to those of a person who could not answer for himself. In the same manner, your general A——y acquitted himself of the charge of misconduct for the attack of T——a, by accusing his engineer, who, having fallen in the battle, could not contradict his assertion. In regard to the affair with the Mantchoux, Brut-an-tiffi was resolved to swear truth out of Tartary by mere dint of impudence. In the very article of running away, he began to propagate the report of the great victory he had obtained. He sent the Dairo a circumstantial detail of his own prowess, and expatiated upon the cowardice of the Mantchoux, who, he said, had vanished from him like quicksilver, at the very time when they were quietly possessed of the field of battle, and he himself was calling upon the mountains to cover him. It must have been in imitation of this great original, that the inspector, of tympanitical memory, assured the public in one of his lucubrations, that a certain tall Hibernian was afraid of looking him in the face; because the said poltroon had kicked his breech the night before in presence of five hundred people.

Fortune had now abandoned the Chinese in good earnest. Two squadrons of their Fune had been successively taken, destroyed, or dispersed, by the Japanese commanders Ornbos and Fas-khan; and they had lost such a number of single junks, that they were scarce able to keep the sea. On the coast of Africa they were driven from the settlement of Kho-rhé by the commander Kha-fell. In the extremity of Asia, they had an army totally defeated by the Japanese captain, Khutt-whang, and many of their settlements were taken. In Fatsissio, they lost another battle to Yan-oni, and divers strongholds. In the neighbourhood of Yesso, Bron-xi-tic, who commanded the mercenary army of Japan on that continent, had been obliged to retreat before the Chinese from post to pillar, till at length he found it absolutely necessary to maintain his position, even at the risk of being attacked by the enemy, that outnumbered him greatly. He chose an advantageous post, where he thought himself secure, and went to sleep at his usual time of rest. The Chinese general resolving to beat up his quarters in the night, selected a body of horse for that purpose, and put them in motion accordingly. It was happy for Bron-xi-tic that this detachment fell upon a quarter where there happened to be a kennel of Japanese dogs, which are as famous as the bull-dogs of England. These animals, ever on the watch, not only gave the alarm, but at the same time fell upon the Chinese horses with such impetuosity, that the enemy were disordered, and had actually fled before Bron-xi-tic could bring up his troops to action. All that he saw of the battle, when he came up, was a small number of killed and wounded, and the cavalry of the enemy scampering off in confusion, though at a great distance from the field. No matter; he found means to paint this famous battle of Myn-than in such colours as dazzled the weak eyesight of the Japanese monster, which bellowed hoarse applause through all its throats; and in its hymns of triumph equalled Bron-xi-tic even to the unconquerable Brut-an-tiffi, which last, about this time, received at his own door another beating from the Mantchoux, so severe that he lay for some time without exhibiting any signs of life; and, indeed, owed his safety to a very extraordinary circumstance. An Ostrog chief called Llha-dahn, who had reinforced the Mantchoux with a considerable body of horse before the battle, insisted upon carrying off the carcase of Brut-an-tiffi, that it might be hung up on a gibbet in *terrorem*, before the pavilion of the Great Khan. The general of the Mantchoux, on the other hand, declared he would have it flayed on the spot, and the skin sent as a trophy to his sovereign. This dispute produced a great deal of abuse betwixt those barbarians; and it was with great difficulty some of their inferior chiefs, who were wiser than themselves, prevented them from going by the ears together. In a word, the confusion and anarchy that ensued, afforded an opportunity to one of Brut-an-tiffi's partisans to steal away the body of his master, whom the noise of the contest had just roused from his swoon. Llha-dahn perceiving he was gone, rode off in disgust with all his cavalry; and the Mantchoux, instead of following the blow, made a retrograde motion towards their own country, which allowed Brut-an-tiffi time to breathe. Three successive disasters of this kind would have been sufficient to lower the military character

of any warrior, in the opinion of any public that judged
from their own senses and reflection : but, by this time,
the Japanese had quietly resigned all their natural perceptions
and paid the most implicit faith to every article broached
by their apostle Taycho. The more it seemed to contradict common reason and common evidence, the more
greedily was it swallowed as a mysterious dogma of the
political creed. Taycho then assured them that the whole
army of the Mantchoux was put to the sword ; and that
Bron-xi-tic would carry the war within three weeks, into the
heart of China ; he gave them goblets of horse-blood from
Myn-than, and tickled their ears and their noses ; they
snorted approbation, licked his toes, and sank into a profound
lethargy.

From this, however, they were soon aroused by unwelcome
tidings from Fatsissio. Yaf-frai had proceeded in his route
until he was stopped by a vast lake, which he could not
possibly traverse without boats, cork-jackets, or some such
expedient, which could not be supplied for that campaign.
Ya-loff had sailed up the river to Quib-quab, which he found
so strongly fortified by nature, that it seemed rashness even
to attempt a landing, especially in the face of an enemy more
numerous than his own detachment. Land, however, he
did, and even attacked a fortified camp of the Chinese ; but,
in spite of all his efforts, he was repulsed with considerable
slaughter. He sent an account of this miscarriage to Taycho,
giving him to understand, at the same time, that he had
received no intelligence of Yaf-frai's motions ; that his
troops were greatly diminished ; that the season was too far
advanced to keep the field much longer ; and that nothing
was left them but a choice of difficulties, every one of which
seemed more insurmountable than another. Taycho having
deliberated on this subject, thought it was necessary to
prepare the monster for the worst that could happen, as he
now expected to hear by the first opportunity, that the grand
expedition of Fatsissio had totally miscarried. He resolved,
therefore, to throw the blame upon the shoulders of Ya-loff
and Yaf-frai, and stigmatise them as the creatures of Fika-

kaka, who had neither ability to comprehend the instructions he had given, nor resolution to execute the plan he had projected. For this purpose he ascended the rostrum, and with a rueful length of face opened his harangue upon the defeat of Ya-loff. The hydra no sooner understood that the troops of Japan had been discomfited, than it was seized with a kind of hysteric fit, and uttered a yell so loud and horrible, that the blindfold Dairo trembled in the most internal recesses of his palace : the Cuboy Fika-kaka had such a profuse evacuation, that the discharge is said to have weighed five boll-ah, equal to eight and forty pounds three ounces and two penny-weight avoirdupois of Great Britain. Even Taycho himself was discomposed. In vain he presented the draught of yeast and the goblet of blood ; in vain his pipers soothed the ears, and his tall fellows tickled the nose of the blatant beast. It continued to howl and grin, and gnash its teeth, and writhe itself into a thousand contortions, as if it had been troubled with that twisting of the guts called the iliac passion. Taycho began to think its case desperate, and sent for the Dairo's chief physician, who prescribed a glyster of the distilled spirit analogous to your Geneva ; but no apothecary nor old woman in Meaco would undertake to administer it on any consideration, the patient was such a filthy, awkward, lubberly, unmanageable beast. "If what comes from its mouths," say they, "be so foul, virulent, and pestilential, how nauseous, poisonous, and intolerable must that be which takes the other course." When Taycho's art and foresight was at a stand, accident came to his assistance. A courier arrived, preceded by twelve postilions blowing horns ; and he brought the news that Quib-quab was taken. The orator commanded them to place their horns within as many of the monster's long ears, and blow with all their might, until it should exhibit some signs of hearing. The experiment succeeded. The hydra waking from its trance, opened its eyes ; and Taycho, seizing this opportunity, hallooed in his loudest tone, "Quib-quab is taken." This note being repeated, the beast started up ; then, raising itself on its hind legs, began to wag its tail, to frisk and fawn, to

lick Taycho's sweaty socks : in fine, crouching on its belly
it took the orator on its back, and proceeding through the
streets of Meaco, brayed aloud, " Make way for the divine
Taycho ! Make way for the conqueror of Quib-quab ! "
But the gallant Ya-loff, the real conqueror of Quib-quab, was
no more. He fell in the battle by which the conquest was
achieved, yet not before he saw victory declare in his favour.
He had made incredible efforts to surmount the difficulties
that surrounded him. At length he found means to scale
a perpendicular rock, which the enemy had left unguarded,
on the supposition that nature had made it inaccessible. This
exploit was performed in the night, and in the morning the
Chinese saw his troops drawn up in order of battle on the
plains of Quib-quab. As their numbers greatly exceeded
the Japanese, they did not decline the trial ; and in a little
time both armies were engaged. The contest, however, was
not of long duration, though it proved fatal to the general
on each side. Ya-loff being slain, the command devolved
upon Thon-syn, who pursued the enemy to the walls of
Quib-quab, which was next day surrendered to him by
capitulation. Nothing was now seen and heard in the
capital but jubilee, triumph, and intoxication ; and, indeed,
the nation had not for some centuries, seen such an occasion
for joy and satisfaction. The only person that did not
heartily rejoice was the Dairo Got-hama-baba. By this
time he was so Tartarised, that he grudged his subjects every
advantage obtained in Fatsissio ; and when Fika-kaka hobbled
up to him with the news of victory, instead of saluting him
with the kick of approbation, he turned his back upon him,
saying, " Boh ! boh ! What do you tell me of Quib-quab ?
The damned Chinese are still on the frontiers of Yesso." As
to the beast, it was doomed to undergo a variety of agitation.
Its present gambols were interrupted by a fresh alarm from
China. It was reported that two great armaments were
equipped for a double descent upon the dominions of Japan ;
that one of these had already sailed north about for the island
of Xicoco, to make a diversion in favour of the other, which,
being the most considerable, was designed for the southern

coast of Japan. These tidings, which were not without foundation, had such an effect upon the multitudinous monster, that it was first of all seized with an universal shivering. Its teeth chattered so loud, that the sound was heard at the distance of half a league; and for some time it was struck dumb. During this paroxysm it crawled silently on its belly to a sand-hill just without the walls of Meaco, and began to scratch the earth with great eagerness and perseverance. Some people imagined it was digging for gold: but the truth is, the beast was making a hole to hide itself from the enemy, whom it durst not look in the face; for it must be observed of this beast, it was equally timorous and cruel; equally cowardly and insolent. So hard it laboured at this cavern, that it had actually burrowed itself all but tail, when its good angel Taycho whistled it out, with the news of another complete victory gained over the Chinese at sea, by the Sey-seo-gun, Phal-khan, who had sure enough discomfited or destroyed the great armament of the enemy. As for the other small squadron which had steered the northerly course to Xicoco, it was encountered, defeated, taken, and brought into the harbour of Japan, by three light Fune, under the command of a young chief, called Hel-y-otte, who happened to be cruising on that part of the coast. The beast hearing Taycho's auspicious whistle, crept out with his buttocks foremost, and having done him homage in the usual style, began to react its former extravagances. It now considered this demagogue as the supreme giver of all good, and adored him accordingly. The apostle Bupo was no longer invoked. The temple of Fakku-basi was almost forgotten; and the Bonzas were universally despised. The praise of the prophet Taycho had swallowed up all other worship. Let us inquire how far he merited this adoration: how justly the unparalleled success of this year was ascribed to his conduct and sagacity. Kho-rhé was taken by Kha-fell, and Quib-quab by Ya-loff and Thon-syn. By land, the Chinese were defeated in Fatsissio by Yan-o-ni; in the extremity of Asia, by Khutt-whang; and in Tartary, by the Japanese bull-dogs, without command or direction. At

sea one of their squadrons had been destroyed by Ornbos ;
a second by Fas-khan ; a third was taken by Hel-y-otte ; a
fourth was worsted and put to flight in three successive
engagements near the land of Kamtschatka, by the chief
Bha-kakh ; and their grand armament defeated by the
Sey-seo-gun, Phal-khan. But Kha-fell was a stranger to
orator Taycho ; Ya-loff he had never seen ; the bull-dogs
had been collected at random from the shambles of Meaco ;
he had never heard of Yan-oni's name, till he distinguished
himself by his first victory, nor did he know there was any
such person as Khutt-whang existing. As for Ornbos,
Fas-khan, Phal-khan, and Bha-kakh, they had been Sey-seo-
guns in constant employment under the former administration ; and the youth Hel-y-otte owed his promotion to the
interest of his own family. But it may be alleged, that
Taycho projected in his closet those plans that were crowned
with success. We have seen how he mutilated and frittered
the original scheme of the campaign in Fatsissio, so as to
leave it at the caprice of Fortune. The reduction of Kho-rhé
was part of the design formed by the Banyan, Thum-khumm-
qua, which Taycho did all that lay in his power to render
abortive. The plan of operations in the extremity of
Tartary he did not pretend to meddle with ; it was the concern of the officers appointed by the trading company there
settled ; and as to the advantages obtained at sea, they
naturally resulted from the disposition of cruises, made and
regulated by the board of Sey-seo-gun-sealty, with which
no minister ever interfered. He might, indeed, have
recalled the chiefs and officers whom he found already
appointed when he took the reins of administration, and
filled their places with others of his own choosing. How
far he was qualified to make such a choice, and plan new
expeditions, appears from the adventures of the generals he
did appoint ; Moria-tanti, who was deterred from landing
by a perspective view of whiskers ; Hylib-bib, who left his
rear in the lurch ; and Hob-nob, who made such a masterly
retreat from the supposed Bonzes of Thin-quo. These three
were literally commanders of his own creation, employed

in executing schemes of his own projecting ; and these three were the only generals he made, and the only military plans he projected, if we except the grand scheme of subsidising Brut-an-tiffi, and forming an army of one hundred thousand men in Tartary, for the defence of the farm of Yesso. Things being so circumstanced, it may be easily conceived that the orator could ask nothing which the mobile would venture to refuse ; and indeed he tried his influence to the utmost stretch ; he milked the dugs of the monster till the blood came. For the service of the ensuing year, he squeezed from them near twelve millions of obans, amounting to near twenty-four millions sterling, about four times as much as had ever been raised by the empire of Japan in any former war. But, by this time, Taycho was become not only a convert to the system of Tartary, which he had formerly persecuted, but also an enthusiast in love and admiration of Brut-an-tiffi, who had lately sent him his poetical works in a present. This, however, would have been of no use, as he could not read them, had not he discovered that they were printed on a very fine, soft, smooth Chinese paper made of silk, which he happily converted to another fundamental purpose. In return for this compliment, the orator sent him a bullock's horn bound with brass, value fifteen pence, which had long served him as a pitch-pipe when he made harangues to the mobile—it was the same kind of instrument which Horace describes : *Tibia vincta orichalco ;* and pray take notice, Peacock, this was the only present Taycho ever bestowed on any man, woman, or child, through the whole course of his life, I mean out of his own pocket ; for he was extremely liberal of the public money, in his subsidies to the Tartar chiefs, and in the prosecution of the war upon that continent. The orator was a genius self-taught without human instruction. He affected to under-value all men of literary talents ; and the only book he ever read with any degree of pleasure was a collection of rhapsodies preached by one Ab-ren-thi, an obscure fanatic Bonze, a native of the island of Xicoco. Certain it is, Nature seemed to have produced him for the sole purpose of fascinating the mob, and endued him with faculties accordingly.

Notwithstanding all his efforts in behalf of the Tartarian scheme, the Chinese still lingered on the frontiers of Yesso. The views of the court of Pekin exactly coincided with the interest of Bron-xi-tic, the mercenary general of Japan. The Chinese, confounded at the unheard-of success of the Japanese in Fatsissio, and other parts of the globe, and extremely mortified at the destruction of their fleets, and the ruin of their commerce, saw no other way of distressing the enemy, but that of prolonging the war on the continent of Tartary, which they could support for little more than their ordinary expense; whereas Japan could not maintain it without contracting yearly immense loads of debt, which must have crushed it at the long run. It was the business of the Chinese, therefore, not to finish the war in Tartary by taking the farm of Yesso, because, in that case, the annual expense of it would have been saved to Japan; but to keep it alive by forced marches, predatory excursions, and indecisive actions; and this was precisely the interest of General Bron-xi-tic, who in the continuance of the war enjoyed the continuance of all his emoluments. All that he had to do, then, was to furnish Taycho from time to time with a cask of human blood, for the entertainment of the blatant beast; and to send over a few horse-tails, as trophies of pretended victories, to be waved before the monster in its holiday processions. He and the Chinese general seemed to act in concert. They advanced and retreated in their turns betwixt two given lines, and the campaign always ended on the same spot where it began. The only difference between them was in the motives of their conduct; the Chinese commander acted for the benefit of his sovereign, and Bron-xi-tic acted for his own.

The continual danger to which the farm of Yesso was exposed, produced such apprehensions and chagrin in the mind of the Dairo Got-hama-baba, that his health began to decline. He neglected his food and his rattle, and no longer took any pleasure in kicking the Cuboy. He frequently

muttered ejaculations about the farm of Yesso : nay, once
or twice in the transports of his impatience, he pulled the
bandage from his eyes, and cursed Taycho in the Tartarian
language. At length he fell into a lethargy, and even when
roused a little by blisters and caustics, seemed insensible of
everything that was done about him. These blisters were
raised by burning the moxa upon his scalp. The powder of
menoki was also injected in a glyster ; and the operation of
acupuncture, called *Senkei*, performed without effect. His
disorder was so stubborn, that the Cuboy began to think he
was bewitched, and suspected Taycho of having practised
sorcery on his sovereign. He communicated this suspicion
to Muraclami, who shook his head, and advised that, with
the orator's good leave, the council should be consulted.
Taycho, who had gained an absolute empire over the mind
of the Dairo, and could not foresee how his interest might
stand with his successor, was heartily disposed to concur in
any feasible experiment for the recovery of Got-hama-baba :
he therefore consented that the mouths of the council should
be unpadlocked *pro hac vice*, and the members were assembled
without delay ; with this express proviso, however, that they
were to confine their deliberations to the subject of the
Dairo and his distemper. By this time, the physicians had
discovered the cause of the disorder, which was no other
than his being stung by a poisonous insect, produced in the
land of Yesso, analogous to the tarantula, which is said to
do so much mischief in some parts of Apuglia : as we are
told by Ælian, Epiphanius Ferdinandus, and Baglivi. In
both cases, the only effectual remedy was music ; and now
the council was called, to determine what sort of music should
be administered. You must know, Peacock, the Japanese
are but indifferently skilled in this art, though, in general,
they affect to be connoisseurs. They are utterly ignorant
of the theory, and in practice are excelled by all their neighbours, the Tartars not excepted. For my own part I studied
music, under Pythagoras, at Crotona. He found the scale
of seven tones imperfect, and added the octave as a fixed,
sensible, and intelligent termination of an interval, which

and affected. He had a turn for knick-knacks and gim-cracks, and once made and mounted an iron jack and a wooden clock with his own hands. But it was his misfortune to set up for a connoisseur in painting and other liberal arts, and to announce himself an universal patron of genius. He did not fail to infuse his own notions and conceits into the tender mind of Gio-gio, who gradually imbibed his turn of thinking, and followed the studies which he recommended. With respect to his lessons on the art of government, he reduced them to a very few simple principles. His maxims were these : That the Emperor of Japan ought to cherish the established religion, both by precept and example ; that he ought to abolish corruption, discourage faction, and balance the two parties by admitting an equal number from each to places and offices of trust in the administration ; that he should make peace as soon as possible, even in despite of the public, which seemed insensible of the burthen it sustained, and was indeed growing delirious by the illusions of Taycho, and the cruel evacuations he had prescribed ; that he should retrench all superfluous expense in his house-hold and government, and detach himself entirely from the accursed farm of Yesso, which some evil genius had fixed upon the breech of Japan, as a cancerous ulcer through which all her blood and substance would be discharged. These maxims were generally just enough in speculation, but some of them were altogether impracticable—for example, that of forming an administration equally composed of the two factions was as absurd as it would be to yoke two stone-horses and two jack-asses in the same carriage, which, instead of drawing one way, would do nothing but bite and kick one another, while the machine of government would stand stock-still, or perhaps be torn in pieces by their dragging in opposite directions. The people of Japan had been long divided between two inveterate parties known by the names of Shit-tilk-ums-heit and She-it-kums-hi-til, the first signifying *more fool than knave* and the other *more knave than fool*. Each had predominated in its turn, by securing a majority in the assemblies of the people ; for the majority had always interest to force themselves into the administration; because the constitution being partly democratic, the Dairo was still obliged to truckle to the prevailing faction. To obtain this majority, each side had employed every art of corruption, calumny, insinuation, and priestcraft; for nothing is such an effectual ferment in all popular commotions as religious fanaticism. No sooner one party accomplished its aim than it reprobated the other, branding it with the epithets of traitors to their prince; while the minority retorted upon them the charge of corruption, rapaciousness, and abject servility. In short, both parties were equally abusive, rancorous, uncandid, and illiberal. Taycho had been of both factions more than once. He made his first appearance as a Shit-tilk-ums-heit in the minority, and displayed his talent for scurrility against the Dairo to such advantage, that an old rich hag, who loved nothing so well as money, except the gratification of her revenge, made him a present of five thousand obans, on condition he should continue to revile the Dairo till his dying day. After her death, the ministry, intimidated by the boldness of his tropes, and the fame he began to acquire as a malcontent orator, made him such offers as he thought proper to accept; and then he turned She-it-kums-hi-til. Being disgusted in the sequel, at his own want of importance in the council, he opened once more at the head of his old friends the Shit-tilk-ums-hitites; and once more he deserted them to rule the roost, as chief of the She-it-kums-hi-tilites, in which predicament he now stood. And, indeed, this was the most natural posture in which he could stand; for this party embraced all the scum of the people, constituting the blatant beast, which his talents were so peculiarly adapted to manage and govern. Another impracticable maxim of Yak-strot was the abolition of corruption, the ordure of which is as necessary to anoint the wheels of government in Japan, as grease is to smear the axle-tree of a loaded waggon. His third impolitic (though not impracticable) maxim was that of making peace while the populace were intoxicated with blood, and elated with the shows of triumph. Be that as it will, Gio-gio, attended by Yak-strot, was drawing plans of windmills, when orator Taycho, opening the door, advanced towards him, and falling on his knees, addressed him in these words : " The empire of Japan, magnanimous prince, resembles at this instant, a benighted traveller, who by the light of the star Hesperus continued his journey without repining, until that glorious luminary setting, left him bewildered in darkness and consternation : but scarce had he time to bewail his fate, when the more glorious sun, the ruler of a fresh day, appearing on the tops of the eastern hills, dispelled his terrors with the shades of night, and filled his soul with transports of pleasure and delight. The illustrious Got-hama-baba, of honoured memory, is the glorious star which hath set on our hemisphere. His soul, which took wing about two hours ago, is now happily nestled in the bosom of the blessed Bupo ; and you, my prince, are the more glorious rising sun, whose genial influence will cheer the empire, and gladden the hearts of your faithful Japanese. I therefore hail your succession to the throne, and cry aloud, ' Long live the ever-glorious Gio-gio, Emperor of the three islands of Japan.' " To this salutation the beast below brayed hoarse applause ; and all present kissed the hand of the new emperor, who, kneeling before his venerable grandame, craved her blessing, desired the benefit of her prayers, that God would make him a good king, and establish his throne in righteousness. Then he ascended his chariot, accompanied by the orator and his beloved Yak-strot, and proceeding to the palace of Meaco, was proclaimed with the usual ceremonies, his relation the Fatzman and other princes of the blood assisting on this occasion.

The first step he took after this elevation was to publish a decree, or rather exhortation, to honour religion and the Bonzes ; and this was no impolitic expedient : for it firmly attached that numerous and powerful tribe to his interest. His next measures did not seem to be directed by the same spirit of discretion. He admitted a parcel of raw boys, and even some individuals of the faction of Shi-tilk-ums-heit into his council; and though Taycho still continued to manage the reins of administration, Yak-strot was associated with him in office, to the great scandal and dissatisfaction of the Niphonites, who hate all the Ximians with a mixture of jealousy and contempt.

Fika-kaka was not the last who paid his respects to his new sovereign, by whom he was graciously received, although he did not seem quite satisfied; because, when he presented himself in his usual attitude, he had not received the kick of approbation. New reigns, new customs. This Dairo never dreamed of kicking those whom he delighted to honour. It was a secret of state which had not yet come to his knowledge; and Yak-strot had always assured him, that kicking the breech always and everywhere implied disgrace, as kicking the parts before betokens ungovernable passion. Yak-strot, however, in this particular, seems to have been too confined in his notions of the *etiquette*: for it had been the custom time immemorial for the Dairos of Japan to kick their favourites and prime ministers. Besides, there are at this day different sorts of kicks used even in England, without occasioning any dishonour to the *kickee*. It is sometimes a misfortune to be *kicked* out of place, but no dishonour. A man is often *kicked up* in the way of preferment, in order that his place may be given to a person of more interest. Then there is the amorous kick, called *Kick'um Jenny*, which every gallant undergoes with pleasure: hence the old English appellation of *Kicksy-wicksy*, bestowed on a wanton leman who knew all her paces. As for the familiar kick, it is no other than a mark of friendship; nor is it more dishonourable to be cuffed and cudgelled. Everybody knows that the *alapa*, or box o' the ear, among the Romans, was a particular mark of favour by which their slaves were made free: and the favourite gladiator, when he obtained his dismission from the service, was honoured with a sound cudgelling; this being the true meaning of the phrase *rude donatus*. In the times of chivalry, the knight, when dubbed, was well thwacked across the shoulders by his god-father in arms. Indeed, *dubbing* is no other than a corruption of *drubbing.* It was the custom formerly, here and elsewhere, for a man to drub his son or apprentice as a mark of his freedom, and of his being admitted to the exercise of arms. The Paraschistes, who practised *embalming* in Egypt, which was counted a very honourable profession, were always severely drubbed, after the operation, by the friends and relations of the defunct; and to this day, the patriarch of the Greeks once a year, on Easter-eve, when he carries out the sacred fire from the holy sepulchre of Jerusalem, is heartily cudgelled by the infidels, a certain number of whom he hires for that purpose; and he thinks himself very unhappy and much disgraced, if he is not beaten into all the colours of the rainbow. You know the Quakers of this country think it no dishonour to receive a slap o' the face, but when you smite them on one cheek, they present the other, that it may have the same salutation. The venerable Father Lactantius falls out with Cicero for saying, " A good man hurts nobody, unless he is justly provoked; *nisi lacessitur injuria."*—" O," cries the good father, "*quam simplicem veramque sententiam duorum verborum abjectione corrupit !— non minus enim mali est, referre injuriam, quam inferre.*" The great philosopher Socrates thought it no disgrace to be kicked by his wife Xantippe; nay, he is said to have undergone the same discipline from other people, without making the least resistance, it being his opinion that it was more courageous, consequently more honourable, to bear a drubbing patiently, than to attempt anything either in the way of self-defence or retaliation. The judicious and learned Puffendorf, in his book *De Jure Gentium & Naturali,* declares that a man's honour is not so fragile as to be hurt either by a box on the ear, or a kick on the breech, otherwise it would be in the power of every saucy fellow to diminish or infringe it. It must be owned, indeed, Grotius *De Jure Belli & Pacis,* says, that charity does not of itself require our patiently suffering such an affront. The English have, with a most servile imitation, borrowed their *punto,* as well as other modes, from the French nation. Now kicking and cuffing were counted infamous among those people for these reasons. A box on the ear destroys the whole economy of their *frisure*, upon which they bestow the greatest part of their time and attention ; and a kick on the breech is attended with great pain and danger, as they are generally subject to the piles. This is so truly the case that they have no less than two saints to patronise and protect the individuals afflicted with this disease. One is St. *Fiacre*, who was a native of the kingdom of Ireland. He presides over the blind piles. The other is a female saint, *Hæmorrhoissa*, and she comforts those who are distressed with the bleeding piles. No wonder, therefore, that a Frenchman put to the torture by a kick on those tender parts should be provoked to vengeance ; and that this vengeance should gradually become an article in their system of punctilio.

But to return to the thread of my narration. Whatever inclination the Dairo and Yak-strot had to restore the blessings of peace, they did not think proper as yet to combat the disposition and schemes of orator Taycho ; in consequence of whose remonstrances, the tributary treaty was immediately renewed with Brut-an-tiffi, and Gio-gio declared in the assembly of the people, that he was determined to support that illustrious ally, and carry on the war with vigour. By this time the Chinese were in a manner expelled from their chief settlements in Fatsissio, where they now retained nothing but an inconsiderable colony, which would have submitted on the first summons : but this Taycho left as a nest-egg to produce a new brood of disturbance to the Japanese settlements, that they might not rust with too much peace and security. To be plain with you, Peacock, his thoughts were entirely alienated from this Fatsissian war, in which the interest of his country was chiefly concerned, and converted wholly to the continent of Tartary, where all his cares centred in schemes for the success of his friend Brut-an-tiffi. This freebooter had lately undergone strange vicissitudes of fortune. He had seen his chief village possessed and plundered by the enemy ; but he found means, by surprise, to beat up their quarters in the beginning of winter, which always proved his best ally, because then the

Mantchoux Tartars were obliged to retire to their own country, at a vast distance from the seat of war. As for Bron-xi-tic, who commanded the Japanese army on that continent, he continued to play booty with the Chinese general, over whom he was allowed to have some petty advantages, which, with the trophies won by Brut-an-tiffi, were swelled up into mighty victories, to increase the infatuation of the blatant beast. On the other hand, Bron-xi-tic obliged the generals of China with the like indulgences, by now and then sacrificing a detachment of his Japanese troops, to keep up the spirit of that nation.

Taycho had levied upon the people of Japan an immense sum of money for the equipment of a naval armament, the destination of which was kept a profound secret. Some politicians imagined it was designed for the conquest of Thin-quo, and all the other settlements which the Chinese possessed in the Indian Ocean : others conjectured the intention was to attack the King of Corea, who had, since the beginning of this war, acted with a shameful partiality in favour of the Emperor of China, his kinsman and ally. But the truth of the matter was this : Taycho kept the armament in the harbours of Japan, ready for a descent upon the coast of China, in order to make a diversion in favour of his friend Brut-an-tiffi, in case he had run any risk of being oppressed by his enemies. However, the beast of many heads having growled and grumbled, during the best part of the summer, at the inactivity of this expensive armament, it was now thought proper to send it to sea at the beginning of winter ; but it was driven back in great distress, by contrary winds and storms, and this was all the monster had for its ten millions of obans.

While Taycho amused the mobile with this winter expedition, Yak-strot resolved to plan the scheme of economy which he had projected. He dismissed from the Dairo's service about a dozen of cooks and scullions, shut up one of the kitchens, after having sold the grates, hand-irons, spits, and saucepans ; deprived the servants and officers of the household of their breakfast, took away their usual allowance of oil and candles, retrenched their tables, reduced their proportion of drink, and persuaded his pupil the Dairo to put himself upon a diet of soup-meagre thickened with oatmeal. In a few days there was no smoke seen to ascend from the kitchens of the palace; nor did any fuel, torch, or taper blaze in the chimneys, courts,and apartments thereof, which now became the habitation of cold, darkness, and hunger. Gio-gio himself, who now turned peripatetic philosopher merely to keep himself in heat, fell into a wash-tub as he groped his way in the dark through one of the lower galleries. Two of his body-guard had their whiskers gnawed off by the rats, as they slept in his ante-chamber; and their captain presented a petition, declaring that neither he nor his men could undertake the defence of his imperial majesty's person, unless their former allowance of provision should be restored. They and all the individuals of the household were not only punished in their bellies, but likewise curtailed in their clothing, and abridged in their stipends. The palace of Meaco, which used to be the temple of mirth, jollity, and good cheer, was now so dreary and deserted, that a certain wag fixed up a ticket on the outward gate with this inscription: "This tenement to be let, the proprietor having left off house-keeping."

Yak-strot, however, was resolved to show, that if the new Dairo retrenched the superfluities of his domestic expense, he did not act from avarice or poorness of spirit, inasmuch as he should now display his liberality, in patronising genius and the arts. A general jubilee was now promised to all those who had distinguished themselves by their talents and erudition. The emissaries of Yak-strot declared that Mæcenas was but a type of this Ximian mountaineer, and that he was determined to search for merit, even in the thickest shades of obscurity. All these researches, however, proved so unsuccessful, that not above four or five men of genius could be found in the whole empire of Japan, and these were gratified with pensions of about one hundred obans each. One was a secularised Bonze, from Ximo; another a malcontent poet of Niphon; a third, a reformed comedian of Xicoco ; a fourth, an empyric, who had outlived his practice ; and a fifth, a decayed apothecary, who was bard, quack, author, chemist, philosopher, and simpler by profession. The whole of the expense arising from the favour and protection granted by the Dairo to these men of genius did not exceed seven or eight hundred obans per annum, amounting to about fifteen hundred pounds sterling ; whereas many a private Quo in Japan expended more money on a kennel of hounds. I do not mention those men of singular merit, whom Yak-strot fixed in established places under the Government, such as architects, astronomers, painters, physicians, barbers, etc., because their salaries were included in the ordinary expense of the crown : I shall only observe that a certain person who could not read was appointed librarian to his imperial majesty. These were all the men of superlative genius that Yak-strot could find at this period in the empire of Japan.

Whilst this great patriot was thus employed in executing his schemes of economy with more zeal than discretion, and providing his poor relations with lucrative offices under the Government, a negotiation for peace was brought upon the carpet, by the mediation of certain neutral powers ; and orator Taycho arrogated to himself the province of discussing the several articles of the treaty. Upon this occasion he showed himself surprisingly remiss, and in-different in whatever related to the interest of Japan, particularly in regulating and fixing the boundaries of the Chinese and Japanese settlements in Fatsissio, the uncertainty of which had given rise to the war ; but when the business was to determine the claims and pretensions of his ally, Brut-an-tiffi, on the continent of Tartary, he appeared stiff and immovable as Mount Athos. He actually broke off the negotiation, because the Emperor of China would not engage to drive by force of arms the troops of his ally the Princess of Ostrog, from a village or two belonging to the Tartarian freebooter, who, by-the-bye, had left them defenceless at the beginning of the war, on purpose that his enemies might, by taking possession of them, quicken the resolution of the Dairo to send over an army for the protection of Yesso.

The court of Pekin perceiving that the Japanese were rendered intolerably insolent and overbearing by success, and that an equitable peace could not be obtained while orator Taycho managed the reins of government at Meaco, and his friend Brut-an-tiffi found anything to plunder in Tartary, resolved to fortify themselves with a new alliance. They actually entered into closer connections with the King of Corea, who was nearly related to the Chinese emperor, had some old scores to settle with Japan, and because he desired those disputes might be amicably compromised in the general pacification, had been grossly insulted by Taycho, in the person of his ambassador. He had for some time dreaded the ambition of the Japanese ministry, which seemed to aim at universal empire ; and he was, moreover, stimulated by this outrage to conclude a defensive alliance with the Emperor of China ; a measure which all the caution of the two courts could not wholly conceal from the knowledge of the Japanese politicians.

Meanwhile, a dreadful cloud, big with ruin and disgrace, seemed to gather round the head of Brut-an-tiffi. The Mantchoux Tartars, sensible of the inconvenience of their distant situation from the scene of action, which rendered it impossible for them to carry on their operations vigorously in conjunction with the Ostrog, resolved to secure winter quarters, in some part of the enemy's territories, from whence they should be able to take the field, and act against him early in the spring. With this view, they besieged and took a frontier fortress belonging to Brut-an-tiffi, situated upon a great inland lake, which extended as far as the capital of the Mantchoux, who were thus enabled to send thither by water carriage, all sorts of provisions and military stores, for the use of their army, which took up their winter quarters accordingly, in and about this new acquisition. It was now that the ruin of Brut-an-tiffi seemed inevitable. Orator Taycho saw with horror the precipice to which he was driven. Not that his fears were actuated by sympathy or friendship. Such emotions had never possessed the heart of Taycho. No ; he trembled because he saw his own popularity connected with the fate of the Tartar. It was the success and petty triumphs of this adventurer which had dazzled the eyes of the blatant beast, so as to disorder its judgment, and prepare it for the illusions of the orator ; but now that Fortune seemed ready to turn tail to Brut-an-tiffi, and leave him a prey to his adversaries, Taycho knew the disposition of the monster so well, as to prognosticate that its applause and affection would be immediately turned into grumbling and disgust ; and that he himself, who had led it blindfold into this unfortunate connection, might possibly fall a sacrifice to its resentment, provided he could not immediately project some scheme to divert its attention, and transfer the blame from his own shoulders.

For this purpose he employed his invention, and succeeded to his wish. Having called a council of the twenty-eight, at which the Dairo assisted in person, he proposed, and insisted upon it, that a squadron of Fune should be imme-diately ordered to scour the seas, and kidnap all the vessels and ships belonging to the King of Corea, who had acted during the whole war with the most scandalous partiality, in favour of the Chinese emperor, and was now so intimately connected with that potentate, by means of a secret alliance, that he ought to be prosecuted with the same hostilities which the other had severely felt. The whole council were confounded at this proposal: the Dairo stood aghast, the Cuboy trembled, Yak-strot stared like a skewered pig. After some pause, the president Soo-san-sin-o ventured to observe, that the measure seemed to be a little abrupt and premature ; that the nation was already engaged in a very expensive war, which had absolutely drained it of its wealth, .and even loaded it with enormous debts ; therefore little able to sustain such additional burthens as would, in all probability, be occasioned by a rupture with a prince so rich and powerful. Gotto-mio swore, the land-holders were already so much impoverished by the exactions of Taycho, that he himself, ere long, should be obliged to come upon the parish. Fika-kaka got up to speak, but could only cackle. Sti-phi-rum-poo was for proceeding in form by citation. Nin-kom-poo-po declared, he had good intelligence of a fleet of merchant ships belonging to Corea, laden with treasure, who were then on their return from the Indian isles ; and he gave it as his opinion, that they should be waylaid, and brought into the harbours of Japan ; not by way of declaring war, but only with a view to prevent the money going into the coffers of the Chinese emperor. Foksi-rokhu started two objections to this expedient ; first, the uncertainty of falling in with the Corean fleet at sea, alleging as an instance, the disappointment and miscarriage of the squadron which the Sey-seo-gun had sent some years ago to intercept the Chinese Fune on the coast of Fatsissio ; secondly, the loss and hardship it would be to many subjects of Japan who dealt in commerce, and had great sums embarked in those very Corean bottoms. Indeed, Foksi-rokhu himself was interested in this very commerce. The Fatzman sat silent. Yak-strot, who had some romantic notions of honour and honesty, represented that the nation had already incurred the censure of all its neighbours, by seizing the merchant ships of China, without any previous declaration of war ; that the law of nature and nations, confirmed by repeated treaties, prescribed a more honourable method of proceeding, than that of plundering like robbers the ships of pacific merchants, who trade on the faith of such laws and such treaties ; he was, therefore, of opinion, that if the King of Corea had in any shape deviated from the neutrality which he professed, satisfaction should be demanded in the usual form ; and when that should be refused, it might be found necessary to proceed to compulsive measures. The Dairo acquiesced in this advice, and assured Taycho that an ambassador should be forthwith dispatched to Corea, with instructions to demand an immediate and satisfactory explanation of that prince's conduct and designs with regard to the empire of Japan.

This regular method of practice would by no means suit the purposes of Taycho, who rejected it with great insolence and disdain. He bit his thumb at the president, forked out his fingers on his forehead at Gotto-mio, wagged his under-jaw at the Cuboy, snapped his fingers at Sti-phi-rum-poo, grinned at the Sey-seo-gun, made the sign of the cross or gallows to Foksi-rokhu ; then turning to Yak-strot, he clapped his thumbs in his ears, and began to bray like an ass ; finally, pulling out the badge of his office, he threw it at the Dairo, who in vain entreated him to be pacified ; and wheeling to the right-about, stalked away, slapping the flat of his hand upon a certain part that shall be nameless. He was followed by his kinsman the Quo Lob-kob, who worshipped him with the most humble adoration. He now imitated this great original in the signal from behind at parting, and in him it was attended by a rumbling sound ; but whether this was the effect of contempt or compunction I could never learn.

Taycho having thus carried his point, which was to have a pretence for quitting the reins of government, made his next appeal to the blatant beast. He reminded the many-headed monster of the uninterrupted success which had attended his administration ; of his having supported the glorious Brut-an-tiffi, the great bulwark of the religion of Bupo, who had kept the common enemy at bay, and filled all Asia with the fame of his victories. He told them, that for his own part, he pretended to have subdued Fatsissio in the heart of Tartary, that he despised honours and had still a greater contempt for riches ; and that all his endeavours had been solely exerted for the good of his country, which was now brought to the very verge of destruction. He then gave the beast to understand that he had formed a scheme against the King of Corea, which would not only have dis-abled that monarch from executing his hostile intentions with respect to Japan, but also have indemnified this nation for the whole expense of the war ; but that proposal having been rejected by the council of twenty-eight, who were influenced by Yak-strot, a Ximian mountaineer, without spirit or understanding, he had resigned his office with intention to retire to some solitude, where he should in silence deplore the misfortunes of his country, and the ruin of the Buponian religion, which must fall of course with its great protector, Brut-an-tiffi, whom he foresaw the new ministry would abandon.

This address threw Legion into such a quandary, that it rolled itself into the dirt, and yelled hideously. Meanwhile, the orator, retreating to a cell in the neighbourhood of Meaco, hired the common crier to go round the streets and proclaim that Taycho, being no longer in a condition to afford anything but the bare necessaries of life, would by public sale dispose of his ambling mule and furniture, together with an ermined robe of his wife, and the greater part of his kitchen utensils. At this time he was well known to be worth upwards of twenty thousand gold obans; nevertheless, the mobile, discharging this circumstance entirely from their reflection, attended to nothing but the object which the orator was pleased to present. They thought it was a piteous case, and a great scandal upon the Government, that such a patriot, who had saved the nation from ruin and disgrace, should be reduced to the cruel necessity of selling his mule and his household furniture. Accordingly they raised a clamour that soon rang in the ears of Gio-gio and his favourite.

It was supposed that Muraclami suggested on this occasion to his countryman, Yak-strot, the hint of offering a pension to Taycho, by way of remuneration for his past services. " If he refuses it," said he, " the offer will at least reflect credit upon the Dairo and the administration ; but, should he accept of it (which is much more likely), it will either stop his mouth entirely, or expose him to the censure of the people, who now adore him as a mirror of disinterested integrity. The advice was instantly complied with ; the Dairo signed a patent for a very ample pension to Taycho and his heirs, which patent Yak-strot delivered to him next day at his cell in the country. This miracle of patriotism received the bounty as a turnpike-man receives the toll, and then slapped his door full in the face of the favourite ; yet nothing of what Muraclami had prognosticated came

25

to pass. The many-headed monster, far from calling in question the orator's disinterestedness, considered his acceptance of the pension as a proof of his moderation, in receiving such a trifling reward for the great services he had done his country, and the generosity of the Dairo, instead of exciting the least emotion of gratitude in Taycho's own breast, acted only as a golden key to unlock all the sluices of his virulence and abuse.

These, however, he kept within bounds until he should see what would be the fate of Brut-an-tiffi, who now seemed to be in the condition of a criminal at the foot of the ladder. In this dilemma he obtained a very unexpected reprieve. Before the army of the Mantchoux could take the least advantage of the settlement they had made on the frontiers, their empress died, and was succeeded by a weak prince, who no sooner ascended the throne than he struck up a peace with the Tartar freebooter, and even ordered his troops to join him against the Ostrog, to whom they had hitherto acted as auxiliaries. Such an accession of strength would have cast the balance greatly in his favour, had not Providence once more interposed, and brought matters again to an equilibrium.

Taycho no sooner perceived his ally thus unexpectedly delivered from the dangers that surrounded him, than he began to repent of his own resignation, and resolved once more to force his way to the helm, by the same means he had so successfully used before. He was, indeed, of such a turbulent disposition as could not relish the repose of private life, and his spirit so corrosive, that it would have preyed upon himself, if he could not have found external food for it to devour. He therefore began to prepare his engines, and provide proper emissaries to bespatter and raise a hue-and-cry against Yak-strot at a convenient season, not doubting but an occasion would soon present itself, considering the temper, inexperience, and prejudices of this Ximian politician, together with the pacific system he had adopted, so contrary to the present spirit of the blatant beast.

In these preparations he was much comforted and assisted

by his kinsman and pupil Lob-kob, who entered into his measures with surprising zeal, and had the good luck to light on such instruments as were admirably suited to the work in hand. Yak-strot was extremely pleased at the secession of Taycho, who had been a very troublesome colleague to him in the administration, and run counter to all the schemes he had projected for the good of the empire. He now found himself at liberty to follow his own inventions, and being naturally an enthusiast, believed himself born to be the saviour of Japan. Some efforts, however, he made to acquire popularity, proved fruitless. Perceiving the people were, by the orator's instigations, exasperated against the King of Corea, he sent a peremptory message to that prince, demanding a categorical answer; and this being denied, declared war against him, according to the practice of all civilised nations; but even this measure failed of obtaining that approbation for which it was taken. The monster, tutored by Taycho and his ministers, exclaimed that the golden opportunity was lost, inasmuch as, during the observance of those useless forms, the treasures of Corea were safely brought home to that kingdom; treasures which, had they been interrupted by the Fune of Japan, would have paid off the debts of the nation, and enabled the inhabitants of Meaco to pave their streets with silver. By-the-bye, this treasure existed nowhere but in the fiction of Taycho and the imagination of the blatant beast, which never attempted to use the evidence of sense or reason to examine any assertion, how absurd and improbable soever it might be, which proceeded from the mouth of the orator.

Yak-strot, having now taken upon himself the task of steering the political bark, resolved to show the Japanese, that although he recommended peace, he was as well qualified as his predecessor for conducting the war. He therefore, with the assistance of the Fatzman, projected three naval enterprises; the first against Thin-quo, the conquest of which had been unsuccessfully attempted by Taycho; the second was destined for the reduction of Fan-yah, one of the most considerable settlements belonging to the King of

Corea, in the Indian Ocean ; and the third armament was sent to plunder and destroy a flourishing colony called Lli-man, which the same prince had established almost as far to the southward as the Terra Australis Incognita. Now the only merit which either Yak-strot, or any other minister could justly claim from the success of such expedition, is that of adopting the most feasible of those schemes which are presented by different projectors, and of appointing *such* commanders as are capable of conducting them with vigour and sagacity.

The next step which the favourite took was to provide a helpmate for the young Dairo, and a certain Tartar princess of the religion of Bupo, being pitched upon for this purpose, was formally demanded, brought over to Niphon, espoused by Gio-gio, and installed empress with the usual solemnities. But, lest the choice of a Tartarian princess should subject the Dairo to the imputation of inheriting his predecessor's predilection for the land of Yesso, which had given such sensible umbrage to all the sensible Japanese who made use of their own reason, he determined to detach his master gradually from those continental connections, which had been the source of enormous expense and such continual vexation to the empire of Japan. In these sentiments he withheld the annual tribute which had been lately paid to Brut-an-tiffi, by which means he saved a considerable sum to the nation, and, at the same time, rescued it from the infamy of such a disgraceful imposition. He expected the thanks of the public for this exertion of his influence in favour of his country, but he reckoned without his host. What he flattered himself would yield him an abundant harvest of honour and applause, produced nothing but odium and reproach, as we shall see in the sequel.

These measures, pursued with an eye to the advantage of the public, which seemed to argue a considerable share of spirit and capacity, were strangely chequered with others of a more domestic nature, which savoured strongly of childish vanity, rash ambition, littleness of mind, and lack of understanding. He purchased a vast wardrobe of tawdry clothes, and fluttered in all the finery of Japan ; he prevailed upon his master to vest him with the badges and trappings of all the honorary institutions of the empire, although this multiplication of orders in the person of one man was altogether without precedent or prescription. This was only setting himself up as the more conspicuous mark for envy and detraction.

Not contented with engrossing the personal favour and confidence of his sovereign, and, in effect, directing the whole machine of government, he thought his fortune still imperfect, while the treasure of the empire passed through the hands of the Cuboy, enabling that minister to maintain a very extensive influence, which might one day interfere with his own. He therefore employed all his invention, together with that of his friends, to find out some specious pretext for removing the old Cuboy from his office, and in a little time accident afforded what all their intrigues had not been able to procure.

Ever since the demise of Got-hama-baba, poor Fika-kaka had been subject to a new set of vagaries. The death of his old master gave him a rude shock ; then the new Dairo encroached upon his province, by preferring a Bonze without his consent or knowledge ; finally, he was prevented by the express order of Gio-gio from touching a certain sum out of the treasury, which he had been accustomed to throw out of his windows at stated periods, in order to keep up an interest among the dregs of the people. All these mortifications had an effect upon the weak brain of the Cuboy. He began to loathe his usual food and sometimes even declined showing himself to the Bonzes at his levee, symptoms that alarmed all his friends and dependents. Instead of frequenting the assemblies of the great, he now attended assiduously at all groanings and christenings, grew extremely fond of caudle, and held conferences with practitioners, both male and female, in the art of midwifery.

When business or ceremony obliged him to visit any of the Quos or Quanbukus of Meaco, he, by a surprising instinct, ran directly to the nursery ; where, if there happened to be a child in the cradle, he took it up, and if it was foul, wiped it with great care and seeming satisfaction. He, moreover, learned of the good woman to sing lullabies, and practised them with uncommon success : but the most extravagant of all his whims, was what he exhibited one day in his own court-yard. Observing a nest with some eggs, which the goose had quitted, he forthwith dropped his trousers, and squatting down in the attitude of incubation, began to stretch out his neck, to hiss and to cackle, as if he had really been metamorphosed into the animal whose place he now supplied.

It was on the back of this adventure that one of the Bonzes, as prying, and as great a gossip as the barber of Midas, in paying his morning worship to the Cuboy's posteriors, spied something, or rather nothing, and was exceedingly affrighted. He communicated his discovery and apprehension to divers others of the cloth, and they were all of opinion that some effectual inquisition should be held on this phenomenon, lest the clergy of Japan should hereafter be scandalised as having knowingly kissed the breech of an old woman, perhaps a monster or magician. Information was accordingly made to the Dairo, who gave orders for immediate inspection, and Fika-kaka was formally examined by a jury of matrons. Whether these were actuated by undue influence, I shall not at present explain ; certain it is, they found their verdict : the Cuboy *non mas* ; and among other evidences produced to attest his metamorphosis, a certain Ximian, who pretended to have the second sight, made oath that he had one evening seen the said Fika-kaka in a female dress, riding through the air on a broomstick.

The unhappy Cuboy being thus convicted, was divested of his office, and confined to his palace in the country, while Gio-gio, by the advice of his favourite, published a proclamation, declaring it was not for the honour of Japan that her treasury should be managed either by a witch or an old woman.

Fika-kaka being thus removed, Yak-strot was appointed

treasurer and Cuboy in his place, and now ruled the roost with uncontrolled authority. On the very threshold of his greatness, however, he made a false step, which was one cause of his tottering, during the whole sequel of his administration. In order to refute the calumnies and defeat the intrigues of Taycho in the assemblies of the people, he chose an associate in the ministry, Fokh-si-rokhu, who was at that instant the most unpopular man in the whole empire of Japan; and at the instigation of his colleague, deprived of bread a great number of poor families, who subsisted on petty places which had been bestowed upon them by the former Cuboy.

Those were so many mouths opened to augment the clamour against his own person and administration.

It might be imagined, that while he thus set one part of the nation at defiance, he would endeavour to cultivate the other; and, in particular, strive to conciliate the good will of the nobility, who did not see his exaltation without umbrage. But, instead of ingratiating himself with them by a liberal turn of demeanour, by treating them with frankness and affability, granting them favours with a good grace, making entertainments for them at his palace, and mixing in their social parties of pleasure; Yak-strot always appeared on the reserve, and under all his finery, continually wore a doublet of buckram, which gave an air of stiffness and constraint to his whole behaviour. He studied postures, and, in giving audience, generally stood in the attitude of the idol Fo; so that he was sometimes mistaken for an image of stone. He formed a scale of gesticulation in a great variety of divisions, comprehending the slightest inclination of the head, the front-nod, the side-nod, the bow, the half, the semidemi-bow, the shuffle, the slide, the circular, semi-circular, and quadrant sweep of the right foot. With equal care and precision did he model the economy of his looks into the divisions and sub-divisions of the full stare, the side glance, the pensive look, the pouting look, the gay look, the vacant look, and the solid look. To these different expressions of the eye he suited the corresponding features of the nose and mouth ; such as the wrinkled nose, the retorted nose, the sneer, the grin, the simper, and the smile. All these postures and gesticulations he practised, and distributed occasionally, according to the difference of rank and importance of the various individuals with whom he had communication.

But these affected airs being assumed in spite of nature, he appeared as awkward as a native of Angola when he is first hampered with clothes ; or a Highlander, obliged by an Act of Parliament to wear breeches. Indeed, the distance observed by Yak-strot in his behaviour to the nobles of Niphon, was imputed to his being conscious of a sulphurous smell which came from his own body ; so that greater familiarity on his side might have bred contempt. He took delight in no other conversation but that of two or three obscure Ximians, his companions and counsellors, with whom he spent all his leisure time, in conferences upon politics, patriotism, philosophy, and the Belles Lettres. Those were the oracles he consulted in all the emergencies of state ; and with these he spent many an attic evening.

The gods, not yet tired of sporting with the farce of human government, were still resolved to show by what inconsiderable springs a mighty empire might be moved. The new Cuboy was vastly well disposed to make his Ximian favourites great men. It was in his power to bestow places and pensions on them, but it was not in his power to give them consequence in the eyes of the public. The administration of Yak-strot could not fail of being propitious to his own family, and poor relations, who were very numerous. Their naked backs and hungry bellies were now clothed with the richest stuffs, and fed with the fat things of Japan. Every department, both civil and military, was filled with Ximians. Those islanders came over in shoals to Niphon, and swarmed in the streets of Meaco, where they were easily distinguished by their lank sides, gaunt looks, lanthorn-jaws, and long sharp teeth. There was a fatality which attended the whole conduct of this unfortunate Cuboy. His very partiality to his own countrymen brought upon him at last the curses of the whole clan.

Mr. Orator Taycho and his kinsman Lob-kob were not idle in the meantime. They provided their emissaries, and primed all their engines. Their understrappers filled every corner of Meaco with rumours, jealousies, and suspicions. Yak-strot was represented as a statesman without discernment, a minister without knowledge, and a man without humanity. He was taxed with insupportable pride, indiscretion, pusillanimity, rapacity, partiality, and breach of faith. It was affirmed that he had dishonoured the nation, and endangered the very existence of the Buponian religion, in withdrawing the annual subsidy from the great Brut-an-tiffi; that he wanted to starve the war, and betray the glory and advantage of the empire by a shameful peace; that he had avowedly shared his administration with the greatest knave in Japan, that he treated the nobles of Niphon with insolence and contempt; that he had suborned evidence against the ancient Cuboy Fika-kaka, who had spent a long life and an immense fortune in supporting the temple of Fakku-basi; that he had cruelly turned adrift a number of helpless families, in order to gratify his own worthless dependants with their spoils; that he had enriched his relations and countrymen with the plunder of Niphon; that his intention was to bring over the whole nation of Ximians, a savage race, who had been ever perfidious, greedy, and hostile towards the natives of the other Japanese islands. Nay, they were described as monsters in nature, with cloven feet, long tails, saucer eyes, iron fangs and claws, who would first devour the substance of the Niphonites, and then feed upon their blood.

Taycho had Legion's understanding so much in his power, that he actually made it believe Yak-strot had formed a treasonable scheme in favour of a foreign adventurer who pretended to the throne of Japan, and the reigning Dairo was an accomplice in this project for his own deposition. Indeed, they did not scruple to say that Gio-gio was no more than a puppet moved by his own grandmother and this vile Ximian, between whom they hinted there was a secret correspondence which reflected very little honour on the family of the Dairo.

Mr. Orator Taycho and his associate Lob-kob left no stone unturned to disgrace the favourite, and drive him from the helm. They struck up an alliance with the old Cuboy, Fika-kaka, and fetching him from his retirement, produced him to the beast as a martyr to loyalty and virtue. They had often before this period exposed him to the derision of the populace ; but now they set him up as the object of veneration and esteem ; and everything succeeded to their wish. Legion hoisted Fika-kaka on his back, and paraded through the streets of Meaco, braying hoarse encomiums on the great talents and great virtues of the ancient Cuboy. His cause was now espoused by his old friends Sti-phi-rum-poo and Nin-kom-poo-po, who had been turned adrift along with him, and by several other Quos who had nestled themselves into warm places under the shadow of his protection ; but it was remarkable, that not one of all the Bonzes who owed their preferment to his favours, had gratitude enough to follow his fortune, or pay the least respect to him in the day of his disgrace. Advantage was also taken of the disgust occasioned by Yak-strot's reserve among the nobles of Japan. Even the Fatzman was estranged from the councils of his kinsman Gio-gio, and lent his name and countenance to the malcontents, who now formed themselves into a very formidable cabal, comprehending a great number of the first Quos in the empire.

In order to counterbalance this confederacy, which was a strange coalition of jarring interests, the new Cuboy endeavoured to strengthen his administration, by admitting to a share of it Gotto-mio, who dreaded nothing so much as the continuation of the war, and divers other noblemen, whose alliance contributed very little to his interest or advantage. Gotto-mio was universally envied for his wealth, and detested for his avarice : the rest were either of the She-it-kums-hi-til faction, which had been long in disgrace with the mobile, or men of desperate fortunes and loose morals, who attached themselves to the Ximian favourite solely on account of the posts and pensions he had to bestow.

During these domestic commotions, the arms of Japan continued to prosper in the Indian Ocean. Thin-quo was reduced almost without opposition, and news arrived that the conquest of Fan-yah was already more than half achieved. At the same time, some considerable advantages were gained over the enemy on the continent of Tartary, by the Japanese forces under the command of Bron-xi-tic. It might be naturally supposed that these events would have, in some measure, reconciled the Niphonites to the new ministry, but they produced rather a contrary effect. The blatant beast was resolved to rejoice at no victories but those that were obtained under the auspices of its beloved Taycho, and now took it highly amiss that Yak-strot should presume to take any step which might redound to the glory of the empire. Nothing could have pleased the monster at this juncture so much as the miscarriage of both expeditions, and a certain information that all the troops and ships employed in them had miserably perished. The King of Corea, however, was so alarmed at the progress of the Japanese before Fan-yah, that he began to tremble for all his distant colonies, and earnestly craved the advice of the cabinet of Pekin, touching some scheme to make a diversion in their favour.

The councils of Pekin have been ever fruitful of intrigues to embroil the rest of Asia. They suggested a plan to the King of Corea, which he forthwith put in execution. The land of Fumma, which borders on the Corean territories, was governed by a prince nearly allied to the King of Corea, although his subjects had very intimate connections in the way of commerce with the empire of Japan, which, indeed, had entered into an offensive and defensive alliance with this country. The Emperor of China and the King of Corea having sounded the sovereign of Fumma, and found him well disposed to enter into their measures, communicated their scheme, in which he immediately concurred. They called upon him in public, as their friend and ally, to join them against the Japanese, as the inveterate enemy of the religion of Fo, and as an insolent people, who affected a despotism at sea, to the detriment and destruction of all their neighbours, plainly declaring that he must either immediately break with the Dairo, or expect an invasion on the side of Corea. The Prince of Fumma affected to complain loudly of this iniquitous proposal; he made a merit of rejecting the alternative, and immediately demanded of the court of Meaco the succours stipulated in the treaty of alliance, in order to defend his dominions. In all appearance, indeed, there was no time to be lost; for the monarchs of China and Corea declared war against him without further hesitation, and uniting their forces on that side, ordered them to enter the land of Fumma, after having given satisfactory assurances in private, that the prince had nothing to fear from their hostilities.

Yak-strot was not much embarrassed on this occasion. Without suspecting the least collusion among the parties, he resolved to take the Prince of Fumma under his protection, thereunto moved by divers considerations. First and foremost he piqued himself upon his good faith; secondly, he knew that the trade with Fumma was of great consequence to Japan; and therefore concluded that his supporting the sovereign of it would be a popular measure; thirdly, he hoped that the multiplication of expense incurred by this new war, would make the blatant beast wince under its burden, and of consequence reconcile it to the thoughts of a general pacification, which he had very much at heart. Meanwhile he hastened the necessary succours to the land of Fumma, and sent thither an old general called Le-yaw-ter, in order to concert with the prince and his ministers the operations of the campaign.

This officer was counted one of the shrewdest politicians in Japan, and having resided many years as ambassador in Fumma, was well acquainted with the genius of that people. He immediately discovered the scene which had been acted behind the curtain. He found that the Prince of Fumma, far from having made any preparations for his defence, had actually withdrawn his garrison from the frontier places, which were by this time peaceably occupied by the invading army of Chinese and Coreans; that the few troops he had were without clothes, arms, and discipline; and that he had amused the court of Meaco with false musters and a specious account of levies and preparations which had been made. In a word, though he could not learn the particulars, he comprehended the whole mystery of the secret negotiations. He upbraided the minister of Fumma with perfidy, refused to assume the command of the Japanese auxiliaries when they arrived, and returning to Meaco, communicated his discoveries and suspicions to the new Cuboy. But he did not meet with that reception which he thought he deserved for intelligence of such importance. Yak-strot affected to doubt; perhaps he was not really convinced, or, if he was, thought proper to temporise, and he was in the right for so doing. A rupture with Fumma at this juncture, would have forced the prince to declare openly for the enemies of Japan; in which case the inhabitants of Niphon would have lost the benefit of a very advantageous trade. They had already been great sufferers in commerce by the breach with the King of Corea, whose subjects had been used to take off great quantities of the Japanese manufactures, for which they paid in gold and silver, and they could ill bear such an additional loss as an interruption of the trade with Fumma would have occasioned. The Cuboy, therefore, continued to treat the prince of that country as a staunch ally, who had sacrificed every other consideration to his good faith; and, far from restricting himself to the number of troops and Fune stipulated in the treaty, sent over a much more numerous body of forces and ships of war; declaring, at the same time, he would support the people of Fumma with the whole power of Japan.

Such a considerable diversion of the Japanese strength could not fail to answer, in some measure, the expectation of the two sovereigns of China and Corea; but it did not prevent the success of the expeditions which were actually employed against their colonies in the Indian Ocean. It was not in his power, however, to protect Fumma, had the invaders been in earnest, but the combined army of the Chinese and Coreans had orders to protract the war ; and, instead of penetrating to the capital, at a time when the Fummians, though joined with the auxiliaries of Japan, were not numerous enough to look them in the face, they made a full stop in the middle of their march, and quietly retired into summer quarters.

The additional incumbrance of a new continental war, redoubled the Cuboy's desire of peace, and his inclination being known to the enemy, who were also sick of the war, they had recourse to the good offices of a certain neutral power, called Sab-oi, sovereign of the mountains of Cambodia. This prince accordingly offered his mediation at the court of Meaco, and it was immediately accepted. The negotiation for peace which had been broken off in the ministry of Taycho, was now resumed, an ambassador plenipotentiary arrived from Pekin, and Gotto-mio was sent thither in the same capacity, in order to adjust the articles, and sign the preliminaries of peace.

While this new treaty was on the carpet, the armament equipped against Fan-yah under the command of the Quo Kep-marl, and the brave admiral who had signalised himself in the sea of Kamtschatka, reduced that important place, where they became masters of a very strong squadron of Fune belonging to the King of Corea, together with a very considerable treasure, sufficient to indemnify Japan for the expense of the expedition. This, though the most grievous, was not the only disaster, which the war brought upon the Coreans. Their distant settlement of Lli-nam was likewise taken by General Tra-rep, and the inhabitants paid an immense sum to redeem their capital from plunder.

These successes did not at all retard the conclusion of the treaty, which was indeed become equally necessary to all the parties concerned. Japan, in particular, was in danger of being ruined by her conquests. The war had destroyed so many men, that the whole empire could not afford a sufficiency of recruits for the maintenance of the land forces. All those who had conquered Fatsissio and Fan-yah, were already destroyed by hard duty and the diseases of those unhealthy climates; above two-thirds of the Fune were rotten in the course of service, and the complements of mariners reduced to less than one-half of their original numbers. Troops were actually wanting to garrison the new conquests. The finances of Japan were by this time drained to the bottom. One of her chief resources was stopped by the rupture with Corea, while her expenses were considerably augmented, and her national credit was stretched even to cracking. All these considerations stimulated more and more the Dairo and his Cuboy to conclude the work of peace.

Meanwhile the enemies of Yak-strot gave him no quarter nor respite. They vilified his parts, traduced his morals, endeavoured to intimidate him with threats, which did not even respect the Dairo, and never failed to insult him when he appeared in public. It had been the custom, time immemorial, for the chief magistrate of Meaco to make an entertainment for the Dairo and his empress, immediately after their nuptials, and to this banquet all the great Quos in Japan were invited. The person who filled the chair at present was Rhum-kikh, a half-witted politician, self-conceited, headstrong, turbulent, and ambitious; a professed worshipper of Taycho, whose oratorical talents he admired, and attempted to imitate in the assemblies of the people, where he generally excited the laughter of his audience. By dint of great wealth and extensive traffic he became a man of consequence among the mob, notwithstanding an illiberal turn of mind and an ungracious dress; and now he resolved to use his influence for the glory of Taycho and the disgrace of the Ximian favourite. Legion was tutored for the purpose, and moreover well primed with a caustic spirit in which Rhum-kikh was a considerable dealer. The Dairo and his young empress were received by him and his council with a sullen formality in profound silence. The Cuboy was pelted as he passed along, and his litter almost overturned by the monster, which yelled, and brayed, and hooted without ceasing, until he was housed in the city-hall, where he met with every sort of mortification from the entertainer as well as the spectators. At length Mr. Orator Taycho, with his cousin Lob-kob, appearing in a triumphal car at the city gate, the blatant beast received them with loud huzzas, unharnessed their horses, and putting itself in their traces, drew them through the streets of Meaco, which resounded with acclamation. They were received with the same exultation within the hall of entertainment, where their sovereign and his consort sat altogether unhonoured and unnoticed.

A small squadron of Chinese Fune having taken possession of a defenceless fishery belonging to Japan, in the neighbourhood of Fatsissio, the emissaries of Taycho magnified this event into a terrible misfortune, arising from the maladministration of the new Cuboy : nay, they did not scruple to affirm, that he had left the fishing-town defenceless on purpose that it might be taken by the enemy. This clamour, however, was of short duration. The Quo Phyll-Kholl, who commanded a few Fune in one of the harbours of Fatsissio, no sooner received intelligence of what had happened, than he embarked what troops were at hand, and sailing directly to the place, obliged the enemy to abandon their conquest with precipitation and disgrace.

In the midst of these transactions, the peace was signed, ratified, and even approved in the great national council of the Quos, as well as in the assembly of the people. The truth is, the minister of Japan has it always in his power to secure a majority in both these conventions, by means that may be easily guessed ; and those were not spared on this occasion. Yak-strot, in a speech, harangued the great council, who were not a little surprised to hear him speak with such propriety and extent of knowledge, for he had been represented as tongue-tied, and in point of elocution, little better than the palfrey he rode. He now vindicated all the steps he had taken since his accession to the helm, he demonstrated the necessity of a pacification, explained and descanted upon every article of the treaty, and finally, declared his conscience was so clear in this matter, that when he died, he should desire no other encomium to be engraved on his tomb, but that he was the author of this peace.

Nevertheless, the approbation of the council was not obtained without violent debate and altercation. The different articles were censured and inveighed against by the Fatzman, the late Cuboy Fika-kaka, Lob-kob, Sti-phi-rum-poo, Nin-kom-poo-po, and many other Quos; but, at the long run, the influence of the present ministry predominated. As for Taycho, he exerted himself in a very extraordinary effort to depreciate the peace in the assembly of the people. He had for some days pretended to be dangerously ill, that he might make a merit of his patriotism by showing a contempt for his own life, when the good of his country was at stake. In order to excite the admiration of the public, and render his appearance in the assembly the more striking, he was carried thither on a kind of hand-barrow, wrapped up in flannel, with three woollen night-caps on his head, escorted by Legion, which yelled, and brayed, and whooped, and hallooed with such vociferation, that every street of Meaco rung with hideous clamour. In this equipage did Taycho enter the assembly, where, being held up by two adherents, he, after a prelude of groans to rouse the attention of his audience, began to declaim against the peace as inadequate, shameful, and disadvantageous; nay, he ventured to stigmatise every separate article, though he knew it was in the power of each individual of his hearers to confront him with the terms to which he had subscribed the preceding year, in all respects less honourable and advantageous to his country. Inconsistencies equally glaring and absurd, he had often crammed down the throats of the multitude; but they would not go down with this assembly of the people, which, in spite of his flannel, his night-caps, his crutches, and his groans, confirmed the treaty of peace by a great majority. Not that they had any great reason

to applaud the peace-makers, who might have dictated
their own terms, had they proceeded with more sagacity
and less precipitation.   But Fokh-si-rokhu and his brother
undertakers, having the treasure of Japan at their command,
had anointed the greatest part of the assembly with a certain
precious salve, which preserved them effectually from the
fascinating arts of Taycho.

This orator, incensed at his bad success within doors,
renewed and redoubled his operations without.   He exasperated Legion against Yak-strot to such a pitch of rage
that the monster could not hear the Cuboy's name three
times pronounced without falling into fits.   His confederate
Lob-kob, in the course of his researches, found out two
originals admirably calculated for executing his vengeance
against the Ximian favourite.   One of them, called Llur-chir,
a profligate Bonze, degraded for his lewd life, possessed
a wonderful talent of exciting different passions in the
blatant beast, by dint of quaint rhymes, which were said to
be inspirations of the demon of obloquy, to whom he had
sold his soul.   These oracles not only commanded the
passions, but influenced the organs of the beast in such a
manner, as to occasion an evacuation either upwards or
downwards, at the pleasure of the operator.   The other,
known by the name of Jan-ki-dtzin, was counted the best
marksman in Japan in the art and mystery of dirt throwing.
He possessed the art of making balls of filth, which were
famous for sticking and stinking ; and these he threw with
such dexterity, that they very seldom missed their aim.
Being reduced to a low ebb of fortune by his debaucheries,
he had made advances to the new Cuboy, who had rejected
his proffered services, on account of his immoral character :
a prudish punctilio, which but ill-became Yak-strot, who
had paid very little regard to reputation in choosing some
of the colleagues he had associated in his administration.
Be that as it may, he no sooner understood that Mr. Orator
Taycho was busy in preparing for an active campaign,
than he likewise began to put himself in a posture of defence.
He hired a body of mercenaries, and provided some dirt men

and rhymers. Then, taking the field, a sharp contest and pelting match ensued, but the dispute was soon terminated. Yak-strot's versifiers turned out no great conjurers on the trial. They were not such favourites of the demon as Llur-chir. The rhymes they used, produced no other effect upon Legion, but setting it a-braying.

The Cuboy's dirt men, however, played their parts tolerably well. Though their balls were inferior in point of composition to those of Jan-ki-dtzin, they did not fail to discompose orator Taycho and his friend Lob-kob, whose eyes were seen to water with the smart occasioned by those missiles; but these last had a great advantage over their adversaries, in the zeal and attachment of Legion, whose numerous tongues were always ready to lick off the ordure that stuck to any part of their leaders; and this they did with such signs of satisfaction, as seemed to indicate an appetite for all manner of filth.

Yak-strot having suffered woefully in his own person, and seeing his partisans in confusion, thought proper to retreat. Yet, although discomfited, he was not discouraged. On the contrary, having at bottom a fund of fanaticism, which, like camomile, grows the faster for being trod upon, he became more obstinately bent than ever upon prosecuting his own schemes for the good of the people in their own despite. His vanity was likewise buoyed up by the flattery of his creatures, who extolled the passive courage he had shown in the late engagement. Though every part of him still tingled and stank from the balls of the enemy, he persuaded himself that not one of their missiles had taken place; and of consequence, that there was something of divinity in his person. Full of this notion, he discarded his rhymesters and his dirt-casters as unnecessary and resolved to bear the brunt of the battle in his own individual person.

Fokh-si-rokhu advised him, nevertheless, to fill his trousers with gold obans, which he might throw at Legion in case of necessity, assuring him that this was the only ammunition which the monster could not withstand. The advice was good, and the Cuboy might have followed it, without being obliged to the treasury of Japan; for he was by this time become immensely rich, in consequence of having found a hoard in digging his garden; but this was an expedient which Yak-strot could never be prevailed upon to use, either on this or any other occasion. Indeed, he was now so convinced of his own personal energy, that he persuaded his master Gio-gio to come forth and see it operate on the blatant beast. Accordingly, the Dairo ascended his car of state, while the Cuboy, arrayed in all his trappings, stood before him with the reins in his own hands, and drove directly to the enemy, who waited for him without flinching.

Being arrived within dung shot of Jan-ki-dtzin, he made a halt, and putting himself in the attitude of the idle Fo, with a simper in his countenance, seemed to invite the warrior to make a full discharge of his artillery. He did not long wait in suspense. The balls soon began to whizz about his ears, and a great number took effect upon his person. At length, he received a shot upon his right temple, which brought him to the ground. All his gewgaws fluttered, and his buckram doublet rattled as he fell. Llur-chir no sooner beheld him prostrate, than advancing with the monster, he began to repeat his rhymes, at which every mouth and every tail of Legion was opened and lifted up, and such a torrent of filth squirted from these channels, that the unfortunate Cuboy was quite overwhelmed. Nay, he must have been actually suffocated where he lay, had not some of the Dairo's attendants interposed, and rescued him from the vengeance of the monster. He was carried home in such an unsavoury pickle, that his family smelled his disaster long before he came in sight; and when he appeared in this woeful condition, covered with ordure, blinded with dirt, and even deprived of sense or motion, his wife was seized with *hysterica passio*. He was immediately stripped and washed, and other means being used for his recovery, he in a little time retrieved his recollection.

He was now pretty well undeceived, with respect to the

divinity of his person ; but his enthusiasm took a new turn. He aspired to the glory of martyrdom, resolved to devote himself as a victim to patriotic virtue. While his attendants were employed in washing off the filth that stuck to his beard, he recited in a theatrical tone, the stanza of a Japanese bard, whose soul afterwards transmigrated into the body of a Roman poet Horatius Flaccus, and inspired him with the same sentiment in the Latin tongue—

> *Virtus repulsæ, nescia sordidæ*
> *Intaminatis fulget honoribus*
> *Nec sumit, aut ponit secures*
> *Arbitrio popularis auræ.*

His friends hearing him declare his resolution of dying for his country, began to fear that his understanding was disturbed. They advised him to yield to the torrent, which was become too impetuous to stem ; to resign the Cuboyship quietly, and reserve his virtues for a more favourable occasion. In vain his friends remonstrated ; in vain his wife and children employed their tears and entreaties to the same purpose. He lent a deaf ear to all their solicitations, until they began to drop some hints that seemed to imply a suspicion of his insanity, which alarmed him exceedingly ; and the Dairo himself signifying to him in private, that it was become absolutely necessary to temporise, he resigned the reins of government, but with a heavy heart, though not before he was assured that he should still continue to exert his influence behind the curtain.

Gio-gio's own person had not escaped untouched in the last skirmish. Jan-ki-dtzin was transported to such a pitch of insolence, that he aimed some balls at the Dairo, and one of them taking place exactly between the eyes, defiled his whole visage. Had the laws of Japan been executed in all their severity against this audacious plebeian he would have suffered crucifixion on the spot ; but Gio-gio, being good-natured even to a fault, contented himself with ordering some of his attendants to apprehend and put him in the public stocks, after having seized the whole cargo of filth which he had collected at his habitation for the manufacture of his balls. Legion was no sooner informed of his disgrace, than it released him by force, being therein comforted and abetted by the declaration of a puny magistrate, Praff-patt-phogg, who seized this as the only opportunity he should ever find of giving himself any consequence in the common-wealth. Accordingly, the monster hoisting him and Jan-ki-dtzin on their shoulders, went in procession through the streets of Meaco hallooing, huzzaing, and extolling this venerable pair of patriots, as the *Palladia* of the liberty of Japan.

The monster's officious zeal on this occasion, was far from being agreeable to Mr. Orator Taycho, who took umbrage at this exaltation of his two understrappers, and from that moment devoted Jan-ki-dtzin to destruction. The Dairo finding it absolutely necessary for the support of his Government that this dirt monger should be punished, gave directions for trying him according to the laws of the land. He was ignominiously expelled from the assembly of the people, where his old patron Taycho not only dis-claimed him but even represented him as a worthless atheist and sower of sedition ; but he escaped the weight of a more severe sentence in another tribunal, by retreating without beat of drum, into the territories of China, where he found an asylum, whence he made divers ineffectual appeals to the multitudinous beast of Niphon.

As for Yak-strot, he was everything but a downright martyr to the odium of the public, which produced a ferment all over the nation. His name was become a term of re-proach. He was burnt or crucified in effigy in every city, town, village, and district of Niphon. Even his own countrymen, the Ximians, held him in abhorrence and execration. Notwithstanding his partiality to the *natale solum*, he had not been able to provide for all those adven-turers who came from thence in consequence of his pro-motion. The whole number of the disappointed became his enemies, of course ; and the rest finding themselves exposed to the animosity and ill offices of their fellow subjects of Niphon, who hated the whole community for his sake, inveighed against Yak-strot as the curse of their nation.

In the midst of all this detestation and disgrace, it must be owned for the sake of truth, that Yak-strot was one of the honestest men in Japan, and certainly the greatest benefactor to the empire. Just, upright, sincere, and charitable, his heart was susceptible of friendship and tenderness. He was a virtuous husband, a fond father, a kind master, and a zealous friend. In his public capacity he had nothing in view but the advantage of Japan, in the prosecution of which he flattered himself he should be able to display all the abilities of a profound statesman, and all the virtues of the most sublime patriotism. It was here he over-rated his own importance. His virtue became the dupe of his vanity. Nature had denied him shining talents, as well as that easiness of deportment, that affability, liberal turn, and versatile genius, without which no man can ever figure at the head of an administration. Nothing could be more absurd than his being charged with want of parts and understanding to guide the helm of government, considering how happily it had been conducted for many years by Fika-kaka, whose natural genius would have been found unequal even to the art and mystery of wool-combing. Besides, the war had prospered in his hands as much as it ever did under the auspices of his predecessor; though, as I have before observed, neither the one nor the other could justly claim any merit from its success.

But Yak-strot's services to the public were much more important in another respect. He had the resolution to dissolve the shameful and pernicious engagements which the empire had contracted on the continent of Tartary. He lightened the intolerable burdens of the empire: he saved its credit when it was stretched even to bursting. He made a peace, which, if not the most glorious that might be obtained, was, at least, the most solid and advantageous that ever Japan had concluded with any power whatsoever; and, in particular, much more honourable, useful, and ascertained, than that which Taycho had agreed to subscribe

the preceding year; and, by this peace, he put an end to
all the horrors of a cruel war, which had ravaged the best
parts of Asia, and destroyed the lives of six hundred thousand
men every year. On the whole, Yak-strot's good qualities
were respectable. There was very little vicious in his
composition; and as to his follies, they were rather the
subjects of ridicule than of resentment.

Yak-strot's subalterns in the ministry rejoiced in secret
at his running so far into the north of Legion's displeasure.
Nay, it was shrewdly suspected that some of their emissaries
had been very active against him in the day of his discomfiture. They flattered themselves, that if he could be
effectually driven from the presence of the Dairo, they would
succeed to his influence; and in the meantime would acquire
popularity by turning to, and kicking at, the Ximian favourite,
who had associated them in the administration in consequence
of their vowing eternal attachment to his interest, and
constant submission to his will. Having held a secret
conclave to concert their operations, they began to execute
their plan by seducing Yak-strot into certain odious measures
of raising new impositions on the people, which did not
fail, indeed, to increase the clamour of the blatant beast,
and promote its filthy discharge upwards and downwards;
but then the torrents were divided, and many a tail was lifted
up against the real projectors of the scheme which the
favourite had adopted. They now resolved to make a
merit with the Mobile, by picking a german quarrel with
Strot, and insulting him in public. Gotto-mio caused a
scrubbing-post to be set up in the night, at the Cuboy's
door.—The scribe Zan-ti-fic presented him with a scheme
for the importation of brimstone into the island of Ximo:
the other scribe pretended he could not spell the barbarous
names of the Cuboy's relations and countrymen, who were
daily thrust into the most lucrative employments. As for
Twitz-er the financier, he never approached Yak-strot
without clawing his knuckles in derision. At the council
of twenty-eight, they thwarted every plan he proposed,
and turned into ridicule every word he spoke. At length

they bluntly told the Dairo, that as Yak-strot resigned the reins of administration in public, he must likewise give up his management behind the curtain, for they were not at all disposed to answer to the people for measures dictated by an invisible agent. This was but a reasonable demand, in which the emperor seemed to acquiesce. But the new ministers thought it was requisite that they should commit some overt act of contempt for the abdicated Cuboy. One of his nearest relations had obtained a profitable office in the island of Ximo; and of this, the new cabal insisted he should be immediately deprived. The Dairo remonstrated against the injustice of turning a man out of his place for no other reason but to satisfy their caprice, and plainly told them he could not do it without infringing his honour, as he had given his word that the possessor should enjoy the post for life.

Far from being satisfied with this declaration, they urged their demand with redoubled importunity, mixed with menaces which equally embarrassed and incensed the good-natured Dairo. At last Yak-strot, taking compassion upon his indulgent master, prevailed upon his kinsman to release him from the obligation of his word, by making a voluntary resignation of his office. The Dairo fell sick of vexation, his life was despaired of, and all Japan was filled with alarm and apprehension at the prospect of an infant's ascending the throne: for the heir apparent was still in the cradle.

Their fears, however, were happily disappointed by the recovery of the emperor, who, to prevent as much as possible the inconveniences that might attend his demise, during the minority of his son, resolved that a regency should be established and ratified by the states of the empire. The plan of this regency he concerted in private with the venerable princess his grandmother, and his friend Yak-strot, and then communicated the design to his ministers, who knowing the quarter from whence it had come treated it with coldness and contempt. They were so elevated by their last triumph over the Ximian favourite, that they overlooked every obstacle to their ambition, and determined to render the Dairo dependent on them, and them only. With this view they threw cold water on the present measure ; and to mark their hatred of the favourite more strongly in the eyes of Legion, they endeavoured to exclude the name of his patroness, the Dairo's grandmother, from the deed of regency, though their malice was frustrated by the vigilance of Yak-strot, and the indignation of the states, who resented this affront offered to the family of their sovereign.

The tyranny of this junto became so intolerable to Gio-gio, that he resolved to shake off their yoke, whatever might be the consequence; but before any effectual step was taken for this purpose, Yak-strot, who understood mechanics, and had studied the art of puppet playing, tried an experiment on the organs of the cabal, which he tampered with individually without success.

Instead of uttering what he prompted, the sounds came out quite altered in their passage. Gotto-mio grunted ; the Financier Twitz-er bleated, or rather brayed ; one scribe mewed like a cat, the other yelped like a jackal. In short, they were found so perverse and refractory, that the master of the motion kicked them off the stage, and supplied the scene with a new set of puppets made of very extraordinary materials. They were the very figures through whose pipes the charge of mal-administration had been so loudly sounded against the Ximian favourite. They were now mustered by the Fatzman, and hung upon pegs of the very same puppet-showman against whom they had so vehemently inveighed. Even the super-annuated Fika-kaka appeared again upon the stage as an actor of some consequence; and insisted upon it, that his metamorphosis was a mere calumny. But Taycho and Lob-kob kept aloof, because Yak-strot had not yet touched them upon the proper keys.

The first exhibition of the new puppets was called *Topsy-turvy*, a farce in which they overthrew all the paper houses which their predecessors had built ; but they performed

their parts in such confusion, that Yak-strot interposing
to keep them in order, received divers contusions and severe
kicks on the shins, which made his eyes water ; and, indeed,
he had in a little time reason enough to repent of the revolution he had brought about. The new sticks of administration
proved more stiff and unmanageable than the former ; and
those he had discarded, associating with the blatant beast,
debaubed him with such a variety of filth, drained from all
the sewers of scurrility, that he really became a public
nuisance. Gotto-mio pretended remorse of conscience,
and declared he would impeach Yak-strot for the peace
which he himself had negotiated. Twitz-er snivelled and
cried, and cast figures to prove that Yak-strot was born for
the destruction of Japan, and Zan-ti-fic hired an incendiary
Bonze called Toks, to throw fire-balls by night into the palace
of the favourite.

In this distress Strot cast his eyes on Taycho the monster-
tamer, who alone seemed able to overbalance the weight
of all other opposition ; and to him he made large advances
accordingly ; but his offers were still inadequate to the
expectations of that demagogue, who, nevertheless, put on
a face of capitulation. He was even heard to say that
Yak-strot was an honest man and a good minister : nay, he
declared he would ascend the highest pinnacle of the highest
pagod in Japan, and proclaim that Yak-strot had never,
directly or indirectly, meddled with administration since
he resigned the public office of minister. Finding him,
however, tardy and phlegmatic in his proposals, he thought
proper to change his phrase, and in the next assembly of the
people swore, with great vociferation, that the said Yak-strot
was the greatest rogue that ever escaped the gallows. This
was a necessary fillip to Yak-strot, and operated upon him
so effectually, that he forthwith sent a carte blanche to the
great Taycho, and a treaty was immediately ratified on the
following conditions : that the said Taycho should be
raised to the rank of Quanbuku, and be appointed conservator
of the Dairo's signet ; that no state measure should be taken
without his express approbation ; that his creature the

lawyer Praff-fog should be ennobled and preferred to
the most eminent place in the tribunals of Japan, and
that all his friends and dependants should be provided
for at the public expense, in such a manner as he himself
should propose.

His kinsman Lob-kob, however, was not comprehended
in this treaty, the articles of which he inveighed against
with such acrimony, that a rupture ensued betwixt these
two originals. The truth is, Lob-kob was now so full
of his own importance, that nothing less than an equal
share of administration would satisfy his ambition; and
this was neither in Taycho's power nor inclination to
grant.

The first consequence of this treaty was a new shift of
hands, and a new dance of ministers. The chair of precedency was pulled from under the antiquated Fika-kaka,
who fell upon his back; and his heels flying up, discovered
but too plainly the melancholy truth of his metamorphosis.
All his colleagues were discarded, except those who thought
proper to temporise and join in dancing the hay, according
as they were actuated by the new partners of the puppet-
show. This coalition was the greatest masterpiece in
politics that Yak-strot ever performed. Taycho, the
formidable Taycho, whom in his single person he dreaded
more than all his other enemies of Japan united, was now
become his coadjutor, abettor, and advocate; and, which
was still of more consequence to Strot, that demagogue
was forsaken of his good genius Legion.

The many-headed monster would have swallowed down
every other species of tergiversation in Taycho, except a
coalition with the detested favourite, and the title of Quo,
by which he formally renounced its society: but these were
articles which the mongrel could not digest. The tidings
of this union threw the beast into a kind of stupor, from
which it was roused by blisters and cauteries applied by
Gotto-mio, Twitz-er, Zan-ti-fic, with his understrapper
Toks, now reinforced by Fika-kaka, and his discarded associates: for their common hatred to Yak-strot, like the rod

of Moses, swallowed up every distinction of party, and every suggestion of former animosity, and they concurred with incredible zeal, in rousing Legion to a due sense of Taycho's apostasy. The beast, so stimulated, howled three days and three nights successively at Taycho's gate; then was seized with a convulsion, that went off with an evacuation upwards and downwards, so offensive that the very air was infected.

The horrid sounds of the beast's lamentation, the noxious effluvia of its filthy discharge, joined to the poignant remorse which Taycho felt at finding his power over Legion dissolved, occasioned a commotion in his brain, and this led him into certain extravagances, which gave his enemies a handle to say he was actually insane. His former friends and partisans thought the best apology they could make for the inconsistency of his conduct, was to say he was *non compos*; and this report was far from being disagreeable to Yak-strot, because it would at any time furnish him with a plausible pretence to dissolve the partnership, at which he inwardly repined; for it was necessity alone that drove him to a partition of his power with a man so incapable of acting in concert with any colleague whatsoever.

In the meantime Gotto-mio and his associates left no stone unturned to acquire the same influence over Legion, which Taycho had so eminently possessed; but the beast's faculties, slender as they were, seemed now greatly impaired, in consequence of that arch empiric's practices upon its constitution. In vain did Gotto-mio whoop and holloa, in vain did Twitz-er tickle its long ears, in vain did Zan-ti-fic apply sternutatories, and his Bonze administer inflammatory glysters; the monster could never be brought to a right understanding, or at all concur with their designs except in one instance, which was its antipathy to the Ximian favourite. This had become so habitual, that it acted mechanically upon its organs even after it had lost all other signs of recognition. As often as the name of Yak-strot was pronounced, the beast began to yell, and all the usual consequences ensued; but whenever his new friends presumed to mount him, he threw himself upon his back, and rolled them in the kennel at the hazard of their lives.

One would imagine there was some leaven in the nature of Yak-strot, that soured all his subalterns who were natives of Niphon; for howsoever they promised all submission to his will, before they were admitted into his motion, they no sooner found themselves acting characters in his drama, than they began to thwart him in his measures, so that he was plagued by those he had taken in, and persecuted by those he had driven out. The two great props which he had been at so much pains to provide, now failed him. Taycho was grown crazy, and could no longer manage the monster, and Quam-ba-cun-dono the Fatzman, whose authority had kept several puppets in awe, died about this period.

These two circumstances were the more alarming, as Gotto-mio and his crew began to gain ground, not only in their endeavours to rouse the monster, but also in tampering with some of the acting puppets, to join their cabal and make head against their master. These exotics grew so refractory, that when he tried to wheel them to the right, they turned to the left about; and instead of joining hands in the dance of politics, rapped their heads against each other with such violence, that the noise of the collision was heard in the street, and if they had not been made of the hardest wood in Japan, some of them would certainly have been split in the encounter.

By this time Legion began to have some sense of its own miserable condition. The effects of the yeast potions which it had drnnk so liberally from the hands of Taycho, now wore off. The fumes dispersed, the illusions vanished, the flatulent tumour of its belly disappeared with innumerable explosions, leaving a hideous lankness and such canine appetite as all the eatables of Japan could not satisfy. After having devoured the whole harvest, it yawned for more, and grew quite outrageous in its hunger, threatening to feed on human flesh, if not plentifully supplied with other viands.

In this dilemma Yak-strot convened the council of twenty-eight, where, in consideration of the urgency of the case, it was resolved to suspend the law against the importation of foreign provisions, and open the ports of Japan for the relief of the blatant beast.

As this was vesting the Dairo with a dispensing power unknown to the constitution of Japan it was thought necessary at the next assembly of the Quos and Quanbukus that constitute the legislature, to obtain a legal sanction for that extraordinary exercise of prerogative, which nothing but the *salus populi* could excuse. Upon this occasion it was diverting to see with what effrontery individuals changed their principles with their places. Taycho the Quo, happening to be in one of his lucid intervals, went to the assembly supported by his two creatures Praff-fog and another limb of the law, called Lley-nah, surnamed Gurg-grog, or Curse-mother; and this triumvirate who had raised themselves from nothing to the first rank in the state, by vilifying and insulting the kingly power and affirming that the Dairo was the slave of the people, now had the impudence to declare in the face of day, that in some cases the emperor's power was absolute, and that he had an inherent right to suspend and supersede the laws and ordinances of the legislature.

Mura-clami, who had been for some time eclipsed in his judicial capacity by the popularity of Praff-fog, did not fail to seize this opportunity of exposing the character of his upstart rival. Though he had been all his life an humble restrainer to the prerogative, he now made a parade of patriotism, and in a tide of eloquence bore down all the flimsy arguments which the triumvirate advanced. He demonstrated the futility of their reasoning, from the express laws and customs of their empire; he expatiated on the pernicious tendency of their doctrine, and exhibited the inconsistency of their conduct in such colours, that they must have hid their heads in confusion, had they not happily conquered all sense of shame, and been well convinced that the majority of the assembly were not a whit more honest than themselves. Mura-clami enjoyed a momentary triumph; but his words made a very slight impression, for it was his misfortune to be a Ximian, and if his virtues had been more numerous than the hairs in his beard, this very circumstance would have shaved them clean away from the consideration of the audience.

Taycho, opening the flood-gates of his abuse, bespattered all that opposed him. Lley-nah, alias Curse-mother, swore that he had got into the wrong box; then turning to Praff-fog, " Brother Praff," cried he, " thou hast let down thy trousers, and every rascal in Japan will whip thy a—se ! " Praff was afraid of the beast's resentment, but Taycho bestrode him like a Colossus, and he crept through between his legs into a place of safety. This was the last time that the orator appeared in public, immediately after this occurrence it was found necessary to confine him to a dark chamber, and Yak-strot was left to his own inventions.

In this dilemma he had recourse to the old expedient of changing hands, and as a prelude to this reform, made advances to Gotto-mio, whom he actually detached from the opposition, by providing his friends and dependants with lucrative offices, and promising to take no steps of consequence without his privity and approbation. A sop was at the same time thrown to Twitz-er. Zan-ti-fic, lulled with specious promises, discarded Toks the incendiary Bonze; Lob-kob signed a neutrality, and old Fika-kaka was deprived of the use of speech ; in a word, the ill-cemented confederacy of Strot's exotic foes fell asunder, and Legion had now no rage, but the rage of hunger to be appeased. But the Ximian favourite was still thwarted in his operations behind the curtain ; for he had so often chopped and changed the figures that composed his motion, that they were all of different materials, so wretchedly sorted and so ill-toned, that when they came upon the scene, they produced nothing but discord and disorder.

The Japanese colony of Fatsissio had been settled above a century, and in the face of a thousand dangers and difficulties raised themselves to such consideration that they consumed infinite quantities of the manufactures of Japan, for which they paid their mother-country in gold and silver, and precious drugs the produce of their plantations. The advantages which Japan reaped from this traffic with her own colonists, almost equalled the amount of what she gained by her commerce with all the other parts of Asia.

Twitz-er, when he managed the finances of Japan, had in his great wisdom planned, procured, and promulgated a law saddling the Fatsissians with a grievous tax to answer the occasions of the Japanese Government ; an imposition which struck at the very vitals of their constitution, by which they were exempt from all burdens but such as they fitted for their own shoulders. They raised a mighty clamour at this innovation, in which they were joined by Legion, at that time under the influence of Taycho, who, in the assembly of the people, bitterly inveighed against the authors and abettors of such an arbitrary and tyrannical measure.

Their reproach and execration did not stop at Twitz-er, but proceeded, as usual to Yak-strot, who was the general, but at which all the arrows of slander, scurrility, and abuse were levelled. The puppets with which he supplied the places of Twitz-er and his associates, in order to recommend themselves to Legion, and perhaps, with a view to mortify the favourite, who had patronised the Fatsissian tax insisted upon withdrawing this imposition, which was accordingly abrogated, to the no small contempt of the lawgivers ; but when these new ministers were turned out, to make way for Taycho and his friends, the interest of the Fatsissians was again abandoned. Even the orator himself declaimed against them with an unembarrassed countenance, after they had raised statues to him as their friend and patron ; and measures were taken to make them feel all the severity of an abject dependence upon the legislature of Japan. Finally, Gotto-mio acceded to this system, which he had formerly approved in conjunction with Twitz-er, and preparations were made for using

27

compulsory measures, should the colonists refuse to submit
with a good grace.

The Fatsissians, far from acquiescing in these proceedings,
resolved to defend to the last extremity those liberties which
they had hitherto preserved ! and, as a proof of their independence, agreed among themselves to renounce all the
superfluities with which they had so long been furnished,
at a vast expense, from the manufactures of Japan, since that
nation had begun to act towards them with all the cruelty of
a step-mother.   It was amazing to hear and see how Legion
raved, and slabbered, and snapped its multitudinous jaws in
the streets of Meaco, when it understood that the Fatsissians,
were determined to live on what their own country afforded.
They were represented and reviled as ruffians, barbarians,
and unnatural monsters, who clapped the dagger to the
breast of their indulgent mother, in presuming to save
themselves the expense of those superfluities, which, by-
the-bye, her cruel impositions had left them no money to
purchase.   Nothing was heard in Japan but threats of
punishing those ungrateful colonists with whips and scor-
pions.   For this purpose troops were assembled and fleets
equipped, and the blatant beast yawned with impatient
expectation of being drenched with the blood of its
fellow-subjects.

Yak-strot was seized with horror at the prospect of such
extremities ; for, to give the devil his due, his disposition
was neither arbitrary nor cruel ; but he had been hurried
by evil counsellors into a train of false politics, the consequences of which he did not foresee.   He now summoned
council after council to deliberate upon conciliatory expedients ; but found the motley crew so divided by self-interest,
faction, and mutual rancour, that no consistent plan could be
formed ; all was nonsense, clamour and contradiction.   The
Ximian favourite now wished all his puppets at the devil,
and secretly cursed the hour in which he first undertook
the motion.   He even fell sick of chagrin, and resolved in
good earnest, to withdraw himself entirely from the political
helm, which he was now convinced he had no talents to

guide. In the meantime, he tried to find some temporary alleviation to the evils occasioned by the monstrous incongruity of the members and materials that composed his administration. But before any effectual measures could be taken, his evil genius ever active, brewed up a new storm in another quarter, which had well-nigh swept him and all his projects into the gulf of perdition.

THE END

Printed by Hazell, Watson & Viney, Ld., London and Aylesbury.

www.ingramcontent.com/pod-product-compliance
Lightning Source LLC
Chambersburg PA
CBHW020832030726
47496CB00001B/200